The Rise

Alistair Hall

Raven Fell Limited *Publishers*

First published in 2025 by Raven Fell Limited

© 2025 Alistair Hall

The moral right of Alistair Hall to be identified as the author of this work has been asserted in accordance with the Copyright, Design and patents Act of 1988.

All rights reserved. No part of this publication may be reproduced, stored in a retrieval system or transmitted in any form or by any means, electronic, mechanical, photocopying, recording or otherwise, without the prior permission of both the copyright owner and the above publisher of this book.

ISBN 9781916299764

Edited by Kat Harvey, Athena Copy

Graphics by Room for Design, Northallerton.

Printed and bound in Great Britain by Martins

Raven Fell Limited, Berwick upon Tweed

a fire heaped up by impious easterners spread from sea to sea. It devastated town and country round about, and, once it was alight, it did not die down until it had burned almost the whole of the island and was licking the western ocean with its red and savage tongue... All the major towns were laid low by the repeated battering of enemy rams; laid low too, all the inhabitants... as the swords glinted all around and the flames crackled. It was a sad sight. In the middle of the squares the foundation stones of high walls and towers that had been torn from their lofty base, holy altars, fragments of corpses, covered with the purple crust of congealed blood, looked as though they had been mixed up in some dreadful wine-press.

The Monk Gildas, (De Excidio 24.1-3)

Map

HIBERNIA

MANAVIA

SEGONTIUM   **MONA**
IR WYDDFA

ITUNOCELUM
ERECHWYD

ISCA DUMNONIORUM

ISCA AUGUSTA   **DEVA**
VIROCONIUM
BREMETENNACUM

DURNOVARIA   **LINDINIS**   *WENLOCK*   **MAMUCIUM**
EDGE
GLEVUM   *VILLA*
CORINUM   *GUTASIUS*   *CRAVEN*

SORVIODUNUM   **LETOCETUM**

VENTA BELGARUM   **DERVENTIO**
VECTIS   **CLAUSENTUM**   **RATAE**   **CAMBODUNUM**
LACTO DURUM   **DANUM**   **ISURIUM**
EBORACUM   *BRIGANTIUM*
NOVIOMAGUS   **CALLEVA**   Gainnion
CAUSENNIS   **LINDUM**
VERULAMIUM   Ypwines Fleot
LONDINIUM   **DUROBRIVAE**   Creeganford
Wippeds Fleot

CAMULODUNUM

DUROVERNUM   **VENTA ICENORUM**
RUTUPIAE

BONONIA
GAUL

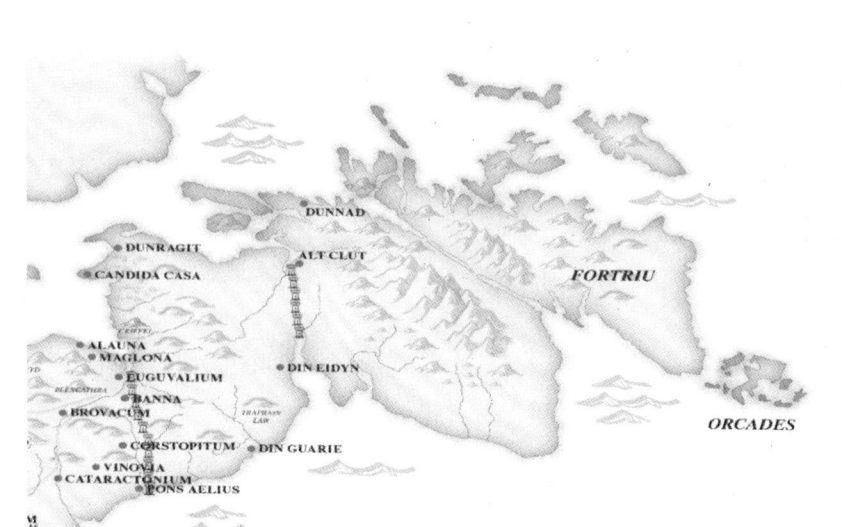

DUNNAD
ALT CLUT
DUNRAGIT
CANDIDA CASA
FORTRIU
ALAUNA
MAGLONA
EUGUVALIUM
BANNA
BROVACUM
DIN EIDYN
TRAPRAIN LAW
CORSTOPITUM
DIN GUARIE
VINOVIA
CATARACTONIUM
PONS AELIUS

ORCADES

BRITANNIA 440AD

Introduction

Everyone who reads this book will know something about the Roman Empire, whether that is from school, novels, films or from visits to archaeological sites such as the Colosseum in Rome or Hadrian's Wall. It is difficult to imagine how the western Roman Empire, which had endured for four hundred years, could have collapsed with such great drama and bloodshed in its final seventy years.

It was an intensely violent period. Empire-wide, treachery and intrigue resulted in a long list of bloody civil wars, undermining available manpower and debilitating the Empire's former military might. This led to a reliance on foreign mercenary troops, known as barbarians, and these tribes quickly grasped the opportunity to steal power from their weakened paymasters.

Britannia had always proved difficult to control, and after all those rebellions finally led to secession, the western Empire abandoned the province. At first, many Britons hoped Rome might return, possibly under the direction of a more vigorous emperor, but the Theodosian dynasty clung to power, the crisis deepened, and the barbarian tribes grew stronger. It was during this period of uncertainty that Coel Hen and his contemporaries established themselves as regional kings in Britannia, raising militias to fight Picts, Scotti, Saxons and, sometimes, each other. It seems there was a step back to regional tribal culture, but many aspects of the Empire endured, evident in the use of Latin, and the survival of the Church, weapons and warfare techniques.

Christianity, taught in Latin, enjoyed remarkable progress at this time, and whilst pagan beliefs and heightened superstition were still a part of life, there is no doubt the presence of Christian missionaries, such as Ninian, Palladius and Patrick, in the Empire's former borderlands was significant to that development. At this distance through time, it is difficult to appreciate how raw the 'new' religion would have felt. The crucifixion of Christ was just eight to nine generations past, and the adoption of Christianity by the Roman Empire was only one or two generations old.

Between AD 367 and AD 476, many cities and their provinces suffered multiple catastrophes, from pillage to plague. Death and despair flourished as the western Empire became less and less capable of defending its citizens. Faith in God became crucial to understanding such dire events, and it is apparent that the clergy of the time believed the Second Coming of Christ was imminent. In particular, the sack of Rome by the Visigoths in AD 410 was seen as the act of an antichrist, presaging the Parousia.

It is interesting to contrast the security enjoyed by the parents of Coel Hen, who lived their lives, probably as pagans, in the extensive, powerful and eternal Empire, with that of their great-grandson, Arthwys, a Christian king ruling a petty northern kingdom and rallying his subjects and fellow kings to defend against Saxon incursion, Rome's power but a distant memory. There is only faint recorded history for the period, and a considerable amount of speculation is required to imagine what occurred.

There is some heroic poetry thought to emanate from the Dark Ages, which displays passion, rigour and fear, giving us a sense of a warrior's perspective, and whilst this story is a fiction, there are real historical figures and events woven into the plot. It is my hope that some readers will research the period to discover how much of an impact the harrowing collapse of the western Empire had upon the foundations of medieval Britain and Europe. The main characters of this story are Brittonic, Roman and Germanic, making their names difficult to read and recognise. I have therefore listed the central characters with a brief description for quick reference.

Aetius	Senior general of the western Roman Empire.
Agiluf	Son of Cian, Arthwys' closest friend.
Ambrosius Aurelianus	Roman exile, son of deposed joint Emperor Sebastianus, influential Belgae landowner.
Arthwys	Heir to the kingship of Elfed, son of Mor and Igerna, brother of Morgaine.
Blwchfardd	Son of Cian, bard to the royal household, brother of Agiluf.

Cian	King Mor's trusted secretary and adviser, father of Agiluf and Blwchfardd.
Coroticus	King of Alt Clut.
Germanus	Former Duke of Armorica, bishop of Auxerre, traveller to Britannia.
Gorwst	King of Reged, father to Meirchiawn and Mordred.
Gwenhyfach	Elder princess of Erechwyd.
Gwenhyfar	Younger princess of Erechwyd.
Hengist and Horsa	Tribal Jute kings who came to Britannia as mercenaries.
Igerna	First Queen of Elfed, wife of Mor, Cornovii princess, mother of Arthwys and Morgaine.
Livia	Daughter of Ambrosius Aurelianus.
Lott	King of the Gododdin.

Marchell	Wife of Gorwst, sister of King Coroticus of Alt Clut, mother of Meirchiawn and Mordred
Martin Merlinus	Priest with a mysterious background.
Meirchiawn	Son of Gorwst, heir to the kingship of Reged.
Mor	First King of Elfed, father of Arthwys and Morgaine.
Mordred	Son of Marchell
Morgaine	Sister of Arthwys, daughter of Mor and Igerna.
Myrddin	Druid and adherent to the old gods. 'Myrddin' is a description rather than a name and means 'holy seer'.
Riothames	Son of Ambrosius Aurelianus
Vortigern	A powerful Roman Briton, King of the Dobunni tribe, known to his peer group as Vitalinus.
Vortimer	King of the Cornovii, son of Vortigern and Sevira.

Myrddin Returns

Elfed

November 446

There was little light left to the day, but it was yet too early to sleep. Wind and rain lashed Martin's small wooden chapel, and outside, leaves rustled and swirled, looking to find their resting place before winter.

'A good Christian should pray at this time,' he spoke aloud to himself in an attempt to change the pattern of his thoughts, although by experience, he knew he would not heed his own good advice. He could not and would not forget his brother's murder or his family's betrayal. Of all the human weaknesses, betrayal was the most pernicious and unforgiveable. 'Not very Christian,' he said, speaking to himself again as he rested his back against the timbers of his tiny chapel.

This struggle with his faith was no longer a daily occurrence. He might go about his duties for weeks without dwelling on the past, but then something would unexpectedly remind him of the regicide that so changed the course of his life. As the buffeting wind shook the chapel, he remembered. *It was on just such a night the betrayal occurred, whilst my brother and I were at prayer... Murderers!* The bitterness would always be there, even though his faith demanded he forgive his attackers. The sound of footfall outside ended his reflections abruptly. He stood, reaching for his sword. The latch lifted but he had barred the door for the night, and it would not open.

'Is anyone within?' An old man's croaking voice was followed by something striking the timbers. 'Martin, it is Myrddin.'

Surprised and immediately apprehensive, Martin lifted the bar.

'My friend! Come in and shelter from this storm.'

The old man in Martin's doorway was soaked and swaying on his feet.

'What brings you to my place of solitude at this late hour?'

Myrddin did not answer. Five winters had passed since the seer had departed Elfed, and Martin had often wondered if Myrddin had somewhere met his end.

'I am pleased to see you still alive! Come sit with me here.' He guided Myrddin to a stool where the old man sat down carefully, using his stave for support.

The old seer caught his breath. 'All I have foreseen is about to come to pass, my dreams are full of warnings, terrible events will soon occur, and the gods of war are sharpening their weapons. I have seen both defeat and the death of kings.'

Martin's heart beat faster. Did Myrddin ever bring glad tidings?

'Is this why you have returned to Elfed?'

'Yes, but I have also dreamt *Artio* is searching for me. If the bear goddess has me in her sights, my time in this life will shortly end. I need your help, Martin.' The seer lifted his head and looked straight into the priest's eyes. 'Fate chooses you as my successor, Martin. You must take my place. You are the next Myrddin.'

Martin laughed, shrugging off the weight of the seer's words 'That cannot be. I have no powers, no magic, no training.'

'You have the sight, and you are yet unaware of the extent of your powers.'

'I have some confused dreams, and I am Christian.'

It was Myrddin's turn to chuckle. 'Our faiths are not so different. Your solitary God concerns himself with the soul's assent to Heaven, whereas mine are more concerned with earthly matters. You believe in an afterlife, whereas I believe in reincarnation. Neither of us fear death, and in life, we both strive to help the living. What I can teach you will not affect your faith; it will only expand your boundaries and enhance your understanding of the world.'

'I cannot follow a path that corrupts my faith. The good Lord chose to save me. Since then, I have been His to direct. I am only here through His will.'

Myrddin nodded knowingly. 'Yes, of course you are, but a Druid's duties extend beyond the bounds of faith; we are the custodians of sacred knowledge.'

'I am not from your tribes, so your people will never accept me.'

'That is not so,' Myrddin said firmly, watching the priest intently. 'You assume I do not know who you are Cynwyb.'

Martin's heart stopped for a beat, startled to hear his true name spoken for the first time in twenty years.

Myrddin continued. 'Cynwyb, brother of Cynloyp, both sons of Cinhill, son of Cluim – did you think I wouldn't know you are from royal blood, a claimant to the throne of Alt Clut? I knew your father and your grandfather – great warriors both.'

'Cynwyb was murdered, betrayed by his half-brother. I am not the same person.'

Myrddin shook his head. 'I know their betrayal continues to haunt you, but you must not let it stand in your way. Your visit to the Otherworld has given you a gift you refuse to use.'

'It was God who brought me back, so I am His to direct.' Martin paused. 'Besides, my dreams are frightening, impossible to interpret.'

'I can show you how, but you must open your mind and be unafraid.'

'Have you told King Mor of my deception?' What would become of him if the king knew?

'There has been no need. Mor appreciates how well you have tutored Prince Arthwys, and he knows I hold you in high regard.'

Martin felt compromised but dipped his head, grateful for Myrddin's discretion.

'What is it you wish of me?'

'You must watch over the Bear and advise him. Now is his time. The Saxon serpent has broken its shackles and ravages south of the Humber. King Mor watches nervously but does not commit.'

'King Mor is a renowned warrior, but his militia no longer has sufficient numbers to hold off the Saxon horde – surely, the other kings will see sense and join him?'

'They will never agree precedence and, like children, are jealous of each other. Ancient tradition dictates it is the Bear who should raise the standard of the northern Britons. The tribal kings give their oath to this allegiance.'

'Arthwys is not ready,' Martin interrupted, anticipating where the seer's thoughts were leading.

'He has to be,' replied Myrddin; 'just as you must be ready to embrace your powers and prove yourself equal to your destiny.'

Martin sensed he was included in the seer's plans, regardless. But what were these plans? And what had brought him to the chapel door so unexpectedly?

'Is the danger imminent?' Martin asked pointedly.

'We must hasten to Cambodunum tomorrow. King Mor has informed me Gorwst has sent to him for help in facing a threat to his western shore. Arthwys must accompany his father, as must we both. The gods summon us all to Reged.'

'What is this threat?'

'An army of Gaels Gorwst has been unable to dislodge. For several months they have been using Insula Manavia as a harbour from which to raid, but now they have grown bold enough to land on Reged's shores.'

'King Gorwst has two sons and many allies, surely it is folly for Mor to allow this to distract him from the Saxon threat?'

'Mor must be persuaded to support his brother so that Arthwys can prove himself to the gods.'

'And which gods might they be? As persuasive as that sounds, surely there is some other purpose?'

'There is treachery within the kingdom of Reged.'

First betrayal, now treachery?

'How do you know this?'

'Marchell is showing more loyalty to her brother than her husband. She has moved her court north to be closer to your brother's murderer, deserting Gorwst and taking Mordred with her for protection. Gorwst suspects the King of Alt Clut assists the Gaels in raiding Reged, jointly selling their captured slaves north to the Picts. The King of Reged has made no secret of how much he abhors this constant raiding for slaves, resulting in enmity between the two kingdoms.' The old seer paused. 'Look into the future, Martin. Mor distracted by Saxons, Gorwst weakened, Gaels invading from the west – Coroticus may intend to annex Reged.'

Years of suppressed anger swelled in Martin's chest. 'I see it, and I am appalled that my late brother's kingdom is being used as a marketplace to sell Christian slaves to heathen Picts. My brother and father must be restless in their graves.'

'They are, Cynwyb, and will not rest easy until Coroticus is in the earth with them.'

Myrddin's insistence on Martin joining the expedition was still puzzling, though he could not deny his strong familial ties to the situation. 'You speak of your gods, but how can they have any impact on our fate?'

'You should know our people are blessed to have two gods of war watching over them, but these two gods are rivals.'

'Rivals for what purpose?'

'Influence. To gain it, they vie to direct our actions.'

'As if we are their gaming pieces? Do these interfering gods have names?'

'Cocidius and Belatucadrus.'

'And do you fear your gods of war, Myrddin?'

'I am wary of their purpose.'

'Why so?'

'Their rivalry stems from their desire to win the favour of Coventina, and we all know how love and desire warp sense and purpose.'

'I've heard of Coventina... Isn't she a water spirit? But regardless – surely, these gods are so ancient they no longer have any potency in the realm of man?'

'Ah, but they have, Martin, for it was Belatucadrus who influenced Coroticus all those years ago.'

'Why should he do such a thing?'

'To deal a blow to his rival. Cocidius lends favour and protection to the Coelings, and your father was a staunch ally of Coel Hen.'

'Are you saying that this god assured the murder of my brother out of spite?'

'Belatucadrus is determined, passionate and violent, whereas Cocidius is measured and tactical. But Cocidius holds an advantage when it comes to influencing the outcome of the battles of men, for Caledfwich is within his gift.'

'Caledfwich? The legendary sword?'

'Yes, and I know where it is.'

Martin was not sure if he believed any of this fabulous tale, but his mind was made up.

'I will accompany you. Arthwys is brave but headstrong – he will need wise counsel. But I still doubt I have the aptitude to be your successor. For now, I have bread and cow's milk I can share with you, then I must pray for guidance before we set out for Cambodunum in the morning.'

Martin looked around his tiny chapel. The light had gone and so had the tranquillity, for now his mind was racing. Was this God's will? Perhaps He had decided it was time for the influence of the Druids to pass and had thus sent Myrddin to him with a message from his dead brother and father. He found this thought comforting, for it allowed him to see the coming mission as a Christian calling rather than the directions of a heathen wizard influenced by ancient spirits. But then, it did not take much wisdom to see the fundamental motivation for Myrddin's machinations was more statecraft than witchcraft.

A snore emanated from under the seer's cowl, ending any prospect of further discussion. No matter, Martin was already resolved to join the expedition to Reged. He had sensed for some time a change was coming – his own dreams had indicated such and were just as terrifying as those described by Myrddin.

A Journey West

Verbeia

November 446

The howling wind suppressed the roar of the rushing river. In spate after several days of rain and sleet, the brown water betrayed the peaty heights above as the river's source. This was not the best time of year to travel but there was no choice. The urgency of their mission had demanded immediate departure despite the many risks.

Surprised though Cian had been by his king's decision, he had followed Mor's order to assemble a turma to support Reged. It was now the second day of their journey, and they carefully guided their iron-shod horses through the narrow valley, following a track that was sometimes rock and otherwise bog. They proceeded two by two, but progress was slow because the horses were valued as highly as their riders. The king had been clear: a lame horse would result in its rider's return to Elfed in shame; careful handling was more important than speed.

The riders, muffled in their hooded capes, kept their heads down, deflecting the sleety wind, concentrating on the difficult terrain. Ahead, a dull white glow amongst a billowing grey mass demarked the Pennine fells. Snow had settled on the high ground promising a bitter welcome in the direction of Erechwyd. Cian had visited the land through which they were passing before. It was known as Crafen, a desolate region full of strangely shaped rocks and deep caves that were gateways to the Otherworld. He shivered at the thought, but thankfully their path was well-trod, and Cian took comfort from the presence of both Derwyn the scout sent to guide them and Myrddin whose ancestors were known to have been the Druids of the high Pennines. Keeping the old seer company was the priest Martin, girded with his great sword. His presence had been requested by Mor, not so much for his Christian succour but for his remarkable fighting ability. Cian had no idea where the priest had acquired such skills and, out of respect, never asked. The king at his side stared resolutely into the distance, wearing a mask of grim determination overlaid with foreboding, for no one knew what danger they were riding toward.

They had been told to expect armed confrontation, perhaps even a battle. But Mor's brother Gorwst was the powerful, God-fearing King of Reged so why did he need the assistance of Elfed? Cian tried to push the worry out of his mind. His king was an excellent judge of such circumstances, but why on this occasion was he so strangely reticent to discuss their objective? No matter – they were only one day into a four-day journey, and the fear that always accompanied the eve of battle was yet to grip their souls.

His thoughts switched to their sons. This was to be their boys' first real confrontation, for Agiluf and Prince Arthwys had yet to draw enemy blood. Cian shook his head and forced a grim smile through gritted teeth. The boys' excitement was understandable – after all, they had been weaned on heroic tales, and then their training had been more intense than even a Roman cavalry officer might expect. The youthful warriors were ready – everyone believed so – and they would fight with valour, particularly from horseback. Their skills were far better than his at their age, but Cian knew the brutal differences between the battlefield and the training ground. Fear would challenge their bravery, and ultimately, the boys' fate would be in the hands of the Lord. He resolved to continue praying hard for their safe deliverance. Lost in his thoughts and hardly noticing the journey, Cian was startled by the king's voice, raised to penetrate the wind.

'This journey will prove more difficult than I thought. There looks to be much snow in the west. We must arrive at our destination no later than the kalends or we risk undermining Gorwst's surprise attack. Derwyn advised four days in fair weather, but I now think five, leaving only one day to contact Gorwst and set out plans.'

Cian turned to speak. 'We must not rush the horses, my king, and surely your brother will already be there and prepared?'

'True,' replied the king. 'Let us hope the messenger we sent confirming our agreement to Gorwst's request has not been delayed by this weather.'

'King Gorwst will not wait for the messenger. He will set off, regardless, to ensure he meets his proposed timing... expecting us to do the same.'

Mor's grim look turned to a smile. 'That is my opinion. He is brave and somewhat impetuous, but he will have planned for such pitfalls.' Mor paused then spoke again. 'My brother will be disappointed that I have been unable to muster more men to fight. There was too little time, and we cannot leave Elfed unprotected.'

'The threat of Saxon attack is great, my king,' replied Cian.

'It will yet happen,' sighed Mor, 'but for now, Hengist's forces attack softer targets. His army still ravages the countryside to the south and west of Lindum. Our fellow countrymen have fled to the protection of Vortimer, Vortigern and Ambrosius. These Saxons do not seek territory but resources. They need crops and cattle to sustain their ever-increasing army.'

Cian nodded in agreement. 'The recent rumours are harrowing... Ratae Corieltauvorum burnt to the ground, and everyone murdered. The rebellion is becoming a war.'

'Fortunately, it is not yet our war, Cian. Hengist is no fool. I sense he has gauged how strongly we will retaliate. A war on two fronts will not suit him, so we are safe for the time being. For now, we must sit on our hands to protect our interests.' Mor grimaced once more.

Cian knew the king had received several requests to intervene, for as King's Secretary, it had been his duty to write the replies. Gorwst and Mor had both declined to send troops south, even in support of the Cornovii, because of the plague which was spreading from the west. Many had died, and in all regions, militia numbers had been drastically reduced. The plague had left its greatest mark on the more susceptible elders, leaving only the young to tend the fields and flocks. This left precious little time for warriors to train, and now both Mor and Gorwst could barely protect their own kingdoms. The Saxon army was rumoured to number in the thousands, and though, aside from random raids, they had not yet forayed north, that day would surely come, just as Myrddin prophesised.

Cian's own family had not escaped the plague. Both his father and mother had been taken by the disease, leaving his brother and sister to run their villa. Everyone knew someone who had died. Tragically, Queen Igerna's cousin, Sevira, had also succumbed, mercifully just before the Saxon onslaught that had resulted in Viroconium being sacked. The world of the Britons was in turmoil. Mor and his queen regretted abandoning their friends and allies, but the choices were stark and the risks too great. The mighty Roman Empire was a distant memory in the North, and the Coeling kingdoms were now more isolated than ever. Mor's decisions, throughout, had been the right ones for Elfed and Reged, and Cian had agreed with them all… until now.

Why was the king so intent upon risking so much for so little? For eight years, Cian had been Mor's most trusted adviser. Bryn was equally close to the queen, sharing both her joys and sorrows, but neither Cian's nor his wife's opinions had been sought about this dangerous venture. Everything had happened so quickly. A messenger had arrived from Gorwst, accompanied by the experienced scout Derwyn. Mor had then consulted for several hours in private with Myrddin who, after a three-year absence, had appeared from nowhere. Following this, the king had issued an instruction to assemble a force of warriors, just enough so as not to weaken the defence of Elfed. Not a word to Cian about what could possibly be more important than the Saxon threat.

Derwyn led the party out of the valley, and in the lee of the fell where the wind was less pressing, Cian grasped his opportunity.

'My king, I've been meaning to ask you about the purpose of this expedition.'

Mor's troubled expression broke once more into a grim smile. 'It is a serious problem, my friend, a family matter. You are doubtless offended that I have not sought your counsel?'

'Not so much offended, my king, more surprised.'

'You are my most trusted friend. I rely on your pragmatism – it has served Elfed well, and in truth, it is that pragmatism that dissuaded me from seeking your counsel, on this occasion. If presented with the facts of this venture, you would surely have tried to deter me, for the odds are not in our favour, even if the omens are.'

'How so, my king?'

'King Nathi, a mighty warrior king of Hibernia, has been raiding Reged from Insula Manavia, but he has now begun taking territory, launching a stealthy invasion. This king's confidence grows with each success, and he has now captured the port of Itunocelum where he has laid siege to Formenus, King of Erechwyd, and his two daughters.'

'Surely, Gorwst, with his allies, can easily crush this Gael.'

'My first thoughts too, but there are family complications, and his ally Coroticus has declined to help. As you know, to your family's cost, the plague is widespread in the north-west, and my brother's militia has been sorely affected. Military success is not, therefore, a foregone conclusion. The circumstances are further complicated because Gorwst's family are friends of Formenus and his family.'

'Is that sufficient pretext to take Elfed to war?'

Cian saw the king's jaw tense. 'It is a matter of prestige and family honour. Myrddin has convinced me there is treachery. And the Coelings must fight for each other.'

'Of course, my king,' Cian said respectfully. 'What is the plan?'

'Gorwst intends to coax Nathi to battle whilst we approach Itunocelum through the mountains to the south and release Formenus.'

'You were right not to seek my advice,' Cian said. 'I would certainly have sought to dissuade you from this venture. You mentioned omens?'

'Yes, Myrddin is insistent that we help Gorwst.'

'Really!' exclaimed Cian, doubting the seer's opinion should hold any such weight. 'Is he so concerned about tribal unity?'

'Always, but he tells me he has seen this all in his dreams, and it is imperative that we rescue Formenus and his daughters.'

Whilst Cian trusted the king, he did not share Mor's faith in Myrddin's mysterious visions. The seer was so old, often seeming confused, and had only recently returned to Elfed after a long, mysterious absence.

They had reached the brow of the hill, where once more, the wind whipped directly into their faces. Pushing on, head down, Cian had much to reflect upon. He asked no further questions, though he still had need of many answers.

The Bishop and the General

Civitas Turonum, Gaul

November 446

Count Romanus had left Rome a full week before Magister Militum Aetius but still had not completed his preparations. As aide to the West's most senior general, it was his task to set up a field headquarters in support of what looked like an increasingly complex campaign to hold Gaul against attacks from both barbarians and rebels. The news reaching Rome had not been good, bacaudae rising in both Armorica and Hispania, Frankish attacks in Belgica Secunda and unrest amongst the Suebi in Gallaecia. To say that resources were stretched was an understatement. With the help of his many secretaries, he had laid out Aetius' map of the continent showing both the Empire's and the enemy's troop deployment, and the bare facts were obvious. Without Aetius' extraordinary influence over the Huns and their military support, the West might easily be lost. Romanus' musings were interrupted by the thunderous noise of cavalry approaching down cobbled streets, announcing the arrival of his master.

'Good God, he's here already. Did you send the bishops away?'

'No, they refused to leave. They claimed to be well-informed that the magister militum would be arriving soon,' replied Constantius, his most able secretary.

'The Church, it seems, has the power to predict military manoeuvres.'

Constantius laughed. 'They are all spies for the Pope.'

'This report of Bleda's murder, you say it has come direct from the frontier and that Rome is yet unaware?'

'That is my understanding.'

'Well, Aetius will understand better than anyone the implications, but all that power now in the hands of Attila is a worry.'

With a grim smile, the count left the map chamber, carefully closing the doors behind him, and stood in the centre of the huge entrance hall. The doors were opened by two bodyguards, and Aetius swept in, wearing a uniform similar to that of his comrades.

'Ah, Romanus, a fine morning, but a little cooler than Rome.'

'Yes, cooler and much less stifling, my lord,' he replied, with a twinkle in his eye.

'Quite so.' Aetius' tone communicated he'd detected the inference. 'Are my headquarters ready?'

'Operational, my lord, but with tasks to complete.'

Servants scurried out with small tables and chairs for the group.

'Where is Majorian?'

'He is pushing the Franks north and will return once he has ensured they have crossed the Seine.'

'He is a fine and courageous soldier; we are much the safer for his presence in our ranks.'

'That is so, my lord, but we must first discuss the far more serious threat the Huns now pose.'

'Has something changed to increase your concern? Have they not always rallied to my support?'

'I have heard only today that Attila has murdered Bleda.' Romanus paused to allow the grave news to sink in. 'The Huns have already pillaged the eastern Empire into near submission, with only the walls of Constantinople left to protect the Emperor. But with Bleda dead, Attila will be beyond control. Our ambassadors say he genuinely believes he is a god sent to subdue Rome, and if he is prepared to murder his own brother, then your friendship may be similarly disposable.'

The shock was clear on Aetius' face. 'I knew Bleda well, and it is true he provided balance to Atilla's ambitions. Now it will only be a matter of time before he attacks Rome, but we must be prepared for him coming west first, to extinguish the threat of our military at his back.'

'Exactly, my lord. You are the only credible rival to the success of Attila's plans.'

Aetius looked distracted, no doubt grappling with a plan to contain the Huns. Much would depend upon whether there was any remaining chance Aetius could still trust Attila. Moreover, the Hunnish army was a ravenous beast that gobbled up cities for their booty. Romanus had long wondered if Attila controlled his army, or the army controlled him. Either way, Aetius would be wise to remain cautious. Romanus could think of no contingency if Attila were to come west, and if his commander's luck ran out, then so too would Rome's.'

'My lord, I have further news.'

'I hope it is an improvement on the last?'

'Well, it is a surprise. You have two visitors. Bishops Germanus and Severus await your audience.'

Aetius paused, looking curious, and then laughed.

'Are they here on a Christian mission, or is there other mischief?'

'They claim to be visiting the shrine of Martin, but my staff tell me they are recently back from Britannia and have been in communication with the Armorican rebels.'

'I have great respect for Germanus. He presided well as a duke of this region, under Emperor Honorius, but he interprets events in the light of former glories and has little understanding of our current vulnerabilities. It is well that I should brief him. Who is this Severus?'

'The recently invested Bishop of Treverorum, my lord.'

'Then he will know how we deal with rebels, following our suppression of the Burgundians in that region. Bring them both to me.'

As Romanus gave instructions for the bishops to be summoned, he breathed a sigh of relief at his superior's good spirits. Aetius had an iron will and feared no one, making it a challenge to anticipate his reactions to any unexpected circumstance. His swift grasp of detail and rapid decision-making contrasted starkly with standard Roman procedure and rationale, but more than anyone Romanus had met, Aetius understood the minds of his barbarian enemies. As a boy, he had experienced life as an ambassadorial hostage, first to Alaric the Goth and then to Uldin, King of the Huns. He spoke both their languages, understood their ambitions and knew how to engage with their heroic bravado. No one was better informed to defend the Empire. But no matter how much Romanus admired him, he remained aware that Aetius' impeccable courtly manners shrouded a fierce, ruthless ambition, and those privileged to be on his staff or chosen as his generals should never feel completely secure.

The bishops duly arrived, attired as pilgrims – a necessary precaution when travelling, but this seemed to amuse Aetius.

'Welcome, your Graces, I trust your journey will not be fruitless. I observe that your appearance rather belies the true wealth and power of the Church!'

Germanus looked frail, but his voice was eloquent and strong. 'Thank you for this audience, Aetius. We come to worship at the shrine of Martin, and it is only providence that brings us before you.'

'Romanus, please seat the bishops. Pilgrims, I am told, often benefit from revelation which is surely better experienced seated.'

'Thank you, Aetius,' Germanus replied, passing over the count's taunt, 'my limbs are weak, but God has given me strength of purpose, and I am convinced He is responsible for this opportune coincidence.'

Romanus caught Aetius' eye and shared a knowing smile at the pilgrim's fortunate coincidence.

'How may we help you, Germanus?'

'You will know that Armorica was once my responsibility and that the cives there are Roman and Christian. They are hard-working and hard-pressed by the heathen tribe of Alans you send to collect their taxes.

Many atrocities have been reported, testing our people's allegiance to the Empire. In my day, we would have engaged in debate through the publicanus, but by sending violent heathen barbarians as tax collectors, you are alienating and infuriating our own people. The Church stands ready to assist the state in fulfilling the role of tax collector.'

Aetius frowned, his jaw set. He closed his eyes for some ten seconds and then spoke.

'Taxes have never been higher. Our young emperor balances his accounts by raising taxes to match the Empire's expenditure. Your peace-loving Armoricans have already murdered the publicanus and now threaten us as rebels. They have lost their cives status and represent a threat to the Empire. King Goar and his Alans are foederati allies, and I am here, as you may have rightly guessed, to suppress this Armorican rebellion.'

'My lord, this has gone too far. I beg you to reconsider. They are *our* people, honest Christians who are appalled by the lack of Roman justice.'

Romanus winced. The bishop's last comment would surely tip Aetius over the edge, but the count remained calm.

'Remind me, Germanus, when you were Duke of Armorica, what was the strength of the Roman legions in Gaul?'

'I believe it was approaching fifty thousand.'

'Yet, your generation, with its adherence to law, allowed the barbarians to cross the Rhine and breach the Limes Germanicus, the same barbarians who now wreak havoc across the continent. I am tasked with clearing up this mess but with less than half the legions that protected you!' Aetius voice was getting louder. 'Yes, Germanus, you can help me. Tell these Armorican bacaudae to disband and pay their taxes, or I will surely crush them and confiscate their property. Roman citizenship and their religion count for nothing if they break our laws.'

Germanus remained calm. 'I can see the Empire is in a vicious spiral of decline, my lord. I only hoped I could convince you that the Armoricans provide more value as your allies.'

'Rebels think like rebels and behave like rebels; they will not change. Mercenaries do not have cause or conscience, requiring only payment. I trust the Alans more than your Armoricans, and I will not negotiate with these rebels. Romanus, is my map room ready?'

'It is, my lord.'

'Come, bishops, let me show you the extent of the threats to our empire's very existence.'

Germanus hesitated then asked a further question. 'There is another matter, my lord. The Britons tell me they have appealed for your help. They are beset by seaborne raiders but have yet to receive your reply?'

Aetius turned to Germanus as Romanus opened the map-room doors.

'Ah yes, the Britons. I received their appeal but can do nothing. They are in a similar situation to us. Come, let me show you.'

The room was dark around the edges, but the light from the high windows fell perfectly on the large representation of the continent. Aetius waved his hand toward Romanus. 'Explain our predicament to the bishops.'

Romanus cleared his throat. 'This is an approximate representation of the Roman Empire and our neighbours. To the north, from the Rhine to the Volga, is the ever-growing Hunnic empire. Now these wooden blocks grouped together represent troops in four different sizes. The largest is twenty thousand, the middle is ten thousand and the smallest complete brick is five thousand. Half a small brick denotes one thousand. As you can see, we believe King Attila can field one hundred thousand Hunnic troops in the West, and one hundred thousand in the East. We know the eastern Emperor Theodosius has at least one hundred thousand troops, but they are spread evenly about his territories to counter both the Huns and the Persians, though even now, he is paying the Huns an enormous tribute to avoid conflict.' Romanus pointed at the bottom of the map. 'Here, the Vandals have swept across North Africa and have captured the Empire's cornfields and many boats at Carthage. We estimate their strength as twenty thousand men, and although the Vandal king, Gaiseric, was recently repulsed from Sicily, he still covets the islands of the Mare Nostrum, and he will no doubt use his newly acquired fleet to attack them. Coming north, Hispania is dominated by ten thousand Suebi. Further north, in the Pyrenees, we estimate perhaps two to three thousand bacaudae pursuing a similar cause to your Armoricans.' Romanus pointed further north on the Atlantic coast. 'Our long-standing rivals, the Goths, have thirty thousand men in Aquitania, and here, further up the coast, we believe the Armorican rebels are no more than two to three thousand strong?'

Romanus looked to Germanus for confirmation, but none was forthcoming.

'North of here, on the north-west Atlantic coast, the Frankish king, Chlodio, commands about twenty thousand troops. Coming east, in line with Treverorum, we meet the Hunnic empire once more, occupying an area formerly held by the Burgundians – who are now resettled to the south of Lake Lemanus.'

Bishop Germanus looked at Aetius. 'I presume these five small purple bricks are our legions?'

'Exactly. Without mercenaries, we would be unable to defend the Empire, but for now, I am fortunate to enjoy Hunnish support.'

'For now,' Romanus repeated, looking nervously toward Aetius. 'By which I mean we imagine all outcomes,' he added. Turning to the bishops, he continued, 'Your Graces, we have very little information on Britannia but are aware of your visit. Do they still have an army?'

Germanus did not hesitate in sharing this information. 'I estimate no more than five thousand militia stationed at various points.'

Aetius now questioned the bishop. 'And what of the Saxons? We hear their numbers have grown to such an extent that they now dominate the east of the island?'

'They have established a colony in the region of Lindum from which they raid aggressively. The Britons are alarmed by the rate of their migration, and it seems their army now numbers between three and five thousand, a considerable force to contend with.'

Aetius looked at the bishops. 'It was my understanding these Saxons were mercenaries in the pay of the Britons, offering their assistance against the Picts?'

'The picture is confusing, but they appear to have rebelled.'

'Ah, more rebels,' said the general pointedly. 'Even if there was a will to assist the Britons, as you can see, we have no reserves. They will not sympathise with our plight, but we cannot help, not whilst the taxes from our diminished empire remain insufficient to even pay for the soldiers we require for our own defence.'

'We understand your position, Aetius – the Britons must defend themselves. But do you understand our viewpoint with respect to Armorica?' The bishop paused, looking directly at Aetius. 'We have become spectators to a gruesome spectacle. We watch from behind our town walls as the northern wolves tear at the carcass of our Christian empire, an empire in which it no longer counts in your favour to be either a Roman or a Christian.'

Aetius rounded on the bishop, now visibly irritated at the cleric's persistence. 'It was not my generation that unleashed this wolf pack, Germanus.'

The bishop steadied his gaze. 'True, but there is no justification for the Empire joining with the frenzied pack.'

Germanus seemed to be deliberately pushing Aetius, and Romanus noticed Severus grimacing at his colleague's boldness, but the wily commander surprised them all.

'Your Graces, we must maintain a balanced view of the overall position. I receive my instructions from the Emperor and the senate, but there is one other person who influences us all – Galla Placidia, and she is a most devout

Christian. Please take your disagreements to her, for the empress is better placed to understand your views. In the meantime, I urge you to return to your cities to ensure that the cives in your flocks are suitably prepared for war, for it will surely come from one direction or another. Aetius stood. 'Your Graces, this audience is over. I shall detain you no longer from the shrine of Saint Martin.'

'Thank you, Count Aetius,' said a relieved Severus. 'We shall be on our way.'

The bishops stood, bowed and turned. As they walked slowly to the door, Aetius added, 'May God protect you on your journey to Rome, Germanus.' The bishop waved his hand and nodded, his grim expression betraying his understanding that he had achieved nothing.

When the doors had closed behind them, Aetius turned to Romanus, his brow furrowed. 'The Armorican rebel leader is clever to seek Church support. What is his name?'

'According to our sources, he is called Eudoxius – we executed Tibatto.'

'We shall execute this one too, regardless of the old bishop's plea.' Aetius paused and looked to be reviewing the meeting in his mind. 'Do we know anything about these Saxons? They appear to have a sizeable fighting force with sufficient boats to transport it.'

'We believe their leader is called Hengist. I was interested to note that their settlements are around Lindum Colonae in the province of Flavia Caesariensis. Technically, this region still belongs to the Emperor, not the Britons.'

'Why does this interest you, Romanus?'

'Perhaps we should offer these Saxons foederati status? They would make good mercenaries to help us with the Armorican rebels, and they will also provide a buffer against the Goths. There are islands off the coast of Armorica where they could station their keels.'

'I see no harm in making contact. Send a messenger; we will certainly need every able-bodied warrior in the West, if Attila breaks his treaties, and the Britons will not miss their enemy's attention.'

Romanus sensed that his master was already treating the dreadful prospect of war with Attila as inevitable.

Mor Prepares for Battle

Erechwyd

November 446

The journey was the coldest Agiluf had experienced in his fifteen years. The route had brought them first past an estuary where the sands stretched as far as the eye could see and then to the tips of two enormous freshwater lakes, both surrounded by high, snow-capped mountains that continually disappeared into cloud, giving only occasional glimpses of their rocky grandeur. There was an atmosphere of great mystery to the region of Erechwyd, and the young warrior was captivated, despite his near-frozen hands and feet.

'It will be difficult to hold our swords in these conditions,' commented Prince Arthwys.

The intermittent sleet showers had covered both the young warriors' capes, as well as their plodding ponies.

'It will be the same for the enemy,' replied Agiluf. 'I am looking forward to warming up.'

'This region is so barren the wind sweeps straight off the sea, and I have never seen so many lakes and mountain tarns.'

'Derwyn says that, once we are past this last tarn, we will arrive at a forest where we may risk camp-fires to warm up before the battle tomorrow. He says, even though there is shelter in the forest, we will be perilously close to our enemies, so we must remain quiet and take great care. Do you know who it is we are preparing to fight? My father has said nothing.'

'Neither has mine, but I overheard that we will be linking up with King Gorwst and my cousins – although there is some worry as to where this meeting is to take place. Derwyn and Father intend to scout the whole area under the cover of darkness.'

As the troop began to descend from the mountain slopes, they were all relieved to see the edge of a forest shrouded in the mist, just as Derwyn had described. Sheltered from the searching wind, Agiluf, Arthwys and their fellow soldiers dismounted and began stamping their feet and rubbing their hands to get some warmth back. They tethered their ponies and gave them a thoroughly deserved feed from the nosebags of bran they all carried, and although the feed was soaked through, it did not bother the hungry steeds. Finding dry kindling was a challenge, but a search around rocky crags located autumn leaves that had blown into crevices where the rain and sleet could not penetrate. They chose a hollow to build their fire, hoping it would shelter the light from the enemy's view. The men only whispered as biscuits were shared and cups of warmed water were passed around. They were all ravenous from five days' travel over difficult terrain, and discussion turned to the feast that would surely follow their victory. The promise of a feast was as good a reason as any to defeat the enemy.

They all huddled close to the fire in a circle, the flames dancing, lighting up their worried faces. It was the eve of the kalends, but there was still no sign of Gorwst. Agiluf watched as King Mor, Derwyn and Winnog set out in the dark to scout the river valley and estuary. He was grateful that he could stay close to the fire and hopefully sleep, but first, he prayed silently, hoping the Lord would watch over him in his first battle because fear was beginning to knot his empty stomach.

The wind howled through the tall, swaying trees, under which they sheltered, and Agiluf drifted in and out of a dreamworld of galloping horses and clashing swords. He was startled awake many hours later by the return of the scouting party. No one spoke, and they quickly settled down to rest. Agiluf drifted back to sleep again. When dawn broke, there was no birdsong, the wind still howled, and the sleet had turned to a light snow. A distant rumbling of thunder and a darkening sky left them in no doubt the weather would deteriorate further. Agiluf's mind quickly filled with the fear from the night before. He overheard whispers – the scouting party had not made contact with Gorwst. He hoped that might be reason to make the king delay, especially because it would be difficult to fight in such poor conditions. He swallowed hard and began moving around to push the worries out of his mind and warm up, checking first on his pony then collecting firewood. The camp was stirring but little was said. Agiluf was just wondering if all the warriors shared his apprehension when the king called for their attention.

'Gather round, men.'

The troop drew as close as possible, and Mor spoke in a quiet voice.

'We have seen our enemy and know our objectives. Only half a mile from here is the Esk estuary at Itunocelum. Pulled onto the beach are three keels, guarded by about ten men. They are Gaels, fierce warriors from Hibernia who raid this coast. Close by these keels are twenty or so women and children, all tied together, taken prisoner for slaves by these raiders. We were unable to scout the town, but slightly further inland is a castrum surrounded by what appears to be the rest of these warriors, perhaps thirty or so. We believe King Formenus is either barricaded inside or is being held prisoner, but we were unable to get close enough to be sure. It seems that these Gaels were preparing to sail away but are delayed by the weather or, perhaps, are waiting to ransom the king. King Gorwst gave me his word he would be here to fight this very day, but we were unable to locate him last night. In his absence, Cian, Winnog and I have agreed a plan of attack, which we will delay until after midday in the hope that Gorwst appears. We are outnumbered, but with surprise on our side, the odds will even.'

Mor looked around at his men. Agiluf sensed an increased apprehension with the news that the mighty warrior Gorwst might not arrive. The king must have read their thoughts.

'Do not fear these Gaels – you are better trained and better equipped. We should try to fight from horseback, for the terrain lends itself to that. The Gaels look to have some horses, but they are probably stolen, and it is unlikely they are trained for battle. Believe in yourselves and have faith in our God and each other.'

Mor picked up his javelin and drew the outline of the estuary in the earth by the fire.

'The river Esk curls like a snake and is shallow at low tide. The keels are positioned here, and the slaves close by, just here.' He pointed, using the tip of his javelin. 'Cian and I will lead fifteen of you inland, circling around to the ford on the estuary to attack with a surprise charge from across the river. We will attempt to release the slaves and expect that the commotion will draw the warriors away from the castrum. Winnog, with his fellow archers, and Arthwys, Agiluf, Martin and Myrddin will make their way upstream, cross the Esk then follow the top of the fell down to the rear of the castrum. Once the raiders are drawn away from the tower, you must first rescue Formenus and whoever else is with him, then drop back up the fell, holding your position there until we reach you. If we fail to break through, do not wait for the enemy to find you, but take the road to the fort of Mediobogdum.'

Arthwys was listening intently. 'Should we charge at these Gaels like you, Father?'

'No, Arthwys. Rescue and withdraw. With Winnog's archers covering you, you should have sufficient time – much will depend upon how quickly Formenus exits the tower, so make sure he is on his toes.'

'After four weeks' incarceration, he will likely be on his knees, my king,' remarked Cian, giving Arthwys and Agiluf a cautionary glance.

King Mor paused and then turned to the priest. 'Is God with us, Martin?'

'He is, my king, and expects us to destroy these heathen thieves.'

'And what of the omens, Myrddin?'

'We have dark skies to cloak our arrival, snow to obscure their vision, and I hear distant thunder readying to announce our victory. The omens are good, King Mor.'

'Good, then we shall break camp and carefully move to our agreed holding positions.'

Agiluf breathed a sigh of relief. He had a clear objective, and they would be under the command of Winnog who was a first-rate leader.

Arthwys turned to Agiluf. 'I wish I was joining in the charge across the river. The fighting will be intense when these warriors come running down the hill to defend their keels.'

'You are brave, Arthwys, but the rescue of Formenus will require quick-thinking and fast reaction. The king has entrusted us with this task, and no one yet knows what condition these prisoners will be in – we may need to carry them to safety.'

Agiluf understood why Arthwys wanted to be in the thick of it – he was keen to show his prowess after all the years of training. Even at his young age, the prince was an excellent horseman – more so than most warriors – but he had yet to prove himself in battle. The older boys had begun to tease him about this, in particular his older cousins. They had scoffed at his being named 'Bear of the Tribes', claiming it was a mistake and that he would be challenged. This had caused fights between the youths when Mor's family had visited Gorwst at Banna. But Myrddin was never in doubt, saying that the fates had chosen Arthwys and would be watching over him. The young prince was Agiluf's best friend, and they had secretly sworn to fight side by side to protect each other, even dying side by side, if it came to it. A brave and strangely comforting oath when first given, but a terrifying thought on this morning of battle. Agiluf swallowed hard. Now was the time to go about his duties and consign his fears to beyond the immediate tasks. Now was the time to show what he was trained for.

*

Cian watched Winnog and his men quietly leave camp in an easterly direction. Agiluf filled him with pride, but he knew Bryn would be full of apprehension at the prospect of this battle. His thoughts drifted back to his own battle encounters, and he prayed his son would be sensible and stay close to Arthwys so that they might protect one another. He reached under his saddle to tighten his horse's girth. His steed stood perfectly still, watching his master, his flicking tail signalling the tension he was picking up, sensing the importance of the day.

'There, there, boy,' said Cian, stroking the beast's neck to comfort him. Then whispering, 'By tonight, we will be coated in Gael blood or perhaps our own.'

Cian had many times witnessed the terrible wounds horses received for their loyalty to man.

'Perhaps the Lord will spare us both,' he added, stroking him again.

It would take them three hours to circle around under tree cover to reach the ford, by which time the rescue party would be in position and waiting for the signs and sounds of their attack. Mor signalled to his men to mount up and follow the path back to the track beyond the ridge. Cian drew alongside his king.

'I hope your brother is close.'

Mor looked at his companion, his brow furrowed with worry. 'So do I, but we cannot delay. We must carry this day, with or without him.'

Nothing more was said as they left the protection of the trees, riding into an unwelcome headwind full of icy snow. At least this weather would be at their backs as they attacked across the estuary. They would need both surprise and the elements on their side if they were to succeed. He had no doubt the question on his mind was vexing Mor just as much.

Where in God's name was Gorwst?

The Edge of the Empire

Venta Belgarum

November 446

Dawn was just breaking over Venta Belgarum, and servants were beginning to scurry about in the large townhouse, but Ambrosius had woken much earlier. He had a great deal to consider before the departure from Britannia of the embassy from Armorica. Reading by candlelight was becoming more difficult as each year passed, and whilst the light of the dawn provided welcome respite for his eyes, it did nothing to help with his decision.

Strewn across his table were many scrolls containing correspondence from his contacts in Gaul, all painting a grim picture of the Roman world. There were many tales of woe, amongst them the news that his family's old estates near Civitas Aurelianum were now occupied by barbarians – not invaders, but on the direction of the powerful Aetius, the Empire's senior general in the West. Memories of his parents' villa were sparse, just occasional glimpses from his childhood which often came to mind as he watched his own children grow. He had never given up hope of a return to Gaul, but nobody could have expected his family's nemesis and executioner, the Emperor Honorius, to remain in power for so long. Yet even now, years after Honorius' passing, the time was still not right. He stood and stretched away the stiffness that sitting in the same position brought upon him so much quicker these days and watched the rain running off the roof tiles into the garden below. Grimacing, he remembered how much warmer the climate was in his childhood Gaul, but then, Britannia's inclement weather was small price to pay for freedom.

'Father, are you joining us for breakfast?' His son's voice interrupted his reflections.

'Good morning, Ames. I will be along shortly.'

Ambrosius tidied his scrolls into a large wooden box and blew out the candle. His mind was now made up, and he would discuss his decision with his senior general Natalinus later.

The family were all seated, waiting for him as he helped himself to salted bread and boiled eggs, before sitting in his usual place. Both his wife and young daughter smiled without saying a word, seeming to sense his preoccupation, whereas Ames was full of questions.

'Will you assist the Armoricans, Father?'

Ambrosius smiled. He encouraged his son to take a keen interest in such matters and did not mind his probing.

'Not on this occasion,' he replied.

'But we have so much in common with them, and they need our support. Won't they be disappointed with your decision?'

'They may be, and truly my heart wants to help, but my mind is wary of the risks – in particular, the rising power of the Saxons here in Briton and the barbarians Aetius controls with the Empire's gold on the Continent.'

The answer would not satisfy his son, already a cavalry officer in the militia. The lad rose to every challenge, inspired by tales of former glories, and was hungry for martial encounter.

'The Saxons are no match for our cavalry, Father.'

'That is not what I have heard from King Vortimer. He says they are fierce and well organised. I don't doubt the superiority of our military, but the size of their infantry units makes them a considerable challenge. An expedition to Armorica at this time would leave our adopted homeland vulnerable. *Never choose to fight on two fronts at the same time,* my father would say, *for you will surely lose both wars.*'

Ambrosius was rightly proud of his spirited son. He had been tutored and trained as a Roman soldier, and perhaps one day, he would recover the family's lands and reputation. Ambrosius had hoped for such an opportunity, all his life, but Rome had never before felt so distant, and supporting an Armorican uprising was not the right pretext.

'I plan to discuss this subject with General Natalinus before we meet Eudoxius and give him an answer. Now, eat your breakfast or you will be late for your drills.'

'When will your guests arrive?' asked Helen.

Ambrosius looked at his wife and smiled. 'Natalinus and his father will be here shortly. Eudoxius and his embassy will come mid-morning.'

'Bishop Germanus expressed hope that you might help this Eudoxius, especially as so many of our Christian brethren have emigrated to Armorica to seek the protection of Rome and the Church.'

'And that is the conundrum, wife. Rome demands increased taxes but does not provide justice or protection for its citizens. I have great respect for Germanus, but he stands for what Rome was, rather than what it has become.'

Ambrosius held no misconceptions about the rights and wrongs of war, for he knew from experience that only military might mattered. Opposing the Empire was always a high stakes gamble – as far as he was aware, his own father's and uncle's heads were still skewered on spears on the walls of Ravenna. Heroes or traitors? Only the outcome of battle conferred who was remembered as which.

'One day.' Ambrosius sighed. 'One day, we will return to Gaul in triumph.'

'I will make it so, Father,' said his brave son.

The Battle at the Shore

Itunocelum

Kalends, November 446

Cian stood alongside Mor as the king cupped his hands over his eyes to reduce the glare from the swirling snow and looked across the estuary. The tide was nearly out, but there had been a worrying development.

'I see it,' said Mor. 'You're right – another keel has arrived.'

'More warriors,' whispered Cian, 'but we are already committed.' Fear gripped him at the enormity of their challenge.

Mor turned to him. 'Gorwst will come – I know it.'

Cian was not so sure; there was no sign of approaching warriors. 'We must attack quickly. Surprise is our only hope.'

The king nodded in agreement. Cian looked up at the sky, hoping for a break in the weather, but all he saw was strange, unbroken black cloud.

Mor made a circular motion with his hand above his head, indicating the rest of his men should mount their steeds. They did this quietly, without speaking, drawing close behind Cian and their king. As the two of them encouraged their horses into the ford's shallows, the men followed, and although the horses' hooves sank initially into shale and fine gravel, the footing beneath was firm. The wind and snow muffled the sound of their horses splashing through the river, but Cian could see their attack was already detected. Enemy guards ran in different directions, raising their spears.

Mor signalled again, and his cavalry increased their pace to a canter, then fanning out into an attacking formation, they lowered their javelins. Cian, now close enough to hear the shouts of the enemy, chose his target from amongst the sentries formed up to face the charge. The sound of horses' hooves pounding on sand suddenly gave way to the brutal clash of battle – metal to metal, wooden shields splintering, men screaming in anger, fear and death. Cian's javelin skewered the neck of his intended victim. Then bursting through the line, he headed for the tethered slaves.

*

Gorwst and his band of warriors watched Mor's charge from the cover of the town buildings. They had arrived by stealth at dawn, quietly murdering all the enemy within, then waiting, fearful their allies might not come. Their position was some distance from Mor's, and without their horses, they would need to cover the ground on foot to link up with his brother's attack. Picking up his shield and spear to lead the charge, Gorwst stalled when there was a sudden crash of thunder and lightning overhead.

He turned to his son. 'Which god does this, ours or theirs? Is it a sign?' There was no time to dwell. 'Meirchiawn, stay close by me. *Forward*,' he screamed, as his warriors emerged from behind the buildings and ran in the direction of the shoreline.

*

From the cover of trees to the east, Winnog and Arthwys surveyed a large number of Gael warriors gathered around three camp-fires. There were more than fifty – many more than they had expected – but only a small number of horses.

The sounds of Mor's attack, with the accompanying crash of thunder and lightning, shattered the enemy's tranquillity, turning peace to chaos. Soldiers reached for their weapons, and the leaders quickly mounted their frightened steeds. One screamed orders, and they all began moving off toward the shoreline. Winnog waved to both his left and right flank, signalling his archers to move forward to each side of the castrum. Arthwys and Agiluf mounted their ponies and galloped to the front of the building where they dismounted and hammered on the barricaded door, shouting, 'Formenus, Formenus, we are here to rescue you.'

There was no answer.

Warriors at the enemy's rear caught sight of the surprise rescue and turned back toward the castrum shouting to their forward troops.

Realising their peril, Winnog shouted, 'Arthwys, for God's sake hurry.'

Once again, the young warriors hammered their sword pommels against the door, and this time a female voice called out from within.

'My father is sick; he cannot help us. The door is wedged with many rocks. We can move only one at a time.'

Realising their original plan was now undermined, Arthwys called to Winnog to join him at the entrance.

'The door is wedged, the castrum impregnable. We must find staves and try to force it open.'

'I fear there is no time,' answered Winnog, as his men loosed their arrows to pick off the approaching warriors.

*

Mor observed the battlefield. His men were holding off the guards by the shore whilst Cian released the tethered slaves, their surprise at the rescue apparent from their expressions.

Thank the Lord, Gorwst had made it, after all – even if his warriors had not yet reached the fighting. The enemy reinforcements were now streaming down the hill from the castrum, urged on by their king from horseback. The battle was about to intensify, and Mor could see they were heavily outnumbered. He wanted to keep an eye on the Gael king who was now joined by a retinue of other riders, but his concentration was drawn back to the raging battle already turning the snow-covered shore into bloody sludge. He slashed at the Gael foot soldiers attempting to unhorse him, but when he looked up again, the Gael king had disappeared from the ridge. He must have rumbled their plan and was likely galloping back to the castrum. Gorwst and his warriors were now fully engaged on Mor's left flank, making ground and drawing the attention of the greater part of the enemy fighting force.

Mor screamed to Cian, 'Arthwys, Agiluf, danger.'

He watched Cian leave the remaining slaves to free themselves, mount his horse and gallop past the fringe of the enemy to join Mor who already feared they would not reach Arthwys and Agiluf in time.

*

Martin and Myrddin had joined the men trying desperately to prise open the door at the front of the castrum. The rapidly falling snow now shrouded the advancing enemy, making their task even more perilous. Suddenly, horses loomed into view, and by the triumphant shouts from the Gael warriors, they did not carry King Mor or his militia.

'Their cavalry has returned,' screamed Winnog. 'My archers will struggle to bring them down in these conditions.'

Arthwys tugged at his friend's arm. 'Come, Agiluf, we can stall this attack.'

The boys jumped onto their ponies and, lifting their javelins, turned to face the approaching warriors.

'There are too many,' screamed Martin. 'Stay here with me.' His sword was at the ready, but Arthwys, seeming not to hear him, lowered his javelin, and the boys quickened their pace to a gallop. Martin could see the Gael king and his warriors raising their swords, gleefully preparing to cut down the brave, youthful challenge.

Suddenly, Myrddin called to him, 'Catch this whilst I find a sword,' and he threw his yew stave at the priest.

Instinctively, Martin caught it with his left hand. All at once, there was a blinding, fizzing flash accompanied by a deafening thunderous clap, so loud it made Martin's body shudder. By the time everyone's eyes and ears had recovered, the Gael king and his warriors all lay on the ground, vapour rising from their blackened bodies like their souls leaving them. Stunned by the noise and the flash, Arthwys and Agiluf had been thrown from their ponies, though mercifully, they had survived the fall unscathed and now wasted no time running their swords through the bodies of their prostrate enemy.

Winnog and his men watched the scene in awe, and Martin, who was still holding Myrddin's stave, could hardly believe what he had just witnessed. The old seer had disappeared around the back of the castrum, looking for his pony which had reared and bolted. Some of the men fell to their knees in prayer, convinced they had just witnessed a miracle.

'What happened?' asked Myrddin, upon his return.

'The most unlikely providence, a miracle by any standard,' Martin replied, watching the old man carefully.

'Providence is an invaluable battle companion,' said Myrddin, reaching to reclaim his yew stave from an incredulous Martin who was only too happy to return it.

*

Cian was galloping alongside Mor, fear at what they might encounter urging them on, when they met their sons trotting toward them with the body of the Gael king cast over a horse. Cian's heart leapt for joy, fear of the worst replaced by swelling pride.

Arthwys was first to speak. 'Formenus is safe, and the enemy are all dead.'

Cian turned to his king. 'We must quickly return to the battle to secure an immediate surrender. The Gaels will quit the fight when they see their king is dead.'

Mor nodded in agreement and, pulling his stallion's head in the direction of the shore, said, 'Remarkable, boys, but tell us of your adventure later. We can ill afford to lose any more men.'

They galloped back toward the fray.

*

Cian was first to reach the brow of the hill. He looked down to see Gorwst had pushed the Gaels up against the slope, though the enemy warriors still fought fiercely. He saw the Gael defence begin to falter, wide eyes turning to where Arthwys had crested the hill. Without ceremony, the young prince threw King Nathi's body to the ground, quickly taking the fight out of the Gaels. They stood frozen, still holding their weapons, uncertainty writ on their shocked faces.

Cian followed Mor as he rode toward Gorwst who was resting on his upright sword, the blade still running with blood. Leaping from his horse, Mor clasped his brother's shoulders.

'I am so glad to see you.'

But Gorwst's response was much more subdued than Cian would have expected.

'Thank you, brother. We shall give thanks to God for this victory. Nathi was not just an ordinary slaving pirate. Judging by the size of this force, he had every intention of occupying Erechwyd.'

Now surrounded, the Gaels threw down their weapons.

'What do you intend to do with these prisoners?' asked Mor.

'I will cut off their heads,' replied Gorwst, angrily.

Cian interrupted. 'Forgive my boldness, but would it not be wise to send a handful back to Hibernia with their dead king, so they can tell their fellows of the perils of setting foot in Reged.'

Gorwst looked toward Mor who nodded.

'That is indeed an excellent idea – clemency is a Christian virtue.'

Meirchiawn now joined the group, followed by Derwyn pulling along a bedraggled and frightened boy. 'Father, do you recognise this slave?'

Gorwst eyed the prisoner carefully. 'He looks familiar, like the messenger Coroticus sends to my wife?'

'He claims he was captured by the Gaels, but we found him hiding from us in a bush.'

'Why hide from your liberators?' asked Mor.

The boy spoke. 'I was frightened, my lords.'

Cian narrowed his eyes. Something was off here. 'Frightened to fight or frightened for other reasons?'

The boy lowered his head. 'Just frightened, my lords.'

Gorwst's demeanour suddenly changed.

'Keep him under guard, Derwyn. He will accompany us to Alt Clut, for the time has come to clear the air with my brother-in-law. What say you, Mor, will you accompany me?'

Mor looked toward Cian who nodded in agreement.

'Yes, we will come. It is important that our northern allies remain steadfast during these uncertain times, but let us wait to discuss this at the feast you must now furnish for us, brother!'

He clapped his brother on the back, and Gorwst laughed heartily.

'Of course, but first, I must find all my men, tend to the wounded and set these prisoners afloat with their dead king.'

*

The storm had passed by the time Cian and Mor picked their way through the corpses that littered their path back to the castrum. The macabre spectacle of Cymry warriors locked in fatal embrace with their enemy was a horrifying yet fascinating sight thanks to the covering of snow that gave the bodies the look of frozen sculptures depicting the very point of death.

'We have been fortunate with casualties,' said Mor, who was scanning the gruesome scene for men he recognised.

'Yes,' replied Cian, 'fortunate that our sons are not also dead heroes.'

Mor stopped his horse and turned toward Cian – had he offended his king?

'I regret I did not fully disclose the detail of this expedition to you, but as you must now see, my brother was barely clinging to his kingdom.'

'There is certainly treachery which must be addressed. For too long, we have assumed the treaties secured by your grandfather would hold firm through the generations, but it seems there are new pressures that do not to fit the old model.'

'That is Myrddin's view – the North must remain united to defend against the Picts. Their threat remains significant, even if it is not imminent.'

'Have you met King Coroticus?'

'No. When my brother married Coroticus' sister, the ceremony was at Alt Clut. Only my grandfather and mother attended, but I do remember Coel telling me Coroticus came to power in a manner which my grandfather found abhorrent. Even so, he was most insistent the security of the frontier was paramount, and so the marriage went ahead with his blessing.'

'I see, so perhaps this victory provides an opportunity for us to reaffirm this king's loyalty, even though we are suspicious of his motives. In which case, it would be as well to visit our other allies at Din Eidyn with the same purpose.'

'I agree, but there must be no show of force. Winnog should return to Elfed with some of the men, for our defences against the Saxons need bolstered there, anyway.'

Cian had never visited Alt Clut or Din Eidyn, but he knew where they were – in the far north, and at either end of a Roman turf wall. Much like the Roman stone wall, it was sited where the land-mass was narrow enough to be crossed in less than two days.

'We will be away at least a further three weeks – our women folk will feel deserted. I will send a message home with Agiluf.'

Mor laughed. 'He cannot deliver it. I am sending our sons with Martin to accompany Formenus and his daughters to their stronghold in the east of Erechwyd.'

'Then Winnog must explain all of our absences,' Cian replied, laughing.

As they approached the castrum, Cian could see Myrddin sat on the trunk of a felled tree. At the approach of their horses, the old man removed his cowl and waved.

His long, tangled white hair and beard showed great age, and as far as Cian knew, he was the only living man who had been a contemporary of the mighty King Coel. They dismounted their horses to join him.

Mor smiled at Myrddin who nodded. 'Gorwst is not himself, as you foresaw Myrddin, and there seems to be treachery amongst his allies.'

'So, if you can put a stop to it, the North will be safe for now?'

'Yes, tell me, is this report true, that Nathi and his warriors were killed by a lightning bolt?'

'Yes, Martin will tell you it was providence, but I tell you he is a wizard with even greater powers than I.'

'How so? He is but a priest,' said Mor incredulously.

'And a strangely skilful warrior,' added Cian.

'He is both,' replied Myrddin, 'but believe me when I tell you he is much more – he has the sight and can predict the future.' Both Mor and Cian looked at each other shocked. 'His name is Cynwyb, a man of royal blood, thought murdered by Coroticus, but he was brought back from the dead. He has not consciously deceived you, for the memory of who he was is buried deep within him where he stifles his desire for revenge. It seems he is protected by your God.' The next request was a surprise. 'You must appoint him as my successor, for my time is nearly past. I am confident he will advise you and give succour to the Bear, for the young cub will sorely need his help.'

'My old friend, are you ill?' asked Mor.

'Yes, each day may be my last, but no one must hear of my mortality, for I must live on in the minds of our allies and enemies alike.'

'We will consolidate Gorwst's victory with visits to our allies to refresh the treaties.'

'That is timely, for I have seen that a mighty Saxon war comes – not since the Romans has there been such a war, and like those terrible times, the whole island will burn. All will be threatened, and all may be lost. Only the Bear can stop this. I will be long gone, so I cannot influence its course, but Martin and his providence can.'

'It is my intention to send him across Erechwyd with Arthwys and Agiluf.'

'I shall accompany them, for there is much he needs to learn and quickly. Now, go about your business and complete your embassies to the north. Good luck and farewell.'

Mor and Cian walked alongside their horses toward the castrum, still stunned by Myrddin's revelations.

Mor turned to Cian. 'I have a strange feeling that was perhaps the last time we will ever speak to the old Druid.'

'Yes. You should speak with Martin, so he is aware of what you know and what you expect from him.'

Cian's mind was full, for this day had opened his eyes to his own shortcomings. The battle he would have wanted to persuade Mor to avoid had proved critical to the future of the North. By thinking only about defence, his judgement had been too narrow and would have resulted in him giving his king poor guidance. Myrddin, by contrast, was looking to future leadership, and not just for Elfed but the whole of the North. How was Arthwys to follow in the footsteps of his great-grandfather when he had to contend with so much division and so many enemies?

*

Before the feast commenced, Meirchiawn sought out his father for a private conversation. He had not seen him look so relieved for some time, and the Reged king was immensely pleased with the great value of booty they had recovered, as well as the huge cache of enemy weapons. This was a victory for his father in the face of a powerful enemy, and his mother and uncle would have to rethink their opinion of the Reged king as a weak leader. Who could have predicted the renowned Mor and his son Arthwys would so readily rally to his support, bringing not one but two magicians! Meirchiawn had heard of Myrddin's powers from his parents, but the priest was a new and potent force. The thundersnow had passed as quickly as it arrived, so it was clearly magic, and none of his men could recall seeing such a phenomenon before.

'The people are calling the priest Martin Merlinus, Father.'

Gorwst smiled. 'We should all be wary of such power. I have asked Mor and Cian to accompany me to Alt Clut for that reason. Coroticus must hear of what has happened here. I believe King Nathi's manner of death will frighten him. We will also gauge his reaction to the return of our prisoner who I believe was sent here to make mischief.

You may join us, son, although I would prefer you visit your mother and brother to inform them of what has occurred here. Mordred will be furious to have missed such a victory – he spends too much time with the queen.'

Despite his father being a renowned warrior, Meirchiawn had grown up watching his overly ambitious mother torment the king with her sharp tongue. It had troubled him and Mordred throughout their childhood, leading to divided loyalties. His mother's move further north had been upsetting for Gorwst, but Meirchiawn had to admit the atmosphere at Banna had become much improved in her absence. She had begged Meirchiawn to go with her and 'leave the fool to his hunting', but there was more to his father than she saw. And like his father, Meirchiawn was suspicious that Coroticus had been in league with the dead Gael king, particularly now he had recognised the so-called 'messenger'. He hadn't been sure at first, so many years had passed since they had played together as children, but the likeness was striking.

'Father, I believe our prisoner from Alt Clut is actually Cinuit, the son of Coroticus.'

There was a short silence.

'I too saw the likeness,' replied Gorwst. 'The keel that arrived at dawn belongs to Coroticus, no doubt sent here to buy the slaves from Nathi.'

'So, they *were* in league.'

'My brother-in-law is an evil man who maintains his power and authority with the riches and allies he earns from trading slaves to the Picts and Scotti. He takes advantage of our region's insecurities without conscience or care.'

'Then we have caught him red-handed.'

'Yes, but we have killed all his men, save for his son.'

'Surely, we should unmask the boy?' said Meirchiawn, surprised by his father's calm.

'To do so would risk his torture and execution. My brother lost men when they fought alongside us to save our kingdom. He would treat the lad like a traitor.'

'But that is precisely what he is.'

'We must be careful – we do not seek war with Coroticus or, for that matter, your mother! We should keep his secret for now, and return him safely to Alt Clut.'

Meirchiawn nodded. His father had been wise enough to think through the consequences.

'When will you tell King Mor?'

'After the excitement of battle has died down, when he will understand my predicament more clearly. We shall sail to Alt Clut in Cinuit's ship, and we will put you ashore to visit your mother on the way.'

Meirchiawn was impressed with his father's cunning, but something else was bothering him.

'I hear Mor has instructed Arthwys and the priest to return Formenus and his daughters over the mountains to his eastern stronghold?'

Meirchiawn greatly admired Gwenhyfach, and although they were not betrothed, there had been suggestions and promises. Could he trust Arthwys, after all the bad blood there had been between the cousins growing up? He was sure his brother would feel the same mounting jealousy, since Mordred considered Gwenhyfar, the younger sister, to be his sweetheart too.

Gorwst must have sensed his son's unease.

'Formenus wishes to reward Arthwys for his bravery in the rescue.'

Meirchiawn snorted. He did not hold his cousin in the same regard. His mother had always spoken of Arthwys with derision, leaving her sons in no doubt that she thought Mordred more suited to battle leader for the North.

'The Bear of the North is bolstered by his magicians,' he said, intending the sarcasm.

'Perhaps that is so, but our kingdom might have been lost without him. Do not let my nephew vex you, for he will shortly return to his own domain, leaving us to pursue our local interests. Reged is safe, and for that we thank God and King Mor. Remember – Coelings united will never be defeated. The Gaels of Hibernia must hear this, and Coroticus must also recognise the combined might of Reged and Elfed. Your cousin is your best ally, whether you like him or loathe him. Now, let us join the feast before our guests consume our share.'

*

Formenus was still recovering in the castrum, tended by his daughters, but was expected to be well enough to travel soon. The surprise raid had left them no alternative but to barricade themselves in the tower, and Formenus had convinced Nathi from the battlements that Gorwst would rather pay a ransom than launch an attack. Mor thought the Gael king's overconfidence indicated how weak they believed the King of Reged had become.

The Elfed king had found a suitable building within the walls of Itunocelum from which to make his plans, and after several days on horseback, Cian was glad to be sat with his stylus, noting the king's orders.

'Is Martin outwith?'

'He is, my king – as requested.'

'Then show him in, but post guards, for no one other than you must hear this conversation.'

The priest arrived, looking particularly nervous.

'Please sit with us.' Mor paused whilst Martin pulled up a stool. 'A great victory, Martin, and my soldiers believe I have you to thank for it.'

'I had little to do with it, King Mor.'

'I remember it was Talhaearn who brought you to Elfed on the advice of Bishop Ninian.'

'That is so, my king.'

'Did they know of your background?'

'I believe so.'

'But did they know of the powers Myrddin tells us you possess?'

'I have no more powers than any man, my king.'

'He tells us you see the future?'

'I have strange dreams which I fail to interpret, and discount as the devil's work.'

'So, you cannot summon lightning bolts?'

'No.' Martin laughed.

'Well, everyone now thinks you can. They are calling you Merlinus the Priest Magician.'

'It was simply remarkable providence, God's will. I am an ordinary man.'

'We already guessed you must have had military training, and I am told that you bear many scars, but we have, until now, respected your privacy.'

'I have been grateful for that respect. Talhaearn gifted me his military manuals to help me tutor your boys about war: Vegetius, Onasander and Frontinus. Arthwys and Agiluf are well versed in Roman strategy and tactics.'

'Ah yes, but there has always been something more about you, and now we know the truth.'

'Has Myrddin told you about Alt Clut?'

'He has, but fear not, for we do not feel deceived.'

'Please forgive me. It was a necessary deception to help me to continue my life. My father was King Cinhill, one of Coel's generals, so I was tutored, much like you, in warcraft, as a Roman officer. I fought many battles against the Picts, but my scars are a gift from my half-brother.'

'Coroticus?'

'Yes. He murdered my brother, King Cynloyp.'

There was a pause whilst Mor considered what he now knew.

'We shall sail for Alt Clut tomorrow. It is well that you are not coming with us.'

'I will not return to Alt Clut unless Coroticus is dead. Until then, I will pursue my Christian duties.'

'Myrddin has nominated you as his successor. He is a man of great intellect and foresight who uses his deductive powers to great effect. In my grandfather's time, he was at odds with Christianity, but the Druids lost that battle long ago, and their powers do seem to have waned in the face of the true religion.'

'There will always be superstition and fear,' said Martin.

'That is so, but will you allow Myrddin to tutor you?'

'Yes. We have already agreed this between us.'

'Then I will welcome you as an adviser, and do please continue to watch over Arthwys, for I fear he has become headstrong and is in need of wise counsel.'

'I will do my best, my king, but he is very much his own man.'

'I am proud of him, but there is yet so much he must come to know. I benefitted from the wisdom of my grandfather. My own father lay dead on the battlefield long before Arthwys was born, although the role of grandfather was more than adequately filled by Talhaearn for my son.'

'None of us will forget Taly, my lord, least of all Arthwys,' said Cian, then turning to Martin, 'but our sons are reckless. I'm told they charged against impossible odds?'

'That is so. Were it not for providence, they would be dead, and the battle lost.'

'Martin, you must teach them all that you know. We all believe they are destined for greatness, and although valour is essential, they must learn better judgement of when it is appropriate. Coel never relished battle. He saw his primary role as protector. The people loved him and he died in his bed – a rare experience for a general.' Mor smiled. 'Even so, the Picts presented him with a considerable challenge, and he proved himself time and again. Now, it is the Saxons who threaten our existence – there will be more than enough opportunities for valour.'

'I will speak with both your boys about curbing their reckless enthusiasm. Let them know there will be many more future opportunities to show their valour if they learn to temper it with the humility of your grandfather.'

'Thank you, Martin. Most men have one chance at life, but this is your second, something which I believe is deserving of a relevant title at court. I think Merlinus is truly appropriate. What say you, Cian?'

'Yes, Merlinus, the Christian wizard.'

Martin took his leave, looking relieved, if a little puzzled by his new role and title.

Cian waited to be sure the priest has left the building.

'My king, do you believe he has the powers Myrddin described?'

'I do hope so, but it matters not. That our enemies and allies alike believe he has will be a power in itself. Have you read *The General* by Onasander, Cian?'

'I have not, my king.'

'Well, borrow it from Merlinus – deception can prove a decisive tactic, both on the battlefield and in negotiations. The priest may not have magic, but he seems predestined, and now we know his talents, he will be an excellent addition to the war council I intend to assemble upon my return from Alt Clut.'

'Perhaps Coroticus should be told his murder victim is now a mighty wizard.'

Mor laughed. 'Onasander would be proud! We must use all our guile to secure the northern frontier.'

Arthwys Rebuked

Mediobogdum

Late November 446

Arthwys had only ever seen mountains of this scale from a distance. Never before had he experienced such rugged grandeur or the sense of foreboding imparted by their towering cliffs up close. The first part of their journey had been aided by fortunate weather. The snow had melted from the lower slopes and a cold sun had assisted them in finding the best route through their magnificent surroundings. Even so, and with Derwyn leading the way, progress had been slow. Formenus was not fully recovered, and the increasingly rocky path had required careful navigation by ponies and riders alike. And still, there seemed no obvious pass over the top.

All round, white waterfalls gushed from impenetrable heights. A chilling wind now pushed dense swirling clouds along the highest peaks, and a light rain began to lash their faces. When the grey, glistening walls of the deserted Roman fort came into view, they seemed strangely out of place amongst the towering peaks, but that did not diminish the welcome shelter they offered nor the relief that came from now knowing the travellers' route was true.

This was Mediobogdum, built by Rome to guard the mountain pass. In these times, Formenus had said, it was frequented by shepherds in spring and otherwise deserted, unless travellers were caught out by foul weather, but Arthwys could not help feeling that it must be haunted by the ghosts of soldiers who had perished defending the remote passage through the desolate mountains.

Darkness was falling, so the travellers went about the business of finding dry lodging within the crumbling fort. Formenus and his daughters found the granary was dry and quickly settled to rest. Derwyn and his two companions camped near the south gate. Arthwys, Agiluf, Martin and Myrddin found a guard room where a fire could be lit, but there was little fuel other than heather, which burnt too quickly, and some leftover roof timbers that were too large to cut without an axe.

'We will have a sorry fire,' said Arthwys.

'It matters not – our stay is brief,' replied Martin, wrapping himself in his saddle rug to gain some respite from the wind that whistled through the stone structure. 'Your fathers wish me to speak with you both.' Martin eyed both boys intently.

This was the first opportunity for the priest to hold a private conversation since the battle, and Arthwys knew it would not be filled with praise. He had intentionally ignored Martin's instruction to remain by the castrum, and it had occurred to him since that this was what had forced Martin to perform the magic that had killed King Nathi.

'God must love you both, for it is only thanks to His thunderbolt that your skins and the day were saved. I have spent ten years teaching you military tactics, in particular battlefield discipline, so believe me when I say, without Divine Intervention, we would all be lying dead at Itunocelum.' The boys remained silent. 'This was not a jousting tournament where bravery is politely applauded; it was a life-or-death situation, requiring level-headed leadership and obedience.'

Martin was right, there was no denying it. Arthwys offered no excuses and lowered his gaze when the priest turned toward him, unable to meet his tutor's eyes.

'Agiluf faithfully follows your every command. He was in your care, and your casual disregard for your own life would certainly have condemned him to the same bloody end.' Arthwys looked at Agiluf, giving him a solemn nod. 'It was a disappointing and foolish act which must never be repeated.'

The boys had never been dressed down with such ferocity, but the tirade was not yet over – now it was Myrddin's turn.

'The Bear of the North's first engagement was nearly his last. Where might that have left your father's kingdom? You have been selected as our best hope to unify the North and defeat our enemies, so you must rise to the responsibility and demonstrate the strength of all your qualities – of which valour is only one, a small part of the whole.'

Arthwys heard his voice tremble as he replied. 'These responsibilities are a burden that grows heavier with each day. I am expected to lead, but my contemporaries yet doubt my abilities and threat of challenge hangs ever over me. Valour is all I have with which to prove myself.'

'I understand, Arthwys, I really do,' said Martin, his tone less harsh. 'So, now that we are clear about responsibility, we must act to consolidate your position. The victory of two days past stands to your credit, but Myrddin tells me there is another means of confirming your right to hold your title.' Martin looked toward the seer.

'Young prince, tomorrow I will persuade Formenus to follow a route that will take us past the mountain, Blencathra.'

Still upset, Arthwys' voice shook as he replied curtly, 'Why? What's there?'

'Remember *The dragon's long back*?'

Arthwys would never forget the rhyme Talhaearn had entrusted to him on his deathbed. Understanding dawned.

'*Caledfwich*?' he said, suddenly. 'Surely, the sword is just a myth?'

'I learnt from my master the location of the sword, where it awaits a leader of the Britons. Following our surrender to the Romans, the tribes were, for a time, forbidden from carrying weapons, so a secret cache was hidden high on Blencathra. Time passed, priorities changed, and our people fought alongside the Romans against the Picts, manufacturing new weapons to Roman design, like those we carry today. Others have searched for Caledfwich, but it has never been recovered, its location almost forgotten, except by the Druids.'

Arthwys felt a sudden pang of self-doubt. 'If I cannot find the sword, does that mean the prophecy is false, that I am not the Bear?'

'You will find it. *I know* this is your destiny.'

'Is the sword magic, Myrddin?'

'Almost certainly. It was wielded by Cocidius himself.'

'Was Cocidius a man?'

The old seer cast a glance toward Martin. 'In the legends of the North, he is part human, part war god. But he is not the only god of war. There is another, stronger and more powerful, called Belatucadrus. It is known that they are rivals for the affections of Coventina, the beautiful water goddess, fighting each other, over and over again. Belatucadrus possesses mighty antlers whereas Cocidius has only his weapons, armour and guile. Legend tells, Coventina admired them both, but her father Taranis, God of Thunder, insisted she choose one to end the strife. The goddess had found a heart-shaped rock that had fallen from the heavens and sheered perfectly into two, so she decided to give each of her admirers a half and bid them prove to her who was most worthy of her attention. Belatucadrus decided upon a show of strength and skimmed the rock across the Solway, a feat his opponent could not equal. However, Cocidius had seen that the rock was not stone but metal ore and, with his armourer, fabricated a sword so strong it shatters other metals. He named the sword Caledfwich and presented it to the goddess for her protection, whereupon she awarded the sword back to him, choosing Cocidius as her consort and protector.'

'Did that end the strife?' asked a fascinated Arthwys.

'Yes. Caledfwich is too powerful to be defeated by any rival, although Belatucadrus remains brooding and bitter. Since then, it has always been the sword that chooses who is worthy enough to wield it, and it is only ever on loan to that chosen leader. In the end, it must be returned to the goddess.'

Arthwys looked toward Agiluf whose wide eyes and open mouth mirrored his own astonishment. The old seer winked at Martin who looked less convinced, bringing the strange tale to a conclusion with an exasperated sigh.

'I think that's enough storytelling for tonight. We should sleep now, for tomorrow brings a long and difficult journey.'

Myrddin curled beneath his rug, and everyone dutifully did the same, but Arthwys could not sleep. Did Myrddin really know the location of the sword? If so, did he have the necessary courage to recover it? The whistling wind seemed to join in as he whispered Taly's rhyme under his breath.

> *'The temple of Myrddin stands proud in the vale*
> *but high on the mountain old spirits prevail*
> *A high cliff doth Venutius' cave protect*
> *Below, a black pool in which stars reflect*
> *The dragon's long back is the only safe path*
> *Obscured by his breath that blows hard in his wrath*
> *Fear not this dragon, he is not the Bear's quarry*
> *For he guides you forth from the deep gloomy corrie*
> *To the top of the cliffs where the rooks stand sentry*
> *On the steep facing rocks guarding the entry.*
> *The risks are many and the Bear must beware*
> *But the prize is great with Caledfwich there*
> *It is said that the sword holds powers beyond ken*
> *And in the Bear's hand proves him leader of men.'*

Leader of men. Martin had been right – he had not considered the risk to his best friend, who he had loved all his life. Faithful Agiluf. Arthwys pictured him cut down on the battlefield as might have occurred, then prayed hard to his own God for forgiveness, until eventually, he drifted into sleep.

The Search for the Sword

Blencathra

Late November 446

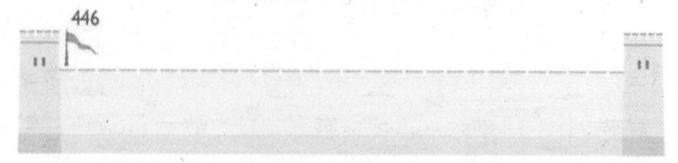

Arthwys was still troubled by Martin's reprimand during their journey through the beautiful and mysterious Erechwyd landscape. His turmoil was exacerbated by the challenge set for him by Myrddin. The burden of prophecy was being thrust upon him, and he could feel the increasing weight of expectation bearing down on him the closer they got to Blencathra.

His tension aside he was pleased that Formenus was nearly recovered from his confinement in the castrum where there had been little food and only rainwater to drink, his ordeal lasting nearly four weeks, so it was surely God's will that both he and his daughters survived. Now, after several days of food and fresh mountain air, the Carvetti nobleman was nearly himself again, no doubt a relief to his daughters. They were the most beautiful young women Arthwys had ever seen, but then, it was not as if military life allowed any time to spend with girls.

Gwenhyfach was the elder. A dark-haired beauty, she was the most engaging, with a lovely smile and a sharp, teasing wit. Gwenhyfar was a flame-haired siren, who was less talkative but watched everyone with her bright green eyes. Several times, he had caught her gaze upon him, but they had yet to speak. Derwyn had mentioned that the princes of Reged admired the two young women – nothing official, only rumours, certainly not enough to discourage Agiluf from riding alongside them, clearly smitten by their charm.

Arthwys noted their father's pensive demeanour. Formenus was a distant relation of his family, an important ally, guardian of the Pennine passes, but he had lost all his best warriors when they were lured into the trap set by Nathi at Itunocelum. Having so many widows to face at Brovacum was a grim prospect and had probably contributed to his easy agreement to Myrddin's detour past Blencathra – a welcome distraction for the doleful king.

The previous day's route had taken them alongside a great lake with many islands, autumn's sunshine accentuating the season's orangey reds and golden browns, but this day had dawned frosty, and the white tops of the mountains disappeared under cloud as the party climbed out of the valley. A prominent stone circle, built by the 'old people', according to Myrddin, now came into view, and the old seer halted the travellers and walked with Martin to its centre. They were there for a short time, Myrddin pointing this way and that with his stave, perhaps explaining the circle's mysterious purpose.

Arthwys drew alongside Agiluf and spoke quietly. '*The temple of Myrddin stands proud in the vale*. Taly's riddle mentions this place.'

'Does that mean we are close to the mountain?'

'Yes, I believe that is Blencathra, looming ahead of us.'

As the journey resumed, they joined the old Roman road that led to Brovacum, and Formenus brought his horse alongside Arthwys.

'Young prince, I will be forever grateful that you came to rescue us. If it were not for your brave intervention, I would be dead, and my lovely daughters would be slaves. I have a reward waiting for you at Brovacum. But tell me, what is Myrddin's interest in this mountain?' His gaze was fixed on the snow-capped misty peak of Blencathra.

'Your offer of a reward is most generous, King Formenus, though it is not necessary. I am just glad you and your daughters are safe and on your way home. However, I do not know why Myrddin wishes to bring us here.' Arthwys thought it best to be circumspect about their mysterious mission.

'I know the ancient ones considered this mountain holy – the summit lines up with standing stones near my home. The mountain's slopes are steep and dangerous. It is a most forbidding place.'

'Perhaps that is it, my lord. As we have just seen, the wizard has a connection with such stones.'

Formenus nodded and laughed nervously, before dropping back with only his thoughts for company.

The track drew closer to the side of the steep fell where the road forked. Following Myrddin's instructions, Derwyn and his two companions brought the party to a halt there. The old seer gathered them all together.

'We are only three hours' ride from Brovacum. Here, we must temporarily part company with you, King Formenus. Derwyn's scouts will accompany you and your daughters home so that you are not delayed in delivering your sad news.'

Formenus' shoulders dropped. 'You are right. I should not delay. Will you join us later?'

'Yes. We will join you in Brovacum when we have undertaken this short pilgrimage up this mountain,' replied Martin.

'To what purpose?' asked Formenus, still curious about the persistent interest in the snow-covered heights.

'To give thanks to God for your deliverance,' replied Martin.

The king lowered his head, perhaps remembering the remarkable circumstances of his rescue.

'Of course, I did not think... I have much on my mind—'

Gwenhyfar suddenly interrupted. 'Father, I insist that Gwenhyfach and I accompany Prince Arthwys and his companions, so that we may also thank the Lord for our safe return.'

'My lady, we shall be making the journey on foot,' said Arthwys, abruptly looking toward Martin.

'We can walk surprisingly well,' said Gwenhyfach, with a raised eyebrow.

Martin nodded. 'Then let us all pray together nearer to Heaven.'

Gwenhyfar turned to her father, her bright green eyes sparkling with excitement. 'You can surely entrust our safety to these mighty Cymry warriors?'

'I believe so, daughter – safer with them than you have been with me in recent times,' said the disconsolate king.

And so, Formenus took his leave, resuming the journey with only Derwyn's scouts as companions. The rest of the group followed the left fork until they reached a beck where Myrddin stopped to look up at the mountain. Cloud shrouded the summit, and a brisk breeze was evident by the distant whistle through the valleys. He turned to Arthwys.

'Not the best conditions for climbing the dragon's back. We will leave the ponies here in Derwyn's care and follow this stream.'

'How do you know this path, Myrddin?' asked Martin.

'My master brought me here as a young boy. It was used by miners long before the Romans conquered our lands.'

They climbed first through trees and then through scrub. The valley was soon a long way below, giving a view of the great Roman highway stretching in a straight line to the east where it disappeared into the Pennine fells. Bracken now dominated the hillside, long past its autumn best, the tired golden fronds moving to-and-fro in the brisk wind.

Martin led the way, followed by Agiluf who accompanied the sisters, both keeping up with the pace. Arthwys, however, remained at the back with Myrddin who was finding the climb more difficult than the others. The young prince was focused on his mission, taking the opportunity to glean as much information as possible from the seer.

'What must I look for when I gain the top of the ridge?'

'In a gully in the cliff face, there is a miners' cave, the entrance to which is narrow and disguised by the boulders that seal it. I have brought a torch for you to light once you are inside.'

'How will I identify Caledfwich?'

'I have never seen it, for the cave has been sealed for over three hundred years. All I know is the sword is dedicated to Cocidius, god of war.'

'Cocidius is usually depicted in red, as if covered head-to-toe in blood.'

'Yes, such an image may well be what proves the sword's identity.'

'Will it still be there after all this time?'

'Have faith, no one has claimed the sword since Venutius.'

Arthwys was still full of questions. 'Have you ever climbed the dragon's back?'

'Yes, once, when I was your age, with my master. It was ever the Myrddin's duty to check the seal remained intact.'

'Are there demons?' Arthwys asked, self-conscious about his superstition but wanting to know, all the same.

'Their presence will play on your mind but think only about the physical world: rocks, wind, ice, darkness, footholds and gaps. Yes, there is danger, but only from these elements. If you allow fear to grip you, you will not find the sword.'

The path continued north, high above a fast-flowing river folded into a narrow valley that they would have been unable to see from below. In the west, Erechwyd appeared dark and brooding. Gathering clouds sapped the colour from the mountains, giving them a dark and foreboding character, but in the east, shafts of sunlight picked out the features of the Eden valley. Arthwys now recognised the significance of Myrddin's mountain to the rest of the region – it was like a sentinel standing watch over man's daily life whilst holding back whatever lurked in the mountains behind.

Martin continued to lead the group, following a stream when the path became indistinct. But as they climbed higher, the beauty of the waterfalls, combining with the less oppressive open fell, lifted everyone's spirits. Eventually, he stopped next to a cascading torrent and waited for the group to catch him up.

'The beauty of God's creation. It is as if we ascend to Heaven,' said the joyful priest.

It was a brief uplifting moment, for only a little further along the path, the rocky face of the summit came into view – sheer, forbidding cliffs that dropped into a deep corrie, dominated by a still, dark tarn. Looking up in awe, they saw a serrated ridge, steeply winding into the clouds like a long serpent.

With a gasp, Arthwys turned to Myrddin. '*The dragon's long back?*'

The seer nodded.

The young prince felt his stomach churn. 'You say you have climbed this before?' It was hard to imagine Myrddin ever being young enough to accomplish such an achievement.

'Yes, but on a summer's day.'

And this is not summer, thought Arthwys, rubbing his hands, already cold in the icy stillness of the vast amphitheatre.

Most of the snow from the previous week had thankfully melted, swelling the streams and rivers in the valleys below, but there was a stubborn white cap clinging to the lofty peak where nightly frosts reinvigorated its daily resistance to the sun.

Arthwys swallowed hard to suppress his fear. Choosing not to delay, he relieved Myrddin of the satchel containing the torch. He acknowledged both Martin and the seer and began walking along the tarn side toward the steep scree that led to the base of the rocky ridge.

Gwenhyfach pulled at Martin's arm. 'Where is he going?' she asked, surprised to see the prince heading off alone.

'A personal pilgrimage. He will be a little while, but we shall wait for him here and pray for his safe return.'

'Wait!' shouted Agiluf, running to catch up with the prince.

Arthwys waited. 'This is not your challenge and there will be much danger.'

'But I am sworn to face all your dangers with you,' replied his faithful friend.

'Martin sorely rebuked me for risking your life at the castrum.'

'Yes, but I did not!' Agiluf said firmly, smiling to reassure his friend.

As they walked together toward the rocky beginnings of the ridge, Arthwys teased, 'I was beginning to think you preferred female company.'

'I really do, but there will be time for everything,' said Agiluf, with a hearty laugh.

'Not if my cousins catch wind of your interest.'

Now they both laughed, and the tension eased.

Fear

The dragon's long back

Late November 446

The two intrepid climbers reached the scree that preceded the rocky outcrop and began picking their way through the jagged rocks.

'This is not as hard as climbing trees in the forest,' said Agiluf, threading a path through the gritty obstacles.

'So far, but look ahead,' replied Arthwys.

In front of them, as the climb got steeper, the ridge narrowed like the blade of an axe. A clinging mist shrouded their objective beyond, and an increasingly hostile wind tugged at their clothing. Already, the sheer drop on either side meant certain death if they slipped. Up and up, they climbed, until the ridge became so narrow they could not stand. With their legs either side, as if riding a horse, they edged their way along until they reached a seemingly impassable gap. The rocks on either side were icy and slippery, making a leap too dangerous to contemplate, especially as the ledge they needed to reach sloped precariously down to the drop.

'We must climb down to climb up,' shouted Agiluf into the wind.

Fear gripped Arthwys. This was far worse than charging the enemy. Perhaps they should just accept there was no way up this mountain in such conditions.

'Here!' shouted Agiluf. 'I've found a better step.'

Arthwys scrambled down to join Agiluf, and they stepped tentatively across the void. But now they were clinging to slippery ice and snow as they climbed, and their hands were like blocks of ice.

'This is too difficult,' shouted Arthwys, losing his footing and slipping back, before managing to stop.

'Try this, it helps to grip.'

Agiluf had found two sharp rocks like spearheads and was stabbing the frozen snow helping him to create handholds and cling to the rock face. Arthwys copied the technique and made better progress.

Soon, white overhanging snow appeared on either side and the gradient of the ridge became almost vertical – they were near the summit.

'Myrddin said the cave is left of here in a gully, but all I can see is the white of mist and snow.'

Agiluf had reached the flat top first and looked around with concern etched on his face. 'We will easily get lost in this mist. We should mark this spot so that we know where to begin our descent.'

There was little visibility, but they managed to scrape snow into a pile to mark the top of the dragon's back and then followed the edge. There was no obvious gully, just shadowy pillars that jumped out of the mist, seemingly detached from the sheer face. They walked for nearly one hundred paces and found nothing.

'We are too far over; we must retrace our steps,' shouted Arthwys through chattering teeth.

They turned, but the way back appeared different, as if the pillars had eerily changed their shape, yet the two young warriors knew they were on the right path because they were following their previous footsteps. Arthwys edged closer to the cliff face.

'Be careful,' shouted Agiluf, 'the overhanging snow will not support your weight and will break away.'

'Over here. Look, it's a gully,' Arthwys called out over the wind.

'I will go first and shout up to you what I can see,' said Agiluf, who appeared to have gained more confidence in his climbing ability. He lowered himself carefully past the overhanging snow, cursing when he caught his knuckles on a protruding rock. Then he disappeared from view, and for some time, there was silence. Arthwys was suddenly very aware that he was alone in the icy mist. He leant forward as far as he dared, trying to hear some sign that Agiluf was unharmed.

'Agiluf,' he shouted, but his voice only echoed, unanswered, down the deep gully. 'Agiluf!' he shouted again.

A voice drifted up from below.

'I see it! I see the entrance. Make your way down, but take your time.'

Arthwys carefully climbed down in the direction of his friend's voice, eventually arriving at a recess in the gully.

'Over here,' said Agiluf.

Arthwys could see snow-covered boulders piled against the cliff. Agiluf braced himself against the rock face and began using his legs to dislodge the large boulders. Arthwys watched each heavy stone spin through the snow before crashing down the gully. Eventually, Agiluf's efforts revealed a small cave opening, just about large enough for a man to climb through.

Arthwys scrambled toward the opening. 'I will go in first.'

He squeezed into the narrow passage where he was met by complete darkness and a dank earthy odour. He slid slowly forward until the rock floor seemed to disappear.

'I'm behind you,' said Agiluf in a lowered voice.

'There's a drop – I can't yet see the bottom.' Arthwys turned to face the rock face and lowered himself carefully, searching for footholds. He found one, then another, and lowered himself further. 'I will call when I find the bottom.' There were two more steps, and although his vision was now better accustomed to the dark, when he looked up, he could see Agiluf silhouetted against the light coming in through the cave entrance. 'I'm down. Four steps so will you be.'

The cave felt appreciably warmer than the wind-blasted summit, but his hands were still cold. He fumbled in the satchel for the bound twigs and strike that Myrddin had provided. Agiluf was soon by his side, cupping his hands helping to deflect the draught. Arthwys tried the strike several times, but everything was damp and there were no sparks. He tried again, striking the two stones together rapidly, until finally there were sparks and the boys blew at the twigs furiously until there was smoke, a crackle, then a flame. As the light of the torch gained strength, they looked around in awe.

The cave had been hewn into the mountain by ancient miners probably following a seam of lead – they had been told there were many such caves in the district. But now with the improving light, Arthwys began to see stacks of ancient spears and shields – not Roman in design, these were the type used by their ancestors. Alongside the spears and shields were ancient swords with longer, wider blades.

'So, these are the weapons hidden from the Romans,' said Agiluf.

They searched through the piles of swords, but there was nothing matching Myrddin's description of Caledfwich.

'It must be here somewhere, Myrddin seemed so certain,' said Arthwys in exasperation.

'Quickly, bring the torch here,' said Agiluf from the far end of the cave. 'I've found something strange.'

Arthwys made his way past the stacked weaponry, and the light from the torch fell upon the object Agiluf was examining. Jutting out of a fissure in the rock was a red-painted effigy, legs and arms outstretched.

'Is this a depiction of the ancient god?' asked Agiluf.

Arthwys looked closer, excitement building. 'It is Cocidius, and this looks like it is the hilt of a sword.'

'I have tried to pull it out, but it will not budge.' Agiluf gave the hilt another tug to demonstrate.

Arthwys could barely contain himself. 'Quickly, bring me one of those swords.'

When Agiluf returned, Arthwys handed the torch to his friend and took the sword. He levered at the Cocidius hilt achieving some movement. They could now see that the blade had been wrapped in waxed linen which, over time, had fused to the rock. Arthwys pulled at the hilt, but the stone still refused to release the blade.

'Why was it placed here?'

'I suspect Venutius was not prepared to accept defeat and had every intention of returning, though he was never able to do so.'

'Yes, but why would someone hammer it into this crack?'

'Myrddin will know the reason. Now stand behind me, wrap your arms around my waist and pull when I shout.' Agiluf placed the torch on a ledge and followed the instructions. Arthwys grabbed the hilt firmly and, placing his feet against the rock face, shouted, 'Pull!'

The young men growled with the effort, but under their combined force, the rock released its hold, and the sword slid out, sending them both stumbling backward against the caves' hewed wall.

Agiluf groaned in the dark. 'That hurt.'

'I have it. I am holding Caledfwich,' said Arthwys, laughing with wonder at the discovery.

'I think my head is bleeding.'

'Are you able to stand?'

'I think so,' said Agiluf, getting to his feet.

The torch had almost burnt out, but Arthwys could make out the light from the cave entrance. 'Come, we should pick our way through this maze of weapons and climb out whilst we still have some light.'

They crawled out of the cave and back into the gully, where they were temporarily blinded by the snow-reflected daylight. Both blinking like startled owls, they waited whilst their eyesight gradually cleared then eagerly examined the sword. The Cocidius effigy on the hilt allowed enough space for two hands to grip, whilst the blade, sharp on both sides, glistened grey and was marked with strange patterns.

'These markings are not man-made, and it is remarkably sharp, despite its great age. It makes me nervous,' said Agiluf, stepping back from the ancient sword.

'Myrddin will tell us more about it, but I do not fear this sword. Rather, I feel emboldened when I hold the hilt, like it was made for me. Here, my friend, hold the hilt. Although it is longer than a spatha, it is strangely lighter.'

'It is undeniably magnificent,' said Agiluf, 'but it is your sword, your destiny, and you drew it from the stone.'

'Come, Agiluf, hold it. It is just a piece of metal!' Arthwys held out the sword to his friend.

Agiluf shook his head. 'It frightens me with its strange markings and shaped effigy for a hilt!'

'Then let us not linger. We should try to reach Brovacum in daylight, for it must be past midday, by now. How is your head?'

'Only a little blood, but I feel somewhat dazed.'

'Go careful then, my friend. Which way shall we descend?'

'It will be too difficult to climb back up and descend the way we came. This scree gully below us is full of icy snow, but if we carefully lower ourselves down, then once we are out of this mist, we should be able to see well enough to climb down to the tarn side.'

'You are the better climber, so you lead.'

Agiluf began his descent, carefully clinging to rocks protruding out of the snow. Each step was precarious, and to the side of the rocky ledges, the drop was vertical. Carrying Caledfwich carefully, Arthwys picked his route by following Agiluf's footsteps. Despite his eagerness to get back to the tarn, he concentrated hard, knowing that one false step could lead to disaster in such treacherous conditions.

Agiluf was half a dozen steps ahead when a large black rook swooped out of the mist, cawing past his head. Arthwys saw his friend startle, slip and flip onto his front. Agiluf laughed at first, but his mirth turned to terror when he began sliding, quickly gaining momentum. His arms thrashed wildly as he desperately tried to find a handhold.

'I can't stop!' he screamed, accelerating out of view down the gully.

Arthwys froze, heart hammering, listening for his friend's voice, but he could hear nothing. Once again, he was alone in the eerie mist. At a loss, he prayed, 'Almighty God, please save Agiluf. Do not let him die.' Aware he could slip just as easily, he used Caledfwich to test each foothold. His panting breath was all he could hear.

'Agiluf!' he shouted, taking a few more careful steps. 'Agiluf!' he called again. Still nothing. He continued to descend in silence. Then he heard the voice he was hoping for.

'Arthwys, down here!'

Where the snow petered out, he found his friend wedged between two rocks.

'Thank God you're alive.'

'Yes,' Agiluf moaned, 'but only just. I am grazed and bleeding everywhere, and I think I have broken my arm, so I cannot lift myself.' Agiluf looked up at Arthwys, his face pale. 'I have nothing beneath me to push my legs against.'

Arthwys' gaze moved down, and he could see that Agiluf was dangling over a sheer drop.

'Good God, you're lucky to be alive. Stay still. I'm going to throw Caledfwich down and hope it lands in the shallows of the tarn.'

He launched the sword, watching it spin into the mist. Then he placed his arms under Agiluf's armpits and heaved. Agiluf slid out of the rocks with a sharp intake of breath. It only took a quick glance to see that he was bleeding from multiple deep grazes.

'Can you stand?'

Groaning and cursing, Agiluf climbed to his feet. Arthwys unbuckled his belt and looped it to make a sling, which he placed over Agiluf's grazed head before carefully lifting the injured arm into it.

'Now, I will loosen your belt so I can hold you from behind as we descend.'

Together, very slowly, they stepped and slid until they were out of the mist. At last, they could see the tarn immediately below them. Now clear of the gully, they were descending on loose scree and grass. Arthwys waved furiously, shouting to the waiting party at the other side of the tarn, and although they were some distance away, Martin and the two girls began running in their direction. Myrddin appeared to be following as quickly as he could manage.

Arthwys laid Agiluf on the grass. Tearing off a piece of his tunic, he ran toward the tarn to dampen the cloth.

Martin arrived first followed by the girls.

'Agiluf fell. He's lucky to be alive.'

The priest inspected Agiluf's wounds. 'Mmm… not too bad.'

'My arm feels broken.'

Martin felt the bone where Agiluf's elbow had swollen into a peculiar shape. Agiluf winced and moaned.

'Certainly looks painful, but the bone feels intact. I think you have been fortunate.'

'You call this fortunate!' said a bemused Agiluf.

Myrddin walked straight to Arthwys. 'Did you find the sword?'

'I did.'

'So where is it?'

'In the tarn. I threw it down so I could bring Agiluf to safety unhindered.'

'In the tarn?' Myrddin looked worried. 'We may have lost it.'

They searched in the shallows along the shore but could not see it.

'It must have landed further out in the deeper water, but it should be in this area,' Arthwys said, pointing and looking back up the gully for confirmation.

'Can you swim?'

'Not well, but I will wade out to my depth.'

'Martin, can you swim?'

'No. I have nightmares about drowning.'

Arthwys could see the tarn sloped steeply as if the mountainside continued down into the depths. He waded in as far as he dared, but could see no sign of the sword.

'What have you lost, Prince Arthwys?' shouted Gwenhyfar from the shore.

'An illustrious sword, my lady, but none of us can swim in deep water.'

'I can swim quite well – my mother taught me. I can hold my breath and keep my eyes open and dive under the water.'

Arthwys looked toward Myrddin who nodded. Gwenhyfach, who was occupied tending to Agiluf, gave a little shriek when her sister suddenly disrobed and dived from a rock. They all watched the brave girl dive under the surface. Arthwys was stunned at the sight of her. She was a beautiful nymph, a water goddess, pale and slim.

Beside him, Myrddin was very still, his brow furrowed. 'Coventina,' was all he said, his gaze fixed as Gwenhyfar's white form pierced the surface of the dark tarn.

She dived time and again, each time coming up for air with empty hands. Arthwys walked along the shore, following her.

'About there, my lady. Dive there.'

Down she went again, but this time she did not come straight back up.

'She will die from the cold,' Gwenhyfach screamed.

Then suddenly, from out of the depths, a sword appeared above the water gripped by a pale hand and followed by Gwenhyfar's red hair breaking the surface. She paddled toward the shore where Arthwys quickly waded in to meet her. He took the sword and threw it to the shore then swept Gwenhyfar into his strong arms. She was as pale as snow and shivering. Wading back to the shore, he quickly took off his own tunic to cover her beautiful body as her sister raced toward them with Gwenhyfar's own clothes.

Now dressed, Gwenhyfar stood up, teeth chattering, allowing them to rub her arms, back and legs to warm her up. She looked up at Arthwys, but her beautiful green eyes rolled toward the sky and she fainted. He caught her and held her close to his warm body.

'We should start down now; it will get warmer as we descend,' he said, carrying Gwenhyfar.

Myrddin followed, inspecting Caledfwich, his intense gaze moving from the sword's hilt to the lake, but Arthwys with Gwenhyfar in his arms concentrated entirely on descending quickly but safely. Just ahead, Martin supported the improving Agiluf, whilst Gwenhyfach walked briskly alongside Arthwys, keeping a watchful eye on her sister. Further down, as they passed the waterfalls, Gwenhyfar opened her eyes, though she remained limp in his arms.

'My lady of the lake,' said Arthwys, 'I shall be forever grateful for your bravery. Is there anything I can do to repay you?'

A weak smile fluttered on her lips. 'You may ask my father for my hand in marriage.'

Arthwys felt his heart stutter, first with shock and then with an excitement unlike any he had ever experienced before.

Gwenhyfach averted her eyes. 'She is delirious,' she said almost apologetically.

But Gwenhyfar looked into his eyes, and her gaze seemed to pierce his very soul.

'No, sister, I am completely serious,' she replied resolutely.

Arthwys was enchanted. He knew he could not decline. They stood waiting for Myrddin to catch up. The old seer was panting heavily.

'Gwenhyfach, please help Myrddin whilst I carry my intended,' Arthwys' spirits were high.

Myrddin paused, leaning on Caledfwich whilst catching his breath.

'I will never return here, but you will have to one day, for she will want them both.'

Arthwys was uncertain what the seer meant but paid it little heed. He had risen to the challenge and proved himself, proved the prophecy was true. Today was the first day of the rest of his life.

A Hostage Returned

Alt Clut

December 446

The journey by sea had been rough and cold, but land was never far from view. They had crossed the Solway before sailing around the point of land nearest to Hibernia. This was a journey the young prisoner had sailed before, and he was glad when they approached the shelter of familiar islands and mountains. From the sea, they entered the Clyde and rowed the keel round the long right-hand corner of the narrowing estuary to where the twin peaks of his father's dark and brooding stronghold stood out against the cloud-strewn gloom of the mountains beyond.

Cinuit was relieved to be travelling to Alt Clut with his head still attached to his shoulders, but he was also terrified. Instead of returning with the slaves he had been entrusted to buy, he was accompanied by a warband led by two of the North's mightiest warriors. Worse still, all his men were dead, his silver had been taken, and the sentries keeping watch from the battlements had no way of knowing the approaching boat did not contain the expected cargo. With his hands tied, he was unable to give them any kind of signal, and Mor would surely kill him if he tried, although he had to admit, he had been treated surprisingly well. He couldn't help thinking the absence of torture and death threats meant both kings knew he was a prince of Alt Clut. Though their accents were unfamiliar, the words of the men from Reged and Elfed were recognisable, unlike those of the Gaels he had been sent to meet. To converse with them, he had required the king's interpreter who was now perished along with rest of Cinuit's party. His father's fury at his failure was going to be unbearable, so much so, he had considered throwing himself over the side.

As the boat beached, several warriors jumped out to quickly provide a defensive shield wall and allow the rest of the crew to disembark safely. There was no reception, so Mor and Gorwst had to call to some fishermen who seemed to be considering whether it might be wise to run away.

'Hey, you! Tell your king that Gorwst and Mor are here to speak with him.'

The men ran toward the steep-sided valley between the two granite peaks. Up above, on the eastern side, helmets and spears appeared above a stockade. The path up the cliff was steep, but the fishermen leapt up it like mountain goats. After a short time, a reception party of twenty or so men descended the cliff by the same path. Arriving at the shoreline, the warriors formed into a line, from the middle of which King Coroticus stepped forward. He immediately addressed his brother-in-law.

'Are you here to attack us, Gorwst?' he asked, brandishing a spear.

'No, Coroticus, that is not our purpose – we are here to return your lost property.' Cinuit was brought out from behind the shield wall, his hands still tied. 'It is unfortunate, but your men were all killed – they were in the wrong place at the wrong time and keeping rather bad company.'

'So, it is a ransom you want.'

'Why, no – are we not allies? On the contrary, we are here to discuss the terms of a renewed alliance.'

'So, you *do* have demands?'

'Let me introduce you to my brother – Mor of Elfed.'

Cinuit watched his father's eyes narrow. Mor was known to Alt Clut as a powerful king and a fierce warrior, his presence this far north could not be without political purpose.

'King Coroticus, our grandfathers were allies and fought side by side. We speak the same language and fear the same enemies, but in recent past we have seen loyalties tested. You should know that King Nathi is dead, his warband has been defeated, and his keels are now my brother's property. Always expect that we Coelings will fight together to defend our lands. We did not expect to find your men with our enemy, and your son is fortunate to be alive. But have no fear for his continued safety, we are here to return him and your keel. We merely require an affirmation of your continued allegiance, and horses and provisions to continue our journey east.'

'That is all?' asked a bemused Coroticus.

'Yes, that is all. A solemn oath of allegiance and some horses.'

'This fort is impregnable, and I no longer fear the Picts or the Scotti.

'Ah, that would be because your relationship with them has changed over time. Now that they do not raid south for the riches of the Romans, they are more interested in Christian slaves – a trade in which we know you are complicit. It is for you to decide with whom you would rather ally your kingdom. Perhaps it is time *we* tested if your fort truly is as impregnable as you claim?'

Coroticus gave a non-committal grunt, then changed tack. 'Where is my silver?'

'Distributed by our priest to those you were seeking to buy with it.'

Coroticus' face turned an alarming shade of red. 'A priest?' he spluttered.

'Yes, a priest who is coincidentally your half-brother, Cynwyb.'

Coroticus was now purple with rage. 'Impossible. I killed him myself.'

'It is Cynwyb. He has told me his story. He is back from the dead and a powerful wizard. We call him Merlinus. Your son witnessed the results of his mastery.'

The colour drained from Coroticus' face. Cinuit quailed under his father's gaze, but he nodded his affirmation, nonetheless. Mor continued.

'Agree to the terms we have set forth in this document, and we will release your son and await our horses. If not, we will board this keel and return to Reged where we will sell Cinuit as a slave, before returning here with Merlinus and an army.'

The document was handed to Coroticus by Gorwst. The Alt Clut king read the scroll whilst Gorwst outlined the terms.

'It commits you to providing warriors should we require them, but it also forbids you from raiding our lands or conspiring with others who would do the same. You have mistaken my tolerance for weakness. I am here to tell you we will not hesitate to destroy Alt Clut if you should move against us in any way in the future.'

Gorwst was still a powerful man, and Coroticus seemed cowed in his presence, though the Alt Clut king resolutely chose not to acknowledge his brother-in-law when he gave his response.

'We have an agreement, King Mor,' he shouted past Gorwst, as he lowered his spear.

Mor untied the bonds from a relieved Cinuit's wrists. 'Good luck, young prince but stay away from our shores. Now go tell your father how Merlinus killed Nathi with a lightning bolt but assure him that, whilst our alliance holds, I will forbid the wizard from ever returning to Alt Clut.'

Facing the Truth

Toward Din Eidyn by the Roman turf wall

December 446

Mor's small band of warriors now rode along the line of the Roman turf wall in the direction of Din Eidyn. Gorwst was the only one amongst the party who had travelled this route before.

'We are hazardously close to Pictland.'

'But surely, this territory is controlled by the Gododdin?' said Mor.

'That is so, but this border is never settled; we must be on our guard.'

Cian joined the conversation. 'I have never seen a fortress as strong as that of Coroticus.'

'These warlords of the far north are isolated, facing constant threat from the Picts; strong defences are key to their survival,' said Mor.

'Of the two, Din Eidyn is the strongest fortress. It sits on a towering rock with commanding views,' said Gorwst. 'It has been some time since I have spoken with King Lott, but his respect for Reged goes back to the days when his grandfather fought with Coel against the Picts, and he is well placed to enlighten us on the situation further north.'

Mor reined his horse closer to Gorwst.

'Brother, both Cian and I are suspicious that recent events indicate Coroticus, and perhaps Marchell, have been plotting against you?'

There was a silence, and Mor was not sure if Gorwst had heard the question in his voice. He was about to try again, when his brother spoke.

'Ambition spreads like a disease. Marchell married me to become a queen but has always been controlled by her brother. Our relations have been distant since the birth of Meirchiawn. Mordred cannot be mine, and he has the look of Coroticus – but tell no one else of this.'

'I see,' said Mor, shocked. 'Are the boys aware of this?'

'No, but I fear Marchell's ambitions for Mordred will bring them into conflict one day.'

'I am sad for your turmoil, Gorwst. But you must protect Reged and its rightful heir.'

'I know,' said Gorwst, with a sigh. 'Damn, Marchell. She is a beautiful woman with a poisonous mind… We are better apart.'

'Take heart, brother. If there was a plot, it is thwarted, and be sure Coroticus will never again challenge you whilst Merlinus stands ready to exact his revenge.'

Gorwst smiled grimly, comforted by his brother's support. 'There is more I should tell you about Marchell and Coroticus.' He hesitated briefly, as if reconsidering the wisdom of his impending disclosure, then he continued. 'They only pretend to be Christian.'

'As do many,' said Mor, quick to reassure his brother.

'There are rumours of ancient rituals with human sacrifice at Alt Clut.'

'You must concentrate on securing and strengthening Reged. We are not Christian missionaries. For too long, you have been behoven to Alt Clut, but look on this moment as a turning point. Coroticus crept into your bed and then your kingdom; he cannot be trusted as anything more than a barrier against the Picts. As for Marchell, she is trouble... dangerous trouble – keep her at arm's length.'

Gorwst fell silent, and Mor wondered if his brother would heed his advice.

The Romans Send an Envoy

Episford

Martius 450

Hengist paced the floor of his timber hall. He had done so all morning, consumed by the likely consequences of his decisions. This would be the first meeting of leaders of the Saxon peoples since the rebellion. Long years of raiding and battles had secured a fertile homeland with which they had done little. Many harvests had been missed, and they were now surrounded by a wasteland. The Wealas had been mostly driven out of their homes or butchered, and although those that remained were prepared to co-operate, they were too few to farm the vast plains.

There was no denying his brother had enjoyed the slaughter. Horsa, and his son Aesc, had raided deep into enemy territory, even reaching the western ocean, bringing back dwindling Roman riches, but his warriors would not easily convert to farmers now the time had come to focus more on occupation than conquest. When their late father had agreed his army would fight under foedus as mercenaries for the Britons, the island had only recently been abandoned by Rome, leaving the remaining inhabitants distracted, fighting amongst themselves. A disease had then swept through their crowded towns and cities, killing so many that those same towns and cities now lay deserted and full of ghosts. Hengist's tribe and his allies were at last secure, bordered by sea and forest, their frontiers bothered little by enemy threat and more than two days' march away. A period of respite was required to turn their territory into a homeland, and throughout winter, he had been considering how he might achieve this.

Constant raiding no longer weakened the Wealas, rather it provoked them to fight back. True, he could call on his army of five thousand men, and his enemies would always lose. But the real dilemma was how to feed such a large force. His allies Freuleaf of the Angles, Gundad of the Gaini, and the Saxon, Wipped, from The Wash had settled their territories long ago, before the Romans left. They all farmed and fished, and fed themselves, but the Jutes had yet to achieve this self-sufficiency. Horsa and Aesc preferred war and restraining them was difficult in their warrior culture. Hengist ran the risk of appearing weak if he suggested a pause in the fighting, but the need for food was pressing. It was food shortages that had been the cause of the rebellion – the Britons, having never expected such a large influx of his people, had refused to meet their needs, so his tribe had stripped the countryside of everything, murdering the inhabitants, ultimately creating even greater famine. The recent arrival at his camp of the young Frank noble presented an opportunity, but persuading his brother to leave his campaign against the Britons would take careful handling.

Merovech was not just a prince of the Franks; he was also an Imperial legate sent by Aetius, the commander of the Roman Army. His people in Gaul were foederati, bound by treaty to the Empire, and he had been sent with a proposal for Hengist. Gundad's tribe, the Gaini, had traded with the Franks on the lower Rhine for many years, so Merovech had approached him to help find Hengist – the prince drawn to the Jutes' stronghold by their proud reputation as warriors. A quick decision was now necessary, and the agreement of all his allies essential, hence this meeting of leaders to enable Merovech, with Gundad's help, to explain the Empire's proposal. Hengist would sit alongside his brother, appearing to need persuading with the rest, even though he was already in favour, as he expected Freuleaf, Wipped and Gundad would be. They were aware of the food crisis facing their Jute neighbours, and with the Jute population three times larger than their own, they were concerned about unrest spilling into their own territories.

Gundad and Merovech arrived first. The young prince was attired in the uniform of a Roman officer, though he wore his long, flaxen hair loose down the length of his back, apparently a custom of noble Franks. They were followed by the others, eager to hear the details of this important request. They acknowledged each other, but little was said as they gathered in a circle on the earthen floor. Hengist spoke first.

'This is Prince Merovech of the Franks. He brings us important news and an offer from the Romans.'

Merovech nodded. 'I speak a little, but Gundad better to explain.' His guttural accent was hard to follow.

Gundad cleared his throat. 'The Romans and their allies in Gaul are threatened by the mighty empire of the Huns.

King Attila, the Hun leader, is moving his army west. Aetius, Rome's supreme military commander, is seeking to assemble the greatest coalition of forces ever seen. He has been made aware of the size of our army and the success of our warriors, and so he proposes a lucrative treaty.' He looked toward Merovech who nodded his approval. 'He requests that you send as many soldiers as possible to the islands down the coast of Gaul at the mouth of the Loire. From there, your men will be deployed inland as required. In return, each man will receive the pay of an Imperial soldier for the duration of their duty, and battlefield booty will be shared out amongst participants in the usual way. The islands may remain a Saxon settlement thereafter. But if all of that is not generous enough, Aetius has made a further concession. He is aware of how the army of Hengist has overrun this region of Lindum in the province of Flavia. This territory belongs to the Emperor, not the Britons, and he intends, one day, to return to Britannia. Under the Emperor's seal, this entire region will be officially granted to the kings of the Jutes, Angles and Saxons. The Britons shall have no future claim to it, so your war here is as good as won. You will be recognised as settled foederati of this territory with Rome's complete approval!'

Freuleaf was first to ask a question. 'The Britons have rejected the Romans, so surely, they no longer recognise Rome's authority?'

'That is so,' replied Gundad, 'but you should know that the Britons have appealed to Aetius to send an army to come and crush you.'

'And does he decline?' asked Hengist.

'Our treaty would put an end to the possibility of him accepting any such request.'

Merovech looked around, once again, and sought to reassure the assembled warlords in their own language.

'Aetius is ruthless but honourable; the Britons have no army to offer him. This offer he makes you – he does the same with my tribe in Gaul. Roman cives are expected to do what the army requires.'

Hengist turned to his brother. 'This is an opportunity. We can spare three thousand men to this lucrative venture and still beat the Wealas if they decide to fight us.'

Horsa stroked his beard, deep in thought. 'You would have me a farmer, brother, I know it. This winter has been harsh, food has been short, our raids return less, and we have to journey further for it. I say we take our entire army to Gaul and fight alongside Merovech.'

'Then how do we defend our new homeland?'

'The Wealas are fearful. Our women and children will be safe with a modest force to protect them. There is nothing here for our enemies, other than revenge.'

'Father, we have too few keels to transport the entire army,' said Aesc.

'That can be resolved,' replied Gundad. 'We have many spare, as do the Angles. Is that not so?' He turned to Freuleaf.

'Yes. We can supply ten keels.'

Wipped now joined the conversation. 'We also have spare keels.'

'So, what do you say, brother?'

Hengist was pleased with both his brother's and his allies' response. 'We shall support Aetius. Has he sent silver to tempt us?'

Gundad looked toward Merovech who nodded.

'There is an amount for expenses,' said Gundad.

'Keep your hands off our silver, Gundad, or I shall chop them off,' said Hengist, looking pointedly at the avaricious merchant.

'But the keels will require payment—'

Merovech intervened. 'My secretary will deal with matters fairly, King Hengist. I am pleased with your decision, but you must make haste. Attila will not wait for us to assemble. I am to return immediately, and you must arrive at the mouth of the Loire no later than one month from now.'

Hengist turned to Horsa. 'We shall lead our army, but one noble must remain to oversee our territories here. Octha and Aesc shall draw lots. Whoever remains must become a farmer.'

Horsa growled. 'Better to die on a battlefield.'

Hengist laughed. 'Perhaps, if you hadn't killed all the Britons, brother, we might have some slaves to farm for us.'

A Visit to Myrddin

Crafen

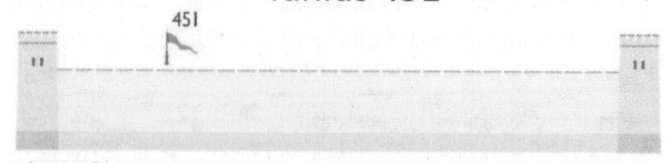

Iunius 451

'This part of our kingdom is so incredibly beautiful,' exclaimed Morgaine.

'There is nowhere quite like Crafen with its white rocks, river valleys and tumbling streams,' replied Martin.

Swallows swooped across the flower-bedecked meadows as the travellers approached a huge crag that looked remarkably similar to a loaf of bread.

'There is our waymark. Beyond that crag is a road that leads all the way to Reged.'

'How far is it to Myrddin's cave?'

'A few more hours. It is across a vast moor, a delightful ride in summer but a devil of a journey in winter.'

'Are you sure he will still be there?'

'He is old and frail, but I am told he still lives.'

'When did you last see him?'

'Around this time last year. I keep expecting to hear of his death, but he endures beyond his own predications.' The priest chuckled, amused by the irony.

'You think he will know the meaning of this ball of fire that travels across the heavens?'

'I hope so, for I have tried and failed to discern its meaning, though I am certain it is a portent of doom.'

Apprehensive as Morgaine was about their mission, she was pleased to be travelling with her old tutor Martin who was now known at court as Merlinus, the king's wizard, though in truth, he was a priest and a healer rather than a magician. Her new role as deacon and healer in his service gave her ample opportunity to express her gratitude to the Lord. When she had nearly died herself, Martin had saved her with his skills, although he said it had been God's will that she should live. Seven years had passed since that awful time, but she could still remember the terrible sickness and the burning sensation on her skin. She was considered lucky, for many had died. Nearly every family had lost someone to the disease that had arisen everywhere. She supposed the extensive scarring to her face and body was small price to pay for her life.

'I hope this celestial sign does not herald a return of the pox,' she said, betraying her train of thought. Martin did not respond. She had noticed how he avoided discussing her misfortune, possibly because he thought it might offend her. He need not have worried, for Morgaine had placed all memories of her illness behind her duty and devotion to healing in God's name.

Their ponies plodded along the straight track that crossed the moor, the constant rhythm of their hooves accompanied by the distant warbling of curlews, alert to the danger of strangers close by their nests. The sweet smell of the midsummer afternoon occasionally gave way to the peaty aroma that clung to the plentiful stream crossings and boggy ground.

'I feel drawn to this place, Martin; it welcomes me. These strangely shaped rocks look almost alive, but benign, not malevolent.'

'The people here are just as friendly – miners and farmers who follow the seasons, only ceasing their toils to give thanks to God.'

'I can see the attraction of such a remote and simple life.'

'Perhaps, but nature can be as cruel as man, and their larders are sometimes empty.'

The warm sun began its descent in the west, reaching a rock escarpment where ravens hovered motionless before swooping to their nests in the crevices. The crimson rays of the setting sun gave the limestone cliffs a pink hew, and there, sat on a rock at the mouth of a cave, they saw Myrddin, his long, white hair and beard obscuring his features.

'Ah, good, he's still with us,' said Martin.

They dismounted, leaving their ponies grazing, and climbed the steep grassy incline, waving as they approached.

'Morgaine and Martin,' Myrddin announced. 'Look, there in the sky, the Flaming Head, just visible in this light, but as the sun drops, it will become a spectacular sight.'

'We are all frightened by what it could mean,' said Morgaine.

'Change. It heralds change.'

'Is it a portent of doom?' asked Martin.

The old seer laughed, his shoulders shaking. 'You Christians! You see doom and second comings everywhere.'

Martin did not respond to the seer's mockery, but Morgaine pressed on. 'My father has asked that we council your opinion. He believes you will know the meaning of this comet.'

'The Flaming Head affects everyone, the whole world. Terrible strife followed the one I saw as a boy. The Picts invaded bringing much slaughter, destroying the Roman garrisons as far south as Eboracum. In response, Magnus Maximus came to the Patria, defeated the Picts. Afterward, he appointed himself Emperor and took an army of Britons to Gaul to fight the Roman Emperor. Neither he nor his army ever returned, leaving Coel Hen in command of the North.'

Morgaine listened with wide-eyed intensity. 'So, my great-grandfather came to power as a result of those turbulent times?'

'That was the outcome in the North.'

'But tell us what you see *now*,' pressed the priest.

'I see many things. Some revolve around King Mor but most concern Arthwys. I shall tell you all in due course, but for now, sit with me and marvel at this sight. See how bright it becomes as the sun sinks.'

Morgaine looked skyward, clasping her gold crucifix for comfort. She had no doubt the Flaming Head was a sign from God, but what could it mean? Myrddin seemed to read her thoughts.

'If, as before, it is a celestial herald for change, then emperors and kings will fall in quick succession. The Bear must prepare for a great war.'

An Omen

South of Aurelianum, Gaul

Iunius 451

Aetius was studying the map of the local area when Count Romanus rushed into the campaign tent.

'Attila has lifted his siege of Aurelianum and is preparing to march east.'

'That is what I would expect him to do – he will not want to fight our infantry on terrain where he cannot bring his cavalry into full effect.'

'Attila must be furious that the rumours about King Sangiban being willing to throw open Aurelianum's gates to the Huns turned out to be unfounded.'

'It was our ruse to draw Attila in this direction and have him unprepared for a difficult campaign. It has worked better than we could have hoped, Romanus. Instead of receiving a generous welcome from Sangiban, his troops were left facing the city walls with empty bellies. King Sangiban's loyalty has bought us valuable time.'

'Aegidius and Ricimer are waiting to see you.'

'Then bring them in. We must leave in pursuit of the Huns; there is no time to linger.'

Romanus stepped outside and quickly returned with the young generals who saluted their supreme commander.

'I have just been informed Attila is preparing to move eastward.'

'Yes, magister,' replied Aegidius.

'Send a messenger to King Theodoric. We move out as soon as Sangiban is ready to join our column.'

Ricimer cast a glance at Aegidius.

'Have you been able to assemble the Franks, Saxons, Burgundians and Armoricans to support our ranks?'

'Almost, magister.'

'Almost?' Aetius frowned.

'Some are more disciplined than others, but most have arrived.'

'I require only that they can hold a shield and thrust a spear!'

'There is some disquiet in the lower ranks, magister.'

'How so?'

'It is this celestial sighting, the so-called Burning Yellow Hair. Many think it is a bad omen.'

Romanus watched Aetius place his hand on his chin, his eyes flickering. Experience told the count that the magister militum was deep in thought.

'Are you referring to the comet of the Caesars?'

'I was unaware that it is known by that name,' said Ricimer.

'It has appeared before many famous battles, all won by the Empire. Go, spread the word amongst your men as they prepare to break camp. We face the Huns as soon as they stop running away from us.'

The generals saluted and departed. The young Count Romanus remained standing, waiting for Aetius to speak.

'Superstition is a powerful weapon, Romanus. We will

need to make the most of everything at our disposal, if we are to defeat Attila.'

Romanus smiled and wondered if Aetius truly believed the comet was a good omen. Perhaps this was not the best moment to point out to his master that Attila had never been defeated and that they faced the largest army that had ever entered Roman territory.

Visitors for Vortigern

The fortress of Ystyuacheu

Martius 453

The three riders followed a winding path through the rolling green hills by the river Teme.

'This will be the first time I have visited my father's hunting lodge,' said Vortimer, nervous about the forthcoming encounter, 'though I believe it isn't far from here. I haven't seen or spoken to him for years.'

'Nor I,' said Britu, 'apart from when he attended Mother's funeral, but even then, he spoke mostly to Catigern.'

'He is still bitter, but I hope he will see us.' Vortimer was not sure that he would. He continued. 'I am told that he has turned the lodge into a fortress, maintaining just a modest court, and since the council was disbanded, he has kept to his own lands, as if he were banished.'

'He was the architect of his own downfall,' said Viracus, the oldest member of the group. 'I'd go so far as to say he's almost single-handedly responsible for the troubles with the Saxons.'

Vortimer laughed. 'He will never see it that way. In his mind, it is the council who are to blame.'

'Do you think he might have mellowed?' asked Viracus.

'Unlikely.'

'It is sad that I barely know my own father,' said Britu.

'That has been his choice, brother. You and I were too close to Mother, God rest her soul, but we are all going to have to co-operate if we are to win this war. Father is still influential, particularly in the west, and he is wealthier than most. We need his help.'

'He will want to take control of any campaign – that was always his way,' said Viracus.

'Let us not prejudge our meeting. Our news will give him concern, maybe enough to make him see sense.'

Britu's optimism was not shared by Viracus.

'Sense? I am not even sure he is entirely sane. He has withdrawn from public life since the plague and doesn't even visit Glevum, the city built by his ancestors.'

Vortimer laughed. 'Cities! Difficult to defend and with little purpose other than to attract raiders and disease.'

'The brothels were better when the Romans were here.'

'You have a long memory, old man,' Vortimer said, teasing Viracus.

'I meant your father's interests are no longer serviced as well as they once were.'

'My father's reputation is an embarrassment,' said Britu. 'He claims to be Christian yet flouts the commandments.'

'That, brother, is a sign of his arrogance. He has never believed that the rules apply to him.'

'Why then do so many remain loyal to him, adopting his warped views as theirs?'

'It is the way with such men – wealth and power cloud judgement. His birthright grants the licence, and his wealth salves the misdeeds, yet it will all count for nothing if the Saxons sweep his little kingdom away.'

'Or when he atones to the Lord for his sins,' joked Britu.'

'We must use his fear of the Saxons to ferment his resolve. He feels safe in his stronghold, so far from the front line, but the Saxons know his name, and they will come for him. Better that he helps us now than perishes alone, watching all that his dynasty has achieved burn.'

*

The fortress in the woods was more impressive than the visitors had imagined. The original hall was surrounded by an earthen bank, on top of which was a timber stockade. Several other buildings had been erected, making the whole complex much like a small town. The land surrounding the clearing was all being worked, and there were many more people than Vortimer had expected. The visitors approached the gate, respectfully calling to the sentries who were watching them with interest.

'Please notify King Vortigern that he has important visitors.'

'Your names?'

'I am Vortimer, son of the king and commander of the joint army of the Britons.'

A sentry ran quickly toward one of the more recently erected buildings. Vortimer could hear a commotion from within. More soldiers appeared and servants began running in different directions.

A groom walked toward the gate. 'My lords, I am to take your horses to the stables.'

Another sentry appeared. 'My lords, I am to take your weapons.'

Vortimer placed his hand on his sword hilt. 'My father has nothing to fear, but I will not surrender my sword. You may take it from me, if you dare?'

Vortimer's name was known to most in the west as belonging to the commander who had valiantly driven the Saxons out of Viroconium and Deva before chasing them back into the east, confining the enemy to beyond the Great Forest. The sentry did not challenge him.

'Please, come with me.'

They paused at a grand door whilst one of Vortigern's men entered to announce the guests. There was a short delay before they were summoned to enter.

The hall was colonnaded, reminding Vortimer of the church in Viroconium. At the far end, in the centre of the hall, sat his father dressed in a toga, surrounded by advisers and servants, all similarly attired. They appeared to have been hastily assembled but were already in the midst of deep discussion. The aged king addressed the visitors.

'Ah, King Vortimer, Prince Britu and, if I am not mistaken, Lord Viracus of the Cornovii.'

Vortimer bowed, as did his companions.

'Greetings, Father.'

'There must be something seriously amiss if you are seeking me out. I hope it is not more treachery?'

Vortimer ignored his father's jibe. 'Father, we come with grave news.' The king leant forward to listen. 'Three years ago, the Saxons took to their keels and sailed away. Everyone assumed the rebel leaders had returned to their homeland because of the council's refusal to maintain their supplies. It was a moment of great relief, particularly for the hard-pressed southern Britons.' Vortigern nodded, indicating that he already knew all this. 'Later, through the contacts of Ambrosius, we discovered they had actually sailed to Gaul where they were fighting for the Romans under the leadership of Aetius against Attila.' Vortigern's brow furrowed at the mention of Ambrosius, but he continued to listen. 'We all came to hope that they would remain in Gaul, and for all this time, they did. But it would seem they have now been released from their arrangement.'

Vortimer paused to give his pronouncement greater impact, but Vortigern was rapt and impatient. 'How do you know this?'

'The Wash and the Humber are full of recently arrived Saxon keels. Great fleets, more in number than I can ever remember from their first campaigns.'

Shock rippled through Vortigern's court.

'So they are back, and stronger than ever?'

'That is so.'

'And what are your plans, General Vortimer?'

Was that sarcasm or respect in his father's tone? 'All the kings of Britannia must co-operate. The Saxon army is huge and battle-hardened. If we do not stand together, we Britons will be swept away by such a large force.'

'You were able to contain them before. Tales of your valour have even breached my fortress walls.'

'Back then, we were using cavalry militia to fight and contain raiders, but their army is now as large as a Roman legion.'

'The council should have followed my guidance.'

Vortimer had no intention of engaging in that old debate, but it seemed Vortigern was intent on venting his displeasure.

'The Saxons were content as our allies. This could all have been avoided.'

Vortimer continued to say nothing, hoping his father would recognise the futility of covering old ground, but he knew that this was his way. He wore a tyrant's mask behind which he kept a scheming, manipulative mind. Here was a man who thought himself incapable of being wrong, or of making bad decisions, constantly adapting his record to suit the circumstances. He also enjoyed belittling others.

'So, you have no idea how to deal with this problem?' said Vortigern, almost smiling.

'It is the sheer scale of this new force. We were hardly able to contain the first rebellion. We suffered much slaughter across our territories before we managed to establish pinch points along the borders of the Colonae. If Hengist mobilises this force, they will be unstoppable, and whilst I can understand you feel safe in your western fortress surrounded by your allies, be sure, they will come looking for the great King of the Britons.'

Vortigern's eyes narrowed. 'And where are your allies, Vortimer – the kings you preferred to your father?'

'The plague has taken many good families; resources and equipment are short. Elafius of Verulamium maintains a militia at Durobrivae where they face the most imminent threat. My own militia hold the Trent valley at Derventio, but our numbers are paltry, at best, a hundred or so.'

'So where is Ambrosius?' Vortigern spat the name.

'He has been building a large militia in the south, but currently, his eyes are fixed on the Continent.'

'To what purpose? Does he think he can be Emperor?' Vortigern laughed. 'His father tried and lasted just two years!'

'The Empire is in turmoil. Attila is retreating but not yet defeated, and the Armoricans have sent several embassies to Ambrosius to ask for support.'

As expected, Vortigern seized his opportunity. 'So, the Roman is still not committed to Britannia, after all this time?' Vortimer did not answer. It suited his purpose to allow his father to hold this standpoint. 'And what of those northern tyrants, Mor and Gorwst?'

'Their militias are devastated by plague, so they concentrate only on defence, fearing attacks not only from Saxons but also Picts, Scotti and Gaels. The Saxon rebellion focused mostly on lands to the south of the Humber – there is little to the north of interest to them and the terrain is difficult.'

'What do your instincts tell you, Vortimer? What do you expect Hengist to do?'

'He will attack south and west again, but he'll probe even further this time. Random raids can no longer feed such a large force. All-out war is their best option.'

'Perhaps we can negotiate by ceding further territory.'

'To what purpose? To reward heathen slaughter of innocent Christians by handing them a secure and fertile homeland?'

'To buy time, my son. You must do your utmost to persuade Ambrosius and Mor to commit troops. In the meantime, we must meet our enemy, face-to-face, to discover their ambitions.'

This was not an unreasonable suggestion. Hengist might consider speaking to the great King Vortigern

'After their time in Gaul and dealings with Aetius, we might find them more favourably disposed to statecraft,' continued Vortigern.

'Perhaps, but they have been rubbing shoulders with Alans and Goths, tribes whose clear ambition has always been to establish kingdoms at the expense of others.'

They both fell silent, lost in their thoughts. Vortimer sighed. 'What has Rome become?'

'We shall discuss this further when we dine tonight. Catigern will return from the hunt soon; he will be pleased to see his brothers.'

Vortimer nodded. Perhaps his father had mellowed enough to provide the necessary assistance.

Almost as if invoked by the speaking of his name, a burdened Catigern staggered in, dropping a deer carcass ceremoniously on the floor.

'Brothers!' he exclaimed, embracing each in turn. 'And Viracus. By your faces, the news is not good?'

'We shall explain later. You look in robust health!'

'I am. A reunion. How splendid.'

'Where is Pascent?'

'Father will not speak to him for his servility to Ambrosius Aurelianus.'

Vortigern looked angry but said nothing. The outspoken comment was a clear indication of Catigern's strong position at court – useful to know.

'And you?' Vortimer asked.

'I visit him as regularly as I visit Father.'

Vortimer looked for his father's reaction, seeing him immediately stand to take his leave.

'Until later, my sons. Marcus, my secretary, will show you to your quarters.'

They bowed as he left the main hall, then Catigern turned to his brothers.

'After Marcus has shown you to your rooms, meet me at the stables. There is a tavern around the back – we have much to catch up on.'

Vortimer was delighted with his brother's welcome. Sides had been taken after the battle of Guoloph. Vortimer had supported his mother – Britu just a small child at the time – whereas Catigern and Pascent had been more ambivalent, allowing for Vortigern to retain their love and support by showering them with gifts. The king's divisive tactics had broken Sevira's heart, but she had died knowing that Vortimer had eclipsed Vortigern both as a warrior and as King of the Cornovii. He missed her every day. He lived such a solitary life, never having married – the Saxon rebellion had left so little time. But his name was known to every king on the island, and he took pride that it was a name that engendered respect and not the loathing that was his father's legacy.

*

Catigern was always the scamp. His tavern proved to be a converted byre where he met with the lower ranks to drink beer. Vortimer found his brother ensconced with his hunting companions, the small group in raucous voice. But they fell silent when they saw which visitors had entered the small building.

'Here, brothers, try this,' called Catigern, proffering jugs of ale. 'If it is too bitter, there is honey to sweeten it.'

The scene was the antithesis of Vortigern's Roman ways. Though, with supplies of wine short, the more refined libation could not have been expected to be on offer at the byre.

Catigern introduced his hunting friends who at first appeared in awe of his famous brother, but the jollity soon returned, enabling Vortimer to draw his brother into a private corner.

'I need help from the west. Cavalry – a competent cavalry soldier is worth five Saxons, our best way of narrowing the odds.'

'We were told you had beaten the Saxons, and they had returned to their homeland.'

'I wish that were so. We contained them for a while before they left, but they have returned with thousands of foot soldiers! The east is already devastated and deserted, so they will come further west and south until we are all either slaughtered or slaves.'

'Do you have a plan, a campaign?'

'Only ideas. But the council no longer meets, and all have different views. Resources are generally insufficient, and even those soldiers brave enough to stand in the front line are terrified because they know these Saxons seek our extinction – we face a fight to the death against wild beasts.'

'Father has been sitting back, hoping they will eliminate his rivals for him. He does not see things the way you do.'

'Reality has never been his strength. He needs to understand that they will eliminate us all, none will be spared.'

'How can I help?'

'If we are to have any chance, everyone must join the fight. It is vital that we find a way to convince Father to join us.'

'He was never a soldier. He feels safe here with his mountains at his back and his wives to console him.'

'How many now?'

'Last count, four. There's a new slave-girl elevated to special duties.'

'He will go to Hell,' said Vortimer, grim-faced.

'Yes, probably with a smile still on his face!'

The brothers laughed.

'The key to securing his co-operation is his ego, I'm sure of it.'

'How so?'

'This is the man who married the daughter of Magnus Maximus, from whose family was drawn one of the Protectors of Britannia. For a while, he saw himself as an emperor, and many still see him this way. The life of a recluse must bore him.'

'Do you think you can get the council to reconvene?'

'I must. It is our only chance.'

'But they are further apart now than they ever were. Father hates Ambrosius, and the cives of the east would prefer Roman oppression and taxes over Vortigern's control.'

'Views are shifting rapidly. Rome has deserted and insulted Elafius. He asked Aetius to return with his army, offering many concessions, but he did not reply. Bishop Germanus provided hope when he visited, but he is long dead, as are his promises. Many Britons fled to Armorica, only to find circumstances are little better there, and now Rome sends Alan barbarians to collect taxes from them. Recently, Elafius discovered that Aetius has made allies of the Saxons, just compounding the betrayal. I want Father to reach out to Elafius. More than anyone, it is Elafius who needs our help and support. And then there is Ambrosius. He will be of little help if he behaves like Janus and looks both ways. He has always been bitter about his family's demise in Gaul, and his hope for a return to his family's estates there has never been fully extinguished. I fear he may hesitate to join the fray until it is too late, so we need to find a way to prompt him to urgent action. Mor will certainly help, but if his militia leave their stockades, there is the risk Hengist will attack to the north. So, I suspect he will want to wait to see which way Hengist moves.'

'But won't Ambrosius take exception, if Father reasserts himself.'

'It was division within the Cymry that defeated Vortigern. His arrogant methods were his undoing. Ambrosius fully appreciates the gravity of the threat but holds little sway north of Glevum, particularly now the

Empire is collapsing. He will prefer to see Vortigern taking responsibility rather than hiding in the hills.'

'So, what is your strategy, brother?'

'We must match the Saxon army and defeat it. Everyone must fight, including you, brother.'

Catigern emptied his flagon, but his expression was solemn. 'War it is, then. Shall we have another beer?'

'Thank you, but no – I must have my wits about me when I speak to Father this evening.'

*

Vortigern made his way across the compound to his living quarters. He acknowledged the two guards who opened the heavy oak doors and saluted their king. It was a large building, partitioned across the centre. In the front half, there were three ladies weaving and spinning wool.

'Good evening, ladies.'

'My lord, are you come to bed early?' said the youngest.

'Tempting, but no. My sons have come to visit me, so I need you all looking lovely when you attend to us at dinner.'

The women huddled together, excitedly discussing what they were going to wear, whilst Vortigern walked toward the large, strong door in the partition. He reached into his leather purse for a key which he inserted into the lock. The levers clicked loudly as the lock was released. Then, removing the key, he entered his strongroom, closing the door behind him and sliding an inside bolt into place. Vortigern sat down on a chair he kept there and looked around at what was left of his family's wealth. The room was dark, the only light coming through narrow slits just below the eaves. The poor visibility was a fair exchange for increased security – the old king was surrounded by piled trunks, full of silver and gold coins, and timber crates, brimming with silver plate. In one area, his family's weapons were stored – swords, helmets, armour and uniforms, some of which had been worn by his father. When Vortigern needed to think, this was his favourite place to do so.

In the wake of his campaign against Ambrosius, he had removed all his portable wealth to this place. Glevum was not safe – a target for Gaels and pirates no longer afraid of sailing into the estuary. Once the greatest port in the west, the city now lay unprotected, in decline and full of disease. The entire province had collapsed, law and order only a memory. He reflected almost every day about what might have been. If only the council had listened. If only his campaign had succeeded. If only Sevira and Vortimer had not betrayed him. For fifteen years, he had bitterly ruminated on the consequences of both his and his rival's errors. He had always known Britannia needed a strong leader to protect the cives, collect taxes and mint coins. He should have been that leader, and despite his failure to secure that role, it was now clear he had been proved right about everything. The Picts had been quelled, the Romans had never returned, Ambrosius was not the saviour the cives had been hoping for, and the unnecessary Saxon rebellion had successfully exploited all of their weaknesses. He was still angry at the young Vortimer who had rejected his father, but he begrudgingly respected the man he had become, admiring his valour. Here was his eldest son, trying to fight an enemy that greatly outnumbered him, without any committed allies. Vortigern's own experience had been remarkably similar, except he had been a civic leader not a soldier, and he had been failed by his generals.

He shook his head, trying to put it all in the past, but he knew he never would. Vortigern had only once met Hengist and his father Whitgils. It had been a long time ago, but their messages to each other had been cordial, and the west had always paid its fair share. It had been the council, guided by Ambrosius, which had caused the rebellion by refusing to pay the foederati. They had only themselves to blame. It was still possible he could persuade Hengist down a peaceful path – such an attempt must surely be the first step for any competent leader. He would help Vortimer, and by facing the fearsome Saxon king across the negotiating table, his bravery would show Ambrosius for the weakling he was, driving a wedge between the self-interested Roman and the beleaguered cives. He imagined how they would rally behind him and remembered how his forerunners – Vitalis, Coel Hen and Octavius – had united to eject the Romans. He looked across at his father's uniform and decided he would wear it tonight and then for the meeting with Hengist. Thanks to the failure of his rivals, he might yet be Emperor of Britannia!

'Vortigern returns,' he said, in a loud and dramatic voice. His mood had lifted – he was going to really enjoy this evening.

A Bid for Peace

The river Dergeuntid at the junction with the Trent

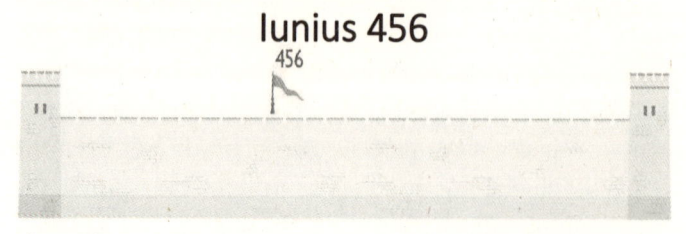

Iunius 456

The day had been sunny and warm. The junction of the two rivers was choked with green weed, the water level low due to the lack of rain. Britu watched the ducks with their young paddling up and down and wondered how long it would be before Vortigern returned with his brothers.

The old king's positive response to Vortimer's request for help had been remarkable. First, he had sent peace envoys to meet both Hengist and someone he said could be trusted – Gundad of the Gaini. It had been quite the surprise when the Saxons had readily agreed to a meeting between their leaders and those of the Britons, suggesting they should convene at a place called Rither Gabail on the opposite side of the Trent to the stronghold known as Gainnion and close to the large Saxon settlement on the Isle of Axholme.

Vortigern had been delighted that it was his influence that had garnered this prestigious meeting and had been determined to remain in control of the negotiations. Britu had heard plenty of tales about Vortigern's arrogance though he hardly knew the man who was his father. The old king had been a recluse for most of Britu's life and his mother had despised him so nothing good was ever said. Even so, it had come as a shock when she disclosed on her death bed that Vortigern was not his *real father*. In their private final conversation, she had assured him that Vortigern's deficiencies as a father had been from choice rather than bias, for not even he knew that Britu was not his son. Once the shock had dissipated, the new reality had not troubled Britu in the slightest. He had always felt different to his much older brothers, and now he knew that Mor, the warrior king, was his real father, it fitted rather better with his self-perception.

His mind wandered back to the old king who, in typical style, had taken an entourage of one hundred nobles, many from his own court, and filled five river barges for the journey to the meeting place. His intention was to impress the Saxon leaders in the process of discovering their objectives. Most of the discussion prior to departure had been about what demands the Saxons might make and what Vortigern was prepared to concede to achieve peace.

A lookout hollered from beyond the timber wharf further up the river. 'I see them.'

In the distant shimmer of the summer evening, two barges loomed into view, their crews slowly rowing toward the wharf.

Britu turned to the patrol captain. 'Where are the others?'

'Something is wrong,' he replied.

As the barges drew closer, Britu caught the rope slung from the prow of the first vessel by Vortimer, and his men heaved the barge alongside the wharf. They were greeted by a distressing sight; the deck was covered with dead and dying men. The young prince jumped on board the barge to help offload its sorry cargo.

'What in God's name happened?' Britu asked Vortimer.

'It was a trap, Britu,' Vortimer replied, his expression anguished. 'They were armed with concealed daggers and attacked when we least expected it. Catigern and Viracus are dead; Vortigern is severely wounded.'

'This is dreadful news. Your side is soaked in blood, brother. It would seem even you did not escape unscathed.'

'We have lost over half our men, but they did not have it all their own way. We killed as many as we could, slaying two of their kings, Horsa and Gundad. Father is on the following barge. He mustered great courage for the fight but now is broken, and I fear he will not long survive his wounds. We were unprepared for this treachery and did well to escape with even this many, for it was their intention to murder us all.'

'Have the Saxons given chase?'

'There has been no sign of pursuit, but the Trent is lined with their keels. They are planning a full-scale attack, I'm sure of it. We have badly misjudged their motives. These Saxons seek only war; they never had any interest in brokering a peace. We must alert our allies, for we have never been so weak.'

A King with Grave News

Elfed

October 456

Igerna and Bryn watched from the door of the great hall as the rain ran off the roofs of the many timber buildings in the compound.

'I remember when we first arrived. Nowhere was private and we all slept in that building over there.' The queen pointed at a small building near the gate.

'Yes. The fort has grown into a town now, and there is barely enough room for all the people who live within the stockade.' Bryn looked across at her own family's lodgings. 'But the alternative is to live outside the defences, and many are too frightened to give up the security offered by the watchful eyes of the king's guards.'

'Arthwys has moved his militia to the compound at Campocalia for this reason. My son's horses and men are too many, and it's only a short distance away.'

'Yes, though the seven miles may as well be seventy. Your son trains the men with such intensity that he keeps them away for weeks at a time. You should hear the complaints from their wives.'

The queen smiled. 'Yes, Gwenhyfar chief amongst them. Arthwys returns even less frequently than his men, though it is not surprising he pushes himself so hard with the Saxon threat on the increase.'

'Your son is dedicated to his duty and the Lord in equal measure. He has ever shouldered the weight of his responsibilities with diligence.'

Igerna sighed. 'Unlike Gwenhyfar who is once again visiting her father and sister in Erechwyd, though I do enjoy looking after Pabo and Eliffer when she is away, even if they are a handful.'

'And now we have news that Meirchiawn is to marry Gwenhyfar's sister, at last.'

'And guess who is to be matron of honour?'

'Her younger sister, I presume?'

'Quite so. Gwenhyfar was so young when she married Arthwys, I am not at all certain they had a clue what they were doing.'

'Well, the children came very quickly, so they knew how to do that!'

Igerna laughed. 'How can I begrudge her a little socialising at the court of Reged? I remember when Sevira took me under her wing – it was constant princes and parties.'

They both laughed.

'Different times.'

'Indeed, King Vortigern, God bless his soul, was a difficult man, but he threw grand Roman parties, and Sevira, as the granddaughter of Magnus Maximus, certainly knew how to enjoy them.' Igerna suddenly felt a pang of sadness. 'I miss her so much, and it is hard to hear that Viroconium is now in ruins.'

'Many cities are. Cian says that it is only our vigilance and our rivers and hills that protect us from the Saxon scourge.'

'Yes, but our isolation has never been so absolute. Mor has felt such remorse since we heard of Prince Catigern's death. He was such a sweet little boy when he was in my care, and the promise Mor made Sevira to protect her heirs weighs heavy upon him.'

'Cian urges caution, though, until the time is right. The slaughter at Rither Gabail has emboldened the savages. Vortigern's bid for peace has proved a costly mistake. These Saxons only seem to understand the sword.'

'Merlinus has seen that God wills us to slaughter them all. He has dreamt that the Cymry, led by Arthwys, will defeat the Saxons in a great battle which will free our people from fear.'

'Cian has told me of this prophecy, but he also says we are outnumbered one hundred to one.'

'I do not doubt that Merlinus sees the future, but he admits he has no influence over how events will unfold, and there is always the chance evil will find a way to thwart his visions.'

'Do you and the king believe all this?'

'Why would we not? Merlinus is ever wise and pragmatic. He says we can either be victims or victors, but preparation and timing are the key.'

'And Arthwys? The weight on his shoulders must be crushing. Does he believe his destiny will accord with the prophecies?'

'He has been led down this path all his life, first by Talhaearn and then Myrddin, now Merlinus. If he doubts, he does not show it. He grows his militia, prays hard, and no one can best him in single combat – he is prepared.'

Bryn smiled. 'Agiluf is devoted to him, but he is kept so busy that it is left to me to find him a wife!'

Igerna laughed with her friend. 'Well, look for a pretty one, or he will never forgive you! It is well that Arthwys married so young – there would be no time now.'

'Grandma, I don't understand this,' little Pabo called from within the hall.

Igerna sighed. 'Latin is difficult. Usually, I have Morgaine here to help, but she has gone to Isurium with Merlinus to help baptise infants in the Swale.'

Bryn laughed. 'The priest makes his deacon work hard.'

'Her devotion to both Merlinus and God is absolute. I am pleased she has found purpose, but I am sorrowful she still feels the need to hide her scarred face from view.'

'She was lucky to survive the pox, as a healer herself she knows this, but her beauty transcends the scarring.' They walked toward the boys. Pabo was waving his wax tablet in frustration.

'Be careful, Pabo,' Igerna scolded him. 'You will ruin the surface if you drop it.'

Bryn touched the queen's arm. 'I'm certain she is happy. Merlinus has a way of making her feel special.'

'Thank you, Bryn.'

'Darkness is falling, my lady; we should get the children to bed.'

Suddenly, there was an alarming thunder of hooves outside, and they could hear raised voices issuing orders. The children, distracted, ran to peek out of the door but quickly ran back when they saw men approaching. The king and Cian burst into the hall, both soaked to the skin.

'Scouts have seen a turma led by a chariot approaching. They believe it is King Vortimer. Send to Campocalia for Arthwys – he should be here with us to greet him.'

Vortimer. The most famous warrior in the land. Stories of his bravery were known to all. She could barely contain her excitement. He was still a boy last time Igerna had seen him. What must he look like now?

'Bryn, we must quickly prepare the hall for this most important guest. It has been so long since I helped Sevira raise him. I wonder if he will even remember me?'

Mor and Cian sat down at the trestle.

'Where is Merlinus?'

'Have you forgotten? He is away at Isurium with your daughter.'

'No matter, send for him too. He can be with us by tomorrow.'

A sentry cried out from the watchtower outside. Cian looked at the king. 'It will be Vortimer's herald.'

Mor stood up from the table and took his seat alongside Igerna. The young herald walked through the main door and handed his sword to the sentry. He bowed respectfully before approaching the king.

'I am sent by King Vortimer who seeks forgiveness for this intrusion but requests that you receive him and General Britu.'

'Please deliver my greetings to your king and let him know we will await their arrival with much anticipation.'

The herald bowed and left. As his horse was heard galloping out of the gate, Igerna's mind was racing. *Britu!* Sevira's youngest son and half-brother to Arthwys. The queen leapt from her chair and began issuing a stream of instructions to Bryn and her team of house servants before returning to sit alongside her husband.

'I wonder why they have come?' she asked.

'Perhaps there have been more battles with the Saxons? We have heard nothing from the south for some time, but I expect Vortimer comes to ask for my help.'

'Are we not sworn to assist him?' she asked her husband pointedly.

'We have long anticipated this request. Arthwys' militia still needs more recruits, but this is the moment for which he has been training.'

'My queen,' said Cian, 'we have considered sending troops to support Vortimer before, but that would have meant leaving Elfed with no defence. The enemy watch our movements and would attack in force if they saw we had left our people and lands undefended.'

'The situation to the south must be deteriorating rapidly for him to have risked coming in person.'

'Well, we will discover his intentions soon enough.'

*

When Vortimer entered the great hall, his appearance shocked Igerna. He walked with a limp, there was a patch over his left eye and his clothing looked ill-kept. He had not removed his mail and carried his helmet under one arm. By his side was a powerfully built young man. Even though she knew the identity of Britu's real father, it was still a surprise to see how closely he resembled Mor and Arthwys.

Mor leapt to his feet and embraced the exhausted king. 'Vortimer, I am pleased to see you. You look as if you have journeyed far?'

'I apologise for my appearance, King Mor. I have come directly from the court of Ambrosius Aurelianus who sends his best regards to you and your family.'

Mor signalled the servants to bring chairs for the guests.

'You may not recognise my general after so many years, but this is my young brother, Britu.'

Mor smiled and clasped the young man's shoulders. 'Britu... you were just a small boy when we last met.'

Igerna stood and walked toward both visitors. 'As was my Vortimer. My lord, how you have changed.' She wiped a tear from her eye then embraced both warriors warmly in turn.

Vortimer smiled. 'Igerna, I have missed you, though you have hardly aged in all these years.'

Igerna laughed. 'That is surely your impaired vision. What have you done?'

'A shard from my shield. It will heal but the wound in my left side does not.'

The queen turned to Britu. 'Your mother, my cousin, her death is a sad loss to us all. I am so pleased to finally meet you, Britu.'

Mor directed the men to sit before him.

'Please make yourselves comfortable. Drinks are being brought, but first we are anxious to hear the purpose of your visit?'

'It is a grim report.' Vortimer looked at the floor, avoiding the searching looks of those around him.

Igerna wiped away her tears and drew up a chair alongside the warrior king. She had comforted him many times as a boy, and she reached for his hand to console him now.

Vortimer lifted his head and looked directly at Mor. 'It is good to be amongst old friends. If only we could go back to the way life was when we first met – I don't understand why God has chosen to test us in this way.'

'It is evil that tests us,' Igerna said firmly. 'God is always with us.'

The sound of galloping horses interrupted the conversation, and Mor held up his hand. 'This will be Arthwys. I have summoned him to meet you.'

They did not have to wait long for Arthwys to enter the hall, with Agiluf at his side. Igerna continually admired how powerfully built both men had become, how they had grown taller than their fathers. When Vortimer rose to greet them, she saw he too was shorter, much like his late father, but Britu was almost as tall as his half-brother. Arthwys and Agiluf bowed and took their places next to Cian.

Mor spoke first. 'This is the mighty King Vortimer, scourge of the Saxons. Cian and I were privileged to fight alongside him many years past. These are our sons, Arthwys and Agiluf, both accomplished warriors and our hope for a better future.' The younger men acknowledged

Vortimer and Britu as Mor continued. 'The loss of your father, Catigern and Viracus was felt deeply at this court. We have thought to strike out in anger but could see no way to provide meaningful support without first establishing an integrated strategy.'

'I'm afraid the situation has become much worse, King Mor. Two months past, the Saxons began massing their troops south of Lindum. Britu and I were with our militia at Derventio and were yet unaware of this development. Elafius bravely led his troops from Durobrivae, taking up position north of the river Welland. The Saxon force greatly outnumbered them, and they were overwhelmed. Many thousands died at a place called Crecganford. The slaughter was terrible on both sides, but the Saxon army is large enough to easily absorb such losses. Elafius was defeated, died in the battle, and the remnant retreated to Durobrivae. Elafius was brave to face such an invincible force, and I believe the damage he inflicted has stopped the Saxon advance for now.'

The news stunned the entire court. Arthwys looked toward his shocked father before speaking directly to Vortimer. 'Raiding has intensified in our region, but the Saxons here do not seek pitched battle. We are protected by rivers and mountains, but the Great Forest is full of the enemy, and it is no longer safe to travel south.'

'We too are aware of this danger in the forest. We travelled through the mountains to get here, difficult in that damned chariot but I can no longer ride a horse.' He touched his left side as he continued. 'The Saxons are ever encroaching further west. At the south-west corner of the forest, near the Trent, a warrior called Aesc has occupied two forts that were built by our ancestors, and they are now using the old salt road from the coast as their main causeway. They consider this all to be their territory, which would be why they attacked Elafius.'

'So the entire Colonae is lost?'

'It appears the Saxons' plan has been to annexe the greater part of the province of Flavia Caesariensis, and they have effectively achieved their goal.'

Mor looked aghast. 'That is audacious. So, there can be no doubt – their return is permanent.'

'They claim that Aetius ceded the province to them in exchange for their military support.'

'Aetius is dead, and Rome will never return – it was not his to offer.'

'Yes, but it has been taken by force, nevertheless.'

The hall fell silent. Never in living memory had such a defeat been so keenly felt. There could be no doubt – Myrddin's prophecy had come to pass, the serpent was indeed devouring the Patria. Mor broke the silence.

'If an army of this size comes north, we too will be defeated.'

Cian looked particularly worried. 'They will emerge from the Great Forest in which they have hidden all these years. The rivers and ravines will not protect Elfed, then.'

Mor held up his hand to silence that thought. 'Planning for defence is not the answer. These heathens have shown their intentions. They have no desire to live peacefully side by side with us. No. Full-scale war is now inevitable.'

Igerna released Vortimer's hand and stood. She looked around at all the men.

'Our priest and adviser will not return until tomorrow, so I shall say this for him. God intends that we destroy these heathens. We have sent missionaries full of hope and all have failed to return, martyred no doubt, though we will never know where or how. Whatever plans you warriors devise, know that the Lord our God wishes you to wipe these Saxons from the face of the earth.' She paused, looking at each man in turn, steel in her eyes. 'All of them, not just their army, but their women and children too.' She turned to speak directly to their royal visitor. 'Vortimer, you are in no condition right now for making decisions. My housekeeper Bryn will attend to your need for food and rest, and I shall send you my bard Blwchfardd who will play the lyre and sing gentle songs to ease your troubled mind. Tomorrow, when our full court is here, we shall reconvene to lay plans, and afterward, we will feast and toast the great deeds we must expect to perform. Britons must unite! What say you, husband?'

'I know that Arthwys has a strategy he wishes to propose, but as ever, the queen knows best. We reconvene in the morning when Merlinus has returned.'

The Bear Roars

Elfed

October 456

Mor sat alone at his trestle. It was nearly midday the following day, and Morgaine had just entered the hall.

'Daughter, has Merlinus returned with you?'

'He has, Father. He will be with you shortly. Where is Mother?'

'She is with Bryn in the mansio attending to our guests. The queen asked me to send you there as soon as you arrived. King Vortimer has need of your healing skills.'

'I will go now.' She turned to leave but ran into the path of Britu as he entered the hall.

'Apologies, my lady.' He looked at her quizzically, but Morgaine covered her face with her veil and scurried out.

'Britu, come sit with me. That was my daughter, Morgaine.'

'She is shy, my lord. Why does she hide her face?'

'She is scarred by an unfortunate disease, but still a lovely girl. How is Vortimer?'

'Rested, fed and reclothed, as am I.'

'The queen was concerned for you both.'

'The queen is remarkable.' Britu smiled.

'As was your mother; we were all very close.'

'So I understand. She spoke highly of you King Mor, making me promise to find you if circumstances became dire. I'm sorry to say that time has come.'

'Did she say anything else?' Mor watched the young man's response.

'Only that I could trust you and that you could be relied upon to fulfil a promise you once made. She never told me what that was.'

Was there a twinkle in Britu's eye?

Mor relaxed. 'It was an oath of allegiance I made to the Cornovii royal family.'

Britu nodded, recognising the implications of such an oath in these times.

'It grieves me that you have lost your father.' Once again, Mor watched the young man keenly.

'I barely knew him. Vortimer has been more the father to me. Vortigern was a recluse for much of my life.'

'His final attempt to quell the Saxons was very brave.'

'Yes. Let us hope he is remembered for that.'

'Ah, Merlinus.' The priest had entered the hall with no fanfare. 'This is Britu, youngest son of Vortigern and Sevira.'

Merlinus bowed and then sat on a stool to one side of the trestle.

'Cian has told me the news.'

The queen entered the hall accompanied by Vortimer wearing clean clothes and without his armour.

'Good day, my friends,' said Vortimer. 'I am rested, refreshed in appearance even if not yet in spirit.'

'Have your men been similarly attended to?'

'Arthwys took them to his barracks at Campocalia, which will have been preferable to the rain-lashed hillside where I left them to camp.'

Cian, Arthwys and Agiluf now entered the hall, and servants began to assemble chairs, placing them in a large circle.

'Father,' said Arthwys, 'I have invited Winnog and Padell to attend this meeting.'

Mor nodded then took his place in the circle. Igerna, Vortimer and Britu sat to his left, with Cian, Merlinus, Arthwys and Agiluf to the right. They chatted whilst they waited for the two captains. Outside, the king's hunting hounds were howling either in frustration at the lack of sport or at the king's many visitors.

'Bryn, tell the huntsmen to exercise the pack or feed them now. I can barely hear a word anyone is saying,' said Mor. 'They are usually working at this time,' he added, by way of explanation.

Eventually, Padell and Winnog joined the group.

'King Vortimer, you may remember these two. Padell is commander of my guard, and Winnog commands a turma of archers – specialist troops, well-suited for forest warfare.'

'I remember them both,' Vortimer said, nodding warmly at the two commanders. 'This is Britu, my youngest brother.'

Satisfied that everyone had now been introduced, Mor began. 'We face a threat that has long been prophesised. When the Saxon army sailed away from our shores six years ago, we hoped they had returned to their provinces, but then we learnt the Romans had harnessed the Saxon greed and aggression for their own purposes, paying them to fight for Rome against the Hun. When Aetius was assassinated by his emperor, their payments stopped, so they returned to our eastern shores. Our scouts watched keel after keel enter the Humber and Trent, but we soon learnt this was but a fraction of their true force, for down the coast, at the mouths of the Glen and Welland, hundreds more keels had come ashore, spilling their vile cargo onto the shores of The Wash. We estimate their army to number close to ten thousand. They are not here for loot, for they know there is none to be had, so they can only be back here for further conquest. They have staked out a region in the east from the mouth of the Trent round to The Wash and in the west from Danum to Corieltauvorum. Is this how you see it, King Vortimer?'

'Yes, our early success led us to relax our vigilance. There was also great hope amongst the cives of the south that Rome would soon come to our assistance, so they too relaxed their vigilance, and the militia at Durobrivae diminished in size. We can blame the passage of time and disease for our dwindling armies, but in truth, motivation has been as much a factor. Roman soldiers and anyone who fights alongside them are paid. Careers in the military previously led to wealth and power. In contrast, our coffers are bare, yet we require men to leave their lands and families unguarded whilst they fight for no financial reward. They are reluctant to do so, and fear pervades our people as never before. Normal life can only be conducted west of the great road from Deva to Verulamium and even the security there is now under threat.'

'Does Ambrosius Aurelianus see it this way?' asked Mor.

'I have great respect for Ambrosius and his son Riothames. They have built a competent militia, commanded by Natalinus, but until this recent defeat at Crecganford, they have been more interested in Gaul. That focus has changed somewhat, now that they think they are Hengist's next target. However, during our recent visit, news arrived that, following the sack of Rome by Vandals, a Gallic senator, Avitus, has been appointed Emperor, and there is much optimism that the Empire will be restored. Ambrosius showed me Imperial correspondence asking that he be ready, if so required, to cross to the Continent in support of the Empire.'

'Do you believe he will undertake such an expedition?'

'Ambrosius is no fool, but he is the son of the murdered Emperor Sebastianus and remains bitter at his family's treatment. At any other time, I would expect him to be reluctant to commit troops north when an opportunity to recover his estates in Gaul could present itself at any moment. He is a Roman first, and so we must remain wary of his divided loyalties, but the news of Elafius' death and the scale of that defeat troubled him deeply – his own daughter lost her husband at the battle. He is also wise enough to know that, with barbarians flooding across the provinces on the Continent, like spring tides across the plains, the western Empire is ever fragile, making an expedition to Gaul at this time too risky.'

'What is the strength of his militia?'

'Four to five thousand men. He garrisons the route from Lactodurum to Verulamium, protecting his northern flank from Saxon incursion.'

'We will need his manpower if we are to win this war.'

'He said the same of you.'

'How so? Our numbers are insufficient to make much difference.'

'His militia is mostly infantry, whereas yours is entirely cavalry – men trained from boys to fight from horseback. He has never forgotten the impact your cavalry had on the battle at Guoloph.'

Cian stood and looked toward Mor for permission to speak. The king nodded.

'We learnt many lessons from Guoloph. Whilst we left our lands to fight in the south, the Saxons attacked Elfed – they watch us as keenly as we watch them. Even with Ambrosius' infantry we are in no position to fight a pitched battle, but maybe the Saxon tide has turned? I'm not sure the battle of Crecganford was a complete defeat. Brave Elafius may have come off worst, but Hengist was stopped in his tracks. If that had been the Picts or Attila, they would have swept on to sack the next city and the next, so in effect, it could be argued that both sides retreated.'

'Exactly,' exclaimed Mor. 'Your tactic of containment has been a success, and the only viable solution for the present. The territory the Saxons hold is lost to the Britons, but most of its previous occupants have fled or are dead. King Vortimer, we too have been stalled by conflicting interests, distracted by the potential for Pict and Scotti raids and Gael incursion.' Mor paused. 'However, from this day forward, we are committed to fighting alongside you. But to do that, the strategy must radically change. Our fear has blinded us, preventing us from seeing our strengths and our enemy's weaknesses. Merlinus, tell this gathering what you have told me, *what you have seen.*'

Merlinus stood and looked at each person in turn as he spoke. 'I have seen our victory. A great battle that takes place on the slopes of a mountain, the final defeat of the Saxons by the Cymry led by the Bear.' He looked at Arthwys. 'The Lord God is with us, and he will protect us if we protect ourselves. With our faith, we have no reason to fear death, but it is foolish to wait for it to arrive. The evil in the east may have been allowed to fester and grow into the invincible serpent that Myrddin prophesised, but we have the Bear on our side. Arthwys, it is *your* time to speak.'

Arthwys took a deep breath and stood. 'Thank you, Merlinus. We stand in the shadow of a beast, so how do we kill it?' He looked around at everyone, seeing them leaning forward, their attention rapt. 'First, we starve it to weaken its resolve and impair its judgement. If it lunges in one direction, we attack it from another. We shall bait it front, back and sides, cutting away at it, piece by piece, diminishing its power. A claw here, an eye there, until finally it is hobbled, robbed of the fire it once breathed. Only then shall we meet it head-on in battle, cutting it into tiny pieces that will disappear on the wind never to reform.' There was not one expression of dissent on the faces that looked at him. He saw only eager approval and hope. 'We will need Ambrosius if we are to surround the enemy territory effectively. Once we have them surrounded, we can undermine their lines of communication even more successfully than they have undermined ours. We must also destroy all their keels, not only those belonging to the Jutes but also the Angles and the Gaini. The Trent is central to their effective communication and movement of troops and supplies, so we must frustrate their use of it.'

'This will mean placing Elfed in the front line,' said Cian, ever cautious.

'Yes, but if we co-ordinate our attacks, the beast will not know which way to turn, and Elfed will be spared from facing its full force,' replied Arthwys.

'I see,' said Vortimer. 'So, we force Hengist to split his army into three, or even four, and destroy his means of bringing more warriors from abroad.'

'Yes,' said Mor. 'We provoke him from every side, becoming raiders ourselves. But we will need to secure Ambrosius' support and have all the elements in place before we can begin the campaign.'

Vortimer stroked his beard and looked at Arthwys with unveiled respect. 'An impressive plan, young Arthwys. If I can persuade Ambrosius to garrison Derventio to defend the west, it would release my Cornovii militia to bolster Durobrivae where we are now at our weakest. But how do we encourage our soldiers to fight? Morale is so low.'

'Recruitment has proved difficult for us too, but Arthwys has a novel idea.' Mor nodded in the direction of his son.

'That this is a war of Christian purpose should be motivation enough, but if we are to attract warriors from throughout the Patria, professional fighters who take pride in their skills, we must provide more earthly incentive. I have sent to every court in the North, asking for such men to join our brotherhood of eques. Each man of quality who joins Elfed may expect to receive a portion of the lands we recover, a demesne of sufficient size and quality to make him wealthy. If a warrior brings with him horses, weapons and men, his demesne will be adjusted in size to compensate his greater commitment. The area under Saxon occupation is enormous, so no one will be left disappointed.'

'Such men will be difficult to lead.'

'Northern Cymry warriors will obey the Bear – that is our tradition.'

'And the Bear, that is you?'

'It seems so, King Vortimer!' replied Arthwys, unconsciously placing his hand on the hilt of Caledfwich.

Vortimer held Arthwys' gaze then nodded. 'So be it. We have no time to waste. I shall return to Derventio in the morning and contact Ambrosius from there, to relay this excellent strategy.'

'Winnog will accompany you down the Ryknild way.'

'Is that route safe to travel?' asked Cian.

'We must ensure that it is. The Saxons have purposefully isolated the North from the Cornovii. For too long, we have fought separate campaigns, counting ourselves lucky when the Saxons turn their attention in a different direction. All Britons must be fearless and unite behind King Vortimer. Death to the Saxons!'

Merlinus caught the attention of Mor, a look of pride passing between them. Arthwys had conducted himself well, every inch the warrior prince. Mor had no doubt that

Coel Hen, Ceneu and Taly were watching from Heaven with pride, for on this day, the Bear of the North had laid down his challenge with a mighty roar.

Uncomfortable Revelations

Dunragit

Quintilis 457

Mordred sat back in the boat and watched the six oarsmen sculling into the bay. It had been a pleasant crossing from Alauna. The high tide had coincided with midday and the travellers had been awarded a clear sky. As had been the case for most of their journey, they could see a long stretch of Hibernia's coast out to the west, and to the south-west, the island of Mannin rose out of the sea, but most eye-catching were the high mountains of Erechwyd, proudly dominating the skyline to the east. A long way to the south, the peak of Yr Wyddfa could just be spied, its snow cap missing for summer, though it would soon return when the days shortened. In the foreground, the sands beckoned them toward the stronghold on the hill. Built for his mother in this magnificent setting, it had been his home for ten years. There were few places from which so many kingdoms could be seen, and he knew all their names and their kings. They knew him too, by reputation at least, for Mordred had yet to meet a man who could best him in single combat. Powerfully built and taller than both his father and brother, he had found his calling as a soldier of fortune, a mercenary, often employed by his uncle Coroticus.

His absence from the court of Reged had not been enforced and had even been lamented, at first. However, since then, his mother's scheming with Coroticus and the Gael king had painted Mordred with the taint of conspiracy. He was sure his brother and father no longer trusted him. So much so that he had been surprised to receive an invitation to his brother's wedding. He had hoped this was a sign that reconciliation was in the air, but his mother's claim she could not attend due to ill health had somewhat soured the gesture.

He sighed and watched the shore come ever closer. What would he find when he got there? His mother had not been the same since Nathi's defeat, and though she would tell nobody why, she feared Merlinus too much to leave her stronghold. Her marriage to Mordred's father was long over, and in truth, Mordred had to admit she was happier with her own people, here in the region of the Novantae. His grandmother, now long dead, had been a princess of the Novantae and, by all accounts, was of such great beauty the King of Alt Clut had been unable to resist. This single-minded desire had been the cause of the dynastic friction which Coroticus had so ruthlessly exploited to gain his throne. But Coroticus was old now, and it was Cinuit who was battle leader of the Damnonii. Together, Mordred and he had fought and raided Scotti, Picts and Gaels alike, but it was always Mordred and his band of Novantae warriors who were the most feared. Although he was careful not to advertise his activities, enough rumours had reached Reged to gain his father's disapproval, even more so now the Bishop of Ireland had chosen to excommunicate the King of Alt Clut and his warband for capturing Christians and selling them as slaves. By association, the bishop's anger applied equally to Mordred, but on the north-west coast, it was raid or be raided. It was their way of life.

The sun burnt down on his neck as his boat crossed the bay, but his mind burnt just as fiercely, with rage and envy. Three days in the presence of his family and their sycophantic friends had only served to remind him of what should have been his at every turn. It had been unbearable. Strutting like peacocks, their arrogance insulting. Gorwst and Meirchiawn had been civil enough, but they had watched him with the constant suspicion he had come to expect, the once strong bond with his brother seemingly broken. To make matters worse, a rumour had reached his ears that Gorwst had decided his kingdom would be better in the hands of one son, rather than divided between the two. That fool, Formenus, had disclosed the devastating news to him whilst drunk, boasting that his daughters were now married to the two most powerful kings in the Patria.

Then there had been sweet Gwenhyfar... still as beautiful, still as flighty. He still loved and desired her, seeking consolation in her company as often as he had been able. She had giggled flirtatiously, leading him on, but Queen Igerna had never been far away, watching him closely. The mighty Mor and the so-called 'Bear of the North' had been too busy waging full-scale war on the Saxons to attend the wedding. They had sent him a personal message, though: a proposal to join the eques of Arthwys. He had, of course, politely declined, citing his mother's need for his protection as the reason, but he had enjoyed basking in their recognition of his fighting skills, and he had taken full advantage of their absence. Despite Igerna's bard singing incessantly about Elfed's 'great heroes', he had found solace whenever he looked into Gwenhyfar's eyes. He was sure she remembered how they had kissed long ago, and she had not seemed put off by his reputation as a rogue... If only he had been dubbed the Bear, she might have married him instead. He had been told many times he was the most handsome of all the Coelings, standing out against their fair features with his raven hair and blue eyes. Yet what use was any of that to him now? He was to be prince of nothing and king of nowhere.

The boat beached and he let out an audible sigh. Yes, the visit to Reged had been unsettling, but he would push it from his mind now. His woman, Fionn, would be waiting – the local chief's daughter, plain but reliable. He would try not to think of Gwenhyfar tonight, difficult as that would be. He walked up the beach and entered the fort. His guards saluted as he passed through the narrow gate heading toward the central stone tower where another guard saluted and stepped aside to let him through.

He ducked under a stone lintel to access the cell his mother used as a day-room. It was well-lit by daylight though cool, and she was in her usual corner sewing alongside her housekeeper Lyn.

'Ah the traveller returns.' She looked up, her lined face almost breaking into a smile. 'You should have worn a hat – you look red from sunburn.'

'I didn't think, Mother.'

'That has always been your problem.'

Mordred accepted her acerbic greeting; his mother knew no other. He did not reply. It was always best to pass over her criticisms.

'How was the wedding?'

'Rather splendid. You should have come with me.'

'I would not have been welcome. Did that Merlinus attend?'

'No, neither did Mor, nor Arthwys. They are engaged in a war with the Saxons.'

'How are your brother and father?'

He noted how she always referred to her husband and son in this detached way. 'Their reception was awkward. I seem tarred with the same brush as Coroticus.'

'I could have told you that before you left.'

'Perhaps, if I had remained at Banna, I might have found better fortune,' he said glumly.

Marchell stopped sewing, put her frame on her knee and made eye contact with her son. 'An interesting comment, stimulated, no doubt, by conversations you have yet to disclose?'

'Formenus tells me I am disinherited.'

'That cannot be so – Gorwst showed me his will!'

'That was a decade ago, Mother, and much has happened since then, not least, your plot with your brother.'

'It was not a plot. Nathi was foolishly over-ambitious.'

'That may be so, but the impact it has had on my future is telling.' Mordred paused then added, 'I really can't understand why my own father could do such a thing to me?'

The queen looked at the floor. 'Someone must have convinced him to do it, doubtless Mor, but it may be nothing more than gossip.'

'Why Mor? And why are you so frightened of this priest, Merlinus?' He could see his mother's anger rising, her cheeks flushed. She did not reply, but Mordred wanted answers. He raised his voice. 'In God's name, Mother, if I am to be disinherited, I want to know why!'

'Keep God out of this and lower your voice or the whole fort will hear. Lyn, please excuse us. I would speak with my son in private.' Lyn left and closed the door. 'Now, speak quietly and explain your distress.'

'Gorwst was a good father to me. I thought he understood I could not desert you, and I always believed that one day I would inherit my share of the kingdom.'

'That was the plan from the day you were born.'

'So why the change? He must know I had nothing to do with Nathi's attempted invasion.'

'If he has changed his will, it must be to punish me. It is the only weapon he has left that will hurt me.'

'Why hurt you? He has always claimed he wants you back.'

'These changes are influenced by this Merlinus.'

'Merlinus! Why? We have never met him; he resides in Elfed.'

'Oh, but I have met him. Coroticus relayed information to me that has filled us both with great fear.' Marchell looked at her hands and drew in a sharp breath. 'This will be hard to believe, but Merlinus is my elder brother, Cynwyb, apparently returned from the dead. It is well known that Coroticus murdered Cynwyb and Cynloyp, but what is less well known… it was me who poisoned Cynloyp's wife and children. Like yourself, Coroticus was destined to be disinherited, so we acted to protect our interests.' Mordred sat down in Lyn's chair, his mind racing. 'No one, other than my brother, knew of what I did, but Cynwyb will have seen them in the afterlife.' Marchell paused and looked directly at her son. 'I may be damned, but I do not regret it. We changed the course of destiny. Cynwyb may one day come to exact his revenge, but for now, he is muzzled by Mor who relies on my brother to ensure the North is defended against the Picts.'

Mordred shook his head in disbelief. 'So, we are outcasts living on the edge of a kingdom in which we have no property, with no way to return. We may as well be dead. You call that destiny?'

'No, no, Mordred. Now we know which way the wind is blowing, it is time to act. It is always better to strike first. You know this is true.'

'In combat, yes, but children? How could you murder children?'

'They grow into adults and seek their revenge.'

Mordred fell silent. His mother was completely merciless.

She allowed him a moment, then said, 'Gorwst may only have got as far as considering changing his will. He may not have written it down, yet. If something were to happen to him before that is done, then you could legitimately challenge your brother for your share. Be ruthless, my son – it is in your blood.'

'What? Kill my father?'

'Hush, hush. Mordred, never speak aloud your true intentions. This life is a bitter and twisted copse that too easily entangles us until we cannot or dare not move, snared so that we are vulnerable to attack, at the mercy of predators. Ambition is the sword with which we cut ourselves free. Others so entwined will block our way, but we do not release them. Instead, we cut right through them as if they are nothing more than briars. Never look back, only forward. It is within your power to change your destiny.'

Mordred reeled from his mother's frank ruthlessness. 'Excuse me, Mother, I need some air.'

*

He could not sleep that night. He tossed and turned, his mind engaged on his mother's revelations and what they meant for him. The sunburn wasn't helping, so he eventually decided to sit outside in the cool and watch the dawn break.

After some time, Fionn peered out of the door of the hut. 'Come back to bed, my lord.'

He shook his head.

'Do you want to talk about what ails you?'

He shook his head again. 'I cannot. It is too complex.'

'Uh, so you think I won't understand?' Fionn looked hurt.

'Come, sit by me, and I will tell you what I must do.' She squeezed on the bench alongside him. 'I have decided to leave this place and go to Elfed to fight alongside Arthwys.'

'But why? You have so much here.'

'I will return, and your brother can look after our interests whilst I am away.'

'Is it another woman?'

'Of course not. I am a Coeling; I have been asked to join another Coeling's eques. It is our code of honour that I answer that call.'

'You've never mentioned this before.'

'As I said, it is complex. I will leave in two days.'

Fionn stood and returned to her bed. The stifled sobbing from within his hut would not change his course of action. He had not mentioned his intention to confront his father on the way to Elfed.

A Strategy Agreed

Venta Belgarum

Quintilis 457

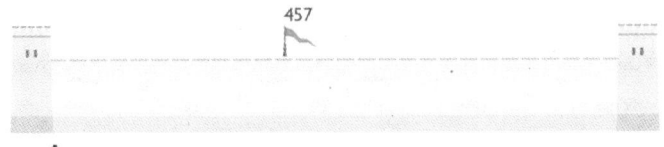

Ambrosius Aurelianus was enjoying the sunrise in the garden of his townhouse. The birds were busy darting in and out of the hedgerow and he could hear their broods tweeting, vying with each other for their feed. By his feet was a wooden box full of scrolls – recent letters from his contacts in Gaul. He found them easier to read by daylight these days.

He closed his eyes briefly to concentrate. How many years had he lived in Britannia? Perhaps forty or even forty-one, he wasn't sure. He tried not to think about the terror inflicted on his family all those years ago, but there was no doubt it informed all his decisions and there were important ones to make today. He had summoned his son and General Natalinus to help him respond to the informative letter he had received from King Vortimer. It lay unfurled in front of him, the corners weighted by pebbles. He had heard the horses reach his courtyard, and now he could hear voices in the corridor. Ames appeared through the gate first.

'Father, there you are. I see you are enjoying this very pleasing weather.'

Clad in uniform, both men strode across the garden.

'Ames, Natalinus, welcome. Please sit down. Refreshments are coming.'

'How is my old friend, your father?' Ambrosius asked Natalinus.

'He is well but finds it difficult to get around the estate these days. He spends most of his days issuing instructions from an old chariot which he has fallen out of on several occasions.'

Ambrosius laughed. 'Please send him my best wishes.'

There was a pause in the conversation as two servants delivered the refreshments. Once the servants had left, Ambrosius recommenced the conversation.

'How is my grandson?'

'I have not seen him for a few days, but Catus is growing into quite the handful, and Silvia is pregnant again.'

'Congratulations! Have you told your mother?'

'Yes, just now, but briefly. We shall talk more after this meeting.'

'Good. So, Natalinus, what is our current strength?'

'Five thousand men, two thousand of which are garrisoned across twenty locations. We have garrisoned Verulamium with a thousand men and have two thousand reservists on two days' notice. I have not yet received a report on what is left of Elafius' militia or who their new commander is.'

'I am informed there are hardly any survivors from that battle. I have received a letter from Vortimer which we will discuss shortly, but first, have either of you received any more news from Gaul?'

'We know only that there is the prospect of civil war, and Avitus has left Rome after the army rebelled against him. His ally, Theodoric of the Goths, is in Hispania.'

Ames' brow furrowed. 'I still find it hard to believe that Aegidius would side with Majorian and Ricimer.'

'He may have no choice, and we can only wait to hear who will endure, but the ambitions we fostered to support Avitus and recover our lands are over for now.'

Ames looked downcast. 'That is a disappointment, particularly for you, Father.'

'Yes, it seems increasingly unlikely that our hopes for a Gallic empire will ever be realised. Avitus was able to calm and work with most of the northern barbarians, but Gaiseric is ever the problem, for he makes Rome feel insecure. It is the senate that has turned the generals against the Emperor. We will await further news, but without the support of the army, I fear for my old friend.'

'What is Vortimer's news?' Ames was clearly keen to move on to domestic matters.

Ambrosius looked down at the correspondence.

'It is in three parts. Firstly, he says the Saxon army continues to grow in numbers and confidence. They are using The Wash and the Trent to concentrate their numbers into the mid-lands. He says that, following their last battle, there is no one militia capable of stopping their progress, and the garrison at Durobrivae is leaderless and decimated.' Ambrosius paused and looked at his general. 'It seems the Saxons are working to a successful strategy.'

Natalinus blanched. 'Good God, they will be battering down the gates of Verulamium soon.'

'In the next part, he says he has persuaded King Mor to provide support, on the proviso we too commit our troops.'

'He cannot be suggesting we form up for a grand battle. Even with the North's cavalry, we would be crushed by the Saxon numbers.'

'No, that would, indeed, be wasteful, but they do propose an interesting strategy.' Ambrosius paused, gathering his thoughts. 'Let us not forget that it was Mor who rallied to our defence in the civil war. He has proved himself an outstanding general.'

'But he has offered us no support since then. Why has he waited until now to declare his hand?' Ames said, his tone curious rather than combative.

'I think we have also been guilty of that,' replied Natalinus. 'In our complacency, we have allowed the Saxons to take root all over the east. They are everywhere; they hold most ports, and we should not forget the colony north of the Thames. If Hengist should incite them all to rebel, we will not know where to focus our troops.'

'Quite so. That is why I believe this proposed strategy is so viable. Vortimer has successfully pushed the Saxons out of the west and now garrisons Derventio, controlling the Trent upstream from that point. Mor monitors their movements in and out of the Humber and up the Trent. As such, The Wash has become a Saxon haven and their preferred migration route – that is why they attacked Elafius with such force. Vortimer suggests our troops take over the garrison at Derventio which will release him to move his militia to Durobrivae to revive the defence on that flank. Mor maintains highly trained cavalry and some keels, which allows him to block Saxon access in the north and north-west. With the boundaries sealed, they propose we turn the tables and become the raiders, harrying the Saxons from these three sides, focusing our attacks on their keels and strongholds. Hengist will have no choice but to split his force into three which will even the odds for our militias. By continually probing in this way, we will establish where they are weakest, and by destroying their keels, we will make them less mobile and also prevent further migration from their homelands.'

'I see. So, we surround them and terrorise them, much like they have terrorised our cives.'

'Exactly. Vortimer finishes by saying that good communications will be essential to our success. Mor will secure the Ryknild, which will open up the route along the edge of the Great Forest. It will fall to us to hold Venonis, keeping the routes to Durobrivae open.'

'We shall study our maps, Ambrosius, but it all sounds most feasible. Are you minded to agree?'

'I am. I believe we finally have a strategy which can arrest this invasion and revive our cives' pride.'

Ames smiled. 'At last. It feels good to be on the offensive instead of sitting about waiting for Rome to come and rescue us.'

Changing Destiny

Crammel Linn

Quintilis 457

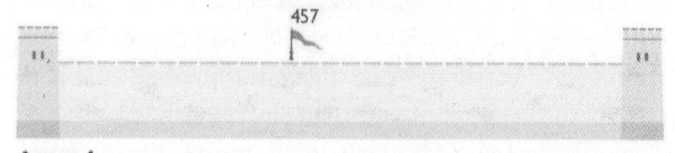

The farewells were more difficult than Mordred had expected. He had lived amongst and fought alongside the Novantae for many years, and they knew him too well. Fionn was still convinced he was chasing another woman, but her brother, with whom he had shared most adventures and many of his thoughts, was the most surprised.

'You go to fight for Arthwys? You told me you hated him.'

All Mordred could do was shrug and distance himself from his previous comments, telling his comrade-in-arms that he should take charge of the keels and men, and that there was more than enough silver to continue their trade.

'Look after things for me,' he said to sister and brother. 'I will return.' Although, in truth, he was uncertain he would.

His mother did not ask and said little, a simple goodbye, devoid of emotion, her parting gift. Could she think he was abandoning her, running away from his responsibilities? But then he saw the glint in her eye, and he knew she believed she was letting loose her assassin. In truth, he wasn't sure of his plan. He just knew it was time to alter course and stake his claims.

He clad himself in black hunting clothes, leaving both his armour and shield but taking his sword and a satchel full of gold and silver coins to buy whatever he needed later. A boat ferried him to Luguvalium where he bought a horse, telling the dealer that he needed sufficient animal feed to take him across the mountains, south to Lavatris. But instead, he travelled north-west, following the course of the Irthing. This was countryside he knew well, a difficult journey in winter, a joy in summer, but in his dark mood, joy did not enter into his heart. Time and again, his mind raced over all the conversations, all the hurt, and although he had not yet decided what would be the outcome, he knew he had to confront his father.

Fury drove him on. He was so close to Banna, yet he could not risk following the Wall. He did not expect to be recognised but it would be foolish to risk description of a stranger reaching his brother. He knew where he might find his father alone, so he headed for the high ground and circled around the town in wild country on the high fells where the wolves howled at night. The long days of summer were perfect for executing his plan, and he penetrated deep into the forest.

Suddenly, his horse reared. He calmed the animal and peered into the sunlit glade to see what had spooked the mare. There, motionless, staring back, was a brown bear, its piercing eyes inquisitive about the strangers in his domain. After a few seconds, the bear turned and lolloped away. Could this be an omen? He remembered how Myrddin would speak of Artio the Bear Goddess who protected Coel. *Was this a sign that he should be the Bear?* His mother had always claimed the title should have been his. There was only one way to find out if her claim were true, and that was to challenge Arthwys to mortal combat. He was confident he would win; no one had yet come close to beating him in single combat. With Arthwys dead, Gwenhyfar would be free to become his wife. He shook his head. His unbridled imagination was getting carried away, influencing his logic.

'One step at a time,' he said aloud, to check his thoughts and rein back his daydreams.

By the time he arrived at the steep-sided gully that banked the Irthing, it was late in the day – too late to expect his father to still be fishing and too late to put his plan into motion. He tied his horse to a tree, leaving the mare with her nose in a feedbag, then carefully followed the riverbank to the twin spouts known as Crammel Linn. The familiar surroundings tempered his anger, for this had always been a place of happy memories for his family. Both he and Meirchiawn had been taught to fish here. His father had told him that Mor had fallen off the waterfall into the pool whilst tiptoeing along the edge, playing dare with him. Later in life, his father would escape from his wife to this place; he would be missing for hours, sometimes an entire day. He made both sons promise not to reveal his whereabouts nor to tell their mother where she could find him. The memory made Mordred smile for the first time in four days.

This was the king's favourite month for fishing, so lying on the flat rock by one of the spouts, Mordred peered over the edge. His father wasn't there, but he had been earlier – he had left his net and rod by the rock where he always sat. Mordred returned to his horse then walked a distance upstream to where he could light a fire to ward off the wolves and wait for the morning.

He slept fitfully, his thoughts and dreams intermingling. He imagined he heard voices, but it was only the rhythmic sound of rushing water combined with the gentle summer breeze blowing through the verdant trees.

The early morning smell of pungent forest vegetation reminded him of happier times – he had played hide-and-seek in these ferns. He began to reconsider his dark intentions. Had he really intended murdering his own father? Perhaps it would be better to reason with him or persuade him, even negotiate, but Mordred still wanted to know *why*. In his eyes, he was the prodigal son, but instead of receiving the fatted calf, he had been treated like a leper. As he continued to reflect, he untied his horse and began walking upstream. Perhaps this confrontation was a bad idea. He could easily mount his horse and ride to Elfed without causing any trouble... His thoughts swung back to the injustice of it all. Leaving would be the coward's way. He was entitled – he had been raised to be a king. He refused to have that taken away. What had he done for his father to reject him so? He stopped to take his sword from his belt. If his intention was to negotiate, it would be better to go to see his father unarmed. He wedged the weapon into the rocks near the river, tying the reins of his horse around the hilt.

'There you go, girl. Enjoy the grass until I return.'

The mare lowered her head and munched the sweet greenery. No one would find her here, but as a precaution, he hid his satchel in the crook of a tree before walking back to the waterfall. When he arrived, there was still no sign of his father, so he hid himself in the trees on the opposite bank and waited. It was not long before Gorwst came along the path, carrying his fishing basket, stooping and throwing a stick for his large wolf-hound.

'So how many fish will we catch today, Hector?'

He was speaking to the dog in his customary manner. Marchell would comment that he spoke more to his dogs than he did to his family.

Mordred lay perfectly still; he did not want to alert the hound to his presence whilst he watched his father set himself up for a day's fishing. He checked his line, casting it a couple of times, then took off his sword and placed it near where his dog had settled. He then baited the line and cast again. Dissatisfied, he flicked the line once more, dropping it into deeper water, then lowered himself onto his favourite rock. Mordred hesitated, gripped by the fear he had always had of his father, but he had come too far to turn back, and he was now too close to sneak away. He stood up, carefully rustling branches to make it sound as if he had just arrived. The dog barked furiously and a startled Gorwst looked up. Mordred made his way across the brow of the waterfall, waving at his father.

'Be quiet, Hector. It is only Mordred.'

Mordred scrambled down the bank and approached his father along the shore.

'Mordred, this is a surprise. I thought you had returned to your Novantae friends?'

'I have decided to accept Arthwys' offer and fight alongside him in the Saxon war. I am on my way to Elfed.'

'That is a good and honourable decision. So, what brings your route this far north?'

'I have come to speak with you about a matter that has played on my mind since the wedding.'

'Why here?' Gorwst looked around.

'It aids reflection to revisit childhood haunts, and I knew we would be alone. This is a very personal matter of great importance to me.'

'So, what is on your mind. Speak openly.'

'Your cousin, Formenus, told me I am to be disinherited.' Gorwst looked away and did not reply, sparking Mordred's anger. 'Well, am I? Tell me!' he said, his voice raised.

'I have decided that Reged will be better led by one king, splitting territory only weakens kingdoms and leads to civil wars.'

Gorwst remained calm and continued to fish, but Mordred's anger was turning to hurt.

'Tell me! What have I done to deserve being treated in such a fashion?'

'There has been disloyalty—'

Mordred cut him short. 'Not from me, Father. Surely, you understand that I could not desert my mother, that one son should remain by her side. God, I see now why she hates you so much.'

Gorwst lowered his head. The last comment had clearly found its mark. 'It was not your disloyalty to which I referred—'

Mordred interrupted again. 'Then why mistreat me? Is my disinheritance decreed? Is your mind made up? Can there be no compromise?'

Gorwst placed his rod by his side and turned to face his son. 'Sit down!' he commanded. 'If you will let me speak, I will explain. It is not yet decreed, but my mind is made up. I intended to speak with you after the wedding, but you left so quickly, as if you could not bear our company.'

Mordred did not speak but glared through the tears that welled in his eyes.

'There is something I should have told you long ago, something that I have been too ashamed to mention to anybody, even your brother.'

'For God's sake, Father, what is it?'

'I'm so sorry, Mordred, but you are not my son.'

'What?' Mordred could not grasp what he was hearing; it made no sense.

'You are the son of Coroticus, born out of incest.'

'No, no, no, that cannot be!'

Gorwst spoke slowly with great force. 'It is true, Mordred. You are not a Coeling, so that is why you cannot be a king of Reged.'

'You lie because you hate my mother.'

'It is the opposite, Mordred. I loved your mother. So much so, I might have forgiven her, but she continues to plot with her brother against me – it is like a sickness for which there is no cure. Ask her, make her confess it to you.'

'Am I to be publicly ridiculed then, so that you may have your revenge?'

'I have told no one of this and will justify my decision publicly on the principle of primogeniture.'

'I don't believe you. If you have told no one, how did Formenus know?'

'I have spoken with your brother about the succession, that is all. His wife must have mentioned this to her father.'

'Why have you kept this from me all this time? Why wait until now to disinherit me?'

'Your mother... Despite her faithlessness, she is beautiful, irresistible. I had always hoped we might be reconciled.'

'So, you thought only of yourself! If you loved your wife so much, how could you let her go so easily? Why did you not fight?'

'Your mother and her brother have been in a murderous pact since they were very young. No one can break it. It was Coroticus who instructed her to marry me, to become Queen of Reged. I prayed that he would die so that our family would endure.'

'You prayed for him to die? You should have killed him.'

'I wanted to, but the risk was too great. I could have lost everything.'

'You have anyway, inflicting great cruelty on me in the process. You are as weak and pathetic as Mother says you are.' Gorwst did not reply. 'So, what of Meirchiawn? How can you be sure he is your son?'

'Look at him. He looks like me. There is no doubt he is a Coeling.'

Mordred wanted to scream with rage and pain. 'So, the sins of the parents are visited upon the children. Is that how it is?'

'They were not my sins, Mordred; they were your mother's.'

'True. Craven weakness is not technically a sin. You should have killed him.'

'Listen to you. You seethe with hatred just like your mother, and you look at me from your father's face. Do you think we are not aware of your crimes? Your reputation as a raider and slave trader reached us long ago from the holy fathers at Candida Casa. You raid with Coroticus, and I am told you and your father are excommunicated for your sins.'

Gorwst turned toward the pool, picking up his rod as if to dismiss the man who was not his son. Mordred stood as if to leave, but in a lightning move picked up Gorwst's sword and, in one sweep, all but removed the king's head. The old man's body keeled over, still holding the rod. Hector attacked, sinking his teeth into Mordred's calf. He cried out in pain, slashing at the hound until it lay mutilated alongside its master's corpse.

Mordred moved quickly. This had to look like a robbery and a thief would leave nothing of value. He removed Coel's torc from what remained of the king's neck and cut his purse from his belt, but Coel's signet ring would not come off Gorwst's finger. There was no choice but to place the still warm hand on a rock and sever the finger. Mordred threw the sword into the pool and scrambled up the waterfall, running back to his horse. He would ride straight across the fells past the old mines until he reached the road to Eboracum, from there it would be a non-stop ride all the way to Elfed. His leg was bleeding, but there was no time to look at it, not until he was a considerable distance away. He placed his bloody booty in his recovered satchel, put his sword in his belt and mounted his horse. He would cross the Wall at Magna and be over the fells before the body of the king was even discovered.

Mordred swallowed hard. He would mourn the father of his youth when told of his death and try to never think of this day again. Nobody must discover Coroticus was his father. He would make his claim on a share of the kingdom in due course. *Never look back. Change your destiny.* His mother's words, but now he hated her too. Mordred felt numb as he rode through the gate in the Wall. His family was a sham. He was neither Carvetti nor great-grandson of Coel Hen. All the things he had considered so important about himself were as nothing. He had started the day a disinherited prince with a just cause, but he ended it a murderer with no claim to anything.

A Challenger at the Gate

Cambodunum and Campocalia

Sextilis 457

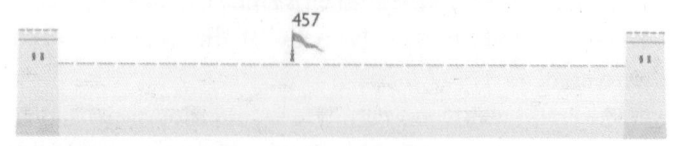

Mor and Cian were in fine spirits as they rode across the moor toward Campocalia.

'This is a turning point, Cian. Not since Coel have the kings of the Patria co-operated so readily.'

'Arthwys will be thrilled with the news.'

'And surprised at the speed with which Ambrosius has agreed. According to the letter, Riothames will send a cohort to Derventio in less than two weeks.'

'That will enable Vortimer to take his Cornovii militia around to Durobrivae.'

'I would expect Hengist to react to these troop movements.'

'He will be watching, but the Saxons concentrate their forces at three positions and will remain close to their keels.'

'Until Arthwys attacks from the north, which will shake their confidence.'

'That is a difficult prospect for any commander, my king, for the Humber sits between our militia and their major settlements.'

'He will find a way to do it,' said Mor, his tone rich with pride. 'He will raid like the Saxons and beat Hengist at his own game.'

The training camp loomed into view. Cian had not seen so much military activity since his early years at Banna. The fields were full of horses and ponies, and the arena where they were schooled was busy with young boys and men practising skills on and off horseback. On the left, as the visitors entered the stockade, there was archery practice, and on the right, wrestling. At the far end, Arthwys was taking a keen interest in a sword-fighting demonstration.

'Arthwys, may we have a moment of your time?'

'Father, Cian! Are you here to join in?'

They looked at each other and laughed.

'No, son, we have done well to mount our horses.' They laughed again, both knowing their sparring days were past. 'We are here to discuss developments.'

'Where is Agiluf?' asked Cian.

'On patrol, back later.'

'No matter. I am sure I will see my son again, one of these days…'

The men dismounted, handing their horses to one of the prince's men.

'Come sit with us.'

They walked toward some logs that had been positioned for spectating.

'Ambrosius has agreed. A cohort is on its way to Derventio.'

'This is excellent news.'

'It is, but Cian and I are concerned that the movement of so many troops may excite the Saxons' interest, before you are ready.'

Arthwys' brow furrowed. 'You're right. We must divert their attention. A raid from the north would draw the Saxon focus in this direction, allowing the southern militias to get into their required positions, but this will prove more difficult than it sounds.'

'The Humber estuary?' Cian said, with a nod toward Mor.

'Exactly. If we are to surprise the Saxons, we will need to attack by boat across the Humber. Although we have river boats, we lack the expertise for marine battles and any trained crews are made up of easterners who are not to be trusted when perhaps it is their kinfolk we will be fighting. I will have to think on a solution.'

Mor stroked his grey beard. 'I will give it some thought, too. Now, your mother and your wife are feeling neglected. They have requested your presence in three days for a celebration. And bring Agiluf; that poor lad is constantly on patrol.'

'It is unlikely we can spare the time—'

'It is a command, not a request. When your mother invites you to eat with her, you make the time. Now, since you are so short of time, we will leave you to your training. Farewell, my son.'

The two old warriors mounted their horses, waving as they headed out of the gate toward Cambodunum.

*

Arthwys had always known he would be called upon to lead. His whole life had been leading up to this moment. He had worked hard, read every Roman military manual and learnt to fight both on foot and horseback from the best warriors, not least his father. Discipline and conviction had become his trusted companions, but he also knew that it was feats of valour that encouraged men to follow. He admired Vortimer, who exemplified selfless valour, but he knew there were many dead heroes whose valour had proved greater than their skills. That was why he put so much time into training. He prayed to God every day, asking that his skills should match his valour and that his strategies and tactics would do right by the men who trusted and followed him. God was with him, of that he was sure, for many of his best ideas came to him after prayer. Religious instruction was a fundamental part of his militia's training, and communal prayers were held at the beginning and end of every day. The souls of his men would be ready for Heaven, but whilst they lived, he would ensure their lives were not needlessly squandered.

The problem of the marine attacks was worrying him. The Saxons were not just better sailors; they were better at naval assault and close proximity warfare. He had prayed on the conundrum, but a solution was yet to present itself.

'Prince Arthwys,' said Agiluf, returned from patrol. 'There is a stranger at the gate. He will not say who he is and wears a cowl and mask.'

'What is his business?'

'He says he wishes to join our militia but will only do so if he is defeated in single combat.'

'How interesting. This should make excellent sport. Who do you have in mind to fight against this brave man?'

'Caius. He is our best warrior.'

'The stranger, does he look strong?'

'He is tall and strong. His accent and clothing suggest a northerner, even a Pict.'

'I am intrigued. Give him every courtesy, feed him and tend to his horse. Does he carry weapons?'

'Only a sword and a helmet.'

'Then provide him with whatever he requires.'

'There is more, my prince.'

'Go on…'

'If he defeats your champion, he insists he will have won the right to challenge you. There is menace in his claim.'

'Really?'

'Yes, he says there is an ancient right of challenge which the Bear must accept.'

Arthwys laughed. A stranger, claiming knowledge of such old customs? This was getting more intriguing by the moment.

'If he beats Caius, then I will have no choice. Tell this stranger that the contest will take place in the morning but caution him that the purpose of this militia is to fight Saxons not each other. I will only allow this to go ahead if practice swords are used.'

*

Arthwys had caught a glimpse of the stranger when Agiluf led him to the stables – clad in black, head under a cowl and wearing his scarf as a mask. Why was he concealing his identity? From the manner in which he carried himself, he was certainly a soldier, quite probably a lord. There were many young men, sons of distant lords, who had joined Arthwys to prove themselves, but he sensed this one was different, more confident, perhaps already a leader. This was a man who wanted to be judged by his martial skills rather than his identity, so had he been disgraced or rejected by his court? But to challenge the Bear? Who could possibly want to take on the responsibility of battle leader for the northern tribes? Realisation dawned – there was only one man he could think of who would have sufficient arrogance and harbour the malice suggested by Agiluf's report. It could only be Mordred.

The rivalry from his cousins had always been unwarranted, even when they had been boys together. He strongly suspected it had been stoked by their mother. Marchell had disputed his right to be the future battle leader from the start, claiming the honour belonged to her second son. But it was not his father Mor who had claimed Arthwys as the Bear; he had been chosen by Talhaearn as prophesised by Myrddin. Arthwys had not sought to be the Bear, and even Marchell's scheming could not contradict Myrddin's divine messengers. But that had not stopped her passing her poison on to her sons, and Arthwys had suffered unfair taunts and blows from both his cousins as a result. Surely, after all this time, Mordred did not still harbour that jealous rivalry? But then, all the tales Arthwys had heard about his cousin over the years, some more recently from Gwenhyfar, indicated that Mordred had grown into an experienced and feared warrior, his loyalty not to Reged but to himself. This would not be the sport Arthwys had envisaged – it was a serious challenge from a most capable warrior.

He signalled to his servant. 'Quickly, bring Agiluf to my tent.'

When Agiluf arrived, Arthwys wasted no time.

'I believe my challenger is my cousin, Mordred.'

'If that is so, it puts this challenge in a different light.'

'Those are my thoughts. He is a Coeling, and he is considered one of the best warriors in the North, battle-hardened from years of raiding with Coroticus.'

'What has prompted him to make this challenge now?'

'I invited him to join our eques, although I never imagined he would accept.'

'But why challenge you?'

'I'm not sure. Perhaps he is driven by pride. Gwen came back from her sister's wedding with word that he is not made welcome at his family's court. Instead, he lives amongst the Novantae on the edge of Reged. I think he is here to prove himself.'

'We must not risk undermining Caius' standing in the militia. If he is defeated, the men under his command will lose their respect for him.'

'I agree. Mordred is a man with real battle experience, perhaps more than you and I.'

'Shall I have him arrested?'

Arthwys laughed. 'No, Agiluf, I invited him!'

'Then what is your plan?'

'Men such as Mordred are prideful above all else. If he were to go up against his father and brother, he would start a civil war, so he has come to fight me and prove he is the dominant bull… or should I say bear? He has no interest in the Saxon threat. That is not why he is here. He has one thing on his mind – boosting his prestige. It is a cock fight he is looking for, Agiluf. He has come to finish what he started as a boy.'

'That is ridiculous. I say we arrest him.'

'I have accepted his challenge, but I will only fight him on my terms. Let's go speak to him.'

They walked across to the stables where the stranger had spent the night and found him grooming his mare.

'Good morning, stranger,' said Agiluf. 'I introduce Prince Arthwys.'

The man stood with his back to them whilst he covered his face with his mask, his broad shoulders betraying a powerful frame.

'Please, Mordred, no more mystery. I have come to tell you that I will not allow you to fight Caius. He is young and capable but not yet battle-hardened.'

Mordred turned and lowered his mask. 'So, who am I to fight?' he said, glaring at his rival.

'Before I answer that, I need to understand your objective. You are not here because you have a burning desire to fight Saxons.'

'No, I am here because I believe I can win against you in single combat.'

'And what would that prove?'

'That I am the greater warrior, better than he who has been named the Bear.'

Arthwys caught Agiluf's glance. 'So, you don't want to be the Bear, you just want to prove you could be?' Mordred did not answer. 'Listen to me, cousin, we sorely need a commander with your skills and experience. Our best men, men like Caius, will be in awe of your prowess. But if you go out there and defeat Caius in front of the men he must command, instead of earning his respect, you will earn his enmity. As for your challenge against me... meet me at the practice ground in one hour, and I will first show you some of the techniques we have developed to fight the Saxons. I presume it was Gorwst who taught you to fight?'

Mordred flinched at the mention of his father. 'Yes, amongst others. I have had several tutors.'

'So, you still use the oval Roman shield?'

'That is the one I prefer.'

'Then I shall find one for you.' Arthwys looked his adversary up and down. He was an imposing figure, powerfully built, but there was a blood-soaked bandage on his leg. 'How did you get that wound?'

'It is nothing. I was attacked by a pack of wolves whilst I slept.'

'We have healers here. You should avail yourself of them,' said Mor. 'And, Mordred, Coelings should fight side by side, not against each other. You are most welcome in Elfed, and if you stay, you will find yourself engaged in as many sword fights as you could ever wish for.'

As Arthwys walked back to his tent, he turned to Agiluf. 'Something terrible has happened to that man. His soul seems very troubled.'

'Can we trust him?'

'We need him, and I believe God has answered my prayers. Mordred is the solution to how we raid across the Humber. He is a seasoned raider, and I can think of no better man to lead our keels and train our men for naval battle.'

*

Arthwys waited with Caius and Agiluf as Mordred walked across from the stable carrying his helmet and sword. There was an arrogance to his gait as he strode onto the practice ground.

News of the stranger's challenges had spread, and a small crowd had gathered to watch.

'Mordred, this is Caius. He is the man I proposed as your contender until we discovered your real identity.'

The men nodded at each other. They were a similar size, but it was plain to see there was a considerable difference in age and experience.

'I have appointed a shield bearer to assist you, and we have a coat of mail which should fit. You should be as well-equipped as we are.'

The shield bearer and a servant ran onto the practice ground carrying a shield, a wooden practice sword and a coat of mail. Mordred set about the task of easing himself into the mail and the servant then laced up the back.

'Ever since my father garrisoned Elfed, we have trained mainly as cavalry. Our equipment and techniques have evolved for fighting on hills, plains and in the forest. We used to use the smaller Roman cavalry shield, but we are fortunate to have learnt from a travelling Goth, a former cavalry officer, lately turned to Christ, who has fought in many great battles. He has shown us how the Goths use their larger shields, not just to block but as a weapon. First though, I would like you to demonstrate to Caius what it is like to be charged by a battle-hardened raider. Practice swords.'

Mordred gave Arthwys a scornful look but swapped his own sword for the wooden practice sword. Caius took up a defensive position and Mordred walked twenty paces away. He turned and ran, accelerating at ten paces and letting out a blood-curdling roar. The impact pushed Caius backward, and Mordred rained down blows from every direction, forcing the young man to stumble, landing on his back with Mordred's wooden sword at his throat. The crowd applauded the stranger, whilst Arthwys helped a disgruntled Caius back to his feet.

'You now know how it feels to face the North's most prolific raider.' He winked at the young warrior. Arthwys turned to Mordred. 'So, this is my shield.' He picked up a leather-clad wooden disc. 'It has a single handle behind the boss.'

'Surely, that is unstable. I prefer mine to be wedded to my forearm like this, with straps.'

'That is the most common method, but I will show you how this is an advantage. I would like you to attack me with the same ferocity you attacked Caius.'

Mordred smiled at the prospect. 'I can improve on that. Real swords?'

'No, practice swords. You will see why.'

Once more, Mordred walked twenty paces, turned and charged. He again accelerated at ten paces and issued his mighty roar. Arthwys stood in classic defence position as if to meet the impact, but the moment before his assailant reached him, he stepped forward into a crouching stance, extending the leading edge of his shield and his sword to full reach. He was inside Mordred's guard, with his weapon against his attacker's chest, before his opponent had even managed to land his first blow. A surprised Mordred swiped furiously as Arthwys brought his shield over his head to fend off the blow. Then stepping neatly to one side, Arthwys dodged his furious cousin, allowing him to stumble past. Once more, the crowd applauded, but Mordred was not amused. He walked toward his shield bearer, and throwing down the practice sword, he grabbed the sword he had brought to Elfed.

'Come, Arthwys, enough of this play, let us fight with real weapons.'

Arthwys signalled to Agiluf who ran quickly across with Caledfwich. Mordred walked toward his opponent.

'Before you raise your weapon,' said Arthwys, 'I wish to speak with you.'

The prince stood his ground and Mordred lowered his sword. 'Are you frightened, Arthwys?'

'Of course! Only a fool feels no fear. Even so, I will fight if that is your wish. But know this. One of us will certainly die. If it is you, I will have lost an opportunity, whereas if it is me, my men will kill you. Whichever the result, only the Saxons will gain.'

Mordred looked chastened. 'An opportunity you say?'

'It is my earnest belief that God has sent you to us.'

Mordred looked taken aback. 'That is a strange interpretation of my challenge but I'm listening.'

'I have a problem for which I have been praying for a solution, and it seems that you have some problems of your own.'

'Why would you think that?' Mordred's reply seemed intentionally dismissive.

'Gwenhyfar has told me there are difficulties – not of your making – in your relations with your family.'

'My family affairs are my own. They have no relevance for today.'

'Oh, but they do. You have nothing to prove to me. I know you are a great warrior, but I dearly wish that, instead of this rivalry, you were *my* brother so that we might prove our valour together, standing shoulder to shoulder when we defeat these heathen Saxons.' The prince spoke in earnest, having often reflected upon the fortitude of brotherhood amongst fighting men.

Mordred looked at the ground. 'So, tell me, *brother*, would you share your spoils with me?'

'Share them? Of course. Is that not what brothers do? We shall quadruple Elfed's domain when we take back the land lost to the Saxon incursion, and each of us who fight for it will have new territory equal to the other.'

It was clear this was not the answer Mordred had expected. 'Why should you be so generous?'

'Because you will have earnt it, by God. Our enemy has turned the land we aim to win back into a vast wasteland. It is ours for the taking, but first, we must win a war.'

'How can I trust you? I have heard such promises before, but they are rarely honoured. Will you swear it before God?'

'On my life. We are both Coelings; we keep our word.'

'This land you speak of, where is it?'

'The northern tribes used to dominate all the land east to the sea, but it is now too dangerous to hold in our name. The many rivers that cross it are riddled with foreigners who feigned friendship then betrayed us. Eboracum, once a great city and centre of trade, is in ruins, the bridge washed away. If we are to challenge Hengist and Aesc, this is the region we must get back under our firm control.'

Mordred took a deep breath and looked at his surroundings. 'The Forest of Elfed is pleasing to the eye, is the east as fair?'

'Join me on patrol tomorrow, and we will ride to the Ouse where I will show you the territories of which I speak.'

'Then I will delay my challenge whilst we survey our prospects.' Mordred sheathed his sword.

'Excellent. Agiluf send word to my father that we will have an extra guest for the celebration.'

'Perhaps my uncle, the king, will disagree with our arrangement?'

'He will accept my decision, for you solve our most challenging problem – how to take back control of the rivers. Come to my tent and we will study a map. You will be surprised by the extent of the estuary and its rivers. But first, it is too warm for this mail; let's rid ourselves of that.'

Mordred smiled for the first time since he had arrived.

'We never wear it at sea. Fall overboard and you are drowned! We have metal plate on straps that we wear when we beach to attack.'

'Hear that, Agiluf, our marine commander is already teaching us.'

Agiluf looked relieved the tension had eased and he laughed nervously.

'An excellent outcome, Arthwys. I believe the wagers were favouring your cousin.'

Arthwys grinned whilst slapping his comrade's arse with the flat-side of Caledfwich.

'Be careful, prefect, or we shall arrange a challenger for you!'

The men laughed together as they strolled in the direction of Arthwys' tent.

Mordred's Malady

Elfed

Sextilis 457

Though Mordred had rested, he had not slept well. His left calf was stiffening from his wound which was hot and painful to the touch. The long day riding on patrol with Arthwys was only increasing the swelling. However, he had been so immersed in the day's thorough explanation of the Saxon threat, he had barely noticed the discomfort.

Before heading out, Agiluf had shown him maps of the rivers and estuary and had highlighted the vast swathes of unfarmed wasteland that bordered Elfed territory, land cleared of cives and settlements by the emboldened Germanic tribes after the territory was left mostly undefended following the Roman army's withdrawal from the Patria.

Mordred was familiar with the islands and highlands of the north-west landscape so saw the east as a strange flat wetland. He had never seen rivers of such magnitude so far inland. The small group of cavalry had ridden out to where the Aire joined the ever-growing Ouse. Here, they had climbed to the top of the watchtower the Cymry had built higher than the trees, from which they could view the meandering river and watch for the enemy.

Arthwys explained that it was dangerous to row a boat beyond this point and that an important Saxon harbour lay around the hook-shaped bend in the river. The extent of the challenge for Arthwys and Elfed was becoming apparent, and it struck Mordred that they had been riding all day and seen only a small portion of the abandoned territory that Agiluf had shown him on the maps. A vast wasteland, yet there was neither site nor sound of the enemy.

'This Saxon war is on a scale I had not fully appreciated. We had heard there were battles and that lands had been lost, but it seems to me that fear of attack has driven you all to the hills, abandoning territory to ghouls and ghosts. I have yet to see a Saxon.'

'It is their naval capability that so challenges us. The Saxon keels can travel far inland on this network of waterways forcing our farmers to retreat from their reach, and our militia must protect our cives.'

'Where are the Saxon settlements? Are they within reach?'

'There are many throughout the Colonae, and they have spread up the Don into the Great Forest, but their warriors mostly assemble at their ports on the coast.'

'I see your problem. Cavalry is of limited use for this kind of fighting. Your strength is in fighting land battles.'

'Exactly.'

'It seems that Saxons dominate this region.'

'Germanic people have lived in the Colonae since the Romans were here. The Angles and the Gaini, who first colonised the rivers, traded with us, but since then, they have been joined by the Jutes who are warriors by trade. They are the ones who incited the rebellion. However, if we are to defeat the Saxons, we must destroy all of their tribes, because as long as they have any foothold in our ports and rivers, we cannot hope to win this war and retain our territory.'

'Then we must fight fire with fire. Terrorise them with river-borne raids and destroy their settlements.'

'That is now our plan, but through our tolerance, we have allowed this canker to fester for too long and their army has grown strong. If we are to cut out the infection, every Christian kingdom in the Patria must take a knife to it.'

Having descended from the watchtower, Mordred was surprised to find himself already disarmed by Arthwys' easy camaraderie. The young prince was an impressive general and a shrewd tactician. However, Mordred's excitement about leading a squadron of keels into battle was becoming overwhelmed by the worsening pain in his leg. His head was banging like a drum. He clung to his horse, feeling sick. Had the bite poisoned him? Perhaps it was the fate he deserved. The hound he had slaughtered was not just his father's favourite but a descendant of Mordred's boyhood companion, Hercules. Oh God, what had he done? He tried not to think about his crime, deciding instead to concentrate on staying in the saddle.

The patrol arrived at Cambodunum where Mordred and Arthwys would be staying the night. By now, Mordred was barely conscious. He was in a dreamworld, clinging to the neck of his horse. He was aware of shouting and people helping him dismount. Now there were closer voices. He was surrounded by women, and through the haze, he saw Gwen. Then more voices.

'I think his wound is poisoned.' It was Arthwys' voice.

'Good God, feel his brow. This wound is on fire.' A female voice this time.

King Mor was there. Mordred tried to speak, but his mouth would not open. Now Arthwys was lifting him up, supporting him on his shoulder, leading him to a timber building.

'These ladies will look after you.'

They laid him on a bed. The roof was spinning. Darkness.

*

'How is he, Morgaine?' King Mor asked, his voice heavy with concern for his nephew.

'He is poorly, Father. The wound was full of poison. We have bathed, reopened and bled it. It was brown with fester, and I could see red poison lines travelling up his leg. He is hot with fever, but I believe we have done enough for it to pass. I have dressed the wound with honey.'

'You think he will recover, then?'

'Oh yes. He is strong, but the bite of a wolf should not be left for so long without attention.'

'Did he say how it occurred?' Mor inquired.

'In the night, sleeping in the wild,' Arthwys replied.

'It is rare for a wolf to be so bold, but they are vicious beasts, and I've heard of such attacks before, though more often in the depths of winter.'

Arthwys looked earnestly at his father. 'I shall pray for him. He has come to fight by our side, and we need his expertise. He has already shown a good understanding of the obstacles and made some bold suggestions.'

'I am surprised he answered your call. His reputation as a mighty warrior may be well-known, but so too is his dubious morality.'

'That is rather unfair,' said Gwenhyfar, who had recently arrived in the hall. 'He was left to find a way to make something of himself. What else could he do?'

Mor turned to his daughter-in-law. 'I rather think that Gorwst lost control of his younger son, but now he is here, we should put his skills to good use.'

Arthwys turned toward Gwenhyfar, Morgaine and his mother. 'Please treat him well so he recovers quickly. I depart for Derventio the day after tomorrow. I hope he will be recovered when I return.'

'The fever should pass in a day or so. He needs to be kept cool and drink plenty of water laced with honey. You will not keep a man like that on his back for long,' said Morgaine.

*

Blwchfardd strummed his lyre gently in the corner of the hall. Gwenhyfar had requested only soothing sounds for her well-attended patient. Pabo and Eliffer had been sent out of the way to the stables for the day, so this was a rare peaceful moment for the young bard.

Even aside from the entire fort preparing for war, there were many changes on which to reflect. Merlinus, his boyhood teacher, had left unexpectedly, and now his close friend, Morgaine, was also leaving. In light of their mysterious absence, Blwchfardd had suddenly been made responsible for tutoring the young princes, alongside Amabilis, a Gothic man of God who could barely speak his language! It was going to be a challenge, but he was pleased with the post. Being born with a clubfoot somewhat restricted the roles in which he could be useful. Attempts to correct his foot as a child had turned it, but this had left him with one leg shorter than the other. Everyone had always been so kind to him, and he had not really thought much about it until now, when war was on everyone's lips. His brother Agiluf was Prince Arthwys' most trusted eques, and their father's attention was drawn mostly by his exploits, often saying he had given his sword to Agy and his lyre to Farddy.

Over the years, Farddy had learnt to disguise his discomfort, and he had no trouble charming the ladies with his quick wit and integrity. Gwenhyfar, in particular, confided in him, their friendship a great comfort to her since marrying into this family of legends, their bond formed from a shared sense of inadequacy. Farddy surmised Gwen felt lost in the shadow of her famous husband, who had no time to indulge her with the attention she craved, and her competent mother-in-law – Queen Igerna being of a different breed and almost a warrior herself. Gwen saw herself as flawed, just as he saw himself, which had drawn them together as friends, making a secret pact to support one another.

Mordred's fever had passed, and though he was still pale and weak, he had become more animated as the days had passed. Farddy looked across to see the sick warrior speaking to Gwen in a lowered voice.

'Gwen, did Arthwys bring my satchel?' His familiarity betrayed their old friendship.

'It is here by your cloak. Do you want something from it?'

'No, no. It contains a few coins, that is all. Will you keep it safe for me?'

'I will place it in the king's treasury… if you tell me why you have come to Elfed?'

'To see you.'

'To cause trouble more like. I heard about your challenge.'

'I was invited to be one of Arthwys' eques.'

'You are lucky to be alive. The sword my husband carries possesses him. They say it makes him invincible.'

'Perhaps I would be better dead.'

'Why so?'

'After you left Reged, there was nothing worth returning for.'

'Please, Mordred, do not say such things.'

Even in the dark of the hall, Farddy could see her cheeks flush with colour.

'Arthwys saved not only my life, but also those of my sister and father. I am devoted to him.'

Gwen stood to leave, but Mordred reached for her hand which she did not pull away.

'I have been too honest. If I had known… but I knew nothing of your imprisonment until after you were rescued.'

'That is all in the past, Mordred. Arthwys is pleased you are here, and so am I – more so, once you are recovered.'

She gently placed his hand on the bed and smiled, casting a quick glance over her shoulder at the bard who had continued to strum throughout their conversation, as if he had heard and seen nothing.

*

Queen Igerna and Bryn were outside, both enjoying a colourful sunset.

'God willing, Arthwys will be in Derventio by now.'

Bryn put her darning to one side. 'This war they plan will result in attacks upon Elfed, both Cian and Agiluf have warned me.'

'We are prepared, more so than ever. Mor believes he has been too tolerant for too long.'

'He has protected Elfed.'

'True, but we now see our protection has been at the expense of other kingdoms.'

'Mor is not responsible for their safety; they have their own kings for that. Cian has wisely urged caution where the Saxons are concerned.'

'And that advice has been to our benefit. Our husbands have carefully garnered good relations with the Angles and the Gaini, but now we are told they blindly follow this Hengist.'

Bryn smiled as she remembered Freuleaf, the young Angle prince she had befriended some thirty years earlier. 'There was a time when the settlers who fought the Picts alongside us were friends. My father, God rest him, would be surprised that the Patria has come to this.'

'Ah yes, but he fought for Rome, as did my father – different times.'

'Different loyalties.' Bryn picked up her darning. 'This Mordred seems a wild one. Does Mor trust him?'

'He is prepared to do so. Arthwys is laying great store by his experience.'

'He is still weak, but his eyes follow Gwenhyfar everywhere.'

'Well, he has that in common with most men. All except for Arthwys, who thinks only of his duty.'

The conversation lapsed for a moment as Bryn pulled through a difficult thread. 'These summer evenings in the forest are glorious. It will not be long until harvest now.'

'I think the men will be pleased to get it in before they launch their campaign.'

'I cannot say I am looking forward to the end of this summer. I am getting such a feeling of foreboding.'

'Oh Bryn, I know it too. Our fathers went to war, and both died; our husbands have been twice but, with God's mercy, returned. Now, it is the turn of our sons…'

Bryn gave a little shudder. 'Let us talk of something else. Where is Merlinus? I have not seen him for a couple of weeks.'

'With Mor's reluctant permission, he has gone to the west of Crafen to seek solitude, but Morgaine plans to travel this week to be at his side.'

'She has been his deacon for six years and is devoted to him, but their absence will be difficult for you.'

'It is, particularly where the education of my grandchildren is concerned. Harder work for us, for sure.'

'Is this new deacon, Amabilis, proving useful?'

'His Latin is excellent, but he finds our language difficult. His attempts at speaking it sound, well... amusing – it makes the children laugh.'

'I hear he has Germanic roots and speaks a little of the Saxon language.'

'He is not the mystery that Merlinus proved to be, but his background is similar. He is of good family and was a Gothic cavalry officer.'

'Cian says he escaped Saxon captivity.'

'Yes, he has provided a wealth of information to Mor and Arthwys, not just about the Saxons but also the Empire which seems so distant these days.'

'I'm surprised by Merlinus' absence at such time as this – he has always been such a rock, such a comfort, in many ways a hero.'

'I do agree, but his reputation as a wizard has come to plague him. He wants to start afresh as a simple man of faith, but I suspect there is more to his absence than that.'

'Really?'

'Have you not noticed, Bryn? Morgaine is blooming; she has never looked so well.'

'Surely not? Though, I would be happy for her.'

'That is how I feel, but hush for now. She leaves in two days, and it is well that our suspicions remain private.'

A Meeting by the Trent

Episford

Maius 462

'Hengist, it was never our intention for the rebellion to turn into full-scale war.!' said Freuleaf. The old Jute warrior and his son, Octha, remained silent, glaring at their Angle visitors as Freuleaf continued. 'It is your ambition that has brought us to this. You must have foreseen that King Mor would strike back, that your raids along the waterways would motivate him to build boats of his own to steal and destroy ours. The northern Cymry are resolute warriors, but we Angles have lived alongside these Britons without hostility for three generations—'

'As slaves,' Octha interrupted aggressively.

It was Freuleaf's turn to glare. 'No, as foederati and as traders, both positions now lost to us through your war.'

'We have gained a homeland.'

'We have gained an enemy.'

Both parties fell silent, gathering their tempers.

'How many boats have you lost?'

Freuleaf looked toward his son. 'How many, Wodning?'

'Following this recent attack, ten.'

'We have lost twice that number, eight of which were stolen. They are becoming bold. We have warriors along the shore and up the Don waiting for them to cross, but they do not come.'

'They have no interest in these wetlands, then, only our boats.'

'That seems to be their strategy. We no longer dare send our keels west of the Trent for fear of attack, so we have moved them all to here.'

'We cannot both cower by the mouth of the Trent. Why do you not attack them?'

'Because they now control the rivers to the west of our territory. King Mor has moved his frontier from the Ouse to the Dergeuntid, and his cavalry face us across the estuary.' Hengist clenched his fists as he continued. 'So long as we keep our keels at a safe distance, we have little else to fear from that quarter, for they will never attempt to attack in force from the north.'

'How can you be so sure?'

'The estuary, the forest and the wetlands are our protection.'

'But you think the Britons plan to invade our territories from another direction?'

'It is a possibility. They have an army gathered to the south near The Wash and another to the west where the Trent leaves the forest, though we are not concerned.'

'Why so confident?'

'Because we have armies looking back at them: Aesc by the Trent and Wipped by The Wash. These northern raids are nothing more than an attempt to distract us.'

'I see,' said Freuleaf. 'So, we are your gaming pieces.'

'No,' Hengist said emphatically. 'You are our allies.'

Freuleaf looked at his son then back at Hengist. 'We have discussed this situation with our people, and we have decided to withdraw all our keels from the Trent and Humber and move them beyond the Roman ferry to the mouth of the estuary.'

'The Britons will think you are running scared.'

'We are. We cannot afford any more losses.'

'The Gaini have said they will remain steadfast.'

'They have no choice; their only port is on this river.'

'If you withdraw your keels, we will not protect your people from raids or defend you if the Britons attack.'

'So be it. You have brought this on us all; it is for you to set it right.' The Angle king stood to leave. 'Good luck to you, Hengist. May Woden be with you.'

As Freuleaf and Wodning walked back toward their waiting keel, the young man turned to his father. 'It seems strange that the Britons are only interested in destroying our boats. What can be their objective?'

Freuleaf shook his head. 'A storm is coming, Wodning. We must be careful to navigate our people to safety. Hengist has become overconfident, his judgement clouded by his success on the battlefield.'

'But we supported him in the rebellion, why desert him now?'

'The rebellion had cause, but he should have reached terms with Vortigern, instead of provoking our neighbours with that slaughter.'

'But Father, that was many years past, and since then, the Wealas have proven too weak to retaliate against us.'

'Nonetheless, they will not have forgotten. I believe it will prove Hengist's undoing. We have wisely avoided provoking the northern Cymry in previous years, but now we have drawn the attention of those mighty warriors, uniting them with the southern armies. This new strategy of theirs has one obvious objective.'

'Which is?'

'We are now surrounded by the Britons' armies with only the sea behind us. They destroy our boats so we cannot escape.'

'Escape from what, Father?'

'Death, Wodning. I think they plan to kill us all.'

Family Matters

Cambodunum

Martius 463

Arthwys searched for his father. He was not in the hall, but his groom was still readying his horse, so he had not yet set off to hunt. Arthwys spied him looking out over the timber stockade. He climbed the ladder and stood alongside him.

'Arthwys! Good morning. I always enjoy how the forest bursts into life at this time of year.'

'It is indeed beautiful, Father, but all that beauty also provides cover for our enemy!'

'How true that is. What may I do for you?'

'I have received a letter from Ambrosius Aurelianus. He requests that I attend a banquet which he is holding in honour of a visiting Roman general, a Count Paulus. He sends his regards to you and Mother and includes you both in the invitation, should you wish to attend. Vortimer will be there.'

'Where is this banquet to be held?'

'Venta Belgarum, one month from now.'

'It seems strange that Ambrosius should seek to distract our generals from their troops at such a critical time.'

'His reasoning is that we are on the eve of a great campaign, and it may be some time before we can all meet again. But there is more.'

'Go on.'

'Emperor Majorian did not die of natural causes as first thought but was deposed and executed by Ricimer.'

'It is difficult to keep pace with the goings-on in the Empire, but Majorian, I'm told, was a good leader, deserving of respect.'

'And that appears to be the view of every Roman general in the Empire, particularly Aegidius and Marcellinus.'

'So how does Count Paulus fit into this?'

'He is second in command to Aegidius, and I believe there is a family connection with Ambrosius.'

'Ah yes, great Roman families vying for power – a familiar refrain. It was always thus. Forgive me if I don't attend. Venta Belgarum is a considerable distance, too far to go to listen to talk of saving a dying Empire. Will you take Gwenhyfar?'

'There will be better times for her to attend such events. It is, as you say, a considerable distance, and the war is not yet won.'

'Vortimer attends, you say?'

'The letter says he is invited.'

'Have you spoken to your mother about correspondence she has received from Vortimer?'

'No, she has not mentioned it.'

'Vortimer is concerned for his health. He still suffers from wounds that never fully healed. He is making arrangements for his succession but has no heirs. Pascent is the elder brother, a strong-minded and principled man, but he has lived away from Viroconium for too long. Vortimer has asked that we support his nomination of Britu who, though he is the youngest brother, is a warrior like himself.'

'Will Pascent accept this?'

'I believe so. He is a man of the Church and is unsuited to military duties.' Mor paused, his gaze thoughtful as he looked at his son. 'Arthwys, please accompany me to the treasury. I have something to give you and something I wish to tell you.'

They climbed down from the stockade and walked across the busy fort. Mor's treasury was a windowless locked cabin attached to the exterior of the hall and always guarded. He reached for a key from his pocket as they approached the door. The guard saluted and stepped to one side whilst the king inserted his key and turned the stiff lock.

'This door is rarely opened, for there is little within.'

Inside, light streamed into the darkness as Mor fumbled around in some old wooden boxes, until he produced a magnificent bearskin.

'This was your great-grandfather's. It is all I have that was his. He wore it into battle, and I believe he would want you to have it.'

Arthwys beamed. 'I shall wear it with pride, Father.'

'It is unfortunate for Meirchiawn that he has nothing of Coel's – the torc and signet ring were taken from Gorwst's body, doubtless melted down by the thieves who murdered him.' Mor paused again, a rare look of uncertainty in his eyes. 'Arthwys, you are, of course, my heir, but there is something you need to know.' He hung his head, eyes to the ground, before squaring his shoulders and returning his gaze to Arthwys. 'Britu is not Vortigern's son; he is mine by Sevira.' Arthwys tried to gather his thoughts as he looked into his father's guilt-ridden face. 'Only your mother knows. It happened just before we met. Neither Vortigern nor Vortimer were ever told.'

'So why are you telling me?' Arthwys asked, curious at the disclosure. 'Surely this is a secret best kept?'

'You will soon be going into battle together. I thought you should know that the future King of the Cornovii is your brother. It seems Sevira chose not to tell him, but she always said I could if I thought it might advantage him.'

Mor fell silent. Arthwys studied his father. He still commanded great respect, and for a man of three score years, he carried himself well. Many men half his age would still lose to him in combat. Arthwys smiled. 'Are there any more family secrets you would like to share?'

They both laughed, but then Mor's face turned serious once more. 'There is one. Gorwst believed your marine commander to be the son of Coroticus.'

'Ah, now that is not such a surprise. Mordred has always seemed so different to his Coeling family, an outsider. He is our fiercest warrior. His men follow his lead without question, and they all fight like him, like demons.'

'I hear he holds court at Eboracum as if it is his own domain.'

'It truly is. He has recovered those lands that we chose to surrender. I admire him.'

'As far as I am aware, he doesn't know about Gorwst's doubts – my brother probably died before disclosing them to anyone.'

'Mordred was inconsolable when the news of his father's murder reached us. But I sense he knows he is different in some way – he is driven by deep personal turmoil.'

'Be wary of him, Arthwys. I'm sure he eyes you as a rival.'

Arthwys smiled once more. 'I encourage his ambition. Elfed is safer for his presence.'

'Very well, my son,' Mor said, giving Arthwys a measured look. 'On our earlier subject – I will be interested to hear what has stirred Aegidius' interest in our shores. Ambrosius has always looked longingly across the sea to Gaul, unsurprising since his father was joint Emperor with his brother until Honorius put their heads on stakes at Ravenna! You have done well to turn his interest to the Patria, so I hope this is not a sign his attention is wavering toward the Continent once again.'

'The Empire of the Romans confuses me, Father. It is difficult to know where I stand with it. Everything that makes me who I am stems from it. My ancestors, my ability to read and write, my military training and equipment, and we have all studied the strategies and tactics of famous Roman generals. We see their great works in stone, the statues to their leaders and old gods inscribed with tales of bold deeds and bravery. But then we are taught about the martyrs who stood against the emperors to follow our Lord. Now, it is a bishop of Rome who directs our religion, yet the Church is not always in accord with an empire split east and west. Travellers tell us about wonderous sights, particularly in Rome, yet civil wars have weakened the once mighty legions, and the eternal city has been sacked twice by barbarians in recent past.'

'Your great-grandfather Coel and your uncle Talhaearn explained it to me in a simple way. The Empire grew strong like a huge red apple with a healthy strong core, but it became too large and heavy for the tree, so it stopped growing and tumbled to the ground. At the Empire's core were discipline, duty, organisation, innovation and knowledge, all the virtues you mention, but most importantly, a strong and rarely defeated army. Like any apple lying on the ground, the bruising turned to rot, so the emperors cut it in half, hoping to manage the corruption by exposing it. Alas, the decay was already in both halves, and with the core open to the elements, the Empire became further weakened and rotted more quickly, their armies no longer invincible.'

'So, you believe Rome has come to the end of its season?'

'As with all things in nature, an end must be followed by a beginning. Our forebears hoped that the Kingdom of Heaven would succeed the kingdom of the Romans, but then our island became ravaged by raiders, and it seems it must be the sword that protects us, rather than the cross.'

'Do you believe Ambrosius might be drawn into conflict abroad?'

'I will answer your question with a question. If the lands of our tribes were overrun by Picts and Saxons and we were forced to live in exile, would we stand meekly by whilst heathens abused our people, or would we do everything in our power to return and take back our lands?'

'We would return!'

'This is how Ambrosius has always felt, although I fear his opportunity may have come too late.'

'Why is that?'

'He is old now, and although there are still many Gallic families who would support his position, it is the Visigoths who now hold sway on the Continent. Fierce warriors, they have made themselves kings of southern Gaul. We have heard of both their military skills and the grandeur of their courts from Amabalis.'

'The disunity of the Gauls has proved their weakness.'

'That is true, but we Britons are the same. It is only God and the Saxons that have given us cause to unite. Ask Cian – he has a better command of history – but hope for a reborn empire in Gaul has drawn our soldiers abroad many times. Your mother's father, Conan, was one such soldier who never returned.'

'It will be interesting to discover why Ambrosius thinks it is important for us to meet this Count Paulus.'

'A trip to the south will open your eyes to many things. You will find the far south of the island to be more Roman in its customs and buildings, and I know Venta Belgarum will impress you. Now, come with me to see your mother, and we will show you Vortimer's letter. If I have understood his message correctly, I doubt he will be strong enough to make the journey south for the banquet.'

A Roman Visitor

Venta Belgarum

Aprilis 463

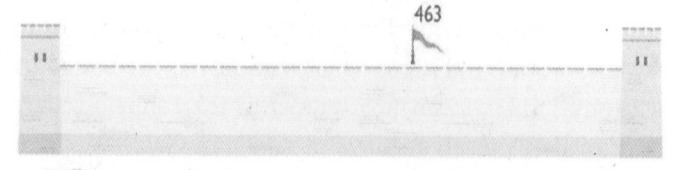

'Prince Arthwys, I am delighted to finally meet you. Both Ames and Vortimer speak highly of you, though it comes as no surprise to me that the son of King Mor should prove to be not only a mighty warrior but also a master strategist. I hear that your plan to split the Saxon force into three is succeeding,' Ambrosius said, greeting his guest in Latin, the language of the Venta Belgarum court. His voice echoed around the stone walls of his domus.

Arthwys had never before stood in such a grand setting. With marble pillars supporting the ceiling and patterned mosaics underfoot, it was as his father had described – impressive. Arthwys replied in near perfect Latin.

'We have managed to harry them sufficiently, so they are forced to turn in all directions to face our threat. But even so, they prepare for full-scale war, so the sooner our campaign begins the better.' A quick glance at Agiluf and Britu told him they were managing to keep up, too.

'I have received news that Vortimer's health deteriorates by the day. Will the potential loss of such a great commander from our ranks hamper the campaign?'

'It would be impossible for it not to have some impact, but Britu is here, so after your banquet, we will ride together to Durobrivae to assess the situation.'

Ambrosius was visibly older than Arthwys' own father, but the young prince was struck by the old Roman's patrician poise and the way it was accentuated by his elegantly embroidered clothing.

'Of course. And I believe you know my son, Ames,' said Ambrosius. Arthwys smiled and nodded at his fellow soldier. 'But I don't believe you have met Natalinus?'

'I have not, but my father has spoken of his bravery.'

Natalinus stepped forward and smiled.

'You have the look of your father. I am disappointed he is unable to attend the banquet, but please send him my regards. His leadership and cavalry saved this city.'

'I shall. He has stayed to man the defences at Cambodunum – we have been on high alert ever since we began attacking the Saxons across the Humber.'

'Quite so,' said Ambrosius. 'I appreciate that this invitation has come at an inconvenient time, but this is the first time we have received an embassy instigated by the eastern Emperor.'

'Emperor Leo?' Arthwys looked toward Agiluf and Britu to see their surprise matched his own.

Ambrosius smiled when he saw their expressions. 'Yes, we are intrigued, too. It is unprecedented.'

'When will Count Paulus be arriving?'

'He is here already, resting after a rough sea passage. But before he joins us, let us find a comfortable place to sit whilst we listen to what he has to say. I think you will find the garden is a pleasant setting, especially with the weather being so fair.'

Ambrosius led the party through from the atrium to the peristylium. Here, in the far south, the weather seemed calmer and warmer, and spring was more advanced than it had been in Elfed.

'You inspected my troops at Derventio, on your way here?'

'Yes. That is where Britu joined us. Your troops have adequately reinforced the garrison, and they are well-disciplined. However, we are hoping to persuade Ames to further bolster their numbers before the campaign begins in earnest.'

Ambrosius looked at his son and nodded. 'He has my authority to do so.'

'I noted a substantial garrison at Lactodurum, might they move up to Derventio?'

'The road to Verulamium has been our Limes Saxonicus, a frontier established many years ago by Natalinus to separate the Thames Saxons from their rebelling cousins. That garrison has kept us all safe ever since, but as you have observed, it is only a three-day march from Derventio, so yes, they will be moved up quickly when you require them.'

'Ames told me that this is your intention, but large troop movements would excite Saxon attention, so they are best kept a safe distance for now.'

Arthwys looked around the garden at his surroundings, taking in the splendour. He had been fascinated by everything about his journey south. Throughout his lifetime, the road from Elfed to Derventio had been too dangerous to travel, so he had only ever journeyed to the west and north of Elfed. Now that Cwmry troops regularly patrolled the road south, the route was restored, and Arthwys was finally able to visit the cities he had only seen on maps before now. The Roman buildings were fascinating, particularly for someone raised behind walls and stockades. He had grown up listening to his father's tales of the south and occasional descriptions from passing travellers. More recently he had been rapt by the stories Amabilis told him. His children's Goth tutor, who was now a convert to the priesthood, had once been a cavalry officer and fought with King Theodoric for Aetius on the vast plains of Gaul. Encounters on such a scale were almost beyond the imagination of a regional Cymry warrior, but Arthwys had absorbed it all, for he already knew the world was large and complicated, just as he knew it would take much more than valour to defeat Hengist's large army.

He sensed the Romanitas here in the south – the feeling that he was part of something much greater and more powerful. His father talked of the Empire's decline, but surrounded by these columns and monuments, speaking Latin, it seemed that the spirit of Rome was alive and thriving. He dared to think that a door may be opening on this different world, one he had trained for all his life but never thought he would see. Was Rome's allure an illusion? His father certainly thought so, but he had witnessed the old discord, whereas this new spirit of co-operation was exciting.

When Ames had joined them at Lactodurum and accompanied them for the remaining journey, it had felt like a royal procession. There was a Roman arrogance to the young man, whose father was the most powerful man in the Patria, and although Ames' enthusiasm for war rather betrayed his inexperience, Arthwys had grown to like his Roman ally, seeing no harm in encouraging his bold manner. After all, confidence would be essential if they were to defeat the Saxons.

Count Paulus swept into the garden, accompanied by two men, one dressed in the uniform of a senior soldier, the other in a toga, carrying the tools of a secretary. Ambrosius and his guests stood to meet them.

'Welcome, Count Paulus. Please, let me introduce you. This is Natalinus, my general, and my son, Ames. To his right is Prince Arthwys, acting commander of the northern armies, with Prince Britu and Prefect Agiluf.'

The Roman acknowledged the men, scrutinising each one respectfully before turning to his own party.

'This is my prefect, Rufus, and my secretary, Julius.'

'Have you recovered from your difficult sea crossing?' Ambrosius asked.

Paulus laughed. 'I doubt I will ever recover from that crossing. Storms bring us all close to the Lord, but this was perhaps too close! I have never prayed so hard, and He mercifully delivered us with nothing more than some seasickness to show for the experience.'

Ambrosius smiled. 'I am grateful that you chose not to delay your crossing, for many of us would have missed meeting you, otherwise. We are in the midst of war against invading Saxons, so it has been difficult to assemble our military leaders in one place at the same time.'

'Thank you for your attendance, gentlemen, it is appreciated. Does the war fare well?'

They all looked toward Arthwys.

'Some minor setbacks, but we are prepared to begin our campaign in earnest.'

'Good. So, to the purpose of my visit.' He turned to his secretary. 'Julius, spread the map before us.'

His companion unfurled a large skin map of the Continent, and everyone gathered around.

'I will start by recounting recent events across the Empire.' The visitor took a deep breath. 'The late Emperor Majorian campaigned vigorously throughout his reign. His objectives were, however, somewhat ambitious, and ultimately, he failed – some say from treachery, but I am here to tell you that it is not as simple as that. The northern Gauls fought alongside Majorian because his cause aligned with theirs – the reunification of an empire torn apart by barbarians. But this did not sit well with his general-in-chief, Ricimer, a barbarian himself, who we believe alerted the enemy to Majorian's plans. This treachery undermined the Emperor's campaign and left him unable to suppress Gaiseric's Vandal kingdom. This mattered little to us in Gaul, but to the senate who had funded Majorian, it was everything. Rome fears Gaiseric and his Vandals most of all – they have sacked the city before and are a constant seaborne threat, controlling many ports from where the Empire imports grain.'

Ambrosius turned to Arthwys. 'Strangling trade causes huge difficulties for Rome – it is a city so large that Italy alone cannot feed it. The senate's priorities have influenced this pressure.'

Paulus continued. 'Indeed, that is so, but they are a lesser threat to the West, and more of a challenge to the East. The senate's dismay at Majorian's failure emboldened Ricimer who deposed and murdered him. Majorian had the courage to address the Empire's woes, but now he is gone, every barbarian on our continent breathes a sigh of relief.' There was a silence amongst the gathering as the consequences of Majorian's death sank in. 'Ricimer has nominated a man called Libius Severus as Emperor. He is a wealthy co-conspirator, but no one other than Ricimer is prepared to accept him, not Aegidius who has sent me here, not Marcellinus or Nepotianus – not one of the generals of the western Empire, and most importantly, Leo, Emperor in the East, does not endorse his appointment. There has been talk that we should all march on Rome to defeat Ricimer, but a civil war at this time will only play into the hands of his barbarians. Leo has urged us all to stay calm but also to gather our resources so that we are ready when the time is right to make our move, and that is why I am here.'

Arthwys sensed the level of expectation rise amongst the gathering. Count Paulus seemed to feel it too, for he paused, increasing the anticipation.

'General Aegidius is at war with the Gothic brothers, Theodoric and Euric. They support Ricimer and constantly press us to gain territory. They are also allied with a Saxon called Adovacrius whose keels control the mouth of the Loire. He is no threat to us, but his cousins Hengist and Aesc, your resident Saxons, are a danger. They have a large army only a short sea crossing from our northern flank. You will know there is precedent for them fighting on our shores when they fought against the Huns at Chalons, as Aetius' foederati.'

'We were not aware at the time,' said Arthwys. 'We thought they had returned to their homeland. It was to our great surprise when they returned to our shores with a larger battle-hardened army. This is what heralded the start of our war.'

Count Paulus nodded. 'It is our fear that your war against them could push them in our direction.'

Arthwys signalled to Agiluf who produced a rather smaller skin map which he unfurled next to the other.

'We have already destroyed many of their keels in this estuary here. They have keels up this river known as the Trent, but we have it blockaded. Tomorrow, we ride to the plains of The Wash, which is a Saxon haven where many keels are moored. Our plan is to draw them out and then destroy their fleet, here.' He pointed to an estuary that emptied into The Wash.

'So, it is not your strategy to force them to leave?'

'No, for they will only return again, possibly even greater in number and more battle-hardened. We intend to kill them all. But first, we must rob them of their keels, which for so long have been their advantage.'

'That is a relief,' said Count Paulus, giving Arthwys a respectful nod. 'What is the Saxon strength?'

'We estimate about six thousand warriors, but we have forced them to divide their forces, so they are deployed in three separate areas.'

'And your strength?'

'We have six turmae of cavalry and four thousand warriors.'

'Are they well trained and properly equipped?'

'Yes. Our core force is similarly split into three to face them, but others may join us along the way.'

'I wish you luck with your campaign, and you have my gratitude for containing this additional threat to our own campaign.' Count Paulus paused, looking thoughtful. 'Tell me, once your battles are won, what will you do with your army?'

Arthwys' brow furrowed. 'We cannot yet envisage such a time.'

Ambrosius cast a glance at Ames then added, 'Perhaps you can tell us what Aegidius might like us to do?'

Paulus looked at each man in turn as he answered the question. 'The purpose of this embassy was to first establish whether or not Hengist's Saxon force is a threat to our western shores. Thanks to your assurances, Arthwys, I will report to Aegidius that I am now confident there is no immediate risk from that quarter. Beyond that, the Empire will be relieved to hear that the Britons no longer fight each other, and that, in the face of this common enemy, you are united. Perhaps, in the future, we may call upon the support of your military to assist us in our ambitions? Emperor Leo has indicated that he is working on a plan to reunite the Empire and diminish the influence of the barbarian kingdoms. Restoring order will require success on the battlefield, and an army of trained Britons would be a great asset in pursuit of this cause.'

Ames replied, his pride in his Roman heritage fully on show. 'I speak only for the south, but it would be an honour to fight at your side.'

The following silence prompted the visitor to ask more directly. 'And what about you, Arthwys. Would your northern army fight for the Empire?'

'Count Paulus, our most recent battles against the Saxons have resulted in defeat with many of our fighters slaughtered. Britu lost both his brother and his father as a result of one battle. We dare not look beyond our immediate objectives. It may take years to defeat the Saxons, but if God wills that happy result, and we survive, we will consider proposals at that time.'

The reply did not seem to disappoint or surprise Paulus. 'Thank you for your honest reply.'

Ambrosius clapped his hands, relieving the tension.

'Come, my friends, I am told the banquet is ready.'

Agiluf rolled up his map and rejoined Arthwys and Britu. 'The Romans are casting about for reinforcements.'

'There is no loyalty, even amongst the Roman elite. If we did not have the Saxons pinned down, be sure they would be requesting their assistance, not ours.'

'One war at a time then!' said Agiluf, making the other two laugh.

*

The banqueting table was filled with the best the Patria had to offer, and there was much more seafood than Arthwys would normally eat. Beer and wine were provided in profusion, but he decided he would avoid intoxication – the ride to Durobrivae would normally take three days, but he was keen to complete it in two, which would require setting off before dawn.

Count Paulus was deep in conversation with Ambrosius, Ames and Natalinus. Britu and Agiluf were raiding the table, eating as much as possible whilst admiring the many attractive servant girls. Arthwys slipped out and headed toward the garden once more.

So, this is how the Romans live, he thought, admiring the statues, running his fingers across the smooth marble surfaces, and reverently examining the exquisite mosaics. He had seen nothing like this detail and elegance in northern rural villas. Most Roman residences, even in Eboracum, had been either destroyed or stripped of their riches, so it was a joy to see such a building intact.

He heard voices as he entered the garden but could not tell from which direction they came. He stood and admired the precision with which the hedges, plants and flowers were tended then heard muffled laughter behind him. The large oak doors had initially obscured his view, but now he turned to see who was there. Sat together, watching him intently, were two of the most elegant and beautiful women he had ever seen. He suddenly felt awkward and boorish in their presence.

'Ladies, forgive my intrusion, I had no idea you were here. I will leave you to your conversation.'

He turned to leave, but the elder of the two spoke. 'Why, it would be nothing less than impolite to leave without formal introduction.'

Arthwys turned back in consternation. 'Of course, pardon my manners. With whom am I fortunate to be acquainted?'

'I am Livia, eldest daughter of Ambrosius, and this is my sister, Aurelia.'

Both ladies stared at him expectantly.

'I am Arthwys.'

'Oh, we know who you are,' giggled the younger sister.

Livia cast a quick glance at her sister. 'But do tell us about yourself.'

'Well, I'm afraid, though I am here today, I will be gone tomorrow.'

'Then sit with us a while.'

Arthwys sat down awkwardly on the stone bench opposite his inquisitors. He could see that Aurelia was heavily pregnant. 'This garden is lovely, so tranquil,' he said. 'Will your husbands be joining us?'

Livia smiled. 'My sister is married to the most eligible Roman in the Patria: Nataline.'

'Ah,' said Arthwys. 'Son of Natalinus, no doubt.'

'Whereas, I am a widow,' she added quickly.

Arthwys looked directly into her sad eyes. 'I meet too many these days. I'm sorry I asked.'

'Don't be sorry. It is some time past.'

A young soldier popped his head around the door then immediately stood to attention and saluted. 'Prince Arthwys!' He bowed his head.

Arthwys stood and clapped him on his shoulder. 'Nataline, I presume.'

'I must ask that you allow me to collect my wife; I resume my duties shortly.'

'Of course, I can see that your responsibilities will soon be increasing.'

The young man looked confused then laughed. 'Ah yes! Good luck with the campaign, sir. I am posted to Derventio.'

'Well, I shall see you there.'

Aurelia stood carefully, supporting her swollen belly.

'Please look after him, Prince Arthwys,' she said, as she followed her husband out of the garden.

Arthwys looked at the beautiful Livia, now sat alone. 'Is it also time for you to leave?'

She brushed a stray strand of blonde hair away from her brow. 'No, I live here now. Please stay and talk to me.'

Arthwys sat down once more.

'These wars, they are never ending,' she said.

'Do you have children, Livia.'

'Mercifully, I was never blessed. Do you?'

'Yes, two boys, but I see so little of them. My wife chides that I will only come to know them once they are old enough to join my militia.'

'My husband was a soldier, Quintus Urcicinius, prefect to Elafius. They both died fighting at Crecganford. At first, I sailed as an émigré with my husband's family to Armorica. We all hold property there, but it is no safer there than here, so I returned to my father's house. King Vortimer is a close family friend, so we have been hearing all about you.' She reached for his clasped hands. 'You are our great hope. Can you make the Patria safe for us again, Arthwys?'

She reminded him of his mother. Roman women were so much more forthright, yet also more sensitive, more affectionate. The womenfolk of the north were rarely demonstrative. She continued to hold his large hands, her touch soft, her manner gentle, but he could see she was holding back tears.

'Ames tells me to be brave, and he is right to do so, but defeat and death are just words to those who have not experienced the ensuing misery.' She sat upright, releasing her grip, once more brushing aside the disobedient strand of blonde hair.

Arthwys smiled, hoping to lighten the mood. 'He is brave and ambitious – he will have us invading Rome one day!'

His comment seemed to amuse her. 'He is proud. Lost causes are a Roman disease.'

Now it was Arthwys' turn to laugh. 'A common ailment for which there is no cure.'

'Will you return to Venta Belgarum soon, Arthwys?'

'If you command it, my lady.' In truth, he did not know when he might return.

'Then I do, and I shall impatiently await that day.'

Arthwys smiled. 'I must rejoin my men.' He stood to leave.

'Wait! A lady's champion must have a token to take with him into battle.' She removed a plain gold band from her index finger and held it out in the palm of her hand. 'Take it.'

'That is kind and generous, but I cannot.'

'Take it, I command you.' She smiled.

Arthwys took the ring and held it in his fingers. It was engraved with one word: *LIVIA*.

'Please, Livia, take it back. It will not fit any of my fingers.'

She unclipped a fine gold chain from her waist. 'Here, wear it around your neck at all times. Think of me, and it will bring you good fortune.'

'Such a gift is not yet deserved.'

'Better that you wear it than it is stripped off my dead body by a Saxon.'

This kind of emotional intensity was foreign to Arthwys, causing complex feelings to crowd his senses. She stood now, but only reached the height of his shoulders. She looked into his eyes.

'Quintus left without a goodbye embrace, and I have wondered since, if his misfortune was a consequence of my imperfect attention.'

She placed her hand on his cheek and gently drew his lips toward hers. A brief parting kiss was perfectly proper, but he longed to stay there. Her scent enveloped him, like a magic potion designed to entrap him.

'Keep us safe, Arthwys.'

'I will do what I can, and thank you for this.' He held up his clasped hand holding the ring and chain, but he did not know what else to say.

A voice interrupted the moment. 'Count Paulus is leaving,' said Agiluf. 'He wishes to speak with you.'

Arthwys took one last look at the beautiful Livia then bowed and kissed her hand.

'We shall meet again, my lady.'

'Soon, Arthwys. Make it soon.'

He walked through the oak doors, shaking his head to cast off the spell. He looked at his grinning prefect. 'She is a lovely woman, Agiluf, and would make a splendid wife for you.'

'I don't think she is interested in me, my lord,' Agiluf said, still grinning.

A Great King Dies

Cambodunum

October 463

Arthwys burst through the door to the great hall. 'Mother! I came as quickly as I could.'

As expected, the queen looked composed, almost serene in her black stola.

'Arthwys,' she held out her arms, and they embraced, holding each other for some time.

'Were you with him at the end?'

'I was, but it was so sudden; only his eyes spoke to me.'

'Where did it happen?'

'We had just risen from the night's slumber when he keeled over, holding his chest. He was gone so quickly.'

Arthwys looked toward the curtained bed cubicle. 'Has the physician examined him?'

'Oh yes. We are certain it was a natural death. There were signs… chest pains, shortness of breath.'

Arthwys knew his father would have been frustrated by infirmity. 'He would rather have died in battle.'

'He would have said that, but I know he was happy, and so proud of both you and Morgaine.'

'I presume my sister is here?'

'A messenger left for her at the same time as yours, but her arrival will be delayed – she has a child by Merlinus.'

'So that was why they banished themselves from court!'

'It was a secret she asked me to keep from both you and your father. I so wanted to tell Mor, but Morgaine felt ashamed and also fearful for Merlinus. The years passed and now we both wish we had told him.'

'He had his secrets too, but he will know now, Mother. Where are Gwen and the boys?'

'With Bryn, awaiting your arrival. Has Agiluf returned with you?'

'No, we are on constant alert. Vortimer and Britu have moved their forces to Durobrivae and Nataline now garrisons Derventio. Agiluf awaits my return to Derventio so our cavalry can join Vortimer. We prepare for battle but fear the Saxons may attack first, for they too have been gathering their troops.'

'And how is Vortimer?'

'Still with us, still determined, but he can still barely ride his horse; he may be unable to fight.'

'Ah, Vortimer. He has given everything to this war.'

'He has, more than any of us.' Arthwys paused before asking, 'Has father's body been readied for his funeral?'

'Bryn and I have prepared him for his journey.'

'May I sit with him a while.'

'Of course, I shall remain quietly here whilst you do so.'

He walked toward the curtain and looked back at his mother. She was the strongest woman he knew and would only show her grief in private or when the occasion required it. He entered the curtained area which was filled with sweet flowers and garlic from the forest. A single candle glowed close by his father's pillow. He looked at rest, so much so that Arthwys had the urge to shake him awake. He thought to recite a prayer but could not think of anything appropriate to say.

'Please God, take care of this great man.'

He sat on an adjacent stool and sighed heavily before speaking quietly.

'Are you with them all now, Father? Coel, Ceneu, Taly and Gorwst?'

Cian would often tell the tale of Coel's funeral and how he had strummed a lyre with no clue what to play! Blwchfardd had later put Taly's famous gorchan to music, greatly pleasing his father and making it easier to recall. Arthwys now recited the last lines quietly.

'Bring me twenty foes, for ten will not do.
And I will charge the last rampart
That stands before the hall of souls
Where my journey to Heaven must start,
The Bear waits there, the warhound too,
Brother cub will be joyous I come,
The court of Coel will convene in the stars,
Great king, your work here is done.'

'I will commission them to write a gorchan for the mighty King Mor... but I cannot stay for your funeral. This responsibility you have raised me to honour is all consuming, and I must not linger. The Saxons are at this very moment watching us over the tops of their shields, and their fleet is harboured by The Wash. Now is the time to strike and reverse the defeat at Crecganford.' Arthwys reached for Mor's cold, lifeless hands, positioned as if he were at prayer. 'Know that I loved you and will miss you forever.'

Arthwys heard his mother's voice from the far end of the hall.

'Morgaine, Merlinus, and who is this? Is it my grandson Morcin?'

'It is Mother. Isn't he a big boy now? I so wish Father could have met him.'

'Hush, Morgaine. God will have his reasons for taking your father at this time.'

Arthwys stepped out from behind the curtain. 'Sister! This day is a strange mix of sadness and joy. And Merlinus... I am glad you are both here.'

To his surprise, they both bowed.

'Arthwys, we are all sad at the sudden loss of such a great king.'

Arthwys picked up his nephew. 'Did I hear the name Morcin?' He looked toward Merlinus.

'Named after both his grandfathers; he will be a great warrior.' Merlinus looked extraordinarily sad. 'My king, I need to speak with you.'

'Will that be as my father's missing priest or as my sister's secretly acquired husband?'

Merlinus lowered his head. 'I am here not just to mourn Mor, but also to seek your family's forgiveness. We intended to come sooner and regret not doing so. I also have a message for you from Myrddin.'

'But surely he died long ago?'

'Yes, but there are some matters he did not want spoken of until you were king.'

Arthwys shifted his attention to his mother and sister. 'I cannot stay beyond tonight, so I will be unable to attend Father's funeral. I am grieved beyond measure by his death, but in my position, he would not tarry either.'

'You are right; your father would understand. We are all relying on you to win this war. Mourn him with your sword in hand.'

Arthwys' heart swelled with pride for his mother's poise and resolution. With a nod, he turned to Merlinus. 'I have summoned my eques to gather this afternoon. You will need to tell me now what it is you know.'

'I would speak with you privately, my king.'

'Of course, let us step outside whilst the ladies share their grief and exchange their news.'

They walked outside into the bright sunshine.

Merlinus spoke first. 'Please forgive our subterfuge, my king. We were drawn to each other over many years. Morgaine did not plan this, and my reasons for leaving court were genuine, although I now feel ashamed for what must appear to be a breach of trust.'

Arthwys laughed. 'Those sound like words you rehearsed for my father, so I suggest you save them for when you make your peace with him.' The old priest looked relieved. 'I am truly glad you have returned at a time when I am sorely in need of wise council, so I forgive you for making my sister a happy woman! I am confident Father would have understood what developed between you, and I can tell that Mother is already won over, so let us speak no more of this.'

'Thank you, my king.'

'You mentioned a message from Myrddin?'

'Yes. We nursed him through his final hours on this earth, during which time he uttered many things. He told me to tell you this: *Whilst the Bear and the Eagle fight far away, a fosterling's jealousy turns to fury and war.*'

'What can it mean? Perhaps it portends a distant future. Do you still have the sight?'

'I am still troubled by dreams I do not always understand.'

'Did you foresee my father's death?'

'No, I would have brought Morcin to meet him if God had chosen to give me that foresight. Myrddin had also said: *Three mighty kings will die before the Saxons are defeated.* But I had assumed he meant Vortigern, Coroticus and Gorwst.'

'Perhaps he did not consider Coroticus mighty.'

'I cannot say, but I can suggest a candidate for the jealous fosterling: Mordred.'

'That is interesting. My father also warned me to be wary of him. What makes you suspect him?'

'Long before your uncle's murder, I dreamt that Coroticus cut off Gorwst's head.'

'That is a strange dream.'

'The murder of my own brother and his family were the source of many nightmares over many years, so I first discounted the dream, thinking my personal obsession was its source, but then the murder actually occurred.'

'So… are you suggesting Coroticus is responsible?'

'No, he did not venture from Alt Clut in his later years, but perhaps it could be someone who looks like him? I have heard that Mordred is his likeness...' Merlinus paused for Arthwys to ponder his intimation.

'I can see how you drew this conclusion. I think we both know that Mordred is not Gorwst's son. Although it was never proven, Gorwst suspected Mordred is Coroticus' son – they are the image of one another.'

'It didn't occur to me until Morgaine mentioned Mordred's arrival at court and how she had tended to a wolf bite. A wolf will not bite a man unless attacked, whereas a dog will defend its master.'

'Prince Mordred has brought valuable seafaring skills and won us the control of our rivers. He is brave and strong, a natural leader; his warriors are devoted to their commander. He is crucial to our campaign and has given me no reason to distrust him.

'My king, I only tell you Myrddin's words and my dreams.'

'Many men masquerade, sometimes to hide their motives and other times to lose their past. Is that not so, Merlinus?'

The priest's face coloured. 'Deception always has a purpose.'

'He has earnt his place at my table, and he shall remain at it. Dreams are not evidence.'

'No, my king, but they are warnings.'

'Merlinus, it is a comfort to me that you have returned to keep an eye on such matters. We have not only missed your wisdom but your reputation. Your timely presence will surely bolster my subjects' confidence. The wizard has returned to fight for his king.'

Merlinus grimaced. 'I no longer carry a sword; my strength and skills have left me—'

'Ah, but you carry the staff of Myrddin, which is far more intimidating than any sword. Now, please excuse me, I must find my wife and boys to allay any offence that I have spoken first to everyone other than them.'

*

Morgaine was sitting in the corner of the great hall playing quietly with Morcin whilst Igerna looked around to check that everything was ready for the gathering in the hall. The death of a king was a dangerous moment, even when the succession was uncontested, and there would be much to talk about.

She reflected upon the death of her own father who had not come back from a distant battlefield, somewhere in Gaul. Arthwys was on the cusp of a campaign that might see him suffer the same fate, and Eliffer and Pabo were yet too young to become leaders in their father's place. She would need to be strong to face the challenges brought by the death of her beloved Mor. God chose his moments for a reason, she had always believed that, but Arthwys would be campaigning for many months, possibly years, leaving vulnerable the kingdom she had helped her husband build. Mor had been so good at measuring the risks and facing the threats, and she took comfort that the cautious Cian was still there to help. The loss of her husband was a stark reminder that her generation were all closely stalked by Death – the old order was changing. She resolved to pay more attention to Gwenhyfar who suffered from her husband's absence and got so overwhelmed by her day-to-day duties. The new queen would struggle if, God forbid, anything should happen to Arthwys.

Cian and Merlinus entered the hall. The sudden death of her husband had hit Cian particularly hard. The loss of a lifelong friend was hard to bear, but much like herself, he buried his grief under the tasks now presenting.

'Queen Igerna, our apologies for interrupting your mourning, but the king has bid that we all meet here. Would you prefer that we move the king's body to the chapel?'

She gave Cian a sad smile.

'No, he will stay here and lend weight to Arthwys' first council. Come sit with me. I have many questions.' Both men sat beside Igerna. 'Who comes to this council?'

'The two most senior barus are here: Winnog, chieftain of the southern Brigantes, and Catevignus of Swale. Each is a powerful lord who can raise a turma of cavalry.'

'They are loyal men whose families are the heart of Elfed.'

'Then, of course, there is our new ally, Prince Mordred, who has two hundred men for his ten keels, mostly Germanic settlers recruited from east of Eboracum.'

'Are they loyal?'

'To Mordred. He has done well to assemble such a force, and their achievements have been remarkable. Elfed no longer fears the estuary – we control it.'

Merlinus remained quiet and shifted uncomfortably on his chair. Igerna knew he had yet to meet Mordred and seemed uncharacteristically nervous at the prospect.

'The Saxon threat and our alliance with Vortimer and Ambrosius take precedence over all else,' continued Cian, 'but we should not lose sight of the effect Mor's death may have on our neighbours. It could motivate them to launch an attack, thinking to catch us with our guard down in our grief.'

'Who do you think capable of such callousness?' asked Igerna.

'We rely on old agreements with Alt Clut and the Gododdin to contain the Scotti and the Picts, but all of these kingdoms have ambitions of their own.'

'Surely they would not be so bold?'

'Mor was a renowned warrior, his reputation strong enough to keep them at bay, but with his death and our forces committed to the south, our northern neighbours may risk raiding our borders to test our strength.'

'Reged will always defend the west, so is it our northern boundary where we might be vulnerable.'

'Mordred has fought alongside Cinuit so will be well placed to guess at that king's thoughts, but King Lott of the Gododdin is a strange one. I met him once with Mor. His fortresses are impregnable, and he fears no one. His grandfather fought with Coel, but such loyalties are long forgotten. There is a vast area of disputed territory between the Wall and Din Eidyn, but it is barren, mountainous and a long way to come for little reward.'

The oak doors opened once more. King Arthwys and Queen Gwenhyfar entered with their boys. Igerna and her advisers stood and bowed. Arthwys bowed before his mother and then in the direction of where his father's body lay.

When Arthwys sat down, he leant toward Igerna and Cian. 'Gwen and I have been discussing continuity of command and authority in my absence. We believe it would be in the best interests of Elfed if you both could continue in your current roles until this campaign against the Saxons is over.'

Igerna looked toward the new queen. 'Are you sure, Gwenhyfar? I am more than happy to hand you the reins.'

Gwenhyfar looked alarmed. 'No, no, I much prefer this arrangement. Once my husband returns, I will, of course, take my place at his side, but you have been handling state affairs so well for so long, we would be foolish to put aside such valuable experience in these precarious times.'

Igerna knew this to be the best course of action but part of her wondered if Gwenhyfar would ever step up to shoulder her responsibilities. It was not that she was idle, far from it – the younger woman filled her days with weaving and sewing. It was more that she lacked confidence and feared making mistakes. She had once said that she only really felt at ease in her father's court, and that life in Elfed had presented many more rigours than she had expected.

The seating was arranged to reflect the shift in authority. Igerna sat to the right of the queen, and Cian to the left of Arthwys. Merlinus preferred to stand with the boys.

Arthwys looked unaccustomed to his father's chair, though he smiled reassuringly at Gwenhyfar who looked similarly uncomfortable.

'I think we are ready,' he said, looking toward Cian.

Cian stood and walked the length of the hall to instruct the guards to let the waiting crowd through the doors. Over the years, there had been many gatherings in this hall, but Igerna could not remember one so sombre. She did not want to think about her loss, determined that she would mourn her husband when appropriate, but the doleful faces and respectful quiet of those arriving brought tears to her eyes. She breathed deeply and wiped them away but not before Arthwys had glimpsed her momentary distress.

Lords and eques stood toward the front, all dutifully assembled at Cambodunum in anticipation of Arthwys' accession. Although tradition expected that sons followed their fathers onto the throne, Igerna knew powerful families should always be careful not to assume the transfer of power was a foregone conclusion. Such moments were open to challenge and could quickly deteriorate into civil war, particularly between brothers or other close male relations. The domain Mor had made his kingdom had previously been Roman territory, taken by them from the Brigantes. Most of his subjects were from that tribe, but in the chaos following the Roman withdrawal from the Patria, Mor had been accepted as their king, his proven military authority bringing the security they craved. Her husband's noble Cymry credentials had been without doubt – he was a Carvetti prince, born at the north-west corner of the Great Wall, but Arthwys was undeniably both Cymry nobility and Brigantes – he had been born at Isurium Brigantum, the tribe's civitas, and he had been raised on their land, amongst their children. Most important of all, Myrddin and Taly had dubbed him the Bear, the future hope of all the northern tribes. Any claimant would struggle to find support for their challenge, but nonetheless, his first address as king was a test of his leadership, and she couldn't help crossing her fingers for luck as her son stood to speak.

'My father was not only a brave, undefeated warrior, he was a wise king. His tragic, untimely loss comes at a time when we could really use that wisdom. Under his reign, Elfed has become a powerful kingdom, largely due to the foresight of three great men: my father, Talhaearn and the late Lord Crannog, chieftain of the southern Brigantes. These three, guided by the seer Myrddin, stood their ground against Pictish and Saxon incursion and faced civil war together. Thanks to them, Elfed has become a safe haven, welcoming all who seek fair and Christian protection from the threats in the east. In the west, my cousin King Meirchiawn pushes back the Gaels and the Scotti, and to the north, our allies the Gododdin hold the line against marauding Picts, but the Patria now faces an even more serious threat: the Saxon hordes....

'Long ago, Myrddin prophesised they would overrun our lands and push the Cymry into the sea, unless brave Elfed stood its ground and destroyed the aggressors. Father heeded the seer's words, holding back the serpent, holding our ground until we were ready to destroy our enemy. That time has come. We now face the Saxons across the Humber and along the Don. Their stolen territory is three times the size of ours, and they control lands to the south as far as the mid-lands. Our challenge is great, for whilst their numbers have multiplied, infesting that region, ours have diminished from disease. Even now, with our three armies surrounding them, we are still outnumbered.

'Elfed has resisted Saxon invasion, so we have not experienced their sport, but ask the priest, Amabalis, what tortures these heathens inflict on those they defeat. He has seen Christians buried alive as companions for their fallen warriors, and I have heard from surviving southern cives, who lost everything in the first wave of rebellion, about the atrocities they witnessed. It must not happen here.

'When I was a boy, Myrddin sent me on a quest to find the sword of destiny: Caledfwich. He said we would only defeat the Saxons if that sword was wielded in the battle. Well, here it is, in my belt, waiting eagerly to spill Saxon blood. Our armies are poised to attack, the fates are with us, and our Christian purpose is true, so why has the good Lord decided to take my father now, at this most critical moment? I have prayed for an answer, yet it was only this morning that I understood, though it took Merlinus to explain it to me – he could see what I could not through my grief.'

Arthwys paused, and all onlookers eyed the seer in awe. It seemed that, of them all, Mordred was particularly fixated by Merlinus' presence.

'He relayed to me a message from Myrddin – one that he was forbidden to tell me until after my father's death.' Arthwys paused once again, the silence absolute, full of expectation. 'Myrddin prophesised that three mighty kings must die before Elfed could crush the Saxons. We have now lost Vortigern, Gorwst and my father. Three mighty kings, all summoned to the best seats in Heaven's great amphitheatre to watch Elfed crush the Saxons. I knew there was a reason for our great loss. I knew there had to be a purpose. Now I know they will all be with us.'

Igerna and Gwenhyfar looked up at him with tear-filled eyes.

'So, you will all understand why I cannot stay for my father's funeral. I must be there for the battles which they are waiting to spectate. At this very moment, our forces are facing up to three mighty Saxon armies, and my comrades are doubtless praying for my speedy return with two extra turmae.

'Are you with me?' he shouted.

'Aye!' came the resolute reply.

'Queen Igerna and Lord Cian will manage matters of state, and Lord Winnog will take command of Elfed's defence in my absence.' He turned to speak directly to the old warrior. 'Although, your son's turma, the forest archers, must accompany me to Durobrivae.'

Winnog bowed. 'I too would gladly accompany you, King Arthwys.'

'There will be plenty more fighting yet, my friend. I am depending on you to defend the queen.' The king turned to the tall, brooding warrior leaning against a roof post. 'Prince Mordred.'

'Yes, Arthwys.'

'Please, stay behind; I have strategy to discuss.'

'I will. I have important information about the Angles for you, too.'

The attendees took that as a sign that the king's speech was over, and excited chatter filled the room. Cian who had been listening carefully stood and walked to Igerna's side. 'That was nothing less than brilliant; he reminds me of a young Mor.'

Igerna smiled. 'I saw it too, but now he goes to war. I fear for him, and I fear for the effect it will have on Gwenhyfar. Bryn and I both remember how it feels to be left behind, not knowing…'

The meeting began to break up, many leaving to prepare for their journey south, to war. As Mordred walked toward the king, Igerna called to him. 'Prince Mordred, may I speak with you?'

'Of course, Queen Igerna.'

She noticed Merlinus was standing close, listening to what was to be said. 'I am told by Cian that you know King Cinuit of Alt Clut?'

'I twice joined Cinuit on raiding expeditions to Hibernia. He is clever but meek. It was his father who drove him to undertake such aggressive raids. If you are telling me he is king now…'

'Yes, Coroticus is recently dead.'

Mordred appeared shaken by the news, though he responded dispassionately. 'Then Alt Clut will be better for it.'

Merlinus stepped forward, interrupting. 'Coroticus will be burning in the fires of Hell.'

'Then you should pray for his soul, priest, for are we not all sinners?'

Merlinus was visibly shaken by the warrior's confident response. He stepped back without another word.

Unperturbed by her priest's outburst, Igerna continued. 'Do you think it likely that either Cinuit or Lott will attack us whilst Arthwys is away on campaign?'

'I doubt it, my lady. They are both watched by the Picts, and it is only their mighty strongholds that protect them from attack. They rely upon their good relations with Reged and Elfed, even if they pretend otherwise.'

'Thank you, Prince Mordred. Your knowledge of Reged's neighbours is most valuable.'

'There is nothing to fear. You can count it my solemn duty to protect our beautiful new queen.'

Mordred looked toward Gwenhyfar. He smiled then winked. Gwenhyfar blushed.

'We take comfort from your loyalty,' she said coyly, avoiding eye contact, although her king had already left his seat to speak with Cian and Winnog.

'Mordred, join us,' the king said, beckoning his marine commander.

Mordred bowed then obeyed his king.

Igerna watched the proud prince saunter toward the group then turned to Merlinus and spoke in a lowered voice. 'What is your impression of our handsome and arrogant Prince Mordred?'

'He is the image of Coroticus, my lady. In my opinion, he is outranked only by the Saxons as a danger to this kingdom. I have warned your son, but he will have none of it.'

'I do see turmoil burning in Mordred's eyes. His reputation is fierce. I'm told he has littered the southern bank of the Humber with Saxon corpses.'

'Aye, my lady, and when he runs out of Saxons to slaughter, where might his attention turn next?'

'Fortunately, there are many Saxons yet to kill,' she replied. The grief she had bravely put to one side suddenly reached for her heart, invading her thoughts. She stood to speak, and a hush descended upon the hall.

'I wish to sit in silence with my husband.'

Everyone respectfully filed out of the hall, led by their new king and his war council.

Enemies Engage

Wippeds Fleot

Maius 464

Wipped was a proud Frisian. His family had lived on these plains for four generations and Roman trade had made his forebears wealthy merchants. They owned many boats, built to ship grain to the Rhine and up the coast to Eboracum, but when the Roman army had withdrawn, there was no alternative but for his grandfather to adapt, and there had been much land for the taking. He looked out across the river to the open sea. The boats he saw there had brought people to work their fields and warriors to defend their gains, but when tensions had begun to build with the Wealas, amongst accusations of raiding – not his men – all trust was broken, and his father had gladly joined forces with Hengist's alliance so that they might create a new kingdom, drawing together all the Germanic-speaking people in the east. The Wealas were weak, and Hengist's rebellion had exposed their disunity. It had been an opportunity well taken. His father had fought alongside Hengist at the decisive battle of Crecganford, where they had killed the leaders and slaughtered thousands. The Wealas army had never since ventured north or crossed the great dyke, even though eight years had passed, and this had enabled Wipped to farm the vast plains unhindered.

As thegn of the tribe, it was his duty to defend his people's most important harbour and the route into the mid-lands. Wealas mounted troops had been gathering for months, and the intensifying hammering of blacksmiths making weapons had been heard coming from their fort. In response, Hengist had sent Octha with two hundred warriors to help defend against the attack he suspected would come soon. Wipped had already been alert to the danger so retained one thousand of his own men. Though most were sailors or farmers, all could carry a spear and a shield. He was not frightened by the prospect of the battle.

His musings were interrupted by one of his scouts. 'Thegn Wipped, the Wealas army has begun their advance from the stronghold at Durobrivae.'

'Then we shall go to meet them. They will follow their road into the fen, the one which crosses the great dyke. We will let them come and slaughter them all between the two rivers. Go find Jelte and Octha and bring them to my hall.'

The thegn looked back to where their boats were moored all along the bank of the river Glen and out to the flat calm of the estuary. They were all secure and out of sight and reach of the approaching army. He entered the dark, cool hall, waiting briefly for his eyes to adapt after the bright sunshine. It was quiet and empty apart from a servant girl preparing food at the far end. He hollered for her.

'Woman!' She rushed toward him. 'Where is everyone?'

'Out in the sunshine, master,' she said in her strange accent.

'An army of your people approaches – when will they learn this is our land now?' He laughed, enjoying her discomfort. 'Bring beer for me and my commanders.'

She scurried back to the kitchen area, as his son entered with Octha. Wipped sat at a trestle and the two younger warriors sat with him.

'Your father has once again anticipated the Wealas' actions. My spies tell me their army is on the march.'

'They will be coming for your boats,' said Octha. 'They have used the same tactics on the Humber. We only evaded their blockade on the Trent because we sailed out of the estuary under cover of darkness.'

'So, this is a co-ordinated campaign – it seems the Wealas really have put their differences aside. No matter, we still outnumber them. We will snuff them out just like our fathers did.'

Octha nodded. 'What is our strategy?'

'Most of our warriors are camped to the north of the river, but the Wealas will likely cross the great dyke and follow their old roads to bring them to the coast. We will ferry our warriors across the inlet and set up a defensive line by the shore, so protecting our boats and settlements. Do you agree, Octha?'

'You know this region far better than I, and your proposal seems strong. Will we begin ferrying the men?'

'Not yet. Let's await confirmation of this army's size and the path it takes before we commit. They are at least one day's march away, but there is nowhere to hide on the fens, and our watchtowers will see them soon after they have crossed the great dyke.'

The serving woman brought three beers.

'Go find my wife,' Wipped instructed. The girl ran for the entrance, bumping into the returning scout, also in a hurry.

'My thegn, they have crossed the dyke and are marching along the eastern side of the river.'

'As I thought. There are so few routes into the fens.'

'We count about fifty mounted soldiers and eight hundred infantry.'

Wipped looked to his two commanders. 'We are twice their number, so take a moment to drink your beer then muster your men for the ferry crossing. We will surprise the Wealas with our strength – they cannot be aware of your reinforcements, Octha. Hengist is truly cunning.'

*

Britu rode slowly alongside Vortimer. The sun was high and strong, making the fens shimmer on the horizon.

'This is God-forsaken country. There is a distinct smell to it, a combination of brackish water and dead fish.'

Vortimer laughed. 'That is how the Saxons smell.'

'Do you think they will have seen us by now?'

'I'm sure of it. They will be watching intently from their watchtowers, hopefully distracted from looking west. Whatever the outcome of this battle, it will all be pointless if we do not succeed in destroying their keels.'

'Arthwys is only travelling by night. I am sure he will have remained undetected.' Britu looked across at

Vortimer, concerned by his pallor. 'Will you be able to fight, brother?'

'I can fight. I will be roped into my chariot, so that I can lead the charge.'

'Is that wise?'

'Battle does strange things to men's minds. Even though most here did not witness the slaughter at Crecganford, fear will grip them when they see the size of our foe's force. I must lead the charge.'

'The men do not understand why we should want to recover this foul-smelling wasteland.'

'And that has been to the Saxon's advantage! It has made the fens around The Wash a haven for them, secure from attack, allowing thousands of their countrymen to arrive without challenge so they can go on to infest the Colonae. The few Britons who lived hereabouts have been long since murdered or enslaved by these heathens, but to stop the stream, we must dam the source.'

'Our strategy is good, but it is dependent on Arthwys' attack being a complete surprise. The Saxons must not know we have a force on the other side of the estuary until it is too late.'

Vortimer nodded. 'Arthwys will have had to navigate a perilous journey. We can only hope that all has gone well for him. This campaign is our last chance to make our kingdoms safe.'

There was a moment's silence, whilst both men considered the challenge ahead.

'Why did you never marry?' said Britu.

Vortimer laughed at the sudden change of subject. He was enjoying his brother's company; it helped take his mind of the excruciating pain from his old wound. 'I never found a pretty princess.'

'But there were many. I saw them with my own eyes.'

Vortimer sighed. Only the Lord got to hear his most personal thoughts and concerns, but Britu was his nominated successor, and perhaps the eve of battle was the time to share such confidences.

'Time passed too quickly. I resolved to defeat the Saxons first, then my wound would not heal…'

'There is still time, brother.'

'Our parents' marriage seemed more pain than joy, but should the battle go our way tomorrow, I shall take a wife, just to please you, brother.'

Both men laughed, though Vortimer knew he would not survive the rigours of the fierce encounter that was to come. He looked across at Britu and took comfort that his brother would make a fine King of the Cornovii.

'Britu, if I fall in battle tomorrow, Arthwys will take my place as commander of our combined armies. In truth, much of our current strategy is his, and he has always been our best hope—'

'God will be with us, Vortimer. Look, our forward scouts are choosing a place to camp, so we are nearly in sight of the enemy. I will be praying between now and dawn for victory and a pretty princess for you, brother!'

The king smiled. He no longer feared death. On the contrary, he welcomed the relief it would bring from the pain that wracked his body.

*

'Agiluf, alert your men. The river Glen is beyond this stretch of dyke. We must cross it as quietly as possible,' Arthwys said in a whisper.

He watched the sun fall below the horizon as Agiluf passed back the instructions. The men had been given green cloaks to cover their armour and weapons during daylight, but supressing the sound of two turma of cavalry preparing to cross a river would not be easy.

'Caius, you are closest, go check the depth of the water.'

The young man stepped gingerly into the green, slow-moving river, a look of relief quickly passing across his face when he realised that the tide was out and the water only reached his thighs. He returned to the bank.

'There is deep mud below a shallow flow, my king. We must keep the horses moving quickly or they will become mired.'

'We will walk the horses across. Nobody is to mount up. Pass the message down the line.'

One by one, the warriors crossed the river, their horses splashing through the dank flow. Fortunately, their progress was obscured by high reeds on the opposite bank.

'If all has gone to plan, Vortimer and Britu's warriors will be camped facing the main body of the Saxon force by now,' said Agiluf.

'Let us hope so. If our enemy have not crossed the estuary, we will be facing a thousand Saxon warriors with only sixty cavalry!' cautioned Arthwys.

Agiluf was just relieved they had managed to get this far without detection. 'It would be a pleasant evening for a stroll along the riverbank, if it were not for the thousand warriors at the estuary spoiling my tranquillity!'

Arthwys grinned in the dimming light. 'Send Cadrog and one scout ahead of us. Tell them to silence anyone they find on our path. We are no more than nine miles from our objective, and daylight is but six hours away.'

Agiluf swallowed hard. Only six hours before they faced the Saxon army. His father had warned him about fear on the brink of battle. *Fear is your worst enemy. Kill your foe, and you vanquish your fear.*

Arthwys never showed fear, but Agiluf wondered how he really felt. He would mostly be concerned about the success of his plan. Defeat here was not an option for the Britons. This strategy was the Patria's last chance to avert Saxon domination.

*

The dawn had not yet broken, and there was little birdsong as the three Saxon leaders positioned their troops in two lines of six hundred warriors. The shadowy mass of the Wealas army began to take shape in the foreground. They too were drawing their troops into two lines with cavalry on each flank. As the early morning mist began to clear, Wipped could see a chariot pulled by two horses at the head of the infantry.

He turned to Jelte. 'That must be their king. Why does he make himself such an easy target for our spears?'

'Arrogance? It looks like their strategy is to get their flanking cavalry behind our lines, but the dyke protects our rear, so they will fail.'

Octha, who had been positioning his warriors on the far left, now joined them. 'We will trap their mounted soldiers in the dyke.' He looked out across the assembled Wealas. 'Why aren't they attacking? What are they waiting for?'

'They are scared of our numbers. Shall we attack, Father?'

'No, Jelte. That would give their cavalry the space they hope to find behind us. We can wait all day, if necessary. It is they who must decide when they wish to die.'

*

Cadrog and the scout were now so close to the settlement they could hear distant voices. Suddenly, right by them in the reeds, there was rustling, then a girl's voice singing a shanty. He knew the words, realising she was singing in his own tongue. He leapt, placing his hand over her mouth, pulling her to the ground and spilling her basket of herbs and flowers. The scout drew his blade, intending to finish her, but Cadrog shook his head frantically and began dragging her upstream toward where Arthwys and his men were hiding.

'She's one of us, a Briton,' whispered Cadrog hoarsely.

Arthwys stooped, put his finger to his lips, and Cadrog lowered the girl to below the tall reeds. She looked terrified.

'Now, remain quiet, or we will have to kill you.' She nodded, making no attempt to escape. 'Will you answer our questions?' She nodded again. 'I am Arthwys. What is your name?'

Cadrog slowly removed his large hand from her mouth. There was a pause as she looked around at the warriors awaiting her answer.

'I am Gaia.'

'Are you a slave?'

'Yes.'

'Where is the Saxon army?'

'Across the bay.'

There was a collective sigh of relief, and Arthwys continued his questioning. 'Are there soldiers in the settlement?'

'There are many guarding the keels.'

'How many?'

'Twenty or so, I'm not sure.'

'Do you want to be freed from slavery?'

Her eyes filled with tears. 'Yes, but I know not where to go.'

'Follow this river west and keep going. Wait for us where the great dyke crosses it. We will meet you there and take you to safety.' Arthwys stood. 'Mount up!' he commanded.

The girl looked up at him in awe. 'Arthwys.'

'Yes, Gaia?'

'Kill them all.'

*

Britu sat astride his horse alongside Vortimer's chariot.

'This is a large army we face, brother.'

'Yes. Now the mist has cleared, I see we are considerably outnumbered. If we delay for much longer, they may be tempted to attack us.'

'Perhaps, but that would be to our advantage. However, our men are getting restless, and the longer they wait, the more nervous they get. I wonder if we should have let them in on our plan?'

'No need now. Look there, in the distance – Arthwys has attacked.'

Plumes of smoke were drifting upward into the sky and the clash of weapons could be heard on the summer breeze.

'See how it has confused our enemy.'

The Saxons were in disarray, their attention drawn by the thickening smoke rising from their settlement across the muddy bay. The rear ranks were breaking away, scrambling over the dyke and up the bank to get a better view of what was happening. From there, they could see the flaming arrows filling the sky beyond the high sea bank. Arthwys was burning their homes and their keels.

'Advance fifty paces!' Vortimer commanded.

Britu signalled to his left and right, and their troops covered the ground quickly, almost at a run. When they stopped, the front row crouched behind their shields. Every soldier in the second row held a bow and began loosing salvos of arrows into the bright morning sky. Many of the enemy had lowered their shields when they turned to see what was happening to their settlement. Arrows hit their marks, and Saxons fell dead and wounded, yet their comrades remained distracted by the terror being inflicted on their families. In the distance, keels were on fire and adrift, the screams becoming louder. The Saxon leaders turned, shouting orders to their warriors, but their attempts to regain control were in vain. Their entire right flank turned to a rabble rushing toward their boats to cross the water as the volleys of arrows continued to rain down upon the panicking soldiers. The Saxon line seemed stretched thin so as to protect each flank from Vortimer's cleverly deployed cavalry, but now he signalled with his spear, and the two turmae quickly changed position and shifted to the centre surrounding his chariot.

'Advance,' screamed the king.

His men kept their V-shape, lowering their javelins, galloping as they drew close to the enemy and crashing into the centre, which by now had no shield wall protecting it. The Saxon leaders were overrun before they had a chance to fight. Britu, at the head of one turma, wheeled left, cutting down the fleeing Saxons like ears of corn, but the Saxons' left flank was better disciplined and held its shape. Vortimer recognised the patterns on these warriors' shields – these were Hengist's men. Perhaps the king himself was amongst their number. As Vortimer watched, they began retreating in an orderly manner, up the banking before the shore. He could not follow them in his chariot, so he called to an eques.

'Give me your horse and take my chariot. I must lead the pursuit of these Saxons.' The eques obeyed the king's command.

'My king,' said Vortimer's charioteer, his face etched with concern, 'your wound?'

'We are wasting time. Help me on this horse.'

With the help of both men, he mounted up and drew his sword. He signalled to the decurion of the turma who drew a group of cavalry about him, and they pressed toward the banking. Now Vortimer could see the enemy's objective – six keels moored off the shore. The battle had become intense, the remaining enemy fighting for their lives. He turned to the decurion.

'Go, find as many bowmen as possible.'

The soldier galloped away to the rear of the infantry. He was gone for some time, and the fighting raged on. The Saxons were aware the battle was lost, but they were bent on survival.

The decurion returned with disappointing news. 'I have rounded up twenty archers who have a few arrows left. The rest are pulling arrows out of dead Saxons.'

Vortimer looked toward the shore. 'They will run for their keels, but there are too many of them for only six keels, so that is when we must try to kill as many as possible. We need more bowmen. Decurion, go find me some more!'

The soldier obeyed.

The Saxon remnants were now on top of the bank, swords and spears flashing in the sunlight, but it was clear to all that they would not hold there for long. Suddenly, a salvo of spears was launched from behind their shield wall. The Britons took cover, and although only a few spears found a target, the distraction had worked, allowing the Saxons to flee down the far side of the man-made bank onto the muddy shore, running for their lives. The tide was coming in quickly and the keels were some distance out. The Saxons struggled through the mud, giving the Cymry archers easy targets. Some stragglers were caught and cut down. Many drowned trying to clamber onto their keels, and some were even killed by their own comrades. One keel capsized, hapless warriors clinging to the side, their weight pulling it over. The Britons watched, jeering from the shore, and those Saxons who didn't drown were cut to pieces when they returned to the shore.

Vortimer dismounted. He could not identify the Saxon commander who had led the warriors onto the keels, perhaps it had been Hengist himself, but no matter – this was a total victory. The Britons roared their success. Every man he passed clapped his shoulder as he limped toward the grassy bank on the shore. Britu rode up, quickly dismounting when he saw his brother.

'My king, your side is soaked in blood.'

Vortimer looked down. Blood was oozing through his chain-mail. His head was spinning. He sat on the bank and removed his helmet.

'We must thank the Lord, then perhaps someone could carry me to my chariot?' He smiled at Britu then slumped to the ground.

*

Only five keels had escaped, and each was over-burdened. In the distance, Wippeds Fleot burnt, the black pall reaching high into the summer sky.

'Octha!'

'Do not speak to me!' The gore-covered warrior held his head in his hands.

'My lord, I must. Which direction do we take?'

'Not north, not the Humber. If the Britons don't kill us, my father most certainly will. Defeat is dishonour.'

'Where then?'

'Sail south, for now. We will seek a temporary haven where we can recover. Hengist and Aesc will only welcome returning heroes. Our gods have turned against us.'

No one spoke. Only the rhythmic splashing of the oars accompanied their sorrow and despair.

The captain signalled to the other keels, and they turned south. There were ports where Octha had been told there were kinfolk, but he knew they would never see their families again.

An Unbreakable Bond

Durobrivae

Maius 464

Britu was sitting alone with the corpse of his brother. The king had finally succumbed to his wounds three days after his greatest victory, where he had won the total rout of the Saxon army and the destruction of their fleet. Revenge for years of atrocities, revenge for Crecganford. God had never before granted them such success against the Saxons, and the cives of the Patria were now more than convinced that their cause was both just *and* holy. The small room in the praetorium was only a temporary mausoleum. After the battle, King Vortimer had suggested that he should be buried alongside his fallen warriors near the coast so that he could join them in a spectral defence against future landings, but his strong heart had continued to beat, and he had only exhaled his last breath upon his return to Durobrivae.

There was a gentle knock on the door and Arthwys entered the room.

'Forgive me for interrupting your prayers, Britu.'

'Please join me, my vigil is complete.'

Burning candles surrounded the dead king, where he lay attired in the uniform of a Roman general.

'He was a hero, an inspiration to us all – his whole life dominated by a war that does not end. May he rest in peace.'

'I have now lost two brothers in this war, but I know I have gained one.'

Britu turned to gauge Arthwys' reaction.

There was a pause before he replied. 'So, you know that I am your half-brother?'

'My mother told me on her deathbed. I have to confess, it was a relief. I had always *known* I was different to the others.'

'For me, it is a bond of great joy amongst all this sadness.'

'Yes, I feel that too, but dare not declare it. I am both successor to Vortimer and a king of the Cornovii. There would be challenges, if my peers suspected that the blood of Coel Hen flows through my veins.'

'Then we shall never speak again of our unbreakable bond.'

'No, but it will always be the strength between us, and I am glad we have spoken.'

'Do you have plans for Vortimer's funeral? As far as I am aware there are only two bishops still administering to their flocks in the south of the Patria. Vodinus is the closest, at Verulamium.'

'Then let us call a council meeting with Ambrosius there too. We must reaffirm our objectives and ensure we have the backing to sustain our campaign, the death of a king can be a dangerous moment.'

'I will accompany you to bolster your position, but I must send my militia north. There is suspicion of a possible Saxon counter-offensive, and we must not flag vulnerabilities to the enemy.'

'Are we near the end of this, Arthwys?'

'No, we have barely started.'

'It seems we are ever committed to be warriors.'

'Christian warriors,' added Arthwys. 'This is God's purpose, and it is well it should be a bishop who sends Vortimer on his journey.'

'We shall bury him close to Saint Alban, where Germanus blessed us as children.'

'I will send a messenger to Ambrosius within the hour... but we must remain cautious of our reception.'

'How so, Arthwys?'

'We are northern warlords, and southern cives view us with fear and suspicion.'

'But surely, now you are battle leader, they all must rally behind you?'

'We think of ourselves as Roman soldiers, but we are Britons.'

'Fighting a common enemy.'

'True, but my father warned me about the capricious nature of those seeking power within the Empire.'

'The Empire brings no weight to our regional conflict,' Britu said firmly.

'Look around you, at this magnificent praetorium. This was the headquarters of the Count of the Saxon Shore. In this place, powerful men murdered their comrades to further their careers.'

Are you suggesting that we cannot trust Ambrosius and Riothames because they are Roman?'

'Your father Vortigern had his differences with Ambrosius, the pretext for which arose during council. More recently, the southern cives pleaded with the Romans to come to their rescue. It came to nothing, but had their plea been answered, perhaps we might have found ourselves once more beholden to the Empire. Your brother, Vortimer, managed the politics skilfully, but we may find the southern cives attempt to divide us, fearing our unified strength.'

Britu smiled. 'That will never happen, brother.'

A Hero Honoured and a Leader Confirmed

Verulamium

Maius 464

Faustinus Urcicinius, with his staff and helpers, had tidied up the basilica to the best of their ability. It was so rarely used these days, and the holes in the roof had turned it into a haven for pigeons who were most reluctant to leave. The mess was worse than he remembered, and he now regretted dressing in his best toga for the meeting, but as tribune of Verulamium, it was his duty to host the occasion. A *council meeting*, they called it, but there had been no such meeting for decades. His father had attended the last one over twenty years past in Londinium before the rebellion. Only their victory had prompted this one, and the leaders of the Britons would arrive soon – men he had yet to meet, apart from the old Roman, Ambrosius, and the Bishop of Londinium, Vodinus. The meeting was to take place before the burial of King Vortimer, and for that, he had been requested to prepare a tomb close to that of Saint Alban. It was a fitting location for the leader who had selflessly defended the Patria. The cives had trusted Vortimer, but who would defend them now?

'My lord, it is nearly time. Ambrosius and his party are approaching from the west, but there is no sign of the funeral party yet.' The tribune noticed the young servant's eyes flashed with excitement at the prospect of a gathering of the leaders of the Patria.

'Go. Find the bishop and alert the kitchens,' the tribune growled, resenting the strain the event was placing on his town, then changing his tone when he saw the bishop had already entered the room. 'Ah, Vodinus, welcome.'

'I have come straight from prayer. God must guide us today.'

'That he must. It seems we have atoned for the sins that the Church has blamed for our great misfortunes?' The bishop had shown a tendency to identify defeat with sin.

Vodinus did not reply, clearly holding a different opinion. Instead, he chose to answer the tribune with a question of his own.

'Who attends this meeting?'

'Ambrosius and his son Riothames; Pascent and his son Riocatus; General Britu who accompanies his brother's body; and the new commander of our forces, General Arthwys.'

'All good Christians, save for this Arthwys.'

The tribune shook his head.

'I'm sure he is Christian.'

'After a fashion, but I hear rumours of magic swords and wizards at the northern courts. The Pelagian heresy is still rife in the north, and before the pontiff's death, he entrusted me with the task of ensuring the purity of the Lord's word in Britannia.'

'Surely, that will be best achieved by first defeating the Saxons?'

The bishop looked offended. 'False prophets are infinitely more dangerous than the easterners. A false prophet's lack of reason poisons the very soul. The Saxons must convert to the true faith, and they will in time. We must learn to love our enemy.'

It was the tribune's turn to not reply – loving the enemy was not helping defeat them. His family had been one of the wealthiest in the east, but his father had fled to Armorica, and the Saxons had taken their lands, later killing his brother Quintus at Crecganford. Northern tyrants were preferable – godless or not.

A toga-clad gentleman entered the room, accompanied by a monk. He acknowledged the bishop who he seemed to know then turned to the tribune.

'Urcicinius, I presume. I am Pascent, brother of Vortimer.'

'I am sad for your loss, Pascent, but delighted with victory, even if it is not yet enough to recover the Saxon Shore.'

'Yes. Vortimer did well, but I am surprised that Britu is not now in command?'

'These are questions for Ambrosius. Is this your son?' He nodded in the direction of the boy in a monk's habit.

'Forgive my manners, yes, this is Riocatus, who has chosen the Church over war – a career I wholly endorse. I will be leaving him in the care of Vodinus.'

Before he could answer, Ambrosius, Natalinus and Riothames swept into the room, their semblance elegant, exuding wealth.

The tribune spoke first.

'Welcome, gentlemen. I'm sure you understand that Verulamium and our people bear the scars of war, but this precious victory has rallied our spirits.'

'And ours also, but as you will hear, the war has only just begun.'

'Can it be won?' the tribune asked candidly.

'We shall ask our generals. We saw them arrive, but they are bringing Vortimer's body, so their progress will be somewhat sedate. Where is Cabrianus of Caint? I expected that he would attend, his region has been hard-pressed by Saxon raiders.'

'We believe he may be dead – our correspondence with him remains unanswered. It begs a question as to why we fight battles in the far north when the adjacent Saxon Shore is not secure.'

'Only the Romans have ever been able to secure the Saxon Shore because it requires a strong navy and control over both sides of the Gaulish Sea. It is otherwise simply impossible to control the movement of the boats.'

'We hear that you are constructing a fleet, Ambrosius?'

Riothames cast a glance at his father.

'That is for a different purpose,' the old man added quickly, seeming grateful that any need for further explanation was interrupted by the opening of the doors to admit the funeral party, consisting of Arthwys, Britu, and Vortimer's coffin carried by six soldiers.

Urcicinius directed them toward a sturdy table he had positioned in the centre of the room. Whilst the soldiers positioned their solemn burden, the party assembled around the coffin and acknowledged each other.

'A hero of the people,' said Ambrosius.

Urcicinius was not prepared to let this opening pass by. 'Yes, a hero, but who will defend us now? In the east we have faced the Saxon threat, time and again. No one in this room has lost more than my family. The Saxon Shore has become a Saxon province where justice means nothing, and theft and murder prevail. We quiver behind our city walls waiting for rescue, but only the might of Rome, with its legions and laws, can remedy this.'

Urcicinius knew he had spoken out of turn, but everything seemed so hopeless.

Ambrosius nodded his head wistfully then replied to his old friend.

'The Romans will not come. The murder of Emperor Majorian has undermined any hope of a reunified empire. There is a rumour that General Aegidius might push for a Gallic empire allied with Emperor Leo, but civil war with Ricimer and Severus would leave Gaul exposed to the Visigoths, and should we join in, it would leave Britannia at the mercy of the Saxons. Yes, we are building a fleet, but it stays in harbour until we defeat our enemies.'

'But can we defeat them? What say you, General Britu?' He cast a glance at the two powerfully built officers standing back, assuming that the more 'Roman' in appearance was Britu. He was mistaken, for the other man replied.

'Tribune, we are aware of your plight, but know that General Arthwys now commands the army and this campaign.'

Urcicinius was encouraged by this solidarity and looked toward Ambrosius who again nodded in agreement.

'You are probably not aware of the extent of the problem, Urcicinius. The whole of the east of this island is awash with Germanic settlers. Their ancestors came with the Romans as soldiers, sailors and slaves. The so-called Saxon Shore is only part of the once powerful Colonae which extends nearly to the northern wall. Arthwys, please explain this to my friend the tribune.'

The taller, more Roman-looking general, stepped forward, bowing in the direction of Urcicinius.

'Tribune, I am Arthwys, King of Elfed, and following the sad death of Vortimer, commander of the allied forces fighting the Saxon menace.'

Urcicinius detected a northern lilt, but the young man's Latin was perfect.

'The easterners watched and learnt how the Patria's weaknesses were exploited by the Picts then adopted their techniques. At first, this was just sporadic raiding, but it was the arrival of the Jutes, led by the charismatic warriors, Hengist and Horsa, which coalesced the easterners into one mighty invasion force, culminating in the defeat at Crecganford. They say, to kill a beast, cut off its head. Vortimer was able to kill Horsa, but his son Aesc and their king Hengist remain a force to be reckoned with, and now Hengist's son Octha has, we believe, landed in Caint.'

Urcicinius interrupted Arthwys.

'We appear to have lost contact with one of the council members, Cabrianus of Caint. Perhaps this warrior Octha is responsible?'

'That is likely, but it is their main force positioned in the centre of the Patria that we must first crush, the battle of Wippeds Fleot is just one victory, but its outcome is more important than perhaps you know, for we achieved our objective of destroying the bulk of the Saxon fleet in The Wash. Moreover, my northern commander, Prince Mordred, is now ready to secure the mouth of the Trent and the Humber, so our hands will be firmly around this beast's throat. We have yet to find a way to control the Thames estuary, though beyond Londinium, Riothames tells me that river is now secure. So, our clear objective is to destroy those Saxons that pose the greatest threat.'

Britu spoke up in support of his comrade. 'The Saxons hold the Great Forest with two mighty strongholds, currently watched over by a cohort under the command of an excellent young officer, Nataline. Your son, I believe?'

General Natalinus beamed at the mention of his son.

'If we are to achieve our objective, none must be allowed to escape,' Arthwys continued. 'The Trent is as broad as the Thames, and our scouts tell us there are still many boats to destroy.'

'Why are you so intent on destroying their boats? Surely, we want them to leave our shores and go back to where they came from,' asked a curious Pascent.

Britu replied candidly to his brother, 'They will never leave. Those boats will only be used to bring more warriors.'

'Once they are defeated and their trade with their former territories is undermined, the Patria will be less attractive to their foreign brethren,' added Arthwys, 'leaving this council with a most difficult question.'

Ambrosius was now intrigued. 'Which is what, Arthwys?'

'Partition. How do we partition the Patria to ensure peace? I used to think we should kill them all, and by God we will try, but in truth, this will not be possible. We must cede land. It will be less than they have stolen, and partition will enable our farmers to once more cultivate land and work right up to agreed borders without hindrance.'

'I see that you are a statesman as well as a soldier, Arthwys,' said Urcicinius. 'I will think on it.'

'But we can only achieve that, if we first win the war.'

Arthwys looked around.

'Are there any more questions?'

'Yes, I have one.' It was the bishop, who was stood by the head of the oak coffin. 'I hear that northern kings such as yourself maintain wizards and magicians at court, and I have also heard mention of a magic sword.'

The atmosphere suddenly became tense, and Arthwys' brow furrowed.

'It is all true, Vodinus, as are the tales of the fire-breathing dragons we ride into battle.'

A momentary stunned silence was followed by raucous laughter.

Arthwys continued. 'Fear and superstition are important weapons for us, so please, bishop, continue to spread these stories.'

The bishop stammered, 'I-I only repeat what I hear.'

Arthwys held up his hand to subdue the mirth. 'The North is different, in that we are not so keen for a return of the Romans, but we *are* devout Christians and do believe the Roman Church can provide justice and stability to the Patria.'

'Aye,' added Britu, with a twinkle on his eye, 'and every Saxon we kill is one less for you to baptise, your grace.'

Urcicinius was amused to see the bishop turn bright red. Vodinus had clearly misjudged the newly appointed high command and, the tribune reflected, perhaps, so had he. He could now see these men were deserving of his confidence and worthy successors to the dead hero before them.

The bishop recovered his posture. 'Let us proceed to the shrine of Saint Alban, lay Vortimer to rest and pray for our victory.'

The Victor Returns

Cambodunum

Sextilis 464

Farddy gently strummed his lyre whilst Gwen embroidered alongside him. His queen had taken to spending her days with her bard in his parents' house, preferring to stay out of the way of the busy goings-on in the hall, especially now the warriors had returned. Farddy had heard all about the victory at Wippeds Fleot from his brother. Not surprisingly, the atmosphere within the fort was joyful, though there was sadness for those who had not survived the battle, Vortimer in particular. Confidence was high, everyone was talking about the push south across the rivers into the Great Forest, but the king himself had not yet returned.

'My father says I must write songs about Arthwys, but it is difficult to conjure poetry from hearsay.'

Gwenhyfar laughed. 'Are you saying you would rather have witnessed his battles first-hand?'

The bard stopped strumming. 'That is precisely what I am saying.'

'But you are not a soldier, Farddy. The risk would be too great, and who would I pass my days with if you went to war?'

The young man silently cursed his club foot. His brother had returned a hero, even more so in the absence of the king, and although proud of Agiluf, Farddy found himself also a little jealous.

'That is true, but I can ride as well as any man. I could be Agiluf's shield bearer on his next adventure.'

'I shall forbid it,' said the queen petulantly, though Farddy knew she could not.

'Then I will seek the king's permission.'

'If he ever returns to Elfed.' The queen sighed, brow crinkling with concern. 'I really don't understand why Arthwys and Britu needed to meet with Ambrosius and Ames at Verulamium.'

'Agiluf says it was necessary, out of duty, now that Arthwys is appointed battle leader following the death of Vortimer.'

The queen sighed once more. 'This must be how it feels to be widowed.'

'You should not say such things; you could tempt fate.'

'I have felt this way for some time. Everyone believes it is such an honour to be his queen, to be wife to an illustrious hero, and in truth, I felt that way, too, at first… but I barely see him.'

'The king pays a heavy personal price to ensure the protection of his subjects.'

'As do I. I know I should fill my mind and my time with royal duties, but Igerna and your mother are so proficient that I feel I have little to contribute.'

'The boys need your guidance.'

'They don't listen to me, not now they are training in the king's military academy. In a few years, they will be fighting alongside him, and I will be fretting for their safety.'

Farddy cast around for something to lift her mood. 'How is your sister?'

'I long to visit her, but I'm told it would be inappropriate at this time.'

'Who told you that?'

'Igerna. She says I should remain here and await my husband.' Gwen looked glum.

'I'm sure Arthwys will return soon.'

'He will, but only to continue preparations for his war. Prince Mordred is most excited by the prospect.'

Farddy was not an admirer of the prince, finding his frequent visits to the queen discomforting. 'We have seen too much of him in the king's absence.'

'Farddy! I enjoy his company.'

'I find him menacing.'

The queen laughed. 'That is just his way. I have known him since we were children. Behind the mask is a sensitive man.'

'Really? Well, he frightens me. And why is he spending so much of his time with us here in Cambodunum?'

'He tells me there is great concern that the Saxons may counter-attack, making us a target.'

'Does he? Well, I will be interested to see if he continues to provide you with such detailed military briefings when the king returns.'

He had just looked down at his lyre, preparing to continue playing, when a lump of bread hit the back of his head. The queen looked flushed and defiant.

'You're supposed to be my friend!' she said, her tone playful.

Farddy grinned. 'Oh, but I am. I merely say what others see, my queen.'

He looked quizzically at Gwen when he heard a sudden commotion outside. She motioned him to go check on the cause of the disturbance. He made his way to the door with his shuffling gait and looked outside.

'Farddy, what is going on?'

Cheers and applause floated through the open doorway.

'Your husband has returned.'

'Oh, my Lord, look at me.' She stood, brushing threads off her robe and tousling her red hair. 'How do I look, Farddy?'

'As you always do, Gwen: beautiful.'

She brushed past him, heading toward the great hall.

*

Cian was surprised at how quickly Arthwys had summoned his court after his arrival. He hurried across to the great hall in the afternoon sunshine and joined the senior eques who were already filing through the door. The king sat waiting – together with his queen, their sons, Agiluf, staff and advisers – his countenance serious. What news could garner such solemnity?

When everyone was assembled, Merlinus nodded to Amabalis who stepped to the front and said a short prayer in Latin. He then bowed to the king and quickly rejoined the old seer. King Arthwys immediately began his address.

'I know that Lord Agiluf has already told you about our victory over the Saxons at Wippeds Fleot and of the sad death of King Vortimer. I will only add that we shall remain forever grateful to our cousin for his selfless duty and heroic stance against the heathens. Without his bravery over all these years, there would have been no victory and no patria left for us to reclaim. We in the North underestimated the Saxons thirst for conquest and left Vortimer to face the threat alone for too long. Our forebears considered them heathen savages that we might use for our own purposes, when in fact, they are a resourceful and clever people who recognised the opportunities open to them long before we appreciated the extent of their threat. I loathe them for what they have done to our lands and for how they have murdered and enslaved our people, but as warriors, they have earnt our respect. This war is not ended; it is only just begun. Our scouts tell us that Hengist is massing his warriors not fifty miles from here, and were it not for Prince Mordred's fierce reputation, I believe they would have attacked already.'

Arthwys nodded at Mordred, acknowledging his valued contribution.

'I have tasked King Britu with patrolling our recovered lands in the south-east of the Patria. That region was once peaceful farmland, but it is has been ravaged beyond recognition. It is a dangerous task we leave in his hands. Hengist and Aesc now hold all the tribes who occupy the Colonae in their thrall – those Germanic tribes our grandparents once trusted and traded with are now our enemy.'

Mordred interrupted. 'My king, the Angles of Linnuis have indicated they want no part of this. They have withdrawn their keels to the coast, and Freuleaf even sent his condolences to Queen Igerna on the death of your father.'

Arthwys turned to his mother. 'Is that so?'

'It is. Cian and I have corresponded with Freuleaf. He has made it clear he is keen to distance himself from Hengist's ambitions.'

'Can we trust him?' the king asked, his tone curious.

Cian now spoke up. 'Your great-grandfather appointed the Angles foederati, and they were awarded lands in the Colonae. Down the years, they have shown themselves worthy of our respect. Bryn and I met Freuleaf when he was a young man, and we believe him trustworthy.'

Mordred continued. 'He has left the mouth of the Trent open to us. We must be careful not to make war against tribes that seek peace with us. Many of my militia are German-speaking easterners who have no love for Hengist, but their skill as sailors is invaluable to us.'

The atmosphere in the great hall was thick with tension. A public challenge to the words of a king would usually be deserving of a stern rebuke, but Arthwys looked thoughtful rather than angry.

'Well said, Mordred. We must adapt and compromise when it is favourable to our objective.' Arthwys paused, gathering his thoughts. 'Other than my mother and Amabalis, who here has travelled beyond our shores?'

Mordred raised a hand.

'It seems you have something to say on every subject, Mordred,' Arthwys said, with a smile. 'Where have you visited?'

'I have raided the Gaels!'

The king laughed. 'I doubt they would have been very pleased to see you!' The entire hall now broke into laughter. 'Anyone else?' No one raised their hand. 'Yet, when we were part of the Empire, we travelled far and traded with the world, welcoming all manner of visitors and merchants to our cities. We have allowed ourselves to become hemmed in and isolated by our enemies, and we have been too afraid to look beyond our borders. I have come to believe that, with God's help, we can return to those days of peace and prosperity. But first, we must wipe our enemies from the face of the earth.'

'Is such annihilation possible, my king?' asked Cian, ever cautious. 'Their army and settlements have grown manyfold.'

'It is possible, with the help of Ambrosius Aurelianus.'

'Surely, he is just a Roman marooned on our island?' Mordred said, his contempt undisguised.

'Yet, he has never deserted the Patria. It is true he is the son of a deposed emperor, who escaped to our shores, and he ever watches Rome with intent, but his kingdom in the south would surprise you. The towns still function as markets, merchants still visit his many harbours, and his militia has developed into a tangible force.'

'Our people have rejected Roman ways. The Empire left us with little more than the ashes of their fire,' Mordred said.

'I appreciate that, and we have become excellent warriors out of the necessity to protect our people, but we cannot defeat the Saxons by ourselves. Ambrosius is the most powerful man in the Patria, and we recently marched a further thousand of his trained and equipped soldiers to Derventio.'

'So, at last we are ready for the final push?' asked Winnog.

'This is so, but now comes our greatest challenge – we must fight our way through the Great Forest and up the Trent.'

'Why does the most difficult task fall to us?' Cian asked. 'Our warriors will be fighting through marshes, rivers and dense forest.'

'It falls to us because we know this territory and it suits our style of fighting. There will be few pitched battles; the Saxons will favour ambush, for they fear our cavalry too much to meet us on open ground.' Arthwys turned to his marine commander. 'Mordred, it is time to seal off the Trent. The few remaining Saxon keels must not be allowed to escape. We will drive these heathens south and onto the waiting spears of Britu and Ambrosius.'

The room was silent, the prospect of further brutal battles weighing heavy. Igerna rose to her feet, still beautiful and poised, despite her age. Her long, grey hair, plaited for comfort, stood out in contrast against the black stola she still wore to honour her late husband. Her tone, when she spoke, was emphatic. 'I will address you one last time before I pass the reins to younger hands.' She smiled at Gwenhyfar. 'All my life, I have prayed to the Virgin Mary, and in times of hardship she has provided great comfort to me. As a little girl, I once thought I heard her say, *No matter the loss, be proud, Igerna*, and so I always have been. My mother died in Armorica giving birth to me, then my father, Conan, a prince of the Cornovii, died on a battlefield in Gaul. I was only four, but I was proud. My aunt, Sevira, adopted me and brought me to Viroconium where Vortigern ruled. He was cruel and sought to marry me to a brute. I resisted, and I was proud. My wonderful husband rescued me from that king's evil clutches then went to war to save the Patria. I was frightened but proud. His actions saved Vortimer and Ambrosius from certain death, men crucial to our recent victories, so I am proud. Now my son takes you all to war once more, and I remain proud, for it is clear to me that it has been my destiny to follow a path to this very moment. A moment prophesised by Myrddin, corroborated by Caledfwich and sanctified by the Virgin Mary Herself. Prepare yourselves for this war, paint your shields with Her likeness, for She will protect you. Now is our moment, and the Cymry will not falter.'

Respectful silence followed her impassioned speech. Cian's admiration and respect for Igerna had never been greater.

Arthwys looked to his mother with pride in his eyes. 'We will fight as Cymry but plan like Romans. We must ensure that our corn is harvested and our homes secure before we attack. Our supply routes must be protected to nourish what will be a sustained campaign in which all here must participate. Hengist has moved inland and masses his troops at Danum.'

Mordred stepped forward. 'The Saxon settlements at Ypwines Fleot are long deserted – we burnt them last year

– and the Episford and Axholme settlements are still fortified, but their warriors have moved into the protection of the Great Forest.'

'Hengist is responding to our involvement in this war. His plan must be to divide north from south, but our tactics seem to have confused him. Perhaps he faces food shortages now we have disrupted his supply routes. Mordred, your orders are to continue clearing the west bank of the Trent; kill everyone and burn everything.'

'I will need more men.'

'You will have them. We will station our army to face his, but we will not attack in the way he expects. Merlinus.'

'Yes, my king.'

'You will be in command of Cambodunum, and our sons will man the stockade. Mother and Bryn, you must turn this place into a huge kitchen and storehouse. Gwenhyfar, you will be responsible for feeding the army at the forward camp with the help of all our warriors' wives. Cian, you will command our retired eques, provisioning and protecting our supply routes.'

'Where are we setting up the forward camp?'

'Beyond the junction of the Ryknild by the Skell, at the small fort with the watchtower.' The king paused, his brow furrowed in thought. 'It is interesting that Hengist has positioned himself in this region. He must believe we are his greatest threat.'

Cian had no doubt that was his reason. 'My king, Hengist will know by now that it is you who leads the Cwmry army. He will be banking on your death as a swift means to undermine the whole campaign.'

He watched Arthwys grasp the hilt of his sword. Cian had heard it said that Caledfwich gripped the king's soul; there was certainly hatred in his eyes when he spoke.

'That is one Saxon I cannot wait to kill.'

*

Gwenhyfar had enjoyed every second of having her husband returned to their home, though she knew his visit would be brief. Their time together was so precious, and so she was pleasantly surprised when her request for a summer stroll along the riverbank had met with his approval. The warm evening was perfect for such an activity, and the wooded beck seemed a long way from the Saxon strife. The peaceful setting reminded her of earlier days when she had felt safe and loved. Sextilis was not the easiest month to follow the path, for the nettles were high and in flower, and the brambles overgrown, promising fruit, but the open pasture had been cropped by sheep.

'I can't remember the last time we walked here together.'

Arthwys seemed to have been lost in thought. 'Neither can I.'

'I used to come most days when the boys were small.'

Arthwys laughed. 'Good luck persuading them now; they have grown so much.'

'Yes, but they do look rather comical, dwarfed by their shields and spears.'

'That may be so, but a spear held above a stockade is a deterrent, no matter who holds it, and they are taking themselves seriously, already thinking of themselves as men.' Gwenhyfar reached for his hand which he grasped willingly. 'Forgive my absence, forgive my distraction – one day we will have the luxury of time.'

'It is all that I live for.'

They walked together in silence for a while.

'Gwen, I have seen a different world.'

'How do you mean?'

'From an early age, I was taught about Rome; I speak Latin and have studied their military manuals; I read their poetry. But neither my parents nor my grandparents benefitted from the Empire's security. Indeed, it was quite the opposite. Mordred summarised it perfectly: we are left with *the ashes of their fire*.'

'He speaks for many. The previous generations are understandably bitter, and many of our people consider the Empire's influence a malignant force. I know my father still feels that way.'

'But that is a narrow view hastened by isolation. What if our cities could rise from the ashes, and boatloads of Brigantes lead and silver ingots were once more sold across the world?'

'Surely, that is just a dream, Arthwys.'

'It seems so for us, but not for Ambrosius. The cities of the far south flourish – Roman buildings and sculptures survive; the cives are well-fed and industrious; their wives are educated and fashionable.'

Gwenhyfar stopped, pulling a face at her husband. 'I do my best.'

'That is not what I meant. You are a queen and look wonderful always. I was referring to the general condition of everyone within his kingdom. It is a marvel, and something I hope we can replicate.'

'The North has always been wild.'

'That is very true, but I'm not thinking solely of the North…'

'You have greater ambitions, husband?'

'Gwen, I am not just King of Elfed; I have become the most powerful general in the Patria. My army is now as large as a Roman legion.'

'Your army?'

'Yes. This is what fate has done to me, and it is why I must lead this offensive. Britu and Riothames follow my strategy, obey my orders.'

'Then it would be pointless to ask that you delay until spring?'

'That is not possible. The Saxons are reeling from their defeat, and we must capitalise on our gains, even though the rivers will flood and hamper our progress.'

Her husband was drifting away once more. They sat side by side on the trunk of a tree brought down by winter's gales, but she sensed his mind was already elsewhere. King Arthwys – the greatest general since Coel Hen, but not an attentive husband anymore. She thought to try to kiss him, but it felt too awkward, and the moment passed.

'Come, my king, we must prepare for your campaign.'

'Thank you, Gwen. I've really enjoyed our walk. We must do it again when I next come home.'

She had married the most driven man in Christendom, but where did it come from? Was it duty, ambition or torment? Perhaps it was all three rolled into a fury. She was sure, though, that he was no longer the young prince who had carried her down the mountain, his mind now too full of war. She would pray for him, probably the best thing she could do for her man. Arthwys would come home one day, and she would of course be waiting…

An Ambush Planned

Danum

Aprilis 465

Hengist and Aesc sheltered in a Roman house to the south of Danum. The strange images on the floors and walls of these old buildings frightened some in their tribe, but the old king had seen many such depictions on his raids into Wealas territory and knew them to have no power. A north wind blew hard, despite it being spring, and the rivers were still in flood. The camp-fire glowed and sparked as the wind whistled through the partially collapsed villa. Aesc casually studied the mosaic upon which he had chosen to sit. He decided the image looked half man, half horse.

'In the end, their gods did not protect them.'

Hengist lifted his head. He was tired and his body ached with an age he had lost track of long ago. How many years had he lived? So many that his son's children were now warriors themselves. His nephew Aesc had never seen these towns as they once were.

'For the Romans, that is true, but the Wealas have one powerful god who they readily give up their lives for. They may fear the pain of death but not death itself.'

'They have found their strength, uncle. They attack with vigour and purpose.'

'It is this young king, Arthwys, son of Mor. It is on his command that they have surrounded us and destroyed our keels.'

'The armies to the south are more hesitant, and our fortresses remain strong in that region.'

'They are awaiting their leader, but I will ensure they do not see him again. He wears a bearskin into battle, an easy target for my spear!'

'You think his attack will come soon?'

'Yes, as soon as the river levels drop. Before the floods, he came twice, testing our defences. He plans to cross into the forest, but his horses will be a hindrance. This forest has helped us in the past and it will again. We will ambush them when they are caught in the dense thorns.'

'Could it be that they will not come, that he just means to continue to starve us out?'

'I doubt that. Though it has been a miserable winter, the worst for some time, but we have hunted and fed ourselves, and we shall soon recover the fertile plains that Wipped farmed.'

'And Octha, has there been news of his whereabouts?'

'My son has landed in Caint where he fights the southern Wealas. Once I kill Arthwys, the Britons' resolve will fade. You and I will then join forces and destroy what remains of the Wealas force in the mid-lands. It will not be long before we are bathing in their blood and dividing up their treasure.'

Both men laughed.

'I shall return to the Heights with that message, uncle. Will we see you before summer?'

'Yes, I shall avenge your father and brother and bring the head of this irritating king with me as proof.'

The Battle in the Forest

Celyddon

Aprilis 466

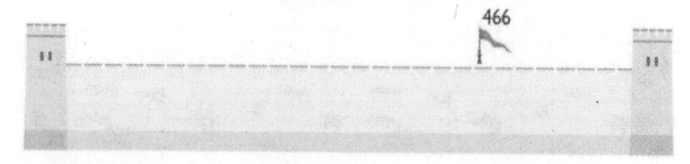

Agiluf carefully picked his way across the battlefield, leading his horse away from the corpses and discarded weapons. The king had tasked him with searching for Hengist, but it seemed the Saxon king had escaped with his retreating warriors. Smoke billowed in the fresh north-easterly wind, the dense briars in which the enemy had attempted to hide still smouldering. Mangled bodies littered the raised ground, whilst gore and blood mixed with the mud, but the smell of death was mercifully lost on the wind. Both Agiluf and his horse were matted crimson, his hands, arms and shoulders aching from the butchery. It had been their fiercest encounter yet, but Arthwys' tactics had carried the day.

The planning had begun many months before, when they had realised Hengist's army was larger than they had expected, making a frontal assault on his position likely to fail, especially as Arthwys' men would be fighting with their backs to the river. It was easy to see why Hengist had dug in there. He would have felt secure and confident of victory, but Arthwys had come up with an elaborate plan, one born from cunning and calling for patience. He had ordered that their forward camp by the Skell be festooned with flags and pennants and that there be constant activity to draw the attention of the Saxon scouts. Then over winter, Arthwys had twice marched his army to the ford across the Don as if planning to attack before returning to camp, seemingly discouraged by the rising floods.

Meanwhile, ten miles downstream, Mordred had been constructing a pontoon bridge. Though the Don was still in flood, the bridge was secure on both banks. The crossing in the dark had been perilous, but three turmae of cavalry and one thousand infantry had made it to the other bank. Back at the camp, Cian and Winnog had assembled every servant, woman and child so that they resembled an army from distant view, even Queen Gwenhyfar had stood with them. Arthwys and Agiluf had then proceeded to follow the river Bassas, where it ran along the edge of the black moor, bringing them behind the Saxon lines. The Lord God and good fortune had favoured them, for though the Saxons were twice their number, they were facing the wrong way and positioned behind great clumps of gorse and briar as their defence against cavalry. The surprise charge by three turmae had terrified the enemy, sending them into disarray. They had thrown themselves into the dense, thorny foliage where they fell prey to the spears of the infantry following swiftly behind the cavalry. Whilst the battle raged, a Saxon camp-fire had been used to set alight the dense briars. The fire had spread on the fresh spring winds, creating further panic and disarray. Realising the battle was lost, the surviving Saxons had run west toward the forest of Celyddon, territory that did not favour cavalry. There was no glory in unnecessary losses, so Agiluf had halted the rout at the treeline.

Looking around at the devastation that surrounded him, he shook his head. For years they had feared Hengist and his army of savages. Agiluf himself had experienced nightmares in which he was surrounded by powerful sword-slashing demons. But the wretches lying at his feet looked half-starved and nothing like the warriors he imagined capable of defeating the Britons time and again.

'Agiluf, Agiluf!' His brother's voice carried on the breeze as Blwchfardd rode his pony toward him.

'Be careful of the blades, Farddy. Stay there; I will come to you.' He mounted his horse, walking it carefully toward his waiting shield bearer. 'Have you come to witness the carnage?'

'Good God, no. It turns my stomach. I am sent by the king. He has summoned his commanders; we are to return to the forum at Danum.' Farddy's eyes were as wide as a drinking vessel, his face pale with shock as he looked around at the slaughter that surrounded him. 'Who are these hooded ghouls killing the wounded?'

'Booty collectors. They care not which side you fought for – best to stay on your pony.'

'This is a frightful sight for a bard.'

'Yes, the aftermath is always grim, Farddy.'

Agiluf did not interrupt his brother's stunned silence whilst they rode, allowing him to keep it until the old town loomed into view. As they rode into the forum, the king was stood waiting, surrounded by a group of eques. Agiluf leapt off his horse, leaving his brother to hold the reins, and strode toward Arthwys.

'Hengist is not amongst the dead.'

'I feared as much. He will be like a wounded animal now, and all the more dangerous for it. We cannot enter this forest on horseback; we must search for him on foot.'

'Aye, and we should not wait for him to build defences. I say we start out at dawn.'

'We will need every man who can carry a spear.'

'Where is Mordred?'

'Recovering his pontoons. It will be two days before he returns.'

'And where is Winnog?'

'I have already dispatched him with a turma to hold the Ryknild road. His orders are to stand his ground if the Saxons emerge from the forest.'

'They will not break cover.'

'That is my opinion, too. In better news, we have new recruits, Agiluf.'

Arthwys indicated several eques stood to one side.

Agiluf could not contain his surprise, when he recognised one of them. 'Is that Meirchiawn?'

'It is. Come, I will introduce you to his companions.'

They walked toward the men – their armour, mail and weapons glinting in the sunlight, in stark contrast to the battle-stained appearance of both Agiluf and his king.

'Agiluf!' Meirchiawn said, smiling. 'I have not seen you in years.'

Arthwys introduced the King of Reged's companions.

'This is Einion, King of Gwynedd, and this is his neighbour, Cunorius, King of Dyfed. They have brought a substantial number of armed men to join us.'

The men bowed respectfully to Agiluf.

He raised his eyebrows and cocked his head to the side. 'At the victory banquet, will these brave men eat only dessert?'

'A strange question, prefect.' Arthwys looked quizzically at Agiluf.

'Well, my king, they seem to have missed the meat!'

Arthwys stifled a grin. 'Yes, they may be late for the battle, but they are fresh and will show their mettle in the forest of Celyddon tomorrow.'

Einion added, 'We have sworn allegiance to your king, Lord Agiluf; you should not doubt our commitment nor our ability.'

'I do not doubt it, but if you had thought to join our cause sooner, brave King Vortimer might still be amongst us.'

'You are right to rebuke us, Lord Agiluf,' said Meirchiawn. 'We underestimated the Saxon threat, but we are here now to make amends as best we can.'

Agiluf bowed stiffly. He had no doubt that these men sought to gain favour now that Elfed's power was proven without doubt. They would be hoping that allegiance and participation might secure their own kingdoms from future threat from this new power on their borders. There was little point in labouring his distrust though, for whatever their motives and despite their tardiness, Arthwys seemed pleased with their support.

'You are all welcome, but there is no time to waste. Go prepare your men, for we will enter the forest at dawn.'

The three kings left to rejoin their warband. Arthwys turned to his friend.

'Are you ready for the morrow? It will be close combat, a dangerous prospect.'

'But necessary. We must not let Hengist slip through our fingers, my king.'

'Agreed. It is unfortunate Mordred is not here. I do not want him surprised by the presence of his brother – we must send a messenger to inform him.'

'I will see to it, my king. Mordred has fought with us from the start, earning our respect and gratitude. We should do our best to assure him that his brother's late arrival to the fray does not usurp his position at your court.'

'Quite so, but I also do not want him using this as an opportunity to settle his claims in respect of Reged.'

'Better we focus on the morrow for now. Our men need to prepare themselves for a most difficult encounter, and we must consider your personal security, my king. I fear you are the Saxon's main target.'

'Caledfwich will protect me.'

*

The wolves of the Great Forest had howled all night – perhaps unaccustomed to so many humans in their domain, perhaps gorging on the dead. Agiluf had slept fitfully but comforted himself with the thought that Hengist was unlikely to have slept at all. The men of Elfed were trained for forest combat, though the fighting would be brutal. He had tried to imagine what tactics the enemy might adopt but kept coming back to the same conclusion – this would be a fight to the death, for the Saxons had no way to escape.

The Elfed scouts had bravely ventured into the forest overnight and identified the enemy's position. They were encamped on higher ground at a bend in the river, surrounded by dense forest. Arthwys' plan was to advance in two lines, spearmen to the fore followed by eques and archers. The forest foliage had yet to burst forth, so leaves would not obscure their view, but the wind had dropped, giving rise to a ground mist. Agiluf had placed some cavalry at each side, expecting the Saxons to attempt to get behind their lines. The newly arrived warriors bolstered the numbers, their clean and shiny appearance making them stand out from those around them. The sun was low in the sky but at their backs as they advanced.

They encountered no traps or ambushes, since the Saxons had had insufficient time to prepare. When it became evident that the enemy had retreated some distance into the forest, Agiluf suspected they planned a flanking manoeuvre.

Front and centre suddenly came under a hail of spears and rocks, then the Saxons turned and ran.

'They intend for us to follow,' said Arthwys, 'but we shall continue at walking pace.'

The front line was ordered to hold ground whilst the archers attempted to pick off the fleeing warriors.

'I wager they go for the left flank next,' said Agiluf.

'I'll take it,' said Arthwys, as they continued their slow advance.

Sure enough, the enemy's next wave of missiles peppered the left wing of their line. Once again, the Saxons fled under a hail of arrows.

'Hengist tries to manoeuvre us toward the river,' said Agiluf. 'There may yet be another attack on our left.'

As predicted, spears and rocks were flung out of the trees once more from the left, and again, the archers responded, but now the shields and spears of the main body of the Saxons had come into view.

Arthwys signalled to hold the advance.

'They look fewer than we expected, but they have formed a circle; they seem to fear an attack from all sides.' Arthwys put on his helmet and battle bearskin. 'What would you do next in his position?' he asked Agiluf.

His prefect did not mince his words. 'Kill you! There is nothing else left for them. Their shield wall will open and disgorge an attack on the centre.'

'Do you think Hengist will lead the charge?'

'I do. You must drop back behind the eques, my king.'

'No, let us tempt him. If Hengist is killed or captured, the remaining Saxons will lose heart. Continue the advance but bunch the men closer; send your cavalry to their rear.'

Agiluf relayed the orders which were swiftly obeyed. The advance continued. At twenty paces, the Elfed archers loosed their final arrows before drawing their swords, but no more spears appeared from behind the Saxons' shields – all were now needed for the bloody fight to come.

It was as if Agiluf had read Hengist's mind, for the Saxon shield wall suddenly opened, and the old Saxon king appeared screaming orders and swinging his sword, his most ferocious warriors charging forth with him.

'Let the first men through, then close our wall,' yelled Arthwys.

The front line stood aside, leaving Arthwys and Agiluf facing several fierce Saxons before the line closed up again. Einion closed in to help Agiluf engage and cut down the warriors, leaving Arthwys to face Hengist.

Parrying the old king's first blow with his shield, Arthwys turned, bringing Caledfwich down on Hengist's back with such force that the old warrior stumbled forward, Arthwys did not hesitate, skewering the Saxon king as he tried to climb to his feet. Then with the mightiest blow Agiluf had ever seen, Arthwys completely severed Hengist's head, leaving a twitching corpse gushing blood.

'Put his head on a spear and hold it high,' shouted Arthwys. Einion grabbed a spear and obeyed the Elfed king. 'Now advance.'

Seeing their king's head held high, the Saxon warriors dropped their guard. Their shield wall collapsed, and they were soon overrun. By midday, every Saxon lay dead. The Elfed army gathered around their king, steam rising from their gore-covered bodies. Arthwys raised his voice for all to hear.

'So, we *can* beat them in battle. This victory is for Vortigern, Catigern and Vortimer. Hengist is dead, but we still have to retake the Colonae and the mid-lands if we are to make the Patria safe once more. We cannot turn back. We will wash, rest and feast in Danum. We can even send for our womenfolk, but we are not returning to Elfed.'

'Not ever?' asked a young soldier in the crowd.

The steaming throng turned to look at the impertinent young warrior. Arthwys roared with laughter, prompting his men to join in.

'Not yet, brave soldier. What is your concern?'

'It is my mother, King Arthwys. She is unwell.'

'Anyone who wishes to visit home, may do so, but I will expect you back in Danum in five days. Do you know Merlinus and my sister Morgaine?'

'I do, great king.'

'Tell them that, upon my instruction, they are to care for your mother whilst you fight for your king.'

'You are a saint! May God always protect you.'

'God sent you to protect me. What is your name?'

'Alwyn.'

'Five days, Alwyn, don't forget. I will be looking out for you.'

*

Danum had been a ruin even before it suffered years of Saxon occupation, but an old granary had been cleared to provide a suitable location for the feast of celebration. Though relief amongst the Elfed army was immense, it was even greater amongst the people of Elfed who had travelled to join the victors of Celyddon. Farddy was in high demand, his fingers sore from plucking the strings of his lyre, his voice hoarse from song, which seemed to amuse his brother.

'Another song, Farddy,' Agiluf teased every time he passed him. Agiluf had joined the two western kings in drinking mead all day; they were all in fine spirits.

Only one eques was missing – Mordred. He was still marshalling his boats and pontoons on the Humber estuary. Bryn had been tirelessly cooking and producing food in difficult conditions ever since the entire camp had moved up from the Skell. Igerna and Gwenhyfar were co-ordinating a mass of servants ensuring everyone inside the old Roman walls had food and drink. Having so much purpose was good for Gwen, and she seemed happier than Farddy could ever recall, and as a consequence, she looked ravishingly beautiful.

King Arthwys, Cian and Meirchiawn had been in discussion for hours, their consumption of mead more measured than their subjects'. He was excited to know what they were planning next, but for now, he was content to let the sweet taste of victory mix perfectly with the honey-infused mead, which he drank in large amounts on the pretence it was helping his voice.

A Compromise Agreed

Danum

Aprilis 466

The mouth of the Trent was now under his control, and his fleet was moored at Rither Gabail. Every Saxon settlement in the region had been cleared and burnt. Alongside King Arthwys, Mordred's reputation had grown rapidly, but his men were not all Cymry. Many were eastern mercenaries, prepared to fight for the man they had nicknamed Dod, meaning 'death' in their language.

Originally tasked with recovering Elfed territory across the Ouse, Mordred had been confronted by a group of sailors recently abandoned by their Gaini masters. They were merchants who no longer had anything to sell, though they still had families to protect. Their leader, Ulf, was a thoughtful, well-connected giant of a man who burnt with a sense of injustice and spoke a reasonable amount of Latin. Not only had his people been left to fend for themselves, but they had then been attacked by Hengist's Jutes who had mistaken them for Britons, and it had been the Britons of Eboracum who had come to Ulf's assistance. With Elfed's backing, Mordred had been quick to offer Ulf not only pay but also a share of the booty.

Word had spread quickly, and sailors from around the river region had joined them. For Ulf, revenge was a greater incentive than pay, because Hengist had killed his brother. Like their leader, many of his men had taken local wives – Britons from the Parisi tribe – so Hengist's call for Saxon unity meant nothing to them, particularly since it had been the Jute's selfish ambitions that had destroyed their merchant livelihoods in the first place.

Agiluf's messenger had brought the good news about victory at Danum but also the troubling news that Mordred's brother had arrived with a small force to fight alongside Arthwys. Mordred watched his Angle sailors expertly sculling their shallow-draft boat upstream in the direction of Danum. He would be facing his brother soon, but he could not decide how the encounter should go. Their last meeting had been at his brother's wedding where Mordred had been treated with disdain and ostracised. Since that time, there had been no contact with his brother, not even after the death of their father. Mordred swallowed hard, pushing away the memory he wished he could forget. There had been no settlement, no recognition, and he knew his brother would be anxious, particularly now Mordred's reputation as a warrior and commander must have reached his ears. Meirchiawn would know that his brother was entitled to a share of Reged, and by coming to Arthwys' court, Mordred concluded Meirchiawn must intend to confront him on the matter. The old anger he had set aside whilst he fought for Arthwys, immersed in the gratifying slaughter of Saxons, was growing inside him once more. But everything had changed since that anger had first taken root. He had an offer of recovered lands for his contribution, and he was a warlord in his own right. Mordred sensed Meirchiawn was scared. The flat horizon offered Mordred no clue as to how close to Danum they were, but Ulf knew the meandering Don well. He turned to his commander.

'We arrive soon.'

Mordred nodded. The years of warfare had brought a maturity that tempered his rage, and he had learnt strategic thinking from Arthwys. He would not rush in and kill his brother, even though he had pictured it in his mind... and yearned for the opportunity. No, he would provoke him with subtlety, but always with one eye on Arthwys' intentions. His oath to the king had been the rudder by which he had expertly steered all these years. Arthwys was invariably several steps ahead of them all, and his lead was the one to follow. Mordred forced his thoughts away from the imminent encounter.

Gwenhyfar, the only woman he had ever loved – she too would be at Danum, being dutiful and beautiful. He closed his eyes and pictured her waiting at the riverside for him to arrive. He was sure she felt the same about him, and Arthwys might yet fall in battle.

'Danum.'

Ulf's voice intruded on his reverie, and Mordred opened his eyes. It was not the queen stood on the quayside waiting, but the king himself. His scouts must have seen their boat approaching.

'Welcome, Mordred. Welcome, Ulf. There has been a great victory; Hengist is dead.'

Mordred stepped ashore and bowed dutifully. Ulf beamed, showing several black and missing teeth.

Arthwys now spoke in Latin. 'Ulf, bring your brave men to the fort. There is meat, drink and friendship.'

The large man nodded and turned to speak to his compatriots.

'Friendship you say, sire?' said Mordred.

Arthwys needed no further prompting to detect the source of Mordred's apprehension, and his response was characteristically direct. 'Yes, friendship. Cian and I have conducted robust discussions with your brother on your behalf; we believe we have a solution to the dispute over your succession… *King Mordred.*'

The warrior's heart lifted. 'I expected a bloody confrontation.'

'I feared it too, but disarm yourself, for there shall be none today.'

Arthwys led his best warrior through the forum toward the granary. Cheers and applause got louder, the closer they came.

'This is a great day, and it is by no means over.'

Mordred caught a glimpse of Gwen in the distance, carrying beer for the men like a tavern maid, as he took off his sword, placing it alongside the king's renowned weapon. As the guards opened the door to the granary, the pungent tang of mead reached his nostrils, as welcoming as Arthwys had promised. But despite the convivial atmosphere, the great barn fell silent when Mordred entered, though he sensed it was more in awe than fear. His resentment and jealousy cleared to allow him to appreciate the unexpected high regard of the warriors of Elfed. Then his attention was drawn to the far corner where his brother sat stiffly next to Cian. *Shall I glare or smile?* He glared; he could not help himself.

'Sit by me, Mordred,' Arthwys said, not hiding his intention to keep the brothers apart. A jug of mead was thrust into Mordred's hand.

'We drink to victory,' said Cian, 'which would not have been possible without you, King Mordred.'

Mordred fixed his brother with a stare, then turned to Arthwys. 'King of Nothing, Lord of Nowhere. What is this talk?'

'Cian will explain. My father, your uncle – himself a second son – trusted Cian's wisdom; together they rebuilt Elfed.'

Other than Arthwys, there were only two men in Elfed who Mordred considered of any importance. Cian, who he respected not only as an experienced warrior but also as an intelligent bard. And Merlinus, who he feared and avoided. Much to his relief, the latter must have remained in Cambodunum, for he was not in evidence.

Cian took a swig of mead and cleared his throat, preparing for a lengthy oratory.

'Succession amongst princes often leads to contention. Primogeniture has never been accepted by the Cymry, and the tradition of our tribe is to split the territory between sons. That accepted, it is always the youngest son who is expected to carve out new frontiers, the seat of power usually passing to the eldest son, who is more often than not the best warrior.' Meirchiawn shifted uncomfortably on the trestle bench, avoiding eye contact with his brother as Cian continued. 'Your own fathers split Reged, north and south, with Banna passing to Gorwst. I remember how tense that moment was, but King Coel was wise and left clear instruction for his ministers to work with. Gorwst's untimely death by murder deprived us of any real clarity on his intentions, but a compromise must be accepted if we are to avoid civil war following this Saxon war.' Meirchiawn still avoided eye contact, and Mordred knew why. 'In gratitude for his loyalty, Arthwys offers Mordred a share of his territory to be determined when Reged has acknowledged Mordred's right to an inheritance and prescribed a region.'

Mordred nodded at Arthwys, glad that their agreement was being confirmed.

Now Meirchiawn raised his head. 'We buried Father without you brother, and now our mother has died too.'

Mordred remained impassive, saying nothing, though his pulse raced, and he clenched his fists under the table.

Arthwys intervened. 'Speak only of the arrangements, King Meirchiawn; this is not the time for rebuke.'

'As Mordred knows, our father was not a raider. What little treasure he held at his death was split in two,' said Meirchiawn. He turned to Mordred. 'Your share awaits you at Banna.'

'And which lands are to be given to Mordred?'

'He is to inherit Bryneich from the Tyne to the Tweed.'

'Then I shall award him the lands from the Tees to the Tyne.'

'King of Bryneich – how does that sound, Mordred? You are king of a territory equal to Reged and Elfed.'

Mordred's mind was racing. It was a wild area and close to the Picts, but much more territory than he had expected.

'There are conditions,' Cian continued. 'As a Coeling, you must swear never to threaten Reged or Elfed, and you must, upon oath, defend the eastern shores and northern border.'

Mordred was aware of Arthwys watching him carefully.

'King Lott of the Gododdin will be unsettled by this,' said Arthwys, 'but he will receive our joint declaration that we will not threaten his territory, and that he may continue to look upon us all as allies.'

Mordred spoke slowly, desperately trying to control his voice and his emotions. 'So, where do you propose I establish my seat of power?'

Arthwys smiled at his cousin.

'Close to the frontier, somewhere your seafaring skills will be to your advantage. I believe there is a stronghold known as Din Guarie – it is a rock much like the one King Lott likes to sit upon!'

Arthwys and Cian laughed, and they all joined in. More mead arrived, this time brought by the queen.

'Mordy!' she exclaimed. 'You're laughing!'

'I am, my lady. I have just become a king, and now I shall need a queen.'

Gwen forced a smile. 'Why so?'

'To sit by me on my rock and stare back at King Lott.'

This amused his peers even more, the humour diffusing the earlier tension. Now the overriding relief of agreement had calmed his anger, it was time for him to ask the burning question. He turned to Meirchiawn.

'How did Mother die?'

'A harsh winter and the grippe. She was buried by your old friends, the Novantae.'

'God rest her troubled soul. Have you visited her grave?'

'Not yet, but when you come to Banna, perhaps we can visit our parents' gravesides together in a gesture of unity.'

Mordred felt a shiver run through him at the thought of standing at his father's graveside. 'Yes, one day,' he said, before turning back to the group. 'But Arthwys, do tell, what is our next objective?'

The king's face became serious. 'There are still scores to settle in the Colonae, and we cannot tolerate having our enemies at our back. Those rebellious easterners on the east bank of the Trent have played us for fools for too long, and now they must be made to pay. Fortress Gainnion is our next objective. Will your pontoons stretch across the Trent, Mordred?'

'Ulf will enjoy the challenge. And the Gaini will struggle to fight, since they are buckled under the weight of their gold and silver.'

Cian looked toward his increasingly confident king. 'We must not unsettle our Angle allies.'

'If they continue to not raise arms against us, we can accommodate their interests. But Lindum must be liberated, so we may visit the shrines of Julius and Aaron once more – this is a commitment I have made to the Lord Himself.'

Cian nodded. 'The net is closing, but we should not become complacent. The Saxons still hold mighty forts in the mid-lands, and Aesc is a renowned warrior.'

'With the Gaini subdued, there will be no escape down the Trent,' said Mordred.

'Exactly. I see you understand the plan – each step is as important as the next.'

'Will you excuse me, sire, nature calls after my long boat trip.'

Mordred headed for the door, where he inhaled the fresh spring air, cooler now evening was fast approaching. In the half-light, he saw the queen, busy and beautiful, moving from camp-fire to camp-fire, and he hid round the corner of a collapsed wall. As she passed, he jumped out, pressed a finger to his lips and pulled her around the corner.

'Gwen, is my satchel still safe?'

'It is in the king's treasury.'

'Will you protect it for me?'

'Of course, Mordy.'

He pulled her closer; he could feel her body through her light cotton toga, his excitement building.

'A kiss for the King of Bryneich?'

She slapped him hard across his face, but he did not release his grip. She wriggled partially free and slapped him again.

'My husband will kill you.'

'He will not.'

'Then ask again when you are sober! Now go, before I scream.'

He was sober, but certainly, he would ask again. He released her and watched her run toward the granary.

An Emperor for the West

Constantinople

Martius 467

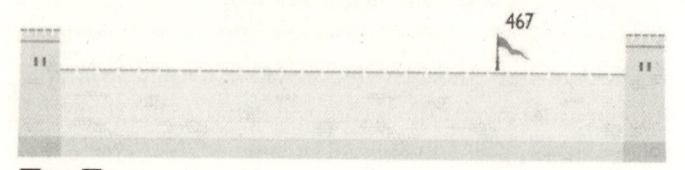

Marcellinus' visit to his family home in Salona had been far too short, but when you were one of the Empire's most senior generals, duty always came first, especially when you were not just a Roman general but also ruler of Dalmatia. He had painstakingly steered his province away from the corrupt and declining western Empire, whilst being careful not to thrust himself into the arms of the eastern Emperor, Leo, maintaining a respectable distance from the scheming German patrician, Aspar. He was confident that Leo acknowledged the prowess of his forces and knew that this emperor understood there was a price to pay for military might. Marcellinus would be comfortable supporting the eastern Empire particularly if it would benefit his old friend and fellow student Anthemius. It was not easy balancing on the tightrope between East and West, but he aimed to always take those actions he believed to be in the best interests of the Empire as a whole. To his mind, preserving Romanitas was more important than self-interest or personal gain. As for religion, he remained unconvinced by Christianity, although he recognised the power and influence of the Church.

He had been back in Salona only a week when he had received the invitation to attend the senate. What had prompted this summons? It was hard to fathom which of the Empire's many pressing woes Emperor Leo might need his help to resolve. One thing was certain, if Leo was summoning a general of Marcellinus' standing, he must be considering going to war.

Obeying the summons, which included an invitation to bring his family, Marcellinus and his entourage had followed the Via Egnatia to Constantinople, eventually approaching the city from the west. The soldier in him couldn't fail to admire New Rome's defences and the impressive vista they presented on the western approach to the city. The road they had taken was in such poor condition it might break axles, but it was safe from bandits. In better times, he would have considered sailing, but the sea was full of Vandal pirates now. It had taken six days to ride this far, though his family were following rather more slowly, probably now two days behind him. But even though he could already see the imposing white Walls of Theodosius with the Hippodrome beyond glinting in the sun, experience told him it would be several hours before they reached the Golden Gate, the magnificent main entrance to the great city. Salona, his capital city, was almost as old as Rome, its architecture betraying the classical influences of Greek culture. In contrast, Constantinople was big, brash and vulgar. Eastern influence added an exotic dimension to everything, particularly the food, its enticing scent reaching them on the air, even from this distance. The road thronged with people, and he could see why it was widely thought the city's population now equalled that of Rome. However, these inhabitants of Constantinople exuded a confidence that had abandoned Rome. This city had never been sacked, the walls never breached. Romanitas was alive and well but a long way from its birth mother.

With so much to think about, the rest of Marcellinus' journey passed quickly. The sentries at the Golden Gate had been briefed to expect his arrival, so his entourage passed easily through the impregnable defences. When they reached the walls of Constantinople, they entered the thronging city beyond. The atmosphere here always lifted his spirits. He was exhilarated by the pervading air of expectation, in marked contrast to the pervading fear that consumed the halls of power in Rome, that city seeming to sense its own decline. As a guest of the Emperor, he would be staying close by the Hippodrome, adjacent to the Emperor's own palace. Anthemius had arranged everything, and Marcellinus looked forward to a convivial and instructive meeting with his friend later. No doubt, the Emperor would expect his audience tomorrow, giving Anthemius time to brief Marcellinus first and hopefully avoid any surprises. Not that such a thing was entirely avoidable with Leo – he was a mercurial character who had not been slow to find his own feet after initially relying on Aspar, his predecessor's magister militum. It had been generally expected that Anthemius would be Emperor Marcian's successor, but Aspar had used his military influence to appoint Leo, one of his own officers. Aspar's intent had been transparent; he had expected to influence his grateful protégé, but Leo had progressively outgrown his old commander, acquiring a taste for supreme power whilst keeping a wary eye on Anthemius, now considered his rival.

Marcellinus cleared his mind. He would discover his fate soon enough, when he met with Anthemius in one of the palace gardens where spies would not overhear their frank exchange.

*

Marcellinus waited in the gardens of the Palace of Antiochos. The sweet smell of plant life hanging on the sea air was a welcome change from the dust of the Via Egnatia. Anthemius strode purposefully into the garden. Elegant to the highest degree, he wore no military uniform, only the toga of a patrician. It was an evening to relax, so Marcellinus had dressed similarly. Anthemius was a powerfully built Greek in his late thirties. As boys, they had studied together in Alexandria, and they had both proved themselves in battle time and again. Marcellinus was the son of noble parents from Illyricum, whereas Anthemius had been born to well-connected parents in Constantinople who had successfully married him to Emperor Marcian's daughter, Marcia, ensuring a glittering career, their friendship never complicated with rivalry.

'I hope your journey was not too arduous?' said Anthemius.

Marcellinus stood and embraced his friend. 'Any discomfort was more than diluted by my burning curiosity!'

They both laughed.

'I have much to disclose, and we have much to discuss. Please sit over here with me. I have ordered refreshment.'

'So, what are we facing? War with the Persians or the Vandals? It cannot be the Huns, because we've only just beaten them!'

Anthemius smiled. 'No, nothing so simple. Leo believes he has arrived at a solution for nothing less than the reunification of the entire Empire!'

'Quite an ambition! I would say, quite an impossible one. The Empire has never been so fractured. The West is finished, dominated by self-interested barbarians who give themselves Imperial titles, yet discard every virtue and ignore every law. The essence of the Empire is lost. What does Aspar think of this proposal?'

'He is old now and lacks imagination. Aspar seems to shy away from any confrontation with the Vandal Geiseric.'

'Both East and West would do well to be rid of Geiseric and his dominance of the sea.'

'You are right, but our first priority is the matter of the western Emperor.'

'It seems to me that General Ricimer has no intention of appointing a successor. No one knows why he poisoned his puppet emperor, Libius Severus, and now Rome is lost. The senate is too scared to move against him for fear it would open the door to Euric and his Visigoths in the west or Geiseric with his Vandals to the south.'

'That is the conundrum, but Ricimer knows he will not solve a thing by sitting still, and his position will just grow weaker by the day if he doesn't address these threats.'

The wine and water arrived, and both men waited for the servants to depart before continuing their conversation.

'Where is this leading, Anthemius? You are fully aware of my loyalties and know I would gladly run my sword through Ricimer. The execution of Emperor Majorian was a disgrace. If only Leo and Aspar had supported his worthy attempts to recover Gaul and Africa, then perhaps we would be holding a different discussion now.'

Anthemius grimaced. 'The fates blow us this way and that. I believe, if Leo was sat with us here on equal terms, he would agree with your assessment of his failure, but may I suggest you do not remind him of this tomorrow!'

'I do not sit on your senate or participate in your military decisions, so it is not my place to make such a comment.'

'Leo is on amiable terms with Dalmatia, is that not so?'

'We are more aligned than ever before.'

'Well, I can tell you there are many others with whom he is on good diplomatic terms who share our opinions.'

Marcellinus was well aware of the mounting disquiet within the West, but he still did not know what the Emperor was planning. 'Anthemius, I am waiting. I think you have softened me up sufficiently to hear Leo's proposal.'

His friend paused. 'The Emperor of the East wishes to appoint me Emperor of the West, and he wishes you to become my magister peditum and accompany me to Rome.'

Marcellinus was taken aback. 'That would be a great honour for us both, but surely, Ricimer will resist such a bold move.'

'It is he who has contacted Leo for suggestions, a strong indicator that he is aware of the precariousness of his position.'

'We know he is not to be trusted, but much like his forerunner, Aetius, he will have a more accurate reading on his fellow barbarians than us.'

'Left to its own devices, Rome could easily fall to Geiseric who would doubtless appoint Olybrius as his puppet. If that occurs, we will face an empire of barbarians. Perhaps a compromise with Ricimer is our only option?'

'That is one view, but surely we have superior ambition than simply propping up the least offensive barbarian? Our objective must be total recovery of the western Empire. Tell me more about these allies of Romanitas, who you believe we can look to for assistance.'

'You are but one in a network of families in the regions who may rally to help eliminate barbarian domination of the western Empire. Aegidius of the Syagrii, in particular, despises Ricimer, and his aid, Count Paulus, regularly corresponds with Leo. Ecdicius, son of Avitus, defends Arvernis from Euric and his Visigoths. I have even heard that Aurelianus, son of the betrayed Sebastianus, waits brooding with an army, ready to cross from Britannia.'

Marcellinus pondered briefly. 'I will accept this honour, but be cautious of these families you mention – they have divergent interests and their own regional issues.'

'Caused mainly by barbarians.'

Marcellinus laughed. 'And they are all Christians.'

Anthemius looked puzzled. 'Why is that a disadvantage?'

'The barbarian elites now share the Christian religion, making the bishops of the West impotent when it comes to war – it has become a dilemma for the devout.'

'Perhaps, but both you and I know there is no better candidate for their so-called Antichrist than Geiseric.'

Marcellinus laughed. 'I think Ricimer is competition for that role!'

A Report of Many Battles

Cambodunum

Maius 467

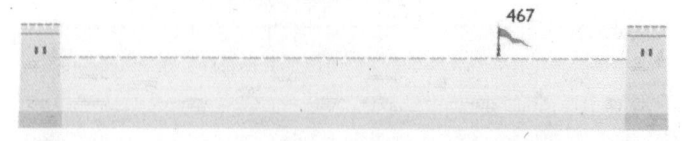

It was now a full year since Cian had last seen his sons. Both had left to fight the Saxons alongside their king, and only brief dispatches from Arthwys himself kept Cian informed of the campaign's continuing success. He knew Agiluf and Farddy were still alive but longed to hear of their adventures. His initial fears of a Saxon counter-attack against Elfed had long passed, and the atmosphere amongst those left behind in the fort who looked after the crops and animals was relaxed. Many of the boys who had been charged with military duties were growing into men and becoming increasingly frustrated that they were not at the king's side, but with the help of other veterans, Cian kept them to their duties and satisfied their martial aspirations by leading them on the necessary security patrols.

Arthwys' eldest son, Eliffer, was now old enough to face the enemy and, like his father, a very capable warrior, but Pabo, only just fourteen, had found solace in study and religion, spending most of his time with Amabilis and Merlinus, who both held him in high regard. They were fine boys, though very different from one another, and yet too young to feel the weight of Elfed on their shoulders. Each would have a political role to play soon enough, particularly if Arthwys continued to increase his lands. Their father's perpetual absence had left their training and education to the rest of the royal household. As a warrior himself, Cian had found more in common with Eliffer, whereas Merlinus enjoyed Pabo's shared interests in reading, religion and healing.

Cian's musings were interrupted when he saw a young soldier running toward him from the gate.

'My lord, a train of wagons is approaching. I think it is your son who leads them.'

'Agiluf?'

'No, my lord, it's Blwchfardd. I'm sure of it.'

Cian waited for the arrival of the lumbering cattle-drawn carts. They made slow but steady progress as they came through the gate, but they did not stop there, continuing instead toward the king's timber hall.

Cian joined the procession and walked alongside his son. There were five wagons in total, each with a driver and an armed guard and pulled by two oxen; all were carrying heavy crates.

'Good to see you, Farddy. What have you here?'

'Father, it has been a slow journey, for we carry the king's treasure. I have so much to tell you, but first, can you arrange for the treasury to be opened. I cannot relax until this is all under lock and key.'

'Of course. Queen Igerna has the key. Wait, whilst I seek her out.'

Cian quickly found the key and watched as the soldiers unloaded the crates and placed them in the small dark treasury. After the work was complete, he ensured the door was properly locked. His son was sweating from the effort, now issuing orders to his men.

'Alwyn, take the first watch. I shall draft some trustworthy locals to help with the guarding of the treasury.'

'Yes, optio.'

'Optio, is it now?' Cian asked, smiling.

'Yes, I have been working as secretary to Arthwys. Alwyn is to guard the treasure until the king returns to divide it amongst those he has promised to share it with. The rest of us must leave tomorrow to return to Derventio.'

'Arthwys has reached Derventio?'

'There have been many battles, but the most important is imminent. I will tell everything after I have billeted these men and made arrangements for tomorrow. I need to swap these oxen for horses!'

*

Bryn was delighted to see her son. She had fussed over him, washed him, fed him and made him change out of his uniform so she could wash and dry it overnight. Farddy had an important message to deliver to Arthwys' family, so she wanted him to look his best.

Cian had watched over her intense activity with amazement, thinking Bryn was ever like a whirlwind that never stopped. He also observed Farddy, realising it was more than just his son's appearance that had transformed. In earning the respect of both the king and his men, Farddy had also, and perhaps most importantly of all, gained greater self-respect. As the son of a noble, he had always been indulged and supported, but until now, he had found little purpose beyond providing amusing entertainment. Experience had taught Cian that a true bard had to be on the field of battle. It was not enough to imagine encounters – the slaughter and loss had to be witnessed first-hand. He watched his son walk, still hobbling from his club foot, toward the king's hall. Yes, he still moved with the same old gait, but he seemed taller, moving with invigorated purpose and determination. The lad's new role might see him rise to the prominence Cian had always hoped for him, and he felt excited for his son.

He caught up to Farddy, and they walked together into the hall where the royal family and their closest advisers sat waiting. If Farddy was nervous, he gave no sign. Cian took his place next to Queen Igerna who was sat to the left of Queen Gwenhyfar and her two boys. To the right, Winnog and Merlinus were sat with the priest, Amabilis, who stepped forward to say a short prayer and then sat back down.

'Queens Gwenhyfar and Igerna, princes, lords and priests, I bring a message from the king.'

'Welcome, Farddy. Have you brought your lyre?' Gwenhyfar's light-hearted question did not chime well with the occasion, but the target of her jest deftly rescued her.

'My queen, I *am* here to sing the king's praises, but his achievements have reached such great heights that no song of mine could do them justice.' The court expressed their delight at his clever reply, and he continued. 'There have been three significant victories of which I will tell the detail, but the biggest battles are yet to come. The kings of the Britons have surrounded an area of hills and forest where the main Saxon army is fortified in two strongholds. Victory is by no means certain. Ambrosius himself is in attendance with his son Riothames. King Britu has recovered Corieltauvorum to the south of the Great Forest, his reports of its devastation a damning indictment of the vile pagans' cruelty.

'As secretary to King Arthwys, I am instructed first to request that you, Eliffer, prepare to accompany me to the battlefront in the morning, and secondly, to charge you, Pabo, with the protection of the king's treasure.' Both boys looked excited to be included in their father's campaign, at last. 'I have brought with me Alwyn, a trusted soldier, who will report to your command—'

'Is there no message for me?' Gwenhyfar interrupted.

'Only that the king will return once the enemy is defeated.'

Cian saw Gwen's eyes fill with disappointment, whilst by contrast, Igerna beamed with pride.

'Tell us about the victories, Farddy,' said Igerna.

'A great many easterners have found common cause with the Saxons; the whole region bristles with enemy spears. One such tribe is the Gaini, who have many times masqueraded as our friends, but whose loyalties are truly aligned with the Saxons. These Gaini are Franks, settled in the Colonae by the Romans. They have lived by the Trent for a hundred years or more.

'Mordred attacked their port and stole their keels, but they clung on, hiding behind the strong walls of their fortress, believing themselves to be safe on the east bank of the great river, but Arthwys crossed the Trent, using Mordred's pontoons. He offered their tribe's leader terms, but the Gaini kept trying to wrangle a more favourable outcome for themselves. The king quickly lost patience and fell upon Fortress Gainnion. Many died, including their leader Gundal, but once inside their stronghold, the king discovered an incredible amount of treasure – much of it stolen from the Britons – secreted away and hidden from us.'

'How had they amassed such a treasure?' asked Winnog, eyes wide with fascination.

'It turns out they have been the hub of the wheel of deceit, ever since all the trouble with the Saxons began. The extent of their ill-gotten gains came as a shock even to Arthwys.'

Igerna spoke with her usual authority. 'King Mor was well aware of their influence, but it was never the Gaini themselves who raided. Gundal's father, Gundad, played a double game for many years whilst hosting and controlling both Pict and Saxon raiders. Pabo, you must guard this treasure diligently – determining its origins will tell us much about the easterners' activities.'

Pabo sat a little straighter, his face flushed with pride.

'So what followed?' asked Cian.

'We burnt Gainnion and progressed to Lindum.'

'Did you meet with resistance?'

'Yes. The city had been barricaded against our arrival, easterners holding the few remaining Britons at spear-point. Arthwys stormed their position, putting them all to the sword.' Farddy turned to the two priests. 'We prayed once more at the shrines of Julius and Aaron, which were miraculously intact.'

'Praise the Lord,' said Amabilis in his distinct foreign accent.

'You said there were three battles?' Merlinus enquired.

'King Mordred had blockaded the Trent and waited for Arthwys at the place where Via Isca runs alongside the river. Then they progressed south-west together, following the road and the river to the edge of the Great Forest. On the northernmost bank, there is a mysterious place known as Tigguo Cobauc. It is a city of caves where bacaudae used to hide. Mordred searched the caves thoroughly for any Saxons, but they had fled. The army and flotilla pressed on. Arthwys knew that the Saxons had an inland port somewhere in that area and discovered it where the Soar meets the Trent, at a place called Tribruit. There were many keels at anchor, guarded by only a small Saxon force which was easily overwhelmed and destroyed, enabling Arthwys and his army to cross the Trent and link up with Riothames and Ambrosius. I was dispatched immediately with the treasure via the Ryknild, and although the road is now safe from bandits, I cannot deny that it was an apprehensive journey.'

'Well done, Farddy. So, we have cleared the Trent and linked up with Ambrosius. Arthwys' masterful plan approaches its fruition,' said a proud Igerna.

'King Arthwys still urges caution. Hengist's son, Aesc, remains in command. He is battle-hardened and not to be underestimated. The next objective is Breguoin, a mighty stronghold south of the Trent. It is an old Cymry hillfort, and the Saxons have it well-fortified with a high stockade.

They know they are surrounded, so they will fight to the last man – it will be a brutal encounter.'

Gwenhyfar looked nervously toward Eliffer whose eyes were wide with excitement. 'Farddy, may we have a private word?'

'Of course, my queen.' He approached her chair and lowered his head.

'Will Eliffer be safe?' she whispered.

'The king would never let him come to harm,' he whispered back.

'Should I advise him to stay close to King Mordred?'

'Good God, no. Mordred is only content when he is soaked in blood from the slaughter. His own men call him Dod, the bringer of death, and he does not care who he sends to Hell – even Saxon children do not escape his wrath.'

'You never liked him,' she whispered petulantly.

'I still don't. He is a demon, the king's weapon, unleashed to send Saxons to their graves.'

'Will you take a message to him from me; I want him to look out for Eliffer.'

'Of course, Gwen, but heed my advice where that man is concerned.'

'I will. Please call by for it later.'

The Battle for Agnus Dei

Ambro Hill, facing Breguoin

Iunius 467

'Ambrosius, may I present my son, Eliffer.'

The old Roman was sitting in his foldable chair in the grand campaign tent. Arthwys imagined this was how his ancestor, the great Coel Hen, had gone to war. Standing behind Ambrosius was Riothames, handsome in the shining armour of a Roman general, and his experienced cohort, Natalinus. Eliffer looked impressed by the illustrious company as he bowed.

'Eliffer, yet another Coeling. I knew your grandfather, Mor. He was the greatest general of this age, until your father showed us how to beat the Saxons.'

Eliffer seemed too overawed by the occasion to speak and simply nodded.

'My son does speak Latin, Ambrosius, but perhaps not today,' Arthwys interjected. They all laughed.

'No matter. I expect he fights as well as his forebears?'

'He does, particularly on horseback – skills that, unfortunately, we won't be deploying on this next battle.'

Riothames stepped from his father's side to add his address to the gathering. 'Arthwys and I have agreed to storm the fort simultaneously on all sides. There is a ramp to the west that leads to the entrance. My infantry will first proceed toward this gate under the cover of their shields. Lord Agiluf and his cavalry will stand off the ramp, out of range of their arrows and spears. This should make the Saxons think we intend to break through their barricades. Our archers will be deployed all around the perimeter to force the Saxons to keep their heads down. At the moment the infantry reach the gate, King Mordred and his men will move from where they will be concealed in the shrubs and gorse to the north and storm the stockade with ladders and grappling irons.'

'This is a good plan. When do we begin the attack?' the old Roman said, his face lit with rapt enthusiasm.

'At dawn tomorrow. Our troops will get into position tonight.' The clean-shaven prince nodded at Arthwys, whilst his father put his hands together in prayer.

'May the Lord bless you with good luck, Arthwys.'

'Thank you, Ambrosius, we shall need it. I believe this stronghold contains their very best warriors, men who will not yield. They will fight to the last man.'

'I shall be praying for your victory.'

Arthwys grimaced.

'You will not be alone. Doubtless, the priests will be busy praying, both today and tomorrow. They believe this battle is the climax of our struggle against evil, the battle for Agnes Dei.'

'Worthy motivation.'

The room fell silent, the prospect of defeat unthinkable. Arthwys soon interrupted the quiet with a practical thought, his mind totally focused on the encounter to come.

'Ames, do not tell your men about the attack from the north. If we are to breach the Saxon defences, it must remain a complete surprise. The enemy will sense a deception if your men are seen to expect one. Come, Eliffer, we must prepare.'

He turned on his heel and left the tent. Agiluf and Mordred were stood outside admiring their southern allies' equipment and watching their drills.

'We attack at dawn.'

Mordred winked at Eliffer. 'I've never seen so many toy soldiers.'

Arthwys smiled. 'They are well-drilled infantry. Ames was trained by Vortimer himself. These men will not let us down.' He began unstrapping the bearskin from his helmet. 'Tomorrow, Eliffer, you must accompany Agiluf with the cavalry. Do not leave his side. You will wear the bearskin of Coel Hen.'

'That would be a great honour, Father, but why?'

'The success of our plan relies completely on surprise. To achieve that, we must show the enemy what they expect to see, and they will expect to see me at the centre of our attack.'

Agiluf looked surprised. 'He is to be your decoy?'

'That is the plan, so protect him well, for he will be the most important warrior on the field.'

'And where will you be?'

'Scaling the stockade with Mordred and Caius. I am certain Aesc is here – the scouts claim to have seen him.'

'Is that a risk you should take, Arthwys?'

'You sound like your father! I think Mordred will need my help.'

Mordred laughed. 'So, I have the responsibility of looking out for you, Arthwys?'

Arthwys smiled and continued with his instructions. 'Agiluf, ensure Cadrog is the archer covering from the northern slope. Once our one hundred men are over the stockade, I want his archers to mount the battlements in close support.'

'I shall see to it.'

Mordred's eyes glinted. 'I'll wager five solidi that it is I who kills Aesc.'

'I'll take it. If you kill Aesc, it will only be because he has already struck me down. Eliffer, you will be responsible for satisfying that wager!' The king's grim humour rather punctured the light-hearted mood. 'Do we know if Britu has repositioned? We cannot let any of the enemy escape the net.'

'He has moved his militia to the southern slopes of Mons Badonicus, where he awaits your command.'

'Good, let us go about our duties. From midnight, we must all assemble in our proscribed positions. When dawn breaks, we will provide Ambrosius with quite the spectacle to watch from this hillside.'

*

The weather had changed, rain starting after midnight then hammering down just before dawn, leaving a mist clinging to the green hillside. Agiluf, astride his horse, was positioned alongside Eliffer who was masquerading as his father. Together, they had drawn Elfed's entire cavalry behind the southern infantry, and as they closed up,

Riothames gave the command to advance. The drilled unit looked like one long serpent as it marched toward the ramp, spears lowered, shields held high. Overhead, missiles of every description rained down from the stockade, bouncing off their shields. The disciplined soldiers kept their shape, despite the steep terrain. As they moved closer to the gate, Agiluf signalled for Elfed's cavalry to tighten up to their rear. The Cymry archers were now in range and began picking off any heads that appeared above the timber battlements.

Riothames drew alongside Eliffer. 'Good morning, Arthwys. Do we signal Mordred now?'

'Good morning, general,' Eliffer replied. 'My father is with Mordred.'

'Aha, yet another of your father's surprises – may the Lord protect him. We must breach this gate soon or he will be in trouble.'

Agiluf signalled, and flaming arrows filled the sky. The infantry, now under a hail of spears, were attempting to dislodge the gate, but the sudden screaming of Germanic orders from within the stronghold indicated the northern attack was underway. They saw the enemy's attention switch away from assailants below. Now, it was a race against time.

At last, Agiluf caught sight of Cymry archers standing on the ramparts loosing their arrows. Arthwys must be inside the stockade. The men up against the barriers threw down their shields, using both hands to clear the obstacles, cutting at ropes and prising at gaps. Logs rolled down the hill, the gate's defences giving way. The infantry picked up their shields again and poured through the opening. By the time Agiluf and Eliffer had encouraged their horses over the remnants of the barricade, the outnumbered Saxons were backed up against the south wall of the stockade, being skewered by the spears of warriors who had long awaited this opportunity. In the foreground stood the three heroes, Arthwys, Mordred and Caius. They rested on swords that still dripped with enemy blood. It looked like it had been an exhausting fight. Riothames rode past, briefly acknowledging them, still thoroughly engaged in the slaughter. Agiluf and Eliffer led their horses across the corpse-littered battlefield toward the gore-covered warriors.

'Eliffer, do you have five solidi in your purse?'

'I do not, Father. Have you lost your wager?'

'We both have. Caius killed Aesc!'

The men laughed despite the grim setting. Above, a thunder crack was followed by a fresh downpour.

'That will be Myrddin's contribution.'

The men laughed again.

*

Nataline galloped his horse up the hill toward Ambrosius' tent and dismounted before the steed had quite stopped. He walked briskly into the welcome shelter of the campaign tent, saluting Ambrosius and acknowledging his father.

'My king, the battle is won with only a few losses. Arthwys and the Cymry stormed the fort, taking the Saxons completely by surprise. Aesc is dead.'

'This is excellent news. I will congratulate them when they return to camp.'

'Their return will be delayed a bit longer. Arthwys has ordered instant redeployment. We are to advance upon Mons Badonicus immediately.'

Natalinus turned to Ambrosius. 'The mind of a tactician; he senses complete victory.'

'Riothames and Arthwys are advancing up the slopes as we speak. Messengers have been dispatched to Britu and the other kings to close in. I must return to my unit.'

'Good hunting, Nataline.'

'Arthwys is a born leader, though it comes as no surprise for the descendant of a Roman general. With men like this in the lead, the Empire can surely rise again.'

'Natalinus, you read my mind. But we have yet to persuade him of the merits of such a venture, and you can be certain he will not even discuss it before this war is concluded. I pray that absolute victory comes soon, for I fear I am short of time.'

The Forested Slopes

Mons Badonicus

Iunius 467

Arthwys and Ames rode side by side as they followed the track south along the edge of the forest. Following behind were the combined armies of Elfed and the south. The column was long, perhaps a mile, and the king had instructed his cavalry to ride either side of the infantry as a precaution against surprise attacks that might attempt to isolate sections of the long train. The enemy's defensive line from the Trent past Breguoin and on to Mons Badonicus had been a formidable barrier for years. Vortimer had never dared cross into the Great Forest which he had once described to Arthwys as 'seething with Saxons', so it was well to be cautious, particularly as evening approached. The Saxons had controlled all land to the east of this region unopposed, so when Arthwys had attacked from the east, he had caught them looking the wrong way, undermining their confidence. Now, with their leaders dead, Arthwys hoped the war could be brought to a swift conclusion.

'Messengers have been sent to Britu to the south, and Meirchiawn and Einion to the west. Their orders are to close in, so we have the enemy stronghold encircled before dawn,' he said.

Ames clapped the Elfed king on the shoulder. 'I must confess that I did not expect to be approaching the slopes of Mons Badonicus this evening, but I see you have the bit between your teeth, intent on finishing this war quickly.'

'It would have been a mistake to pause for feasting and congratulations when our enemy is in such disarray. My scouts tell me the stronghold has few defences. The enemy has been overconfident in this region, relying only on the mountain itself to provide their battlements. But if we pause and allow them time to regroup and dig in, this siege might last weeks.'

'I agree. I am beginning to understand why you credit these heathen savages with so much military wit.'

'They were winning the war!' Arthwys ruefully replied. 'They have killed two of our kings, defeated Elafius, an excellent general, whilst carving out almost a quarter of the Patria which, up until now, they have successfully defended. It is our arrogance that allowed this to happen. Our forebears consistently underestimated the Saxons' determination, making the mistake of focusing only on Hengist and the Jutes when it was the whole of the east that rebelled against accepting us as their overlords.' Arthwys softened his tone slightly when he saw how taken aback Ames was by his forceful candour. 'Hengist was a cunning leader who shared his spoils amongst ordinary people which is why so many tribes came to support him. When the Romans withdrew, our people were left without an army to protect them. They were farmers, not warriors, making it easy to rob them of their land and property, then kill or enslave them. Now their fields are empty, so even if we remove this Saxon threat completely, others will come to the Colonae. The best we can achieve is partition and pledges.'

Ames nodded. 'The Saxon Shore is the Patria's Achilles heel. Only a strong and united empire will fully resolve the problem. But a victory here will make them think twice before they come again. This is why my family has the greatest respect for your achievements, Arthwys. When we burn this settlement tomorrow, the smoke and flames will be seen for miles around, and the message will spread all the way to the coast, like a beacon signalling that we can now defend our island.'

Ames' mention of his family reminded Arthwys of a question he had been meaning to ask. 'Tell me, how is your sister, Livia. She was very kind to me and has much hope invested in our campaign.'

'You are her hero, my friend. She asks me about you constantly and holds on to a promise she claims you made, to return to see her?'

Arthwys smiled, reaching for the charm he still wore around his neck. He believed it had brought him the luck she had promised. Before he could respond to Ames' query, his attention was drawn by two riders galloping toward them.

'It would seem it is time to split into our groups to encircle the settlement. Let us see what these men have to say.'

It was Crannog and Caius returning from Meirchiawn. They saluted before Crannog spoke. 'Everyone is advancing to their positions but will await your orders to attack. There are no enemy along this road, but the forest here is dense and the terrain steep.'

'Thank you. Fall in with your men and spread out but stay in contact with each other. They know we are coming, so there is no need to be quiet, but stay alert. The Saxons have held this area for many years and may have prepared traps. I want every soldier within sight of the enemy stronghold by dawn. Once in position, we will assess our tactics for the attack.'

*

Agiluf had been charged with looking out for Arthwys' son, and found he was enjoying the young man's company. Eliffer had disclosed that he had been relieved to return the bearskin to his father. Whilst the boy had been pleased the ruse had fooled the Saxons, he had been embarrassed by all the attention the bearskin had drawn. Agiluf had seen for himself how soldiers had saluted and eques bowed, only to dissolve into fits of laugher when they saw through the prince's disguise.

Reaching the edge of the forest, they dismounted and led their horses on foot, threading their way through the dense undergrowth that adorned the slopes of Mons Badonicus. Having survived one battle in his company, Eliffer was at ease now with his father's oldest friend.

'Lord Agiluf, I shall never wear that bearskin again.'

'I wouldn't say *never*. One day, you may be the Bear, battle leader of the northern tribes.'

'But surely, the war will be over by then. Father says this will be the final encounter.'

'I believe that too, but there will always be war.'

'Not with Saxons; they will all be dead.'

Agiluf laughed at the naivety of youth. 'Both your father and I have realised this is a much bigger problem than our predecessors realised. We call them Saxons, but they are made up of many different tribes and come from different parts of the Continent. Some are newly arrived, but some came with the Romans. They are better termed as easterners. Do not doubt that they hate us as much as we hate them.'

'Will they still come, even though we have killed their leaders and slaughtered so many?'

'New leaders will rise through their generations, just as you will lead in your father's place one day. We can never stop their boats entirely; the coastline is too long and vulnerable.'

'Cian says that this federation of kings is our best hope for the future.'

Agiluf grimaced. 'If it holds. My father is a cautious optimist, which means he is full of hope whilst still convincing himself of the worst possible outcome – it is often confusing!'

'So, what is your hope, Lord Agiluf?'

'To survive tomorrow, if the Lord grants it, then sleep! We shall speak more of hope over a cup of mead when this is all over.'

*

The combined army of the Britons drew closer to the Saxon stronghold. Messengers had now returned from Britu, so Arthwys knew the enemy was surrounded. The warm summer nights were short, and a full moon lit their way. The yellow flowering gorse that clung to the hillside seemed to glow in the half-light.

From his vantage point, Arthwys could see the large Saxon settlement nestled below the south side of the peak on a stretch of level ground. Over the years, there had been rumours of a Saxon town in the forest, but no one had ever seen it from this vantage before He had a bird's eye view, its full extent revealed. Arthwys ruefully reflected how close the enemy's plan to keep north and south separate had come to succeeding, this settlement's size bearing witness to their audacious plan. He turned and descended to his commanders waiting below.

'It is a large settlement but weakly defended. The enemy have stayed safe here for decades, so we can expect there will be a great many easterners below. They will have used the old salt road to constantly bolster their numbers. This place has provided the base from which the enemy has so easily launched their raids against our people before disappearing back into this forest, all these years. Vortimer always maintained a presence to the west, but he could never gain control of the ground we now stand on. Tomorrow, we destroy this heathen haven. Nothing must be left, and no quarter must be given, for they never showed us any mercy.'

'What formation will we use for the attack, Arthwys?' Riothames stood amongst his captains, keen to know if his infantry would lead the assault.

'The ground looks flat, so this is a task for the cavalry. We will make an initial charge to flush out their warriors, and then the infantry will close in from every side. Burn everything and kill everyone.'

*

Cadell was sitting at his uncle's side watching the burning embers of the camp-fire. All around were Cornovii warriors with their spears and shields to hand, ready to move into position at dawn. He knew this was a special moment, the eve before his first battle, and he was both excited and apprehensive.

'Is King Arthwys nearby?' he asked. Cadell had yet to meet the great warrior.

'He is,' replied Britu.

'I am excited to meet him.'

Britu smiled. 'He will be pleased to meet you too, though he will be preoccupied with leading the attack.'

'The men are saying this is the last of the Saxons.'

'It is the last of those that have chosen war over peace.'

'I will avenge my father.'

'You will stay by my side,' Britu replied sharply.

Cadell felt the rebuke and did not reply.

'Catigern will be with you in spirit, but don't let the thought of revenge distract from your training.'

'I won't, uncle. In truth, I cannot really remember him.'

'He was a great warrior, as was my elder brother, Vortimer. Our family have sacrificed much to this war.'

Cadell remembered a question he wanted to ask his uncle. 'My mother said that my great-grandfather was an emperor of Rome, is this true?'

Britu laughed. 'It is true, but like you, your grandmother could not remember him, for she too was a bairn when her father died in battle.'

'So, am I a Roman?' Cadell said, filled with confusion about his ancestors.

Britu laughed again. 'Not anymore. We are Britons. Your great-grandmother was a Cornovii princess.'

'Is that better than Roman?'

'Certainly! These men are with us for that reason alone. Now stop this blether and think about your first thrust.' Britu paused, then added, 'And do not forget to pray to God, young warrior, for our fate is in His care.'

Cadell clasped his hands and closed his eyes as if in prayer, but his mind raced. Surely all his famous ancestors would be watching from Heaven. He would not let them down, particularly his father.

The Final Slaughter

Mons Badonicus

Iunius 467

Britu positioned his cohort of Cornovii infantry at the edge of the clearing as dawn began to break. Low cloud with light rain obscured a clear view of their objective but their formation was as agreed by messenger the previous day. He had been informed that the whole force would be arranged in the shape of a giant horseshoe, the enemy settlement surrounded with their backs to the high ground of the Mons. Positioned on his left, he could see a turma of cavalry jointly led by King Einion, who he knew well, and the Reged king, Meirchiawn, who he had yet to meet – both latecomers to the war but welcome additions, nonetheless. To his immediate right, as expected, were two contingents of cavalry, the furthest led by King Arthwys, the nearest by Lord Agiluf, but beyond them, although obscured by both the relief of the hill and the morning mist, he knew there was a large contingent of Prince Riothames' infantry – as many as a thousand soldiers.

The Saxons were outnumbered and, doubtless, terrified, but he was certain they would fight as they always did, with a ruthless purpose. He closed his eyes and prayed silently to God. *Keep us safe as we end this war.* Urcicinius, Tribune of Viroconium, had begged him to remain in command in the east and continue to garrison Durobrivae, the threat of the Saxon Shore ever present, but Britu and his men had been away from their homelands far too long, and there were tales of injustice reaching his ears. *No*, his mind was made up – he would return to Viroconium with his men, and along with Cadell, they would re-establish authority and farm their property. His thoughts were interrupted by the excited voice of Cadell.

'Uncle, King Arthwys approaches.'

The king's chestnut stallion drew close, pulling at its reins, snorting, wanting to be off, and clearly not in the slightest weary from the king's long campaign.

Britu felt jealous of the beast's vitality. He could feel his own waning, so it was well that Arthwys should seek to conclude his campaign this day. The mighty warrior king was wearing his battle bearskin over his helmet but as he turned toward them, Britu could see his expression was grim.

'Good morning, Britu. This mist should lift soon then we shall attack. I see you are not mounted?'

'Today, I fight alongside my men, because I have this young buck to keep an eye on.' He gestured toward Cadell. 'Come, Cadell, meet the greatest warrior of our generation.'

Cadell drew closer and bowed rather clumsily, still holding his shield.

'My king.'

'Cadell is the only son of Catigern.'

'Catigern was a great warrior too. Today we will all make our fathers proud.' Arthwys winked at Britu, but once more looked concerned. 'The cavalry will engage first to draw the enemy into the open. I will call for the infantry to advance shortly thereafter. There will be many Saxons hidden within their huts which you are tasked with setting on fire, but be wary of those warriors within – they will not die easily.'

He turned to Cadell. 'There will be much slaughter. Be prepared for the most ungodly sights. Women, children and the old... We must kill them all...'

Britu frowned. 'We understand what must be done, no matter how unpleasant a prospect.'

'Such tasks are usually performed best by King Mordred, but he sails back down the Trent to patrol our gains.'

'The easterners fear him; his reputation is known to all.'

'It is a shame he is not here to witness this final slaughter. I doubt this campaign would have succeeded without his decisive river campaigns. Will you join us after the battle is won? All leaders are invited to the camp of Ambrosius.'

'If God deigns I survive this, I seek your permission to leave the field. I have promised my men our immediate return to Viroconium. This is the closest we've been to home for some years.'

'Yes. Of course, you have it – it has been a long war.' Arthwys paused then raised his voice to a holler. 'Fight well, Britu. Fight well, Cornovii!'

The men roared their assent. He turned his impatient horse and cantered back toward his ranks.

Britu watched Arthwys return to his eques and waited for the first signal.

It came within a minute. Caledfwich was thrust skyward, and on either side of the Cornovii, hooves thundered across the clearing. There was only an earthen bank defending the large settlement. The horses cleared it easily. It was as if the Saxons had never expected their mountain lair to be discovered, and although they thrust their spears wildly into the air in defence of the charge, they were all overpowered. It was a thrilling sight to see – the eques lowering their javelins, choosing their targets, accompanied by the familiar cacophony of battle, whinnying horses, the clash of steel, men shouting and screaming.

An eques galloped back toward them waving his javelin. It was the signal to advance. Britu raised his sword, torches were lit, and the Cornovii began marching quickly over the moorland in the direction of their objective. They breached the first line of turf defence with no resistance. The enemy had been pushed back. Blood-covered corpses filled the hollow, some still writhing in pain. Only a few eques had failed to make it over the ditch, three injured horses evidence of this.

Reaching the dwellings on the south side of the town, Britu shouted, 'Fire them,' and the torch-bearers ran toward the hovels, casting their flaming burdens onto thatched reed roofs. His men watched and waited as the flames took hold, uncertain what to expect, but a shouted Germanic command was followed by screaming Saxons pouring out of several huts, ready to fight for their lives. Britu moved closer to Cadell as they became surrounded by spears, but out of the smoke a warhorse smashed into two of their foes from behind, and a swinging blade felled both. With his shield held to the fore, Cadell stepped forward and skewered his sword into the nearest Saxon. His first kill. Britu similarly felled the closest warrior with a series of fierce blows. As he looked up, Lord Agiluf was grinning back at him. Prince Eliffer mounted by his side.

'We are assigned to your protection, King Britu.'

He smiled. 'Arthwys is as a brother to me!'

Prince Riothames' men now appeared to their right, searching and slaughtering, hut by hut, the screams of women and children now audible. Britu paused his troops' advance. The battle was as good as over. Had Arthwys detected he was weary, tired of the slaughter, and sent Agiluf to watch over him? He remembered as a younger man feeling similarly protective of his weary brother, Vortimer. He spoke softly to himself. *At last, it is over, Vortimer. God has granted us victory. The Bear's plan worked. We are heading home to Viroconium.*

*

Ambrosius and Natalinus had risen at dawn to train their gaze on the heights of Mons Badonicus. They were too far away to hear the cries of battle or the clash of weapons, and the morning was overcast with a light rain. But four hours or so beyond daybreak, the clouds lifted, and large plumes of smoke could be seen rising into the sky beyond the peak. The battle was underway, but it would be several hours before they would receive news of the outcome and learn whether both their sons were safe.

Following two sleepless nights with two early starts, Ambrosius was tired, feeling his age, but suffering more from the debilitating swelling in his stomach. His physician had advised him to stay in Venta Belgarum, saying the old king had not long left, but Ambrosius was determined to be present for the final defeat of this enemy that had so tormented the island he had made his home since his exile from Gaul. He had always fostered the hope that he might one day return to his homeland, but his wife Helena already lay in a mausoleum in Venta Belgarum, and he sensed he would shortly be by her side.

He lay down on his camp bed and fell asleep instantly, waking much later in the day to the sound of cheering. He was initially dazed and uncertain of his whereabouts, but his faculties engaged once he clambered to his feet with the aid of his stick. Now he could hear approaching horses. His campaign tent was deserted, everyone outside, including his servants. He peered out of the loose leather flap, squinting into the bright sunlight of a late summer's afternoon. Natalinus was close by, applauding and waving. He saw Ambrosius and helped him outside.

'Look, the heroes return.'

'Is Ames amongst them? I cannot see in this sunlight.'

'He is leading the column with Arthwys.'

'Thank the Lord. We have much to discuss with them both.'

Dark Secrets

Cambodunum

Sextilis 467

Cian and Bryn had been busy discussing the final arrangements for the victory feast which was just two days away. King Meirchiawn had decided to stay on at Cambodunum for the celebrations and send for his wife and children. He had been passing the days hunting with the king, but Cian had no doubt more than camaraderie was behind his decision.

The booty acquired from the Saxon campaign still filled the treasury to bursting. The intention had been to divide it between the three Coeling kings of the North, but when both Cian and Merlinus had counselled that others deserved a share, particularly Elfed's brave eques, Arthwys had agreed to divide the spoils more widely. Cian, Merlinus and Blwchfardd had been made responsible for this task, and Farddy was currently in the strongroom weighing and counting.

The new King of Bryneich had not yet returned from the Humber but was expected to arrive soon to receive his share. Merlinus had disclosed to Cian that he was uncomfortable with Mordred's new status, though he had declined to give his reasons, whereas Arthwys was ever full of praise for his cousin.

Bryn's fretting about accommodation interrupted Cian's musings. 'There is no room in the mansio for Mordred now that Gwenhyfach and her children have arrived with a host of servants.'

'We must be careful not to offend Mordred. He has become one of the king's most favoured allies.'

Bryn's brow furrowed as she thought hard on the dilemma. 'There must be somewhere suitable.'

'A campaign tent pitched in the lee of the stockade might be appropriate.'

'Will he bring servants?'

'I doubt it. He's a loner, completely self-reliant.'

Cian heard Farddy's familiar footsteps approaching the door, and they both turned to see him standing there stripped to a loin cloth.

Cian laughed out loud. 'A bit hot, are you?'

'Sweltering. The treasury has no windows. I am working by candlelight on the hottest day of summer!'

'I hope you are being even-handed.'

'Of course, Father, but I've discovered something that you need to see. Can you come quickly?'

Cian accompanied his son to the windowless cabin that jutted from the side of the hall. The guard stood to one side, allowing both men into the strongroom. It was, as Farddy described, unbearably hot. A candle flickered on a low worktable where the contents of a leather, bloodstained satchel were spread out. In the half-light, Cian could see a magnificent gold torc and a signet ring. The torc was smeared with old, dried blood, and when he scrutinised the signet ring, he could scarcely believe what he read: *COEL REX*. He was looking at Gorwst's stolen regalia.

'Stay here,' he said in a hoarse whisper. 'I must find the king.'

Despite his advanced years, Cian ran to the great hall where Arthwys was entertaining Meirchiawn.

'How goes the counting?' Arthwys asked, his tone light-hearted.

'My king, there is a matter of great urgency that I must discuss with you in the treasury.'

Arthwys stood, placing his hand on his cousin's shoulder.

'At least we can be assured it is not Saxons!'

They both laughed raucously and Meirchiawn also stood. 'I shall go and see if my family are settled whilst you deal with your business.'

As Cian led Arthwys round to the treasury, he whispered dramatically, 'Gorwst's regalia is in your treasury.'

The king's demeanour changed instantly. He pushed past Cian, threw open the treasury door and rushed to the table where he examined the items.

'Where is Merlinus?'

'In the chapel.'

'Put some clothes on, Blwchfardd, and bring him to the hall immediately.' Arthwys gathered up the bloody items and put them in the satchel. 'Was all this amongst the booty?'

'I found it in this crate, but I don't remember it being part of the consignment from Derventio.'

'I shall ask my mother; she has held the key since my father's death. This is an extraordinary find.'

They strode purposefully back to the great hall. As they entered the main door, Arthwys shouted, 'Mother, Gwen, come see what we have discovered.'

The women looked intrigued as they came toward him, but their expressions turned to concern when they saw what he carried.

Igerna spoke immediately. 'That satchel belongs to Mordred. Gwen gave it to me on his behalf, so that we might keep it safe in the treasury.'

'Were you aware of the contents?' Arthwys said, frowning at his wife and mother.

'He told me it just held a few coins,' said Gwen, whilst Igerna shook her head.

Arthwys placed the satchel on the table and carefully lifted the bloodstained flap to reveal the contents. 'Behold, King Gorwst's regalia.'

Gwenhyfar went white, and her eyes filled with tears. 'I had no idea… How can this be?'

The silence that followed was suddenly broken by the arrival of Farddy and Merlinus. Arthwys looked at the old priest and indicated the items on the table.

'Mordred's satchel,' he announced.

Merlinus was aghast. 'Where is Meirchiawn?'

'He just left to check on his wife and sons.'

'He needs to see this.'

'Farddy, ask Meirchiawn to join us, then go find Agiluf and Caius – we have decisions to make.' Arthwys' face was dark with fury. 'Did you know, Gwen?'

'Know what?'

'That Mordred murdered his father?'

'How can you accuse me of such a thing!'

The king looked sternly at his wife. 'I have to ask. Did you know?'

Cian grimaced, as the king's voice raised to a shout.

'Of course not,' Gwen blurted, before she turned and ran sobbing to her chamber.

Igerna frowned. 'That was unnecessary, Arthwys.'

'If I didn't ask, others would think it.'

Merlinus looked at his furious king. 'This is what I warned you about when I told you my dream, Arthwys.'

'But why would Mordred place such damning evidence here, in my father's treasury?'

'It shows the workings of an arrogant, deranged mind. Can you not see?' The old seer looked around at all those gathered. 'His darkest secret hidden in Elfed's safest place, right under our noses.'

Igerna looked concerned. 'He has been toying with us, Arthwys. He has asked Gwen if his satchel was safe many times, and each time, she offered to return it to him, but he always declined. In his strange mind, it has been a gruesome love token, something he could bother her about, something that bound them. It's as if he has been daring us to discover his secret. Poor Gwen must be devastated to discover her old friend has used her so badly.'

'Perhaps my questioning was too harsh.'

'It was, Arthwys. After all, it is you who has championed this man, allowing him to become a hero of Elfed.'

Outside, the sky had gone dark. Thunder rumbled, rolling ever closer.

Meirchiawn returned to the hall, dripping from the rain. 'What is so urgent?' he asked.

'We have made a discovery. Steel yourself, for it will shock you to your core.'

Meirchiawn looked down at the table and emitted a strangled groan when he recognised his father's regalia.

'In God's name, Arthwys, what is this?'

'The newly discovered contents of a satchel that your brother brought to Elfed when he first arrived.'

'Then all our suspicions converge. A murder plot always seemed more likely than a chance robbery.'

'You suspected this?' asked Merlinus.

'It was the nature of my father's death – his head was removed with one blow; it had to be a warrior who attacked him. Thieves would have slit his throat from behind. Moreover, his hound would never have let strangers get so close.'

'Did you suspect your brother?'

'He seemed the obvious culprit at first, but then we heard he was on his sickbed in Elfed, so we believed it couldn't have been him.'

'Yes, he was here, desperately ill from a wolf bite,' Merlinus added, his tone heavy with scorn.

Blwchfardd arrived with Caius and Agiluf. The rain was falling heavily now, and the three men were soaked through. Lightning fizzed close by in the forest, followed by an almost immediate crash of thunder overhead.

Arthwys turned to his most faithful eques. 'Quite by chance, we have discovered the culprit of Reged's most heinous crime. It appears that our comrade-in-arms, Mordred, murdered his own father before arriving in Elfed. I am in turmoil. He is our friend, a hero of the Saxon campaign. I expect King Meirchiawn, here, will want him summarily executed. Indeed, my own father would have agreed with that swift sentence, but we abide by Roman law in my court, so he shall have the opportunity to answer for his crimes. Agiluf, I charge you with capturing and restraining him when he arrives. Do not try to fight him – you would lose, and he may escape. I will leave it to you and Caius to come up with a way to make the arrest safely. Now, we all must go about our routines as if nothing is amiss. If you will excuse me, I must go and make things right with my queen.'

Cian caught the anguished look that passed between Agiluf and Caius – there would be little enthusiasm for the arrest of their fellow warrior.

*

Arthwys found his wife huddled on her bed, still distraught.

'Gwen, my love.'

She sat up, wiping away the tears.

He sat beside her and held her hand. 'This is devastating news. We must remember Mordred in our prayers.'

'I feel such pity for him, Arthwys. He is a strange one, cocky and confident, but so lost. He pursued me for many years before I met you, but Father never liked him.'

'He has never made a secret of his admiration for you, and I have sensed you have feelings for him… I have heard about the letters…'

Gwen put a shaking hand to her mouth. 'Surely, you don't think I have been unfaithful?'

'No, but you were part of the reason for him staying here at Elfed all these years, for which I was grateful.'

Gwen looked shocked. 'You were aware of his attention, but kept him here, anyway?'

'I knew it was just his way, though there has been gossip.'

'About what!'

'Gwen, it is of no matter nor consequence. I pay no mind to idle tongues.'

She looked at him, studying his face for a while. 'Will you execute him?'

'Many would say I should; patricide is the worst of all crimes.'

'But what do *you* say?'

'The world is suddenly upside down. One month ago, he was fighting at my side, better than any man I have ever seen. He has saved my life more than once. But justice must prevail. We must satisfy God that Mordred has done enough to atone for his sins, for it is He who has exposed his crime to us.' Arthwys gave an exasperated cry. 'We should be enjoying this moment of glory, celebrating our hard-won security. Perhaps it would have been better if Farddy had thrown the satchel into a deep lake. But Mordred placed the evidence of his sins in a foolish place, almost as if he was daring God to expose his crime. It is the way of fate that men should be torn down when they least expect it.'

They sat quietly whilst Arthwys pondered what to do. At last, he spoke. 'I will speak to Meirchiawn, but I'm inclined to clemency. I will propose we banish him to the north. The Picts should keep him busy doing what he is best suited for.'

'That would be a merciful judgement, allowing for recognition of all he has achieved on Elfed's behalf. It would be my preferred solution.'

'Then so be it.'

*

The summer storms had passed, leaving the forest smelling fresh. Igerna walked briskly toward the mansio where Gwenhyfar had chosen to spend the night with her sister and two young nephews. The feast that had taken so long to prepare was far from her mind. The events of the previous day invaded her thoughts, making her heart sink ever lower. She had no doubt it was God's will that Mordred should be held to account for Gorwst's murder, but witnessing the man, who had fought so valiantly alongside her son, writhing in a net like a wild animal had been unpleasant and undignified. Arthwys had hidden his upset behind uncharacteristic fury, and Gwenhyfar had not left her chamber until dark. Arthwys' queen had pleaded with him to allow her to be excused from court for the proceedings, but he had insisted she attend, giving Igerna the task of ensuring she did.

Arthwys had been to see Mordred in his shackles, to outline the charges against him, but the warrior had refused to speak to either Arthwys or his guards. Igerna doubted anyone had slept that night. She arrived at the mansio to find Gwenhyfar dutifully waiting for her, dressed in black, her drawn face showing the effects of the previous day's harrowing events.

'Come, my lady, let us get this over with.'

The sky was clear, but the great hall was dark inside as they took their seats to the left of King Meirchiawn. Arthwys was flanked by Cian on his left and Merlinus on his right. The sudden clanking of chains heralded the arrival of Mordred, accompanied by Agiluf and Caius as his guards. They seated him in front of the assembled court. Blwchfardd was sat in the shadows with his stylus and tablet, ready to take notes. Grave concern was etched on the faces of everyone present as Arthwys began to address Mordred.

'First, I wish to say that I have no appetite for this – you are my finest warrior, and you have fought for me with valour time and again, but we have been brought to this impossible position by your actions. Do you wish to say anything?'

Mordred's eyes burnt with anger, but he said nothing.

'So be it.' Arthwys paused. 'You stand accused of the murder of your own father, King Gorwst. The evidence against you, discovered in my own treasury, is compelling.'

Cian reached for the satchel at his feet and passed it to the king.

'This is yours. Found hidden inside were Gorwst's torc and Coel's ring, both still coated in the king's dried blood.' He opened the satchel to show the assembled party.

Gwenhyfar could hardly look, wringing her hands over and over again. 'You asked my queen to keep the satchel safe for you, and in good faith, she placed it in the king's treasury. Had my father been here when the contents were discovered, he would have had you summarily executed for the murder of his brother.' Mordred remained impassive as Arthwys continued. 'Many would be surprised that you dared break the Code of Coel and raised arms against another Coeling—'

Merlinus interrupted. 'Except that does not apply to you, does it Mordred?'

The prisoner glared at the seer but, still, spoke not a word.

'Before my father died,' said Arthwys, 'he disclosed to me that King Gorwst suspected you were the son of Coroticus, born out of incest.'

Mordred lowered his head and let out a deep guttural growl.

'In a dream, Merlinus saw what he thought was Coroticus decapitating King Gorwst, but on seeing you, and the undoubtable likeness you have for your true father, he subsequently realised the murderer in his dream was you. I chose to ignore his warning, preferring to give you a chance to prove yourself a man of valour and honour.'

Now Mordred raised his head and spoke for the first time. 'And have I not done so, Arthwys?'

'Indeed, you have shown great valour in the defence of the Patria.' Arthwys turned to the Reged king. 'Do you wish to say anything to the accused, Meirchiawn?'

Meirchiawn nodded stiffly. 'This murder is an appalling crime. Father loved you and raised you, despite what he suspected. If this were Reged, I would have you executed, but we are in Arthwys' kingdom, so your fate lies in his hands.'

Arthwys acknowledged his cousin's words with a respectful nod. 'We named you king, but that title and the accompanying rights must now be rescinded, since we are all agreed that you are not a Coeling. The lands we granted you are forfeit, but Valentia between the Tyne and Tweed is wild and unpopulated, so I have decided to banish you there for life. If you cross the Wall or the Cheviot or attempt to land a boat in the Patria, this clemency will be withdrawn, and you will be hunted down and executed. I will not send you away destitute. To honour the service you have done this kingdom, I shall give you the wage and share of any other eques who fought this campaign, along with my gratitude for your valour. Agiluf and Caius will accompany you beyond the Tyne where your manacles will be removed. Do you have anything to say before I have you taken from this court to begin your journey?'

Mordred turned toward Arthwys' queen. Her cheeks were streaked with tears.

'I have always loved you, Gwen, and I am truly sorry that you suffered suspicion as a result of my actions. I came to Elfed to fight Arthwys for you but found myself fighting for Elfed, instead. This family has stolen everything from me, including you.'

Gwen lifted her head. 'I was never yours, Mordred. I felt pity for you and tried to help you find your place in the world, nothing more. Our friendship is over; you are dead to me.' She shook with a loud sob and turned her face away.

Mordred's head dropped, his shoulders slumping.

Igerna reached for Gwen's hand. 'Well said,' she whispered softly.

Arthwys signalled to Agiluf. 'Take the prisoner away. Release him well north of the Tyne. And Caius…'

'Yes, my king?'

'If he causes any trouble, throw him overboard in his chains.'

They watched Mordred leave the hall, chains rattling but head held high now. There was a long silence until Arthwys decided to move events along.

'Cian, please ensure the booty is divided into four. Elfed and Reged are to receive a quarter each, and the balance will be shared out amongst the eques and our legion of brave soldiers.'

Merlinus leant across to the king. 'This clemency will have dire consequences.'

Arthwys did not respond.

A Letter from Ambrosius

Cambodunum

September 467

It had been the busiest month of Farddy's life. The booty had been distributed in accordance with Arthwys' wishes. King Meirchiawn had at last returned to Reged, and the large army recruited to fight the Saxons had broken up, the soldiers returning to their families and fields. The elation of victory had quickly dissipated as they got back to the mundane reality of administering a kingdom.

For the first time in thirty years, Elfed was free of external threat. But Arthwys had not rested on his laurels. He had journeyed first to Eboracum to explain the circumstances of Mordred's fall from grace to Ulf. It had proved a difficult message to deliver, but a share of the booty had sweetened the news, and the new commander of the rivers proved to be more pragmatic and loyal than he had first appeared. Ulf had then accompanied Arthwys and Cian to meet Freuleaf, the King of the Angles, where Farddy had been surprised to witness his father welcomed like a long-lost friend by a king who even remembered 'Bryn' to be the name of Farddy's mother!

They had returned to Cambodunum to discover two important developments. Gwenhyfar had discovered good reason to hurriedly betroth Eliffer to Elaine, the youngest daughter of Winnog, and a letter had arrived for Arthwys under the seal of Ambrosius Aurelianus, brought by a messenger who would not return to Venta Belgarum until he had Arthwys' reply. The king summoned Cian and Merlinus to discuss the message in advance of dictating a reply to Farddy.

'I am summoned to Venta Belgarum where Ambrosius wishes to confer on me the honour of Magister Militum per Brittonum.'

'A Roman appointment?'

'Yes, bestowed by Emperor Anthemius, no less!'

'That is indeed a great honour. So, it would seem Ambrosius has reported our victories to Rome?'

'And to Constantinople. He says here that even Emperor Leo has heard of our success.'

Igerna was listening from her chair by the fire. 'Your father would be so proud, but be careful – my own father died in Gaul fighting other men's battles. This could prove to be nothing more than the hopes of a faction that will falter in the face of those families that have controlled Rome for a century.'

'The Theodosian influence has declined, and the new emperors seek compromise. Ambrosius has waited his whole life for a return to his homeland, but the stars have never aligned favourably enough, until now. What say you, Cian?'

'These honours are well-deserved, the reward for a life of discipline and service. But men who wield the kind of power these Romans do will seek to use you for their own ends.'

'Perhaps the time is right for the Empire to be reunified under a Christian banner. What say you, Merlinus?'

'My king, that is a question I cannot answer. They want you for your manpower and martial prowess. Many generals have embarked from this island, some have even become emperors, but in so doing, they left their families with the burden of defending their home territories against invaders from every direction. There is a price for ambition.'

Arthwys laughed. 'My ambitions are not so lofty.'

'Unleashed, ambition has no limit, and the higher you climb the further you fall.'

Cian had been reading the letter, and he now looked up, his expression thoughtful. 'When I was the same age as Eliffer, my master Talhaearn spoke often about the Empire, how the Romans pressed the tribes into military service and the burden of the Emperor's taxes. Often, he would say, *The yoke of Rome has left deep scars.*'

'So, Taly saw Rome in a negative light?'

'Not all of it. He retained his Roman title and took advantage of its culture. He trained me in Latin, classics and Roman military matters. He did not want to let go completely.'

'So, what is your opinion?'

'This letter suggests a different empire, one that is more a federation of kingdoms. It could mean agreement with Rome rather than domination. Magister Militum per Brittonum recognises you as commander of your own army of Britons. This new Emperor Anthemius may seem enlightened, but is perhaps driven by a desperation for more soldiers. I see that Aegidius has died and Count Paulus has taken command in Gaul, but I cannot be sure what this means for the shifts in power within the Empire.'

Arthwys turned to Farddy. 'Please convey to Ambrosius that I accept the invitation to come to Venta Belgarum next week. I do not reject his proposals, but I wish to understand more about them before making any commitment.'

Farddy nodded and began to write.

'Now, where are Gwenhyfar and Eliffer? I believe we must have a wedding before I depart, for there will certainly be a christening upon my return!'

Persuasion

Venta Belgarum

Autumnus 467

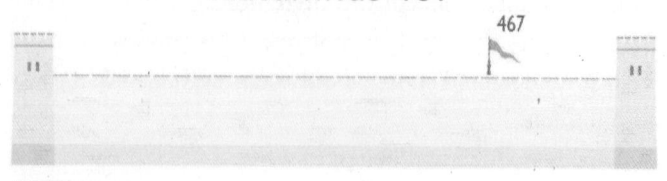

Riothames paced the corridor outside his father's bedchamber.

'He will be ready to see you soon enough,' Livia said, calmly admiring the garden through a window and wondering at her brother's impatience.

'Another messenger has arrived, and I have so much to discuss with him before I go to inspect the fleet at Clausentum.'

'His illness makes the mornings difficult. The servants are careful to present him as best they can.'

'He has so many decisions to make over the next few days. I fear he will find it all too tiring.'

'Do not stress him, Ames. We do not know how long he has, which makes this time precious for us all.'

Riothames sighed and nodded. 'Arthwys will arrive today.'

Livia smiled, careful not to reveal the extent of her excitement to her brother. 'I would be happy to distract him, if you wish to delay his audience with our father.'

Ames laughed. 'I'm sure you will anyway. But it is the opposite; I need to get to him before Father without delay.'

'Why so?'

'Because without Arthwys' agreement, Father may not sanction this campaign.'

'Does that surprise you, brother?'

'No. I understand his caution, but this is the opportunity we have been waiting for all these years. If we miss it… there may not be another.'

'Do you wish me to help persuade Arthwys?'

'I doubt even you could influence him in this. He has a warrior's spirit, but he is ever pragmatic. He will only want to involve himself if he can foresee a positive outcome.'

'It is understandable. He has not lived in exile as we have, so he does not feel the pull of Rome.'

'I know. For him, it is merely a matter of ambition, and the extent of that, I cannot gauge.'

'That is because, until now, his entire focus has been on defeating the Saxons, protecting his own people. His motivation in that instance was clear.'

'That may be so, but he is, after all, a general. I have a large standing army which I have purposefully retained. I have built a fleet to transport it, yet my dying father wavers despite our recent victories.'

Livia looked at her brother, studying the concern etched on his face. 'I will help if I can.'

The large oak doors to the bedchamber opened. The servants bowed and left, carrying used towels and the remnants of breakfast. Ambrosius, propped up on pillows, beckoned them in.

'Come in, you two.'

'Have you slept well, Father?' Livia asked.

'It becomes increasingly difficult to do so, but no matter.'

Ames inspected the table to the side of his father's bed, examining the scrolls bearing Imperial seals.

Ambrosius looked from the scrolls to his son. 'The Emperor wastes no time. Imperial legates are on their way here to outline the plans further.'

'We are ready to embark,' Ames said eagerly.

'I am still undecided. When will Arthwys arrive?'

His son's brow furrowed. 'He comes today.'

'Good. Then we will soon be in a position to inform Anthemius of our decision.'

'Really, Father, how can one man's decision be allowed to have such an influence on something as vital as the Empire's resurgence?'

'Because it is not the Empire I care about, but you and Livia.'

Livia reached for her father's hand, trying to reassure him. 'I think Ames sees the opportunity to grasp the future you hoped for us.'

'Your grandfather saw that same future, but his ambition ended with his head on a spike at Ravenna.'

Ames shook his head. 'Different times. He was betrayed. And we will be fighting for the Emperor, not against him.'

Livia watched her father's face cloud over.

'You are too easily impressed. This Emperor throws around titles, and gifts lands already occupied by formidable barbarian kings. His promises will only be realised if he achieves military success, and I know of only one general equal to that task now that Aegidius is dead –

and that is Arthwys. It was his strategy that won the Saxon war, his strategy that brought us to the attention of Rome and Constantinople in the first place!'

Ames' face coloured. 'And it was our manpower and resources that secured that victory.'

'Quite so, Ames. I meant not to take anything away from your fine ability as a military commander. Your ambition is commendable, but it is also emotional. For Arthwys, Rome is nothing more than a curiosity. His objective opinion of the Emperor's plans will tell us not only if we stand a chance of success, but also what the Britons truly think of the Empire in these times. And be sure, my son, ridding the Patria of Saxons is an entirely different prospect to fighting overseas for an empire you have little reason to trust.'

*

This was Amabalis' first visit to the Romanised region of Britannia, and the Gothic priest was impressed by the walls of Venta Belgarum.

'I am reminded of the cities of Gaul. I have seen nowhere else like this on this island.'

'There are similar cities to the west, but the cives of the north and east have long abandoned their Roman towns and buildings. This city is a spectacular remnant of Rome, which I am sure will help make your stay most enjoyable,' said Arthwys.

The three men rode through the bustling streets to the barracks where they stabled their horses before heading toward the large townhouse belonging to Ambrosius.

Servants received them and led them in the direction of their accommodation.

'There are many visitors staying—' said a servant, turning to Arthwys.

'But none so important as this one,' said a female voice from behind him.

He turned. 'Livia!' She looked as beautiful as he remembered.

'Arthwys!' She embraced him and then stood on her toes to gently kiss him. 'You promised you would return much sooner than this,' she teased.

Arthwys laughed, remembering how much he enjoyed her company. He turned toward his companions. 'Do you remember my prefect Agiluf?'

'Of course.'

'And this is Amabalis, a Gothic priest from Gaul.'

Livia smiled and acknowledged both men. 'I am assigned to your welfare. My instructions are to bring you directly to an audience with my father.'

'How is his health?'

'Poor and deteriorating, but his mind is as sharp as ever and full of the challenges that beset us.'

Followed by three servants, she took the men down a long corridor which led to a smaller complex of buildings to the south of the main house.

'This is my personal residence where you are to be my guests. Ames is holding a banquet in your honour this evening, but he has had to go to Clausentum to inspect his fleet, so you will not see him till then. Have you travelled many days?'

'Four. We were fast on the heels of your messenger!'

Livia smiled in her beguiling manner. 'Yes, he only returned last night. My father is so pleased you have come.'

After the long dusty ride, Arthwys found Livia's sweet fragrance hypnotic, just as he recalled from their first meeting, though it made him acutely aware that his own cleanliness needed attention.

'I must wash before I see your father.'

'Of course. The servants will fetch water and towels. I will wait for you in the garden.'

Arthwys' room was adorned with statues and ornaments, the floor a mosaic depicting a sea creature he did not recognise. Everything was clean and fresh. A tunic and sandals had been laid out for him, but he decided to leave changing into fresh clothes until later, for he was as anxious as Ambrosius to commence their meeting.

All three men were quick to assemble in the garden, from where Livia led them back along the corridor to the king's chamber at the far north of the complex. Two guards collected the visitors' weapons before allowing them to enter. The room was unlike any bedchamber Arthwys had ever seen, large and colonnaded, with Ambrosius on a bed at the far end.

'Arthwys! It is good to see you and your companions. Come to my bedside.' Ambrosius signalled to his servants to bring chairs so that the visitors could be comfortably seated. Livia took a seat on a low couch, just outside of Arthwys' eyeline.

'Ambrosius, you already know Agiluf, and may I also introduce Amabalis – he is a priest who ministers in Elfed, but he fought with the Visigoths in Gaul. His knowledge of them has been of great value.'

'I am honoured to meet you, Amabalis.'

The priest bowed respectfully. 'How fares your health, great king?'

'Not good. The Lord will be judging me soon,' he said, smiling at Amabalis, 'so I am grateful you came quickly. Tell me, Arthwys, what do you make of all these offers of Imperial titles and lands?'

'It seems to me the Emperor is throwing them about because he is short of the soldiers he needs to achieve his objectives, but I have no understanding of what those objectives are.'

Ambrosius laughed, clearly appreciating Arthwys' honesty. 'Imperial objectives are almost never clear. The only thing that is clear is that absolute power is sought by many.'

'So, what do you think makes this new Emperor different?'

'His intention is to defeat and control all the barbarians. For the last decade or so, the western Empire has been dominated by Magister Militum Ricimer, a powerful general but a barbarian himself. He has failed to control the Visigoths in Gaul and the Vandals in North Africa. He has, however, been ruthless in ensuring he retains his own position, going so far as executing Emperor Majorian and, in so doing, infuriating his fellow generals. Both Aegidius in the West and Marcellinus of Dalmatia rejected Ricimer's puppet emperor, Severus, so much so that they even considered invading Rome. Leo, Emperor in the East, is attempting to curb Ricimer's power by appointing

Anthemius, a Greek, as Emperor in the West, whilst also sponsoring the Roman Marcellinus to provide enough military muscle to equal Ricimer.'

'Will they succeed?'

'It is difficult to say. The Vandals and Visigoths have grown strong and now equal the power of the western Empire. The only way to stop these barbarian kingdoms from dominating our future is to go to war against them and win.'

'Has the death of Aegidius weakened Rome's position in Gaul?'

'Count Paulus says not, but Syagrius, Aegidius' son, sees himself more as a comrade of Childeric of the Franks, and although there is co-operation with the Romans, I believe our influence is waning. The chickens have taken over the henhouse!'

'So what do they wish of you, Ambrosius?'

'They have asked that we take our army and station ourselves in central Gaul, effectively blocking any of the barbarian kingdoms from expanding further.'

'So Anthemius sees the Visigoths as the threat to Gaul?'

'Yes, but first he is combining his armies with Leo's to attack the Vandals next spring which means most of the Empire's forces are gathering to move south. This might tempt the Visigoths to consider expansion in Gaul.'

'So, the Emperor wants the Britons to be the deterrent?'

'That is the plan. But Ricimer is the fly in his ointment.'

'How so?'

'It is unclear where he sits in all of this. He has been sidelined but is a barbarian and known to favour the Visigoths. He would not wish to see them suppressed.'

Arthwys frowned. 'And what would we gain by involving ourselves in Rome's war?'

'Recognition of both Britannia and Armorica as kingdoms on equal terms with Rome and control of lands in Aquitaine, south of the Loire.'

'This all presumes Anthemius does not lose. What say you, Amabalis?'

The priest shook his head. 'Euric now leads the Visigoths. He is clever and ambitious, and like Attila, he murdered his own brother to attain the throne. His army numbers twenty thousand, perhaps more. The Emperor's plan will only work if he finds a way to split that army and force Euric to fight on several fronts, much like how you defeated the Saxons. A gathering of troops on what Euric considers his border will certainly threaten him. It may be enough to make him fight on two fronts.'

Ambrosius drew in a sudden sharp breath and bent forward, his face pale. 'Arthwys, may I speak with you privately?' he said through clenched teeth.

Agiluf and Amabalis stood, bowed and walked to the door where Livia showed them out.

'Come closer, my friend,' Ambrosius said, speaking in almost a whisper.

'I am dying. I might have days – months, if I'm lucky. I am reluctant to sanction this expedition unless you join it. I know Ames would prefer to have you along, but he is headstrong and will answer the Emperor's call, regardless, once I am dead. Will you do this for me?'

How could Arthwys refuse the request of a dying man. 'I understand your concerns, but unlike your kingdom, Elfed cannot afford to pay a standing army. We have shared our booty from the Saxon war and my soldiers have returned to their families and lands. I have no troops to offer you, although I know there are many bored warriors reaping and threshing as we speak.' Arthwys looked thoughtful for a moment. 'The most I could muster from volunteers is two hundred cavalry, that is all.'

'Ames has five thousand men, and our Armorican friends claim that three thousand will join us once we cross the channel.'

'That may be so, but you heard Amabalis – Euric is formidable. And this plan of the Emperor's seems overly complicated. Should we not just be grateful the Patria is free of war after years of terror?'

'And that is thanks to you, Arthwys. I too am worried this campaign in Gaul will prove a disaster.'

'Then why is Ames so set on this course?'

'All his life he has been aware that his grandfather was all too briefly an emperor, that after the defeat of Jovinus and Sebastianus, our estates in the Loire were confiscated. If this expedition is successful, he will recover our property and finally set foot on the lands where his powerful forebears lived. Not only that, but he will have achieved something I never could – restitution.'

'Does Livia also wish to return to Gaul?'

'After I am gone, what is there here for her? Count Paulus is pressing us for an answer. He says our force cannot arrive soon enough; he hopes to have us there in the spring. I need to know, Arthwys – are you prepared to support my son?'

'I cannot accept command or the title of Magister Militum per Brittonum, because this campaign will be fought in ways and territories beyond my understanding, but I will bring whichever of my eques wish to accompany me on this adventure. I too would like to set foot in Gaul and see all those places of which I have heard so much.'

'Thank you, Arthwys. It gives me comfort to know Ames will have the benefit of your influence in his decision-making. Now, if you will excuse me, I am in pain and extremely tired.'

Arthwys stood, bowed and left through the large doors. Livia was in the corridor waiting, holding Caledfwich with reverence.

'So, are you going to Gaul?'

Arthwys placed his sword in his scabbard. 'Yes, but not as your commander,' he replied, looking serious.

'No one holds that role,' she said, linking her arm through his, 'though, there is a vacancy.'

He smiled at the mischief in her eyes.

*

Agiluf and Amabalis were waiting for Arthwys in the garden whilst he finished speaking with Livia by the entrance.

'I do not believe Ambrosius and his son recognise the military strength of my people,' said the priest.

'Arthwys will know the right thing to do – he always does.'

Agiluf watched as the king took his leave of Livia and came over to join them.

Arthwys looked troubled. 'I have declined Ambrosius' request that I command this expedition, and I have told him that I will not raise our army to support it.' He hesitated, studying Agiluf's reaction. 'But I will accompany Riothames and take as many eques as wish to join me.'

'May I ask why you would go at all?'

'Ambrosius supported us when we needed his help, so the least I can do is provide his cause with some cavalry assistance.'

Agiluf looked at the priest. 'Amabalis believes it is a dangerous venture, with little chance of success.'

'I agree with him. I have no understanding of Roman politics whereas Riothames and his family are steeped in it. I see it as an adventure. I would like to see Armorica and Gaul.' He winked at Agiluf. 'I am not risking my kingdom, that will remain safe; I risk only my life.'

'And mine! I presume we will be paid well for our support.'

'We have still to negotiate our rewards as mercenaries. How easy is it to find horses in Gaul, Amabalis?'

'Not easy at all – they are dearer than slaves.'

The priest's humour seemed to lift the king's mood. 'I am told a bishop will be attending this evening's banquet; you will need to be on your best behaviour.'

'A bishop! Is this city his see?'

'I am not sure. Why do you ask?'

'I have never been properly consecrated, but a bishop could make it so. I must find him straightaway.'

'I am sure Livia can direct you to him.'

Both Agiluf and Arthwys were amused by the speed with which the priest left.

'Will we be taking Amabalis to Gaul?'

'Yes. I know Merlinus will be sorry to lose him, but this is Amabalis' opportunity to get free passage home.'

Agiluf looked at the frown that furrowed his friend's brow. 'What is troubling you, Arthwys?'

'This campaign seems so pointless. I fear we are being drawn into conflict without understanding the motives of those who call on us.'

'Then why have you agreed?'

'All we have known is war. It has made us renowned warriors. Now that our homeland is safe, why not sell our skills?'

'Many of our comrades will gladly join us, Arthwys. You are right – warfare has become our way of life these last ten years.'

'My father used to say warriors die in battle; they don't retire. He would have far preferred to meet his end with his sword in hand.'

'I think my own father has missed that opportunity.'

'I often wonder what my father would have thought of our success in battle.'

'Like you, he was a strong and committed warrior. He could have been nothing other than impressed.'

'He did have some weaknesses – much as we all do. Prior to his death, he disclosed to me that Britu is my half-brother.'

Agiluf was not entirely surprised. 'He does look very much like you. Does he know?'

'Yes, but he is now King of the Cornovii, so it is best kept secret.'

'So why tell me?'

'For some time, I have felt a sense of foreboding that my life will foreshorten. Britu and the Cornovii are our closest allies, and I wanted you to know that Elfed can rely on him, more so than my cousin in Reged.'

'That is good to hear.'

Both their eyes were drawn to the vision of beauty stood at the doorway to the garden. Arthwys smiled.

'Tell me, on a separate matter, is it wrong to want another woman?'

Agiluf laughed at the abrupt question. 'Only if her husband finds out!'

'Arthwys,' Livia called, 'Ames has returned. If you wish to speak with him before cena, now is your opportunity.'

'Come, Agiluf. Let's go discover what this Roman warmonger has planned next for us.'

Agiluf followed his king but remained curious about what had prompted the intensity of their previous conversation. They walked toward the large atrium, where preparations were underway for the reception. Livia showed them into a room adjacent to the main entrance where Ames was stood waiting.

'Arthwys and Agiluf, I'm so pleased that you have arrived in time for tonight's reception.'

'It was good of you to invite us.'

'Have you given the Emperor's proposal due consideration?' It appeared Ames was too anxious to bother with any subtlety.

'Yes, I have considered it, and your father has explained what he believes the new Emperor hopes to achieve.'

'We have waited years for this opportunity, so it is crucial we act quickly.'

'Ames, I have told your father that I will not accept a Roman appointment and cannot be the one to lead this army, but because of my loyalty to you and your father, I have offered to accompany you with a contingent of cavalry who will need paid as mercenaries.'

'Did my father agree to sanction my expedition?'

'He implied as much, but he agrees with me that you are risking much.'

Riothames' brow furrowed. 'Rome is fighting for its very existence. If we stand by and spectate, we will remain forever isolated. This is our chance to re-establish our connections and supply routes. To do that, we must defeat these barbarians, once and for all. Anthemius intends to finish what Majorian started, so that Roman influence will prevail across the world once more.'

'I have brought with me a priest who, before turning to God, fought with Aetius. He is a Visigoth, and he doubts that our army can defeat his people.'

'I met him. He was on his way to seek consecration from Bishop Mansuetus.'

'He tells me Euric's army is four times larger than ours – nearly twenty thousand, with skilled cavalry.'

'Yes, but our initial role is only as a deterrent. We are just there to bolster Count Paulus whilst Marcellinus defeats the Vandals. It will be thereafter that we fight

Euric. Anthemius plans to send an army from the south to split the Visigoth force.'

'Do you know the territory where we will be deployed, Ames?'

'I have only ever visited Armorica, where we still have influence and property. The Loire Valley is further south.'

'How will you transport the horses?'

'We cannot. We must purchase as many as we are able once we make land.'

'We will need many; it will be costly. Who is funding this?'

'My family. But the Emperor will repay us when he has his victory. That is the arrangement.'

'So you will buy our horses and pay my eques?'

'Of course. Your involvement is crucial to the morale of my men. You are a hero to the Britons. It would be unthinkable to launch this campaign without King Arthwys and his famous eques.'

'Do the Armorican Britons have a commander?'

'A very good one called Maxen. You will meet him this evening.' Ames paused, seeming to take in their appearance for the first time. 'It is customary to leave your weapons in your lodgings.'

Arthwys looked toward Agiluf. 'It feels strange not to wear our swords; we have been fighting for so many years.'

'I am told yours is as famous as you are. May I see it?'

Arthwys drew his sword from its scabbard and handed it to Ames.

'It has a name – Caledfwich in our language.'

'I see you have bound the handle in leather. What is the effigy?'

'Cocidius. He is an ancient god of war, like Mars.'

'Did you inherit it?'

'No. Agiluf and I found is as boys. It was jammed into rocks.'

'Strangely light but longer than a gladius. What are these repetitive markings?'

'My ironsmith says the metal has been folded like cloth, but he cannot explain how it was done. There was a seer called Myrddin who said metal from the heavens was mixed with the ashes of our ancestors, but all I can say is I have never used a harder sword.'

Ames nodded and handed the sword back to Arthwys with great respect. 'King Arthwys, I fully appreciate this is not your war, but my family are proud to have you as our ally, and we welcome your support.'

Arthwys smiled then turned to Agiluf and spoke the language of the Cymry. 'Come, my friend. We will hide our weapons and pretty ourselves up for these Romans.'

Agiluf smirked.

Ames looked curious. 'The translation?'

'I said our warrior ways must sometimes allow for the fine manners of you Romans.'

The three men laughed heartily.

*

Arthwys awoke with the dawn. Waking in strange places was a regular experience, but never before had he slept in such ornate surroundings. The previous day's events rolled through his mind. The reception had been enjoyable, although he still questioned the air of optimism surrounding Riothames' campaign. Maxen was indeed an experienced warrior who had already fought alongside the Romans. He knew much about the Loire Valley and spoke of the presence of Saxons, who presented an additional threat. Bishop Mansuetus had kindly consecrated Amabalis who had beamed all night. Agiluf had spent most of his time with Nataline, his attractive wife Aurelia and some of her friends. Beautiful Livia had not left Arthwys' side, keeping the conversation flowing whenever he flagged.

He had not asked it of her, but he had known she would come, quietly settling beside him in the moonlight, her naked skin seeming to absorb its glow. Nothing was said. There was no need for words. And then she was gone. Afterward, he had lain still, reflecting upon his betrayal, though he knew already he would sin again.

Now, in the morning light, he felt different. The bliss of the moment had been replaced by a guilt far stronger than he had expected. He tried to justify his actions, but he could not. Rather, he was left feeling as if something irreplaceable had been broken.

He shook his head and sat up. They would stay for a week then return to Elfed to plan and prepare – there was much to do before embarking for Gaul.

Optimism

Ver 468

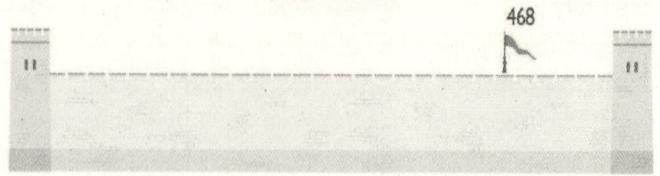

C ount Paulus waited on the beach at Aletum watching the fifty ships approaching the shore. This was the first of three waves of troop carriers bringing Riothames and his Britons to join with the Emperor's campaign. Though it would take six weeks for them to assemble and provision, he was convinced drafting in the Britons had been an inspired move. The spring winds were fresh, but the sea was remarkably calm – a good omen which he prayed would persist for the two weeks of the landings. Riothames was bringing some six thousand troops, and Maxen, his Armorican comrade, had promised a further three thousand men – a force of nine thousand in total, each man sorely required, and they could not come soon enough. Since the death of General Aegidius, Paulus had detected a reluctance on the part of the Franks to engage in battle against Euric. Syagrius, Aegidius' son, seemed only nominally in control of his allies but this was an empire-wide weakness. Rome's legions continued to dwindle to a mere shadow of the might that had secured her historic glory, the power of the barbarians growing in their place, now holding sway. It was only politics and the promise of a share of Roman taxes that kept the foedus allies doing Rome's bidding, though treachery was commonplace. This force of Britons would aid a shift of power back to the Romans in northern Gaul. The addition of a new army, made up of loyal troops might also help to stiffen the Franks' resolve, though Childeric's support was maybe less crucial now that the army of Britons was here.

As the ships began to beach, Paulus congratulated himself – after all, this had taken two years to plan, and now that his hard work had come to fruition, the Emperor was sure to bestow many honours upon him.

*

Agiluf had not enjoyed the crossing. His previous sailing experience had been limited to fording estuaries and hugging the coastline; he did not to have the stomach for the swell of the open seas. He had vomited over the side along with many of his men, feeling great relief when the Gaulish coast had come into view. Arthwys had been lost in thought for almost the entire passage, but he too was cheered at the sight of land.

'I prayed for a safe journey, and God has seen fit to deliver us.'

'You have been quiet, my king. I began to wonder if you were regretting this venture?'

'For a while, mid-ocean, I questioned my decision, but now I see the coast and walls of Aletum, I know this is my destiny.'

'Elfed will be safe in your absence. You were wise to deny your sons' requests to accompany us. Eliffer has yet a young family, and Pabo is too young.'

'This is not their fight; it is Rome's. I am only here out of loyalty to Ambrosius. He was a good leader. I will miss him.'

'Livia has taken it hard, so much so that she even accompanies her brother to these shores. She has clung to you both like lichen since the death of her father.'

'Yes. She is devastated, but it made sense for her join us on our voyage. Their family has wealth beyond our imagination. They still have property in Armorica, and this is where she lived before we ever met.'

Agiluf smiled, choosing not to push Arthwys on Livia's attachment. 'I cannot help but feel excited about all we are about to see and experience.'

'I feel the same, but before we think about touring the sights, Prefect Agiluf,' Arthwys said, feigning a stern tone, 'we have some troops to knock into shape and horses to acquire.'

Agiluf gave a mock salute then grinned with relief as the ship's hull scraped onto the sand.

*

Anthemius had never expected to be handed the Purple of the western Empire, but now he had it, the absolute power he wielded was becoming more and more intoxicating. The Palace of the Caesars on the Palatine Hill was the right choice of residence, for if his reign was to be successful, he would need to conduct it in the style of the old emperors, perhaps even accompanied by the old religions. War was the priority of any successful emperor; tolerance and peace were merely consequences of victory. Rome needed to rise and recover her prestige.

His voice echoed around the vast throne room, and the magnificence of his surroundings lay the weight of history on his shoulders. He had opted not to sit on the elevated dais. His superstitious nature could not shake the thought that it was already occupied by the ghosts of his mighty predecessors. Instead, he stood in front of a vast table-map of the Empire, surrounded by his northern generals and an air of excitement.

'Having recovered both Sardinia and Sicilia, Marcellinus sailed for Carthage but was unfortunately forced to turn back in the face of foul weather.'

Magister Militum Ricimer's mouth twisted in a sneer. 'So, is his campaign against the Vandals over... a failure?'

Anthemius knew Ricimer longed for an end to his rival. 'No, nothing is lost. Today, I can announce that Leo joins us in this struggle. He is sending one thousand ships under the command of Basiliscus. We will crush Gaiseric together.'

Ricimer could only muster a dispassionate nod, but his colleagues applauded the news.

'However,' said Anthemius, 'we are not here just to discuss the Africa campaign – I have two other announcements.' The group fell silent, hanging on the Emperor's every word. 'Count Paulus has messaged me with the news that an army of six thousand Britons, under their commander Riothames, has successfully landed at Aletum. They are joining with our allies in Armorica and will march to Avaricum before summer's end.'

Once again, the group applauded, but Ricimer, who had already been briefed about this, remained characteristically critical. 'King Euric's Visigoths vastly outnumber this expedition.'

'That is true, but Count Paulus' forces number three thousand and then there are the Franks who have yet to declare the number of troops available to us.'

'Still not enough,' said Ricimer.

'And that is why you are all assembled here with me today.'

The generals looked at each other and then toward Ricimer who remained silent.

'I have decided that my son Anthemiolus shall gather an army with you three'—he pointed to Ricimer's colleagues—'and prepare to attack Euric from the south. That way we will split his force and defeat him.'

General Thorisarius looked surprised. 'Why is Magister Militum Ricimer not commanding us?'

'Ah well, that is the subject of my third announcement. Patrician Ricimer, now married to my daughter Alypia, will remain with me here at the beating heart of our resurgent Empire.'

Ricimer forced a smile and bowed as his colleagues applauded once more.

*

Farddy shuffled toward the great hall to fulfil his daily routines. The forest of Elfed had burst forth, its annual verdant canopy hiding the many tweeting birds tending their nests. Each year, it seemed more beautiful than the last, although he still felt disappointed he had not been allowed to accompany his brother abroad. He knew he was not a warrior – he had not enjoyed the brutality of the Saxon wars, and every time he tried to compose a poem about Arthwys' victories, images of the battlefield prevented him by haunting his mind. But he would have liked to see the sights of Gaul. Still, he had to admit his role as secretary to Arthwys was much less demanding in the king's absence, which allowed him the time to resume the role of bard to Queen Gwenhyfar. For her part, she was delighted and seemed much happier than he had seen her for some years. The monster Mordred and his awful deeds were forgotten, and though Arthwys was absent, they both anticipated his victorious return.

Resisting Rome

Aestas 468

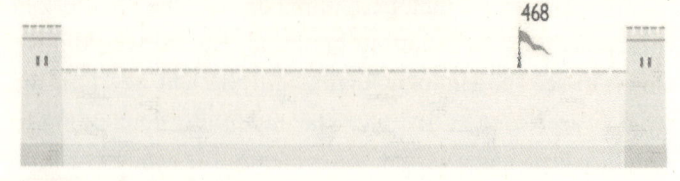

Euric had much on his mind as he looked across the Garonne from the old Roman battlements. It was a beautiful evening, the setting sun in the west casting long shadows across the Pyrenees to the south.

This was all his kingdom, won in many battles, though he had no doubt there would be many more. The Romans had once commanded the most powerful empire on earth – Tolosa, this city he had chosen for his capital, reflected that might – but their strength had ebbed away. Now was the time for his people, for those the Romans called barbarians, the warriors they had manipulated to fight their wars for them. Foedus, that was what the Romans called their military slaves, though the term no longer applied to his people or his kingdom. But despite Euric's fiercely won independence, he was troubled by the new Roman Emperor. His spies had kept him well-informed, leaving him in no doubt that Anthemius intended war. Euric had been quick to grasp Count Paulus' reason for suddenly involving this army of Britons and Armoricans. Rome's strategy would be to split Euric's forces by attacking his territory simultaneously on two or more fronts. It marked a troublingly aggressive change to the Imperial policy in the region. The Britons were already positioned to the north at Avaricum, and Count Paulus, that most determined enemy of his people, was positioned with a small army near Civitas Turonum. His most useful spy, Arvandus, had also reported that a Roman army was preparing to attack from the south, and he had advised Euric to attack the Britons without delay. But what if this was a Roman trick?

'Your majesty.' The voice of a senior eques interrupted his musings. 'Adovacrius the Saxon awaits an audience with you.'

'Has he considered our proposals?'

'Yes. He has agreed to attack Juliomagus.'

'Good. That will divert Count Paulus west whilst we attack the Britons. Tell me, Julius, what do you think the Franks will do?'

'They will defend their territory rather than go to the aid of their allies, provided we do not threaten them by pushing further north.'

'Exactly my thoughts. Once we have defeated the Britons, we will move to face the southern threat. War with Childeric will wait.' The king gripped his eques' shoulder. 'Come, my friend, Adovacrius is about to do us a much bigger favour than he perhaps realises.'

*

Patrician Ricimer could not believe the news his aide had just delivered. He screamed, threw tableware at the walls, and pushed over a bust of some no-consequence Roman worthy. It was a catastrophe. Rome was as good as finished, its power extinguished, the treasury empty.

Ricimer turned as Romanus, the magister officiorum of the palace, entered the patrician's chamber.

'I see you have heard the woeful news,' Romanus said, looking around the room at the destruction. 'What a disaster! It was the greatest fleet ever launched.'

'They had Gaiseric at their mercy, so they foolishly gave him five days to consider proposals – *five days*! Plenty of time for him to mobilise his fireships. One hundred ships lost, ten thousand men killed, and Basiliscus has withdrawn to Sicilia where he is no doubt being consoled by that other incompetent coward Marcellinus.'

Romanus hung his head. 'We made a mistake approaching Leo for help after the ousting of Severus,' he said quietly, his words prompting another furious response.

'We had no choice! Gaiseric had become too strong for the western Empire, and Leo was plotting against us anyway. We stepped aside for the good of Rome. A combined force should have been the solution to defeating the Vandals. But now... now our problems are even greater.' Romanus remained silent. 'The prestige of the Empire is lost, gone, beyond recovery.' Only revenge could assuage the bitterness that burnt within Ricimer now. 'If Leo and Anthemius had made me commander of this expedition, Gaiseric would not have been given five minutes, never mind five days.' He lowered his voice trying to calm himself. 'But they were too afraid of placing that much power in my hands. Instead, I have been manacled by marriage to Anthemius' daughter and reduced to signing papers, whilst those eastern cowards try to make treaties with the enemy instead of killing them. I tell you, Romanus, there are factions that will have Marcellinus assassinated for his incompetence – he will not leave Sicilia alive!'

Romanus was a long-standing confidante, Ricimer's closest ally in the palace; the patrician did not have to tell his friend that this statement alluded to an arrangement rather than a prediction. 'And Basiliscus?'

'He is the business of the eastern Empire. They must deal with their own, whilst we deal with ours.'

'Do you have any instructions for me, Ricimer?'

Ricimer fixed his furious stare on Romanus. 'Yes,' he rasped in a lowered voice. 'We must rid ourselves of this regime. Anthemius is weakened by these defeats; his aura is lost. Who can save Rome now? I am not sure it is even worth saving, anymore.'

*

Syagrius had been taught to respect Childeric by his father. Aegidius had been adamant that the King of the Franks was an ally and there was to be no mention of foedus status between them. Together, they had maintained their independent province after breaking with Rome when they turned their backs on Emperor Severus and the assassin Ricimer. Count Paulus, however, had forecast change for the better, a return of the glorious Roman Empire with the appointment of Emperor Anthemius. Rome requested their assistance in bringing forth her resurgence, but Syagrius and Childeric were uncomfortable coming to Rome's heel after years of independence.

'The Britons who have crossed into our territory expect us to behave as allies?' asked Childeric.

'Count Paulus has led them to believe so. He orders us to lend our support to their campaign against Euric.'

'It is true that our enmity with Euric is a common cause, but surely we do not want to assist Rome in reasserting its authority over an empire of which we do not wish to be part?'

'I agree,' said a cautious Syagrius, 'but if Euric comes north, we will need Rome's help.'

'And if Euric is defeated, Rome will expect us to join the Empire once more. I do not think they would stop short of using force if we were to refuse, regardless of how much we help them now.'

'I have already assured Paulus that our troops will support him.'

'Ah, but I have not. I say we sit on our hands and defend the territory that is ours – you are comfortable with this arrangement, yes?'

What Childeric said made sense to Syagrius, no matter how much he did not want to break his word to a fellow Roman. After some thought, he nodded. 'I agree. It would be foolish to aid a war that gains us nothing other than renewed Imperial authority.'

'If Euric sees we do not support the Britons, I'm sure he will leave us be, in favour of easier pickings.'

Syagrius agreed with Childeric's summation. 'But Count Paulus must hear nothing of our pact.'

'He will not hear of it from me, my young friend.'

*

The climb to the top of King Lott's most southerly hill fort was steep and boggy. Traprain Law was not a place Mordred would choose to live, but the land hereabouts was wild, and even his own fortress was nothing more than a wooden stockade on a rock by the coast. His weapon had been taken, and he was accompanied by two guards with spears, both of whom were only partially clad despite the driving rain. The Gododdin were renowned for their hardiness as much as their horse skills. Even their living quarters appeared to have been designed to embrace the harsh weather rather than to repel it, as if sheltering from it was a form of cowardice.

On entering King Lott's presence, Mordred immediately sensed the great respect the old, yet still powerfully built, king commanded.

'We know who you are, stranger,' he bellowed, as if addressing a vast audience. 'You are Mordred, exiled from Elfed, exiled from Reged. Are you here to fight our champion?'

'If that is what you wish, but I would rather speak with the great King Lott. Pray tell, where is he?' Mordred said feigning respect. 'I hear he is a giant!'

The king laughed. 'In reputation but not in stature. Why are you here?'

'To pay homage to my neighbour beyond the Tweed.'

'I am told you were Arthwys' best eques and you have killed many Saxons.'

'That is true, but my rewards and lands were confiscated, and now I intend to recover what is mine.'

'That is a bold statement. You know well, we are long-standing allies of Reged... though it pays us nothing!'

'I do know this, but will you allow me to put a proposition to you?'

'Yes, come to my hut and we will drink mead. I enjoy propositions.'

The king's hut was dark and thick with smoke, but his hospitality was generous. Lott passed a horn of mead to his visitor.

'A proposition, you say?'

'Yes, I have boats, many boats. I have recovered them without detection from the south.

'Surely, Arthwys has missed them?'

'Arthwys is still fighting for Rome in Gaul. Some say he is dead.'

'So, what do you want from me?'

'Warriors who I can train as marines then have them raid with me to the south. I know the locations of much treasure, all of which I will share with you. No one will know of our arrangement.'

The old king thought for a while. 'I agree, but on the proviso I can rely on your help to fight the Picts and the ever encroaching Scotti menace. Good warriors are in short supply!'

'King Lott, I will happily slaughter as many as you can put in front of me.'

The old king grinned, displaying an array of rotting teeth. Mordred nodded then took a draught of his drink. His plan was taking shape and it would not be long before he would wreak his revenge on Elfed.

Disillusion and Treachery

Aestas 471

A year to deploy followed by a year billeted at Avaricum, the campaign was slow to begin. Then the orders came, advance to the river Indre at Deols where Count Paulus and Syagrius would join forces to march south to face the Visigoths. But three months had passed and neither had arrived. Riothames looked deeply troubled as his commanders assembled to hear the content of the message he had received from Count Paulus. It was almost midday, and the sun was bearing down. Agiluf and Arthwys sought some shade beneath an orange tree to listen. Both men were finding Gaul's warmer climate stifling, and Agiluf was beginning to wish he was back in Elfed enjoying refreshing summer showers – it never seemed to rain in this part of Gaul.

'Gentlemen, I'm afraid the news from our Roman friends is not good. Count Paulus is still pinned down fighting Saxons on the Loire and he does not know where Syagrius and Childeric are. He has received no messages indicating their intentions.'

'So, what are we to do, Ames?' said Maxen. 'Our orders were to march here and meet up with two more armies before moving on to Tolosa. How long are we supposed to wait?'

'Paulus cannot disengage from the Saxon army; he needs a larger force to push them back. He is asking us for cavalry assistance.'

'If our allies are so unreliable,' said Maxen, 'perhaps we should fall back to Avaricum. Our provisions are low, and this place is nothing more than a crossroads by a river.'

Ames looked around the assembled commanders and found Arthwys. 'What say you, Arthwys?'

'I too am concerned by how unreliable our allies are proving to be.'

'If we fall back, it will be another year before we can assemble another force sufficient to threaten Euric which will undermine the effectiveness of Anthemius' southern attack.'

'But we don't even know when that attack will begin, and we do not have the numbers to attack Euric by ourselves. If no one is going to join us, we have no choice but to fall back to our winter quarters.'

Riothames looked thoughtful. He turned to Maxen, the only officer who knew the territory. 'How quickly could our cavalry reach Juliomagus?'

'Three to four days.'

'Then I suggest that Arthwys and his eques depart immediately to assist Count Paulus and return with his assessment of how viable this campaign is. That will mean we only have to wait another two weeks at this place. Arthwys, do you agree?'

'I agree that it would be a disappointment to go backward when we have come so far, but I find two things concerning. First, why did Count Paulus not anticipate the

Saxons? And second, where on God's earth are Syagrius and Childeric?'

Riothames' shoulders slumped. 'I cannot say. I have relied completely on the judgement of the Roman northern command, and I have to say, their intelligence has been patchy throughout.'

'Do we know where Euric's army is?'

'Our assumption has been that it is focused on the south where the Roman army is about to advance into his territory.'

'But is that what is happening? Does anyone know for sure?' Riothames could only shrug. 'I will do as you ask, because it seems the only good option. When are the southern scouts due to return?'

'Three days.'

'Then we will not delay. We will leave at dusk and travel through the night.'

Agiluf and Arthwys strode toward the field where the eques were going about their daily duties.

'It is good that our men will have something to do now,' said Agiluf to his king.

'Forgive my contradiction, but nothing about this is good. Ames has placed too much trust in his Romans, none of whom appear to trust each other. I have a bad feeling about this grand plan, and I will be urging him to drop back to the Loire when I return. This army needs to move; it is too exposed here.'

*

The young optio had been searching Juliomagus for Count Paulus for some time when he eventually found the count at prayer in the church.

'My lord, a large army is headed our way, and the Saxons are withdrawing.'

'Then my prayers have been answered, Lucius. Is it Syagrius?'

'I cannot say, my lord, but they are not Romans.'

'I shall continue to pray until they arrive.'

It was not long before the gates were opened to allow the forward cavalry through. The powerfully built leader leapt from his horse, his long, flaxen plait swinging at his waist.

'I am Childeric. Where is Count Paulus?'

'Follow me,' said Lucius.

They entered the church where the Roman was still on his knees at prayer. Paulus stood to greet the barbarian leader.

'Childeric! Thank God you are here. I have been blockaded in this town for two months, and no one has come to assist. My messengers must have all been killed by the Saxons.'

'No, no, we got your messages.'

'In God's name, why didn't you come, then?' The barbarian king gave no reply. 'Where is Syagrius? Has he joined the Britons?'

'No, he remains at Noviodunum.'

'You both had express orders to rendezvous with the Britons.'

'We have chosen a different path.'

Paulus gaped. 'The Emperor shall hear of this. On whose authority do you disobey an order from Rome?'

'We are not foedus. We are not bound to follow Rome's orders.'

'I will see you are arrested for this insubordination.'

'Who will arrest us? Not you. Rome no longer has any authority in this region.'

Lucius watched in horror as the Frankish king drew his sword and thrust it into Count Paulus' chest, killing him instantly. Childeric withdrew the weapon and wiped it clean on the murdered Roman's tunic. He turned to the frightened officer.

'He killed himself, yes? You fight for me now. Assemble your men. We have Saxons to chase.'

Childeric walked outside the church and signalled to one of his senior officers.

'There is plague in this city. Loot and burn it.'

*

The sunrise was bright and clear, signalling yet another hot day on the plain. The young sentry nearly tripped over as he ran into the small building Riothames was using as his headquarters.

'My king,' he gasped, trying to catch his breath, 'the scouts have just galloped in – they have seen a huge army coming from the south.'

'God help us. It must be Euric. Sound the alarm and bring Nataline to me, now!'

Nataline arrived quickly. 'My king?'

'Take our best horse, leave now. You must catch Arthwys and turn him back.'

Nataline headed directly for the stables, weaving between men running in every direction, taking up their defensive positions along the river. Nataline was soon mounted and galloping out in the direction of Juliomagus. He could not be sure of the route Arthwys had taken, but he had to find him. He would trust in God and ride like the wind.

Defeat and Surrender

Aestas 471

Both Arthwys and Agiluf knew that the urgency of Count Paulus' call for support had to be weighed against looking after their horses. It would be pointless arriving in the middle of a battle with exhausted mounts. The geography was alien to them, leaving no alternative but to follow either the rivers or the established, poorly maintained Roman roads. They had ridden through the night, but the heat of midday was best avoided, and so the large troop had sought shade and rest as the hot sun baked the surrounding countryside. The men were just preparing to mount up and continue their journey when a rider was seen galloping toward them. Arthwys cupped his hands over his eyes and squinted into the bright sunlight.

'The rider looks to be one of ours. Perhaps Syagrius has shown up.'

They waited, wondering why the messenger was travelling with such urgency, and then Agiluf recognised the rider.

'It's Nataline. Something is wrong, I know it.'

The young officer slowed his horse to a walk as he reached the eques. The poor animal was lathered in foam, its head hanging with exhaustion. Nataline fell to the ground.

'Water for them both,' instructed Agiluf, as he stooped to hold his young comrade. A bladder of water was placed to Nataline's lips, and he sucked in as much as he could manage. Arthwys crouched alongside him, waiting for the news.

When Nataline caught his breath enough to speak, his voice was hoarse. 'It's Euric. A large army appeared at dawn yesterday. We must return straightaway; Riothames must be under attack by now.'

Arthwys paled. 'This is the worst possible news. We have been naïve, believing that we are the only ones with a plan. Euric has read our minds. I'll warrant the Saxons are in league with him.'

'Find a fresh horse for Nataline. This poor mare has done all she can; release her. We return to Deols immediately.'

*

Full of apprehension they travelled through the night, arriving in the region of Deols before midday.

'How close are we to our camp?' Agiluf's unfamiliarity with the region making him uncertain of the remaining distance.

'Quite close, but we must remain in the forest, or the enemy will see us.'

They had been following the river but guessed that Euric would attempt to cross it either upstream or downstream of the ford into the town.

'It is my best guess that Euric will have crossed upstream and attempted to surround the camp.'

'Do you think the attack has already begun?'

'Almost certainly. We are but a mile from Riothames, and the men are reporting that the river runs red with blood, and they have seen corpses floating westward.'

'So you think Riothames is defeated?'

Arthwys shrugged. 'If he is not, we will need to break through the Visigoth lines to reach our forces and aid the retreat.'

'For us to succeed, our attack must be a surprise.'

Arthwys nodded. 'We must arc northward and only break cover when we are sure of the enemy's position.'

Nataline had not spoken for some time. 'What if they are all dead?' he suddenly blurted.

Arthwys was never calmer than in the hours before a battle. 'That is unlikely. It takes more than a day to butcher nine thousand men. I suspect they have been severely mauled and that Euric is considering his next move. He has all his territory to defend and will be aware there is a Roman army massing to attack him from the south.

'How can he know that?' asked Nataline.

'He has read our every move, so far. Either he is a remarkably gifted general or he is very well-informed. It may be both, but if he knows of the southern attack, it tells us two things.'

'And they are...?' asked Nataline.

'That he will be keen to withdraw as soon as possible to prepare for the southern attack, and also, if he has the confidence to attack us now, that the Roman army is not yet ready to begin its advance.'

'But the Roman attack was to coincide with ours!' said Agiluf, aghast.

'This whole campaign has been nothing more than the figment of both emperors' ambitions. We have been hampered at every turn. We can only hope that the Roman campaign against the Vandals has fared better, because our campaign has yielded the opposite effect to their intentions.'

'In what way?'

'In attempting to weaken Euric, they have only strengthened him.'

Agiluf looked around. 'We must remain alert and stay as quiet as possible. We are coming to the edge of the forest, but I cannot yet see Deols.'

'We have no choice but to follow the forest's perimeter until we meet the road north.'

'We must hurry. My men are being slaughtered out there,' Nataline said, panic rising in his voice.

'We must remain cautious,' said Arthwys. 'We are no help to your men if Euric attacks us before we even reach the camp.'

*

When Arthwys' eques reached the north road, they advanced stealthily to the edge of the forest. Now they could see Deols.

'Good God,' said Agiluf. 'Euric's army is vast, but I expected him to have more cavalry.'

'They have cavalry, more than us. I suspect Euric has sent most of it to the south where the greater threat awaits,' said Arthwys, eyes narrowed as he appraised the battle formations before them.

'How will we break through?'

'We will charge in a V-formation and force our way through the Visigoth ranks to our defences.'

'We could get caught in a trap from which we cannot return.'

Arthwys grimaced but looked determined. 'We must help our comrades. Our attack will come as a surprise to the Visigoths. That will give us precious time to break through before they can properly reform. If we are lucky, they may even retreat from us, thinking we are the advance party of a much larger army.'

Agiluf nodded and gave the formation order to his four captains, who returned to their men and their horses to watch for the signal from their king to attack. Agiluf's stomach churned with fear as they waited. It was always thus until his sword was swinging. The signal came, and they burst from the trees. First a canter, then a gallop. The thrill of the cavalry charge thrummed through Agiluf's veins as two hundred horsemen thundered down the road, cutting down every human obstacle in their way. Visigoths turned with horror in their faces, their battle lines splitting open in their shock and terror, enabling the riders to push through. A mighty cheer went up from the ranks of the Britons who parted their shield wall to let the cavalry into the camp. But the joy of breaking through was soon crushed by what the new arrivals now witnessed. Corpses lay everywhere, testament to how fierce the battle had been. Maxen greeted Arthwys as he dismounted his horse.

'Our hearts are gladdened by your arrival, Arthwys. Riothames is dead. He fought bravely in the front line but fell from an arrow through his throat.'

Agiluf was shocked at the news, but Arthwys was too focused on the battle for emotion to take its toll.

'That is unfortunate news. What is your assessment, Maxen?'

'We are finished. This is a hopeless place to defend. We are reduced to using the piled bodies of our comrades for cover. They have killed thousands of us, but we have killed thousands of them. The river is choked with corpses and dead horses, and now these flies are everywhere. We must escape soon, for disease will soon follow.'

'Do you counsel surrender or a fighting retreat?'

'If we surrender, they will make us their slaves.'

'Is the priest Amabalis still alive?'

Maxen let forth a bitter laugh. 'Yes, the busiest priest in all of Gaul is still alive.'

'Then bring him to me. I have an idea.'

*

Following his discussion with Arthwys, Amabalis had fashioned a large cross from broken spears. To the top, he had attached a pennant of white linen cut from a toga. Arthwys similarly carried a white pennant on a broken spear. They mounted their horses and set off in the direction of the enemy front line, guiding their steeds around the corpses from both sides which littered the ancient ford. They rode slowly and purposefully toward the centre of the Visigoth line dominating the horizon. The priest turned to Arthwys.

'They have seen us but are not attacking. Look, there in the centre on the white stallion, that is Euric.'

Risking his life for Arthwys was the least Amabalis could do for the king who had rescued him from the Saxons. It was late afternoon, and it seemed that the Visigoths had ceased their attack for the day, but experience told Amabalis that this magnanimity would only last for as long as Euric believed he had the upper hand.

Euric's piercing eyes studied them as they approached, a look of surprise flashing across his face when Amabalis addressed him in his own language.

'Great king, I am here to offer surrender on behalf of the Britons who wish to bury their dead and return to their homeland.'

'Who is this who speaks our language yet keeps company with our enemy?'

'I am Amabalis, a humble priest who once fought with your father against Atilla.'

'And who is this warrior who so boldly broke through our northern flank?'

'This is King Arthwys. He is a good king. He saved my life and has won many battles.'

'So why does he fight for the Romans?'

'Loyalty to a Roman who brought us here and who now is dead, killed by one of your arrows.'

'I will speak with this Arthwys.' Euric switched to perfect Latin. 'King Arthwys, why have you brought this force of Britons to threaten us?'

'An error of judgement, King Euric. The Romans convinced our leaders that the Empire was on the rise once more, that they needed our help to regain their lands, but now we see the truth. Gaul no more belongs to Rome than does Britannia.'

'Are you foedus?'

'No. We are free men who were persuaded to fight for the Christian common good.'

'So why would you help Rome place its yoke upon my shoulders when all on your island live free?'

Arthwys hung his head. 'I see that now. We were manipulated with falsehoods, and we have paid a high price for our error.'

'Will you fight for me, Arthwys?'

'I can see you are a great king, a worthy leader, but you are already surrounded by plentiful soldiers. We Britons have spent far too long in this region and wish only to return to our patria.'

'The Romans brought you here because they have no legions of their own. They invited us all to their table so they might control us, but now, they must eat at our table or starve.'

'The men who devised this campaign sit in Rome, King Euric. That is the direction from which your next challenge will come.'

'I know this, but we are also surrounded by ambitious and untrustworthy allies who would gladly pay you to return to the battlefield against us. Will you give me your oath that, if I allow you to leave this field, you will return to your patria rather than raise arms against us?'

'You have my solemn oath. Our heart is not in this fight. The Rome we Britons imagined no longer exists, its power extinguished, its emperors ineffectual. It seems

Rome's demise is God's plan, and I will not hereafter be persuaded otherwise.'

'Wise words, Arthwys. It is widely held that Anthemius is a pagan. Did you know this? Would you have fought for him had you known?'

'I would not. That may well explain why the fates have been so against us from the outset.'

'Go, bury your dead and leave this place.'

Arthwys and Amabalis turned their horses, not daring to speak until they reached the ford.

'Your people are no different to mine, Amabalis.'

The priest nodded. 'They are ruthless, but they have great respect for brave warriors. Euric knows you will keep your word.'

'A day, perhaps two, to bury the dead, and then we shall return to Armorica. I presume you intend to stay in this region?'

'God has brought me here for a reason, though I have yet to understand His purpose.'

'Well, I would say, saving the lives of thousands of men is a reasonable start.'

Amabalis laughed. 'Ah yes, but it is men's souls that I must save.'

'Everyone here will have made promises to God for their deliverance, I know that I have.'

'And so have I,' said the priest. 'But promises are easy to make; it is the keeping of them that is difficult.'

Death and Despair

Aestas 472

A year had passed, but Arthwys had chosen to stay a while in Armorica at the large property Livia owned between Aletum and Aregenua. The estate bred horses, and Arthwys had always taken pleasure from applying the patience and persistence necessary for schooling horses to battle standard. The absorbing work had provided much-needed solace following the defeat at Deols, and although a full year had passed, time had flown, and it had been good to have the time to reflect.

The Briton army had lost over half its men in the slaughter, and Nataline had returned to Venta Belgarum to face the many widows. In Armorica, Maxen's position had become tenuous. Childeric had followed up his victory over the Loire Saxons with exploratory raids into Maxen's territory, and Arthwys' eques had stayed on to help repulse the threat. Livia had been devastated by the death of her brother so soon after that of her father. On top of that grief, acknowledging that the crushing defeat of her family's army had finally buried all hope of a Roman future was difficult to bear. Arthwys had consoled her best he could. None of his eques had yet chosen to return home, preferring to stay with their king, they said, though he had noticed how many of them had taken advantage of the presence of so many Armorican widows – such was war, and he was in no position to judge.

He had intended returning to Elfed eventually, when it felt appropriate to leave, and a recent spate of unsettling nightmares had been drawing his thoughts to home more strongly than at any other time in the past year. He had dreamt both Myrddin and his father were beckoning him, only when he followed, he would lose them in a forest or become mired in a bog or entangled in thorns. Each time, he would wake feeling completely lost. He was not a seer, so he could not divine the meaning, if indeed there even was one, but the dreams' persistence was disconcerting. He had spoken with Livia about them when she noticed his disturbed sleep, but she had dismissed them. Not surprising, as she had made no secret of wanting Arthwys to stay with her. He could not deny he was sorely tempted, but he had always known a day would come when he would have to leave.

Two approaching riders caught his eye, distracting him from his reverie and disrupting the concentration he was applying to his horse's footwork. One rider he recognised as his good friend Agiluf and the other looked familiar. As they got closer, he recognised the second rider as Blwchfardd. The news he carried must be important for him to have travelled all the way from Elfed. Arthwys dismounted his stallion and walked to the rail to greet his friends.

'Farddy!' he called. 'What brings my faithful secretary so far from home?'

Farddy looked harrowed and haggard, seeming many years older than when Arthwys had last seen him. Agiluf's customary good humour was absent from his expression, and he shook his head with pursed lips. The visitor's message was chilling.

'King Arthwys, I have the gravest news, but forgive me, I would prefer not to declare it from horseback. Better that we three find a private room. All I will say for now is that you must prepare yourself for terrible grief.'

Arthwys felt sudden apprehension. What could have happened?

'My friend, come inside. We will find some refreshment for you whilst you relay your news.'

As they walked toward the villa, Arthwys noted how Farddy seemed to drag his club foot in a more pronounced manner, like he carried a great weight. Clearly, something dreadful had occurred. His mind raced with fearful anticipation. He ushered the two men into a room close by the villa's entrance and called to servants for water and wine. Once settled, he turned to Farddy.

'Was the journey arduous?'

Farddy's voice broke with emotion.

'Yes, I didn't know where to look for you. Until news reached us from Nataline just a few weeks ago, we all thought you were dead… all except Merlinus who remained resolute that you were not.'

'Arthwys,' said Agiluf, his voice similarly strained, 'prepare yourself for grief and rage in equal measure.'

The king nodded to Farddy. 'I am ready, please begin.'

'It is one year since we heard news of devastating defeats for the Romans at sea and in Gaul. The traders who brought us this news spoke of thousands of Britons slaughtered and their king dead. When we heard no news to the contrary, and none of Elfed's men returned home, we presumed you were amongst the dead.'

'I sent messages with merchants, but I had no idea they had not arrived,' said Agiluf, his face pale.

Farddy sighed and shook his head. 'News of King Arthwys' death spread like wildfire. It was no coincidence that Pictish raids suddenly recommenced in our eastern territories around the Tees. Eliffer responded bravely, taking his militia north to counter these attacks. He could not have known the raids were a diversion designed to draw our warriors away from Cambodunum.' Farddy looked to the ceiling and wrung his hands. 'Early one spring morning, when Eliffer had been gone a week and was not expected back for another, the gates were open, no threat apparent. Suddenly, Mordred led thirty or so men into the compound, killing the guards and murdering our women and children. They had come by boat, making the most of his knowledge of our rivers. Our father, Cian'—his voice cracked with emotion as he looked at his brother—'fought bravely, killing three or four of them before he succumbed to multiple blows. Bryn and Igerna barricaded the hall, but the attackers broke in and cut them down in cold blood. I was disarmed and severely wounded by Mordred.' He lifted his tunic to show a deep scar across his torso. 'He would have finished me, too, were it not for Gwenhyfar's courage. She held a dagger to her heart and screamed she would kill herself if he did not stop. You see, she knew he was not just there for revenge, that he had come for her. The treasury was looted, then the hall set on fire. I passed out from my wound, and when I was eventually found and revived, Mordred had left and the queen was missing, abducted.' Tears were now streaming down all their faces.

'Where were Pabo and my grandchild?'

'Merlinus, Morgaine and Pabo were mercifully at the church in the forest. God only knows what that murderer would have done to Merlinus if he had found him. Mordred searched for him growling that he wanted to *finish my father's business.*'

'And what of Elaine and my grandson?'

'It is now grandsons, King Arthwys!' Farddy forced a smile through his tears. 'Peredur and Gwrgy were with Elaine at her parents, a safe distance from the attack.'

'Has Eliffer gone in search of his mother?'

'Eliffer is too badly wounded to ride. Merlinus and Pabo travelled to Reged to request King Meirchiawn's help.'

'What did my cousin say?'

'That he could not spare the men, for they were committed repelling raids in the west. He warned that he could not ensure Pabo and Merlinus' safety in his kingdom. I believe he fears Mordred.'

'So, where are they now?'

'At Candida Casa at Whithorn.'

'And Eliffer's wounds. Will my son recover?'

'He is being cared for, but it is unlikely he will fight again. Winnog and his son are holding Elfed as best they can, their resolve bolstered by the news that you are not dead.' Farddy continued to wring his hands. 'Merlinus buried Mother, Father and Igerna by his small church in the forest.'

Arthwys nodded approvingly and wiped his tears.

'He said something strange at the funeral that gave us all faint hope, even though we still feared you were dead at that time.'

Agiluf looked up. His brother had not told him about this.

'He said that, before Myrddin died, he had told him of a time of great sorrow, but that Elfed and Reged would survive, and to take comfort that the king would fulfil his duty to return Caledfwich to where it belongs.'

Arthwys stood abruptly. 'I must pray for my loved ones. Then I will tell Livia of my plans to leave. Agiluf, muster as many men as are prepared to accompany us. We sail for Reged within the week. Farddy,' he said softly, 'you are a brave and faithful eques. I am sorry for your pain but grateful for your loyalty. Comfort your brother, and then we will go consign Mordred to Hell where he truly belongs.'

As Arthwys made his way to the chapel, he tried hard to remain calm, but every nerve and sinew was screaming for revenge. Poor brave Gwenhyfar, what pain must she have endured? Why had God deserted him? Had he not come to Gaul to fight for Christ? Arthwys felt lost, just as he had in his dreams. But he had to be resolute now and find his way, sword in hand. Myrddin had been right – it was his duty to return Caledfwich… but not before it had removed Mordred's head.

*

Ricimer and his loyal bodyguard marched into the square in front of the church of Santa Maria in the Trastevere district of Rome. The church was surrounded by Gundobad's Burgundian troops. The young commander striding across to meet Ricimer was both his nephew and the newly appointed magister militum.

'We have captured him; he was dressed as a beggar. Do you wish to speak with him?' asked Gundobad.

'Briefly, although we should withdraw soon. I see that your men have begun looting.'

'After such a long siege, our men deserve reward, uncle.'

'Quite so, but these things can quickly get out of hand, and our city allies will resent such acts. Lead me to the prisoner.'

The church was full of soldiers when they entered, the clergy nowhere to be seen. Ricimer was brought a chair which was placed in front of Anthemius who was unbowed but bound hand-and-foot.

'So, it is over,' Ricimer said, betraying no emotion.

Anthemius sneered. 'Have you come to kill me yourself? Assassinating emperors is your speciality, after all.'

Ricimer laughed. 'We already have a new emperor – Olybrius, one who understands his people.'

'How dare you! You skin-clad barbarians will never understand the Roman people or their ways.'

'But you are a Greek, Leo's arrogant puppet. Who are you to tell me about the people of Rome?' Anthemius did not respond. 'Under your leadership, Rome has been totally defeated, and you have drained the treasuries of both empires to an unrecoverable level. You have failed to recognise that the world rejected the old Rome some time ago, that your subjects refuse to be enslaved all over again to provide pleasure for the Empire's elite.'

'Leo supported my campaigns.'

'Leo, Leo,' Ricimer scoffed. 'The bloated eastern Emperor who sits behind his grand walls manipulating us all. He would not be in power himself were it not for the successes of two barbarian generals – Aetius who defeated Attila, and Aspar who created him. The likes of you and Leo only achieved power because barbarians, such as I, allowed it to be so. But no more. What is there to fight for when the Britons, Vandals, Visigoths, Burgundians and Franks have all rejected the yoke of Rome. Olybrius has promised me that he will rule for the welfare of *us all* and not for the benefit of this collapsed state.'

Anthemius pursed his lips. 'I beg you not to murder my family. Please, leave them be. They have done you no harm.'

'Ah the final plea, but surely murder is Rome's answer to everything? Remember how I begged you not to execute my excellent colleague Romanus? Did you grant him mercy?' Ricimer's eyes flashed with revenge. 'Your daughter Alypia despises me, but then we did not choose each other, did we? I will consider sparing her and her brothers as your final request...' Ricimer turned away from the former Emperor. 'Gundobad!'

'Yes, patrician.'

'Execute the prisoner.'

Anthemius was pushed to his knees, his head held over a stone block. Gundobad raised his sword and brought it down on the neck of the deposed Emperor with a powerful strike. The severed head rolled away as blood gushed across the stone floor of the church.

'Do you wish to have the head displayed?'

'No. Release the body to his family. We gain nothing by overt displays of vengeful slaughter. Our objective is achieved, and it is enough that he has been removed from office.'

The King Returns

Aestas 472

It was clear to Agiluf that Arthwys blamed himself for Elfed's devastation and the plight of his family. He alone had determined Mordred's punishment, and perhaps he should have guessed the scorned warrior would seek revenge, but it was the savagery of the attack that had shocked them all. When the king had chosen to linger in Armorica, he had not considered that his absence might be interpreted as his death, emboldening his rival.

The defeat at Deols, although a catastrophe for Riothames and his Britons, had hardly degraded Elfed's militia. During their time in Armorica, they had fought alongside Maxen to repulse Frankish attempts at expansion, so earning the gratitude and respect of the Armorican people. Not sensing any need to rush back to Elfed himself, Agiluf had met a woman, a soldier's widow with two children. His new family needed him, but the murder of his parents could not go unanswered, and his duty and loyalty to the king always came first. He was not the only one of the king's eques who had made a new life for himself, many others felt the same. Regardless of loyalty, it had taken great persuasion to convince them to return to the Patria, even with their collective outrage at Mordred's attack and concern about the fate of their families back home. In the end, Agiluf had promised those who accompanied the king free passage back to Armorica when the campaign against Mordred was over, and they had managed to gather a force of sixty men for the sea crossing.

The journey had been exhausting and, at times, terrifying. The king's eques were not sailors, but the sturdy lusoria vessels required them all to row. Initially, it has been quite the challenge, but the sea captains had been patient and the crews had adapted quickly. Everyone on board knew the tales of sea monsters pulling ships under with their tentacles and had heard reports of mighty storms tossing ships around like toys, so they had all known they were putting their lives in God's hands when they had chosen to embark on this journey. Having a priest amongst them to lead their prayers had been an advantage, and Adrian's knowledge of the west coast and the many religious houses with landings had also proved invaluable.

The first leg of their passage to the island of Lisia had provided some comedy as the men tried to master basic rowing skills in calm waters, but when they moved out into rough seas over the following two days, the voyage turned to an exercise in endurance. The sea had swelled alarmingly and Agiluf had been violently seasick. A strong easterly threatening to blow them off course had ensured the sail could not be hoisted. Mercifully, the days had been long, the visibility fair, but that first night at sea had been daunting. With no moon, the darkness had been so complete they lost sight of the lead boat, and it had seemed they were surrounded by nothing but limitless, inky depths. The swell had continued through the night, accompanied by the constant sound of men praying and retching over the side. No one had slept. But by dawn, the wind had changed, and they could see both the distant cliffs of Dumnonia and their companions' boat off the starboard bow. Thereafter, the captain had stayed in sight of land, and once around the foot of the Patria, the hoisting of the sail had made for lighter work in the prevailing south-westerly wind. God, or whatever deities determined events at sea, had proved kind, and their continuing voyage was accompanied by many sea-birds, sometimes dolphins, porpoises and seals, too. They had come ashore at several religious communities who were all surprised to receive a king. Arthwys had made the pious gesture of praying at them all. The good weather and brisk wind had stayed with them, as they passed the great mountain, Yr Wyddfa, and visited both the islands of Mona and Manavia.

Agiluf continually thanked the Lord that the voyage would soon be over.

'Is that Erechwyd?' asked Farddy, who was sat at the stern by his side.

'It is, that is where Arthwys met Gwenhyfar, and where we found Caledfwich.'

Agiluf looked ahead to where the king travelled in the lead boat and wondered if similar memories were passing through his mind, adding to his pain. Other than the sea captains of the two ships and a priest, no one amongst them had travelled such a distance by sea before. But Arthwys had been resolute they would rescue the queen by the fastest means possible and that meant sailing all the way to Reged. Agiluf had suggested a shorter sea crossing and then travelling north overland, a journey taking four to five weeks, but Barinthus, their most experienced captain, had convinced Arthwys they could sail it in half that time. And so it had proved, for they would reach Alauna before the day was out.

Looking across to the fells of Erechwyd, Agiluf thought how full of their usual mystery they were, the afternoon sunshine casting shadows across the green, brown and grey landscape, accentuating the depth of the dark corries. These were familiar landmarks.

'See there, Farddy? That is Itunocelum where I fought my very first battle.'

'I remember Mother and Queen Igerna being so angry and worried that you and Arthwys had been sent into battle when you were still just boys.'

Farddy looked sad as the memory of his mother and the queen came to mind, but Agiluf laughed for the first time in eleven days. 'This last part of the voyage has turned out to be quite enjoyable, though I'd rather forget the first few days.'

Their seafaring was almost at its end now, and they helped drop the sail to enable the captains to expertly manoeuvre the boats onto the old Roman wharf at Alauna. The mood of both crews lifted as they disembarked, and with his feet once more on firm ground, Agiluf joined Arthwys on the quayside. Walking cautiously toward them but stopping a safe distance away, a local headman called out in Latin.

'Who are you?'

'Friends,' replied Arthwys, in the language of the Cymry.

The headman smiled and came closer.

'You speak my language?'

'Of course! I am King Arthwys of Elfed. Tell me, are there soldiers in that watchtower?'

'They have all just galloped off to warn King Meirchiawn of invaders!'

'I feared as much. Will you send a messenger to him from me?'

'Yes, I will send my son.'

'Please tell him that we will stay here tonight, but tomorrow we will march to Luguvalium to meet him.'

'Right away, my king.' The man bowed and left.

'Agiluf, instruct the sea captains to remain here at berth, pending our return. But first, we must find a skiff to send to Whithorn to collect Merlinus and Pabo.'

Agiluf walked back along the quayside.

'Barinthus, will you find a skiff and sail across to Whithorn to collect the king's son Pabo and a priest called Merlinus?'

The old captain smiled. 'I shall take this priest to assist me.' He gestured toward Adrian. 'He will know the location.'

'Indeed, I do,' said the priest. 'There is a shrine there to the holy saint, Ninian.'

*

Meirchiawn and his sons listened to the report from the flustered and frightened guards from Alauna.

'Two warships you say, and how many soldiers?' the Reged king asked, unable to keep the concern from his voice.

'Hundreds.'

'In two ships? That cannot be so. Nonetheless, this is worrying. Were there any flags or insignias?'

'They were well-equipped with shields and spears, that was all we could see.'

'It is unusual for raiders to sail into port and moor their ships in broad daylight,' said Cynfarch, his eldest son. 'Who can they be?'

Queen Gwenhyfach entered the hall. 'The son of Alauna's headman is waiting to see you. Shall I show him in?'

'Yes, but hurry. We must waste no time gathering up our forces to face this threat.'

The young man entered and bowed. 'My king, I bring a message from King Arthwys. He has arrived at our port.' The room went silent. 'He requests a meeting with you tomorrow, here in Luguvalium. He states he will begin his journey as soon as his son and counsellor have joined him from Whithorn.'

'Please tell my cousin he is most welcome. Do you return straightaway?'

'Yes, my king.'

'Godspeed.'

As soon as the messenger had left, Meirchiawn turned his fury on his guards. 'Return to your posts and, for God's sake, learn to count.'

The guards departed quickly.

Cynfarch was first to fill the silence. 'Arthwys! We thought him dead.'

'He comes to wage war on Mordred. He will want to know why we have not already done so, why we have not rescued your sister,' Meirchiawn said, looking at his wife.

'All we can do is speak the truth, but he will not like what he hears.'

'That is a certainty. But this unexpected shift in power might still benefit our kingdom.'

'He is a hero to the people. Do you not fear he is a threat to you? After all, the throne of Reged is a powerful seat that many covet.'

'He would never break the Coeling code, though that will not prevent him from wielding his sense of superiority over us.'

'Maybe, but we do not know how his experiences will have changed him. We must be cautious, husband. He is a powerful warlord bearing a grudge.'

'We are surrounded by them!'

*

The morning was fresh with a brisk sea breeze. Criffel looked majestic across the bay in the sunshine, its grey peak skirted by the purple hue of heather in flower. Arthwys waited at the end of the wooden pier watching the small skiff slowly make its way across the estuary. He was excited to see his son and old Merlinus but curious about their time in isolation on Whithorn and anxious to hear more of what had befallen his family. It had been nearly four years since Arthwys had left home. Pabo was now nineteen and Merlinus was very old, certainly well into his seventh decade.

The boat headed for the beach, and Arthwys waved as it drew in, watching as his younger son stood and stepped out with the captain. Arthwys saw with pride that the young man was now as tall as himself. The two of them helped Merlinus climb out of the boat with some difficulty whilst Arthwys strode down the pier and onto the beach. He held out his arms, but Pabo remained focused on supporting the unsteady priest.

'Pabo, I am so pleased to see you.'

'Father,' was his son's stiff reply, though he bowed respectfully.

'Merlinus, how are you?'

'I have been getting older whilst I waited for your return.'

Arthwys laughed. 'So you did not think me dead like everyone else?'

'I was certain that you were not, but then, you were away so long, even I would have lost faith were it not for Myrddin's prophecy.'

'Well, I'm here now to set matters straight. Come, let us sit over here.'

Pabo helped Merlinus to walk up the shingle whilst Arthwys thanked Barinthus. When they were all sat comfortably, Arthwys turned to the old priest.

'How are my sister and nephew?'

'Both well and keeping me alive,' he replied.

'And Eliffer, tell me how he is.'

'He was badly wounded fighting the enemy and also broke his left leg falling from his horse. We put the limb in a wooden cage before we left for Reged.'

'Will his wounds heal?'

'If he has avoided infection, yes, but his days as a warrior are most likely over. He no longer resides at Cambodunum. His family are living with Winnog at his villa further north. He is well cared for, but if you intend returning to Armorica, Pabo will have to return to Elfed to help govern.'

'Why do you think that is my intention?'

'Because something there has kept you from returning all this time.'

'It was a protracted campaign that ended in defeat. After that, our allies needed us...'

'Not the Roman adventure you hoped for then?'

'It was not. The Empire is nothing more than an empty shell.'

'I hear it was Blwchfardd who found you, so you must already know the consequences of your absence.'

Arthwys hung his head. 'I am staggered. I was so confident Elfed was secure and that no harm could come to my family. I have prayed for answers, but none have come.'

'Ah, but God does not guide the conduct of men. One failure alone caused this...'

'I know. I should have executed Mordred. But Gwenhyfar did not want it, and he had fought for us with such valour.'

'And now he is responsible for the ruin of Elfed.'

Arthwys sighed and shook his head. Then he straightened his shoulders and looked at his son. 'Why did you choose to remain at Candida Casa?'

'Eliffer and Winnog bolstered our militia sufficiently to protect Elfed, but they did not have sufficient manpower to pursue Mordred. I approached King Meirchiawn to ask him to help me rescue Mother, but he would not. He says attacking Mordred would incite King Lott of the

Gododdin. Instead, he wrote to Mordred, offering ransom for the return of Elfed's queen, but it was declined. I have withdrawn from Reged so as not to antagonise Mordred and begin a war that will do nothing to secure her rescue… if indeed, she even wants to be rescued…'

Arthwys looked sharply at his son. 'What do you mean?'

'Mordred has convinced her you are dead. He has used that belief to chain her to him. Her sister will explain their unholy alliance better than I. I have remained at Whithorn awaiting your return. Merlinus said you would come and *could not* be dead.'

Arthwys put his arm around his son's shoulders. 'You have done well, Pabo. Let us go speak to Meirchiawn to see what can be done. Merlinus, will you join us?'

'Later. For now, I will return to Candida Casa. Myrddin always said that the Bear would return the sword, and so it has proved. I will pray for you both.'

*

Reged was, without doubt, the most powerful northern kingdom, even more so since the sack of Elfed. Meirchiawn was a cautious king, his treasury full and his relations with his neighbours cordial. His sons, Cynfarch and Elidyr, were growing into strong warriors who, one day, would ensure the kingdom continued to thrive. His father had always lived in the hills at Banna, but Meirchiawn preferred the town of Luguvalium close to the coast where he had rebuilt several buildings including the grand hall in which his family now lived and conducted their daily business. The sentries on the walls had alerted the royal court that King Arthwys and his militia of eques were approaching.

'He comes to make war,' said Gwenhyfach, shaking her head.

'But not with us, wife. Be cautious. He is still the greatest warrior of our generation, despite his setbacks.'

'He will ask you to attack Mordred, and that will bring King Lott down on us all.'

'Undoubtedly, we will discuss that option, but do not underestimate him or his militia. The men he brings are not typical soldiers; they are highly trained eques. On foot, they are equal to three ordinary warriors, but once we give them war horses, which they are likely to request, they will be the match for five. I fought alongside them in the Saxon wars, and they are an impressive fighting unit.'

'You hold their prowess in high regard, Father?'

'I do. Which is why I would be interested to hear what went wrong in Gaul, although I suspect Arthwys will be thinking only about his wife and have little time for other conversation.'

A commotion outside heralded the visitors' arrival. The doors were opened by the sentries, and Arthwys entered, accompanied by his son, Agiluf and Blwchfardd. The King of Reged knew them all from his time in Elfed.

'Welcome, gentlemen. You have all travelled a very long way. Come sit at this table. We have food and refreshment for you to take whilst your eques are billeted.'

'I fear they will fill the town's taverns tonight,' said Agiluf.

'Much as my soldiers did when we stayed in Elfed,' Meirchiawn said, trying to keep the tone of the meeting as friendly as possible.

Arthwys looked directly at Gwenhyfach. 'My lady, I am pleased to see you. I only wish the circumstances were better. Your presence, of course, reminds me of why I am here.' He was visibly moved – the sisters might have been twins but for their different hair colours.

'Arthwys,' Meirchiawn drew the king's attention, 'the queen and I plan to discuss this delicate matter with you in private, but first, please eat and drink.'

'Before I sit at this table, cousin, I need to know that you will support my endeavours to rescue Gwenhyfar? I do not mean that you should go to war on my behalf, only that you will provision me and my men. We have particular need for trained war horses.'

'We are Coelings, and so you have every right to expect our full support, but the circumstances are fraught. King Lott looks upon Mordred as a son and will not take kindly to a campaign on his borders.'

'How many fathers does Mordred need?' Arthwys' scornful voice set everyone on edge. He looked around as if searching for signs of dissent then continued. 'I will see him dead this time, regardless of any support from Reged. I do not care if he is killed in battle or if I do it myself.'

Gwenhyfach looked at her husband, too scared to speak in the face of her brother-in-law's thirst for revenge.

'Please, Arthwys, sit and eat,' said Meirchiawn. 'Of course, we will support you. I see you still wear the uniforms from your campaign in Gaul. We heard of

Riothames' defeat, and news reached us that even you were dead. What happened over there?'

'Ames was misled. He believed there was consensus for a Christian reunification of the Empire under both emperors and that only two rogue barbarian states were the impediment to this ambition, but that was far from the truth. The Emperors' grand plan was not supported in the provinces, and although they pulled their levers of power in Rome and Constantinople, they no longer wielded sufficient influence. In the end, we were betrayed, Count Paulus was murdered, and nothing went to plan. The Romans can neither trust the barbarians nor each other, and the Briton and Armorican armies were needlessly slaughtered. The barbarians we were there to defeat are no different to us, fighting to achieve that which we already enjoy – freedom from the Roman yoke.'

'Will they achieve this?'

'They already have. There is no longer anyone to stop it. Anthemius' failures led to a civil war, and we have since heard he has been executed.'

'And how is it you survived unscathed?'

'Providence, a chance decision. Perhaps God protected us. Whatever the reason, the Cymry were not present when the Visigoths attacked. We arrived in time to negotiate a surrender and withdrawal to Armorica.'

'So, what kept you there? Why did you not return?'

'We have been fighting with the Armoricans against their heathen Frankish neighbours who tried to take advantage of the defeat. All that time, we believed it was God's plan for his virtuous Christian eques that we fight the heathens. I did not anticipate that the unity we forged in the Saxon wars would be so easily undermined.' Arthwys eyes narrowed as he looked toward his cousin.

'None of us could have guessed at Mordred's intentions.' Meirchiawn shook his head. 'He is an evil threat to us all.'

'Even Reged?'

'He bears me as much a grudge as he bears you, but we have remained safe for some time. It appears the false news of your death emboldened him to wreak his revenge upon Elfed. Since then, we have remained ever alert to surprise attacks, which is why I felt Pabo was safer at Whithorn.'

'Arthwys,' said Gwenhyfach, having gathered enough courage to speak to the Elfed king, 'I have news of my sister's plight. If you come to our chamber, I will divulge these most private matters.'

With apparent suspicion, Arthwys followed Gwenhyfach and Meirchiawn to the end of the hall where they stepped through a doorway in a wood partition that separated the hall from a private room.

'You must steel yourself,' said the queen in a lowered voice, 'for I will speak plainly.' Arthwys gave a curt nod. 'I have been corresponding with my sister, though I am conscious our letters may well have been read by others. Mordred has taken her to Din Guarie. She says her accommodation is rudimentary, but the setting is beautiful. His fortress sits on a high cliff by the sea where she is able to swim every day.'

Arthwys listened carefully, hanging on her every word.

'He is kind and loving to her, and although she has not been permitted to see her family yet, she hopes this may soon change.' She paused, seeming not to know how to continue.

'Go on,' said Arthwys. 'I must know all that you know.'

'She believes you are dead and has mourned you. She sees her only role now is to protect her surviving family, and so she has taken this bull by its horns.'

Arthwys frowned. 'Are you saying she is in his bed?'

'What else can a woman do in her situation? She may be held on a leash, but now so is he. It is not a question of preference but of survival. Do you understand this?'

Arthwys grimaced. 'You have put it well, but I can only see her betrayal. Could she not have poisoned him rather than submitting?' The king's fury was mounting.

'She may well have tried, but do not forget, in her mind, you are dead, and her family is vulnerable. She has used the only weapon a woman can safely wield to tame the beast who would destroy all she loves.'

'Surely, there was something else that could have been done?' he said in anguish.

'We all thought you dead,' replied Meirchiawn. 'We offered to pay ransom, but that was never his objective. Mordred has always wanted your wife.'

'What do you think your sister will do when she discovers I am alive?'

'She will be glad in her heart and relieved for her family, but the shame will be too much for her to bear. She may lose her mind. I'm surprised she has not already done so.'

Arthwys gave a dismissive nod and turned to leave. 'I have heard enough of this feeble appeasement. Let us rejoin our sons.' He looked back at Gwenhyfach. 'Be sure to let her know that I am coming to collect her, when you next correspond.'

'Arthwys,' Gwenhyfach snapped in a stern voice, stopping him in his tracks, 'my sister risked her life to recover your sword, bore your sons, endured a decade of war, and stopped further bloodshed at Cambodunum by her courageous actions. She has adapted best she can to protect her family, believing her husband and protector to be dead. Now she must look on as one of you kills the other. You men! You saunter off to war with no thought of anything except filling your treasuries or dying your glorious deaths, leaving the women to pick up the pieces.'

Arthwys had listened intently to his feisty sister-in-law. 'For all these reasons, I will bring her home. In the eyes of God, Gwen is still my wife, so be sure to let her know that if He can forgive her, then surely, so will I.' He turned to Meirchiawn. 'All I require from Reged are horses and the use of the fort at Banna. I will send a message to Mordred urging him to return Gwen, but we all know he will not. Upon receipt of his reply or in the absence of one, we will advance upon his stronghold. If King Lott chooses to get involved, he will regret it.'

'Do not misunderstand my wife's impassioned words, Arthwys. You have our full support, never mind the difficult circumstances. Whatever you require will be supplied.'

'Thank you both. To appreciate what drives men like Mordred one must understand envy, obsession and dark desire. Like a spider left in a corner, he has grown and grown, entrapping all who come close. Now my wife is in his web, and he will not release her. I should have listened to you all when you urged me to have Mordred executed – that is my failing. But Reged should have rescued Gwen before this unholy arrangement had a chance to take hold, rather than attempting to justify it in the aftermath. Were the circumstances reversed, I would not have hesitated, nor would I have consigned your sons to a monastery with nothing but prayer for hope.'

As the Elfed king stormed out of the chamber, Meirchiawn turned to his queen and reached for her hand. 'His words are bitter, but he is not wrong.'

'Warlords are never wrong, are they husband? It only ends when blood is spilt. Mark my words, this will not end well. I must write to my sister without delay. She must be prepared for what is coming.'

A Revelation

Sextilis 472

Sextilis was Gwenhyfar's favourite month, not just because it was her birthday, but because it was when the weather tended to yield the last real warmth of summer. True, it was not always so, for she well remembered the thunderstorms of Erechwyd from her childhood. *Warm rain* her mother had called it, though no matter how warm, it would still flood the becks and flatten the corn. Din Guarie's climate was quite different to the region of the lakes. The strong breeze was near constant, but the sunshine that firmed the fruit and browned the corn was ever more reliable. Many seasons had passed and repeated whilst she walked the long beaches, waiting for her rescue.

Mordred had said that it was a Frisian trader who had first brought him the news that a king was dead, and rumours were already rife in Elfed before her abduction, although she had refused to believe them, always hoping Arthwys would return. But then time had stretched on, and still no one came. After six months, a letter had arrived from her sister confirming that she too believed Arthwys was dead. Initially, her captor had insisted upon reading all her letters, but eventually, on realising the great comfort they were to her, particularly in respect of keeping up with her family's news, he had let the screening slip.

'The sea is calm, my lady.'

'Yes, the islands are so clear today.'

Her companion was Brigit, a young slave-girl who Mordred had brought her after one of his adventures north. She was the daughter of a culdeis, a holy man who had assisted Palladius in attempting to convert the Picts to Christianity, and it was the Latin he had taught her that had saved her. Her father had been killed, though she never spoke of it.

'Life could be worse,' the girl added with a smile. It was an expression Gwen also repeated to herself over and over, but today, she could not imagine how life could get any worse.

Time since her abduction had passed quickly. Many times, she had thought to escape, but to where? She had even considered murdering Mordred – poison or a push from the clifftop, perhaps a dagger in the night – but these thoughts had dissipated in the face of his kindness and the love he showed her. She had mourned Igerna, Cian, Bryn and, eventually, Arthwys, and although she heard little of Pabo, Eliffer and her grandchildren, her sister had written that they were all safe.

She dared not dwell on the past, for there lay the large hole into which she had thrown all the memories that might otherwise jar her sanity. It was something she had in common with Brigit. Everything they discussed openly was about now, tomorrow, and if the past must be discussed, they went no further back than one or two years. Occasionally, very occasionally, they ventured into secret conversations about loved ones. And every day, they prayed together. There was a place in the dunes where they had erected a cross, and despite her youth, Brigit would always lead the prayers, her command of liturgy impressive.

At first, Gwen had resisted Mordred's advances, but his subsequent rages had been so frightening. Over time, she had discovered life was better if she found ways to calm his wild temper, and inevitably, she had gone to his bed, where he had reawakened sensations in her that had been lost long ago. She had no doubt that he loved her in his lustful way, probably with more intensity than she had ever been loved before, but that could not stop her guilt growing like a cancer. She could go days without the slightest reflection on the rights and wrongs of her life with Mordred, immersing herself in domestic routines that filled her time and mind. But there was no hiding from her shame anymore, not now she had received a letter containing the most shattering of revelations. If not for her devastation, she might have laughed at her sister's attempts to conceal the name, knowing that, had Mordred chosen to read the letter, he would have easily guessed the subject's identity.

A certain Armorican has visited our court. He is acquainted with E and P and intent on visiting the east of the Patria. Then later in the letter she had written, *This man has lost something precious and will not stop until he finds it.*

Arthwys was alive and coming for her. Oh, how she wished she had not succumbed to Mordred, the full shame of it impossible to dismiss, the terrible sin she had committed against God and her husband. Worse still, she could not bear the thought that one might kill the other or that both might die, and for her sake. She had hoped praying with Brigit would bring some solace this morning, but she had been unable to repeat the words or concentrate on their meaning. She had hidden the letter inside a secret pocket within her purple cloak. Originally a gift from Arthwys, this cloak was her only treasured possession from her life before. Mordred had jealously taken all her jewellery, leaving her with only a tiny crucifix hung on a gold chain.

'My lady, are you swimming today?'

'Not yet. Let's walk a little further beyond the dunes.'

They continued their stroll.

'There are so many sea-birds hereabouts, Brigit. They raise their young then fly away. I find the pattern of birdlife so interesting.'

'So true, my lady. They say – though I don't know how they know – that some birds keep the same mate all their life.'

Brigit's innocent observations felt like a moral taunt. 'Is that so?' *If only I had remained as virtuous as a seagull!*

'Here. I will swim from here.' Gwen took off her cloak and began removing her clothes. 'Now, I intend to swim as far as I can today, for the conditions are perfect.'

'Very well, my lady. I will be here when you return.'

Gwen skipped across the sand to the sea. Wading in was sometimes the best moment, so refreshing and cleansing. *If only it could cleanse my sins.* She turned and waved to Brigit and looked toward the fortress one last time. Arthwys had returned, her family was safe, now she could escape. Her mother had taught her to swim in the lakes of Erechwyd, but she had always found the sea more enjoyable. *Poor Mother*, she reflected. *She died so young, leaving only daughters to look after Father*. How proud she would have been to see they had married kings. How ashamed she would be to know of her daughter's inadvertent infidelity.

Immersed to her neck, Gwen struck out with her rhythmic stroke, her mind immediately detaching from her actions. It had been a good life. She relived the moment she had taken Arthwys' sword from the water's grasp and remembered how he had carried her down the mountain. Their wedding had soon followed, such a splendid occasion... Becoming part of a new family... She had loved his father and, in time, had come to understand Igerna. Eliffer, her firstborn, had been a difficult birth, but Pabo had proved easy, though less so in life. How he had struggled with his father's absences. Cian and Bryn had been like grandparents to Eliffer, but Merlinus had made the difference with Pabo. Merlinus, a mystery of his own making, but not a wizard like Myrddin. The old queen returned to her thoughts... It had taken time, but she had really come to appreciate Igerna as a wise and regal matriarch, missing her support most of all – she would have known what to do... Gwen smiled to herself. She would see them all again soon; they would all be waiting. Then there was Arthwys, who had always made her feel so proud, her handsome Bear of the tribes, the mightiest warrior in the North and the love of her life. Pray God would forgive her sins, and her men take comfort from what she must do now.

She had swum for what seemed like hours. Looking around, she saw that she was level with the islands, though she had no intention of swimming for land or turning back – she had not the strength for either… Somehow, it felt right that she surrender herself to the water, that she should return to that which has given her the gift that had won her a king. Her head slipped beneath the surface. She gasped for air, and her lungs filled with seawater. She was sinking. Death was coming and it hurt far less than childbirth… Darkness.

*

'Dear God,' screamed Mordred. 'Where is she?'

Brigit was shaking. 'She just swam out of view. She had said she would be swimming far today, but when she did not return… At first, I thought the tide had just taken her and she had come ashore elsewhere, so I ran up and down the beach to check before raising the alarm.'

'Did she say anything more about her intentions?'

'Nothing, my lord. She skipped into the water as she always does.'

'We must find her.' Mordred turned to his men. 'Launch as many boats as possible. Search the islands. What has she done?'

'My lord!' The gruff voice of a sentry drew his attention. 'There are riders below with a message from King Arthwys.'

'Arthwys?' he screamed. He ran out the door, his guards flanking him all the way to the gate where the riders waited a spear's throw away, still astride their horses. Mordred recognised none of them, but he could tell they were Arthwys' eques by their mail coats, horsehead buckles and crossed shields.

'Is this a hoax?' he screamed at them.

'No, my lord, it is not,' shouted the youngest eques positioned in the middle. 'King Arthwys demands that you hand over his wife to us immediately, or he will advance upon your stronghold within the week!'

'Is that so,' said Mordred, furious. 'Tell Arthwys that I will bring my army down the Devil's Causeway to meet his. We will finish this once and for all!'

'And what of the lady?'

'She remains here.'

The eques turned their steeds, commencing their return journey. It seemed the reply they had received was the one they had expected. What was happening? Did Gwenhyfar know Arthwys had returned and had made a bid to escape? Surely, she would not do something so callous, not after the time they had spent together. His thoughts were interrupted by Brigit running toward him waving a scroll.

'Look, my lord, it is a letter from her sister. I found it hidden in her clothes.'

Mordred quickly read the letter. *So she knew!*

'When did this arrive?'

'Only last evening.' Tears rolled down Brigit's face. 'I'm sure she had no intention of escaping, that she made a desperate decision in the moment. I can only think that she has drowned, and her body will wash ashore soon.'

Mordred suppressed his emotions. 'I cannot delay. I must assemble my men to march south as soon as possible. Try to find her for me.'

'I will walk the beaches until I find her. God will guide me to her.'

The Final Battle

Sextilis 472

Arthwys was not in the hall where Agiluf had expected to find him. An orderly, clearing up following breakfast, looked up.

'He is at the south gate, my lord. He said to send you there when you arrived.'

Agiluf found Arthwys looking over the cliff at the valley, still lush with summer foliage, a slight mist following the bends of the river below.

'Good morning, Arthwys.'

The king turned to greet his friend. 'Good morning, Agiluf. Banna is a well-positioned fort. This is great hunting country, but we cannot dally and give Mordred time to win support from King Lott… although I doubt the Gododdin will want to get involved, any more than Reged does.'

Agiluf nodded absently. 'My father learnt everything he knew here. He told me so many tales of those days with Taly, Mor and Gorwst; he even remembered Coel Hen.'

'I think, like these trees, his tales grew taller as the years passed, but it is strange to think we are standing in the birthplace of both Reged and Elfed.'

'Coel Hen was a man of great vision, and having witnessed for ourselves the chaos that is Rome, I now see his foresight did more for Britannia than any of us truly understood.'

'Perhaps it had something to do with Myrddin's influence. I know I miss his wise counsel. Only last night, I dreamt of him. Strangely, he was accompanied by Gwenhyfar. They were by a lake, beckoning me.'

'Well, at least you slept! We were training well into the night, and by the time I put my head down, my mind was so full of it all that I could not sleep.'

'Have the men mastered their steeds?'

'Given the shortage of time, they have done well. These ponies from Reged are the very breed that carried Coel Hen into battle against the Picts.'

'Our clash with Mordred will be much like fighting Picts. Pabo and our returned scouts saw few horses but a great number of foot soldiers. Mordred's men are trained as naval raiders. That will make his men difficult to fight in close combat.'

'You expect an ambush, then?'

'That is his style, but anything is possible. Most of all, I sense he will want to fight me himself.'

'In single combat?'

'Perhaps. But his obsession with me will prove his weakness.'

'How so?'

'Because the purpose of our mission is to rescue Gwen. Engaging with him in battle is incidental.'

After all the king's talk of revenge, it came as a great relief to Agiluf to hear him talking tactically. He smiled. 'Ah. You have another plan.'

Arthwys returned his friend's smile, such moments rare in recent days. 'Did you not wonder why I sent Pabo with two of our scouts to Mordred's stronghold?'

'I thought you were giving the boy experience.'

'That was some of it, but their purpose was to survey the strengths and weaknesses of Din Guarie, to find a way in. Although, their report of Mordred's response to my message is puzzling, even if it is a better result than I expected.'

'In what way?'

'He marches south to meet us. An impetuous decision which he will regret.'

'If you were in his position, what would you have done?'

'I would have stayed put, bolstered my defences and made my opponent lay siege, knowing that my great friend King Lott would not take kindly to anyone waging war on his borders.'

'It is as if he is so set on fighting you that he can think of nothing else. He has always been arrogant and impulsive.'

'All that matters is his fortress has been left open to the rescue mission which Pabo will lead. But before we can get to that, we must concern ourselves with the difficult terrain.'

'What will we be facing?'

'The scouts tell me that the causeway north comes to a place where it passes through a narrow gap between high mountains with fierce rivers that become increasingly difficult to ford the further east we travel.'

'You think Mordred will set his ambush there?'

'I'll wager he is already positioned on a prominent hill overlooking the causeway.'

'That could be a problem for us.'

'It is more a problem for the rescue party. Because we dare not show our hand, it seems we may have to engage his men to ensure the causeway is clear enough to allow Pabo to ride past and on to Din Guarie. We will know more when we see where Mordred is positioned. When will your men be ready to depart?'

'Within the hour, my king.'

'Good. I will meet you at the east gate.'

*

Mordred's men had marched for a full day to reach the point on the causeway where he proposed to do battle with Arthwys. He had brought fifty men under two captains, every one an experienced raider. They were a mixed bag – soldiers of fortune all, some Gododdin, some Britons, some easterners, but all completely loyal. His ruthless tactics had seen them through raids north and south, but their cut-and-run fighting style did not usually bring them face-to-face with battle-hardened cavalry.

Mordred considered his choice of high ground. It was perfect. The elevation would frustrate both cavalry and archers, ensuring his men could engage on equal terms. If the encounter should begin to go against them, they were well-positioned to disappear into the hills and regroup later. All that mattered now was that he killed Arthwys. On the march south, he had nurtured the faint hope that Gwenhyfar might be found alive, perhaps on one of the islands, but at the same time, his rage and hatred of Arthwys had bloomed. If the Elfed king had not returned from Armorica, the woman Mordred loved would never have been driven to lose her mind. Until that letter had arrived, they had been happy on their idyllic promontory. He forced the anguish from his mind to concentrate on the planned encounter. He turned to his most experienced warrior.

'Where will we make our stand? In the crags behind or on that hill where there are dwellings and a church?'

'We will see more of the vale from that church, and there will be food left behind by the fleeing inhabitants!' said the warrior.

'Good, then we will sit, wait, and see who comes along the causeway whilst filling our bellies.'

*

Farddy had heard all about the Wall but had never seen it until they arrived at Luguvalium. Now he was riding along most of its length in awe of this monument to Rome. Sections had collapsed and some of the forts showed signs of fire damage. If these stones could speak, he wondered what tales they might tell. The Wall acted as a graphic reminder of why Arthwys and his brother had thought to give the Empire one last throw of the dice, whilst also speaking of the powerful forces they now knew were ranged against the Imperial yoke.

His mind returned to the task before them. He had worried constantly about the queen, ever since she was taken. They were the only two nobles to survive Mordred's murderous onslaught, and he wanted him to die painfully and slowly, fully intending to play any part he could in the vile beast's demise. He hoped to sing to Gwen again and chatter about inconsequential things as they used to, but would either of them ever forget what they had witnessed that day? He had always harboured a small hope that she might think a little more of him than perhaps she should. She had kissed him once, but it had been playful and never repeated. He could recall that rush of feeling and how long it had lasted. He still experienced the sensation when he pictured the memory. Tears filled his eyes. What depravations must poor Gwenhyfar have endured? He had done his best to find the king as quickly as possible, but it seemed that the fates had turned against them this time, the might and glory of Elfed having so suddenly spoiled, like a ripened sweet plum at its zenith fallen to the ground, split and decaying.

He pushed the sorrow from his mind and focused on their mission to rescue Gwen. Since they were making better progress than expected, Arthwys had decided to push on rather than stop at Coria. They had crossed through the gate and travelled some miles along the route north. Farddy's attention was drawn by a group of men, women and children travelling along the route toward them. Seeing the king had gone to the rear to speak to his eques and cheer up the stragglers, Farddy turned to Agiluf who rode alongside him.

'Brother, these people look displaced. We should speak with them to discover from what they flee.'

Agiluf nodded and held up his hand, signalling the column to halt.

The fearful looks and armfuls of paltry possessions suggested the travellers had left their homes in a hurry. They were led by a man who appeared to be a priest.

'Where are you people heading?' asked Agiluf.

'To Coria, my lords, for protection. We have fled our homes in the face of a raiding party from the north. We believe they are Mordred of Din Guarie's men. Do you go to slay them?'

'Yes. Whereabouts are the homes from which you flee?'

'Cambolann, a settlement close to the causeway. They have occupied our dwellings and are butchering our animals for food.'

'Is it far from here?'

'Two days' walk along the causeway there is a ravine concealing a bridge. They are positioned on the hill to the east of the crossing, close by the crags and the moor.'

'Thank you, my friend. Good journey. When you see us come back this way, you will know it is safe to return.'

'Beware, my lord. It is a high place. Your progress will be watched by keen eyes for most of tomorrow. By the time you get there, they will have either fled or be waiting in ambush.'

'Then we shall make as much progress as we can this evening.'

Agiluf signalled for the column to proceed once more. After considering what the priest had said, Farddy asked, 'So, the battle will be tomorrow?'

'It is not like you to be so keen for a fight, brother.'

'I am keen to see the end of Mordred.'

'As are we all, but this fighting will be hand to hand.' Agiluf turned to face his brother. 'Farddy, though you are one of my best riders, you are not a warrior. Your skills would be better served making the hard ride with Pabo to rescue the queen.'

'I understand, brother. I would be honoured to join Pabo's mission.'

'Good, I will inform the king when we make camp.'

*

It had rained in the night, and very few had slept. The dawn was cold and a thick mist clung to the heights that loomed over the causeway. Arthwys knew they were no more than half a day's ride from their anticipated encounter. He gathered his men around him, with Agiluf to his right and Pabo to his left.

'Men, you all know why we are here and who we are about to face. Take heart and have faith in God, for we will carry this day. We are a superior force in every way, but be prepared for a hard fight. It is unlikely the terrain will allow us to ride into this battle. Mordred will want to force us to fight on foot, hand to hand, to give his men, who have little armour and inferior weapons, a better chance. It is unlikely we will be able retain a formation or make good use of a shield wall, and our archery skills will be purposely frustrated, but I have a way to counter these difficulties. We will face the enemy in twenty groups of three. For this to work, we must remain as disciplined as possible. Two of the three will carry shields, spears and spathas, but the third will move behind the front two and carry a bow, quiver and spatha, and have his shield slung over his back. It is quite possible the enemy will carry no shields to protect against arrows, so at close range, the bowmen will be lethal, but remember to stay as a group to protect each other. Mordred will be looking for me, so stay out of his way. Are there any questions?'

'Yes, my king. When the battle is won, where will we go? Some of us have women in Armorica, and some have wives in Elfed.'

'And some in both places!' quipped a voice from the back.

The men roared with laughter.

'Pabo and I will return to Elfed, but'—he turned to his prefect and smiled—'Agiluf returns to Armorica, and Barinthus will take any who wish to go with him.'

The men broke into conversation amongst themselves.

'I will not leave you, my king,' said Agiluf, his expression serious.

'Maxen will welcome you with open arms. There is nothing here for you now, my friend. Elfed can never be the same again.' Arthwys turned back to the group, holding up his arms to indicate he wished to speak. 'This mist is to our advantage, so we must leave straightaway to take advantage of it.' He now turned to Pabo. 'It will also cover your mission; you must ride like the wind.'

'Yes, Father.'

'And Pabo, if anything befalls me, rule Elfed wisely with your brother, for I have to admit I have rather neglected it.'

Agiluf gave the order. 'Mount up and say your prayers as you ride – God will understand.'

*

Mordred stood with his two burly captains who both looked concerned.

'This mist is a bad omen. They could attack us before we are even aware they are here. I say we retreat to the crags until it has cleared.'

'Retreat? I have challenged them to battle,' said Mordred, furious, 'Ambush them, yes, but running away to hide in the crags is for cowards.'

'The men are nervous, my lord. Word has spread that King Arthwys commands the enemy.'

'He is but a man with a sword.'

'A man with a magic sword.'

'I have seen it – it is no more magic than mine!'

'What if he brings the wizard who throws thunderbolts?'

'His wizard is old and feeble.'

'Well, something has conjured up this mist.'

'We stay put. Mark my word, the mist will lift.'

*

Arthwys' troops reached the ravine as the mist began to lift.

'No one must speak; make no noise.'

Arthwys indicated to Pabo, the scouts and Farddy that they should leave immediately. They descended the track to the river, knowing their way – all except Farddy having already crossed the bridge twice within the last week.

'The priest said to follow the river out of the ravine,' whispered Agiluf to his captains. 'Ride two by two with spears to hand. Pass the word.'

As the column closed up, the king pulled his bearskin from his saddle bag and tied it over his helmet. 'This will draw his attention.'

'Arthwys, the high ground is to our left, so we are somewhere behind them.'

Through the mist, they spied a small group of wooden huts huddled in a raised compound surrounded by a shallow ditch.

'Dismount.'

The ponies were left by the river and the men formed into their groups of three. An archer fell in behind Arthwys and Agiluf.

'Advance.'

The disciplined troops moved in the direction of the village where a scurry of movement betrayed the presence of the concealed enemy. A few paces more, and the men were close enough to see shapes and shadows.

'Archers!' cried Arthwys. The shield men dropped to one knee, and the twang of cords and the hiss of arrows were followed by the thuds of impact. The shield bearers remained down listening to the screams of the enemy.

'Again!' shouted Arthwys, and once more arrows hissed, picking off targets.

'Five paces,' shouted the king.

The shield bearers stood and moved forward.

'Archers!' shouted Arthwys, and once again, the shields were lowered and two volleys loosed.

This time, the king changed the command. 'Swords!' Bows were discarded, shields were swung to arm and swords drawn. The enemy suddenly appeared out of ditches, from behind trees and huts, running at full tilt. Arthwys' sixth sense had told him the charge was coming.

'Choose your targets,' he shouted to his eques.

'I'm coming for you, Arthwys!' Mordred's screaming voice rang in Agiluf's ears, but he knew the king would not reply – battlefield harangues only served to break concentration.

The king moved his feet to brace for the impact, watching Mordred's sword. It smashed onto his shield, and Arthwys thrust at his opponent's legs pulling the sword back in a cutting motion across his assailant's thighs. Agiluf covered his flank, easily dispatching his first opponent before more enemy came looking for his blade. One voice rang out over the clamour and clash of battle.

'You should have stayed dead,' hollered Mordred, bringing his sword down once more, this time splintering Arthwys' shield. The king thrust upward, again making contact and piercing his enemy's mail, but Mordred continued his diatribe undaunted. 'I should be the Bear. I am the strongest.'

His sword was at the top of its arc, but Arthwys shifted sideways as the blow swung down, and Mordred missed his target, hitting a rock. Arthwys brought Caledfwich down squarely on his attacker's helmet, splitting it open and cutting into his skull. Mordred staggered, falling to his knees, blood spurting from his cleaved metal dome. He dropped his shield and fell forward onto his hands. Agiluf glanced quickly around to see Mordred's men were falling back, many left prone on the ground. The king looked down at his wounded adversary, raising his sword for the final stroke.

'She's dead,' Mordred screamed up at him.

Arthwys hesitated, his shield lowered. Breaking his own battlefield rule, he responded, 'How?'

In that moment of distraction, Mordred's sword flashed, skewering the king's groin. Agiluf watched in horror as Arthwys recoiled from the pain, but even then, he swung Caledfwich down on Mordred's neck, severing his head. The king staggered, and Agiluf rushed to support his injured friend.

'How bad is it?'

Arthwys put his hand between his legs. 'There is a lot of blood, and it hurts like Hell.'

'Let's get to the river.'

They walked cautiously down the hill whilst the men finished up, chasing down the last of Mordred's men. Agiluf sat the king on the bank and removed his helmet, bearskin and mail coat before inspecting the grievous wound.

'It is so deep. We must get you to a healer quickly.'

'They were no match for us, but I fear we came too late. Mordred said Gwen is dead. Those were his last words.'

'It is truly a tragedy if that is so, but right now, we must stem this bleeding. Alwyn,' he shouted, 'ride directly to Alauna. Send Barinthus for Merlinus and Morgaine. Take a spare horse. Cadrog, you must remain here and wait for Pabo to return, then follow us to Alauna. Keep five men back to bury the dead. But first, find material to dress this wound. The rest of you search everywhere for two or more sturdy poles. We will need to stretcher the king, for it is certain he cannot ride.'

'How many men did we lose?' asked Arthwys.

'I have not yet counted, but it looks like seven dead with several wounded. Please lie back, Arthwys. We need to swaddle you to slow this bleeding.'

Arthwys did as he was told as Agiluf wrapped strips of cloth around his leg and lower torso.

'These men have never seen me wounded,' he said, as he watched them build a sled from tree poles. Broken spears were lashed as crossbars and as much material as possible and some sheepskins found in the village were used to make a comfortable base. The king was placed on the frame and tied to it. The calmest pony was then chosen to pull the sled, and although in obvious pain, the king seemed to retain good humour.

'Look at me,' he said. 'Bear of the North swaddled like a bairn!'

The men laughed, but Agiluf could not raise a smile. The sword had penetrated deep into the king's groin, and no amount of pressure seemed to stop the bleeding. The rags he had first applied were already drenched in blood. His only option was to get Arthwys to Morgaine as quickly as possible. Mordred's final utterance in respect of the queen was also a concern. Agiluf could only hope his friend would not dwell on it. They would hear the truth soon enough when Pabo returned.

They began the journey, having no choice but to travel through the night if they were to have any chance of saving Arthwys.

*

Farddy had imagined Mordred's stronghold would look something like Elfed, but the contrast was stark. Din Guarie was built on a high cliff exposed to the maritime elements. Beaches of fine, bright sand, unlike any he had seen before, stretched for miles in both directions. The golden expanse was partially hidden from view by large dunes covered in coarse, tufty grass interspersed with great clumps of gorse and wildflowers. There were several boats pulled up on the beach, adding to the idyllic view. But none of this could prevent his stomach churning with fear as they approached the gate in the stockade.

To their surprise, the gates lay open, unguarded. They hesitated for a moment. Could it be a trap? When no movement was detected, they cautiously encouraged their ponies up the steep climb to the flat top where they found deserted wood-framed circular huts with simple thatched roofs. A few young slaves in rags ran to hide whilst the men from Elfed looked around the compound. Mordred seemed to have taken everyone who could fight with him, for no guards emerged.

'Queen Gwenhyfar,' Blwchfardd shouted, but there was no reply.

They rode toward the one large hut in the centre. The scouts stayed on horseback to keep watch, whilst Farddy and Pabo entered through the open doorway, ducking to avoid the cross beam.

Farddy let out a strangled cry at the sight he saw, and Pabo rushed forward. The queen lay upon a table, in a white gown, two candles burning by her head. She was bedecked with the wildflowers they had seen growing so profusely in the dunes. It was hard to accept the serenity of the scene through the shock and grief. A young girl of considerable beauty was on her knees, her hands shaped in prayer. She was neither startled nor alarmed by their arrival.

'My lady drowned,' she said simply. 'I have prepared her best I can, combed her hair and dressed her in her best gown.'

'Oh Gwen,' Farddy wailed, before shuffling toward the corpse and dropping to his knees beside the girl.

Pabo walked slowly toward his mother and held her cold hand. 'Rest in peace,' he said, his voice barely audible.

The girl looked up at him. 'You must be Pabo?' He looked astounded by her perception. Then she turned to the sobbing Farddy. 'And you must be Farddy, my lady's bard.'

'And who are you? An angel?' said Pabo, emotion overwhelming him.

'No, I am Brigit. I have been your mother's close companion. Will you help me bury her? I have prepared a place, and I know the words to say to God.'

Farddy wiped his tears. 'We shall carry her there.'

Pabo summoned the scouts, and the four men carried the queen's body on their shoulders down the hill to the dunes where a cross was already placed, and a hole had been partially dug. They placed her body gently by the cross.

'Will you finish digging the grave for me?' asked Brigit.

The scouts duly obliged, the sand easy to dig. Brigit turned to Pabo.

'I know the mass, if you are happy for me to speak it?'

Pabo nodded. She began her prayers, and to their surprise, she knew all the words to the psalms and the correct liturgy for burial. Farddy could barely watch as they lowered Gwen into the deep grave. Once in position, she was quickly covered by the sand that filled her grave.

Now more composed than he had been earlier, Farddy spoke to Brigit as they walked back up the hill to the fort. 'We were close; I would sing to her.'

'She said your voice is beautiful. She told me about all of you.'

'Tell me, Brigit, how do you know so much about God's rituals?'

'My father taught me, and I helped him in his ministry. He was sent to Palladius to support his work. The bishop died ten years ago, but the mission continued until Mordred raided our church…'

'So, where is your home?'

'Before Pictland, it was Hibernia. I don't remember much, but I hope to return.'

'And your family?'

'My parents are dead, though Mother had sisters. For now, it is only God who guides me.'

Pabo had been listening to the conversation. 'He guides me too, Brigit. I know that my father will want to meet you. He will take great comfort from hearing of your friendship with my mother. We brought a pony for her, but now it can be yours. I am confident Mordred will not return, so you are free to leave with us, but we must depart straightaway so we can impart this sad news to my father.'

'I can be ready to travel with you now, for I have no possessions to gather. But if you will allow, Gwen had a cloak I would like to borrow for the journey.'

Pabo smiled. 'I am sure she would be pleased to gift it to you.'

Departure

Sextilis 472

Alwyn had always been one of Arthwys' most faithful eques, and so he had proved once more. He had ridden hard to Alauna and relayed to Barinthus both the urgency to collect Morgaine and the dire state of the king. He had then helped row the skiff across to Whithorn where Merlinus and the king's sister listened carefully to his description of the wound and packed various potions and dressings into their satchels, so that when Agiluf arrived at the harbour, they were all waiting and prepared.

There was much relief that the king was still alive, although Morgaine was gravely concerned for his life. He had continued to lose blood on the journey, and he was ashen and in great pain. They found shelter in a barn on the banks of the Ellen, where Morgaine cleaned the wound and applied a poultice. She also gave the king a potion which helped with the pain and made him drowsy. The mood amongst his eques was sombre, the initial post-battle euphoria having quickly evaporated, not just because the king was grievously wounded, but word had already spread that the queen was feared dead – many fighting close to the king having heard Mordred's taunts. Though their enemy's death was celebrated, all declared it had come at too high a price. Arthwys had never been known to take wound or injury. It had given him an air of invincibility that had passed on to his eques, but now everyone felt an unfamiliar vulnerability, and there was great fear that the king may be dying.

Merlinus was direct with his assessment. 'Arthwys, you have lost too much blood. We cannot cauterise this wound, but if we take you to Whithorn, we can care for you better.'

'We must wait, Merlinus. Gwen will be joining us soon, Pabo too. Surely, this is not how it ends?'

'The Lord calls for us, when he is ready, and we have little say in the matter.'

'And Myrddin, what did he say?'

'Myrddin foresaw your strife with Mordred but never foretold the outcome. The only thing he was clear about was that the sword would be returned.'

'To where? Surely not the cave at the top of the dragon's back?'

'To Coventina. He was adamant it became hers once again, when you threw it in the lake.'

'So Caledfwich belongs to the water goddess?'

'Myrddin believed so. She gave it up into Gwenhyfar's hands, so that it could be used in our time of greatest need, but now she expects its return. I have wondered if the sword was only yours to defeat the Saxons, that it was never meant to be used to fight for Rome.'

Agiluf had been listening to this mystical exchange. He couldn't help feeling there was a ring of truth to it. It had always seemed that there were greater powers at work than simple luck and chance. It had been Myrddin who had guided Arthwys' fate, and the Bear had stayed true to the prophecy, winning all his battles… until he left for Armorica where the omens seemed against Rome, and they had both felt that even God himself saw no future for the Empire.

Alwyn entered the shelter. 'Riders are approaching,' he said excitedly, 'and they are accompanied by the queen.'

Relief flooded Arthwys' features and he looked revived. The arrivals could be heard dismounting their ponies before being ushered into the shelter. Pabo was the first to speak.

'Father, I have heard about the battle and your wound.'

Brigit and Farddy were at his side.

'Gwen, my love, is that you?'

Arthwys held out his hand and Brigit grasped it.

'No, King Arthwys, it is not. I am Brigit, a friend of Gwen's. I am sad to tell you that the queen drowned at sea only five days ago.'

Arthwys sank back, tears filling his eyes. 'So Mordred did not lie.'

'No, but I am here to tell you about the life your queen led whilst you were away, about the time we spent together, about the things she wanted you to know.'

'Pabo, are you still here? The light has got so dim in here.'

'Yes, Father. I am here.' Pabo stepped closer to where his father lay.

'Did you see her?'

'Yes, we helped Brigit bury her by the coast. It is a beautiful place where she will rest in peace.'

Tears spilled from Arthwys' eyes. 'It is plain for all to see that I cannot continue as king. It must be you who returns to rebuild Elfed, my son. You must be a pillar of strength for our people and be a leader to those of my eques who wish to go home. Look to Britu, he is your uncle and a close ally. Oh, how I wish I had told you this before today. Alwyn, are you still here?'

'My king.' He fell to his knees. 'Forgive me for misleading you. I saw the lady wearing the queen's cloak and...'

The king forced a smile to his pain-ravaged face. 'I too was fooled at first. But now I command you to be to Pabo as Agiluf has been to me – his true and faithful eques.'

'I will, my king, I swear it. But what are we to do without you?'

'Be brave, for I will return when I am needed. Agiluf, my dearest friend, this is where we part, but before I go, you must promise me three things.' Agiluf nodded, not trusting himself to speak. 'Take Caledfwich up to the tarn on Blencathra and throw it into the depths. I fear Coventina may be holding Gwenhyfar's soul in exchange for the sword. Do not look at it or hold its hilt, for it has the power to corrupt minds. It has made me feel invincible, but there have been consequences...'

Arthwys was quiet for a moment, prompting Agiluf to speak. 'Three things, you say?'

The king recovered his focus. 'Yes. See this ring around my neck? Please remove it, for I am too weak. Return it to Livia and tell her that much as I treasured this token, it was her love I treasured most of all.'

Agiluf carefully unclasped the chain around his friend's neck, glad that his hands did not tremble. 'And the third request?'

'Take Farddy with you to Armorica, for I know you intend to return. After a period of reflection, tell him to compose a gorchan for his king, and our fallen eques.' The king raised his voice best he could. 'For have we not been the greatest warriors this land has ever seen?'

'Undoubtedly so, King Arthwys. It has been an honour to serve you.' This time, Agiluf allowed the tears to fall. There was nothing left to say.

Merlinus cleared his throat. 'Carry the king to the boat that is waiting to cross the estuary,' he said.

'May I accompany him?' asked Brigit, who still held the king's hand. 'I have many things to tell him that Gwen wished him to know.'

Morgaine gave the girl a searching look. 'I would welcome your help, sweet Brigit.'

It was a solemn procession that made its way to the boat. Many eques lined the route to bid their king farewell, touching him as he was carried past. Once he had helped lay Arthwys in the boat, Agiluf climbed back onto the quay and watched as they cast off. He looked around for his brother and saw him watching from the pier as the skiff was rowed out to sea. Walking back to his side, he placed his arm around Farddy's shoulder to console him.

'He is barely alive,' he said, watching his brother's reaction.

'But he has promised to return,' replied Farddy.

'Come, we have our first duty to perform at the request of the king. I am to return Caledfwich to the tarn on

Blencathra. Let us set off straightaway before this grief we feel cripples our commitment.'

*

The wind was light and the sea calm. The rhythmic splash of the sailors sculling in unison was accompanied by the soft whisperings between those sat around their dying king. Merlinus could see that Arthwys did not have long.

The king strained to speak. 'Please tell me about Gwen,' he said, his fading gaze fixed on Brigit.

'She missed you every day and prayed that God keep you safe, even though she feared you were dead.' Brigit still held his hand, and now she gave it a tight squeeze in reassurance.

'I failed her in so many ways.'

'Hush, my brother,' said Morgaine, 'you will be with her soon.'

The king's eyes closed. 'Will God forgive me, Merlinus?'

'He has been with you always. He will not desert you now.'

'I know I am dying, but tell no one of my death. Bury me in an unmarked grave.'

Morgaine glanced at her husband who nodded his agreement. 'You are wise, my king, for so long as Arthwys is thought to live, Elfed and the North will remain secure.'

Hardly breathing now, the king strained once more to speak. 'All of you, help Eliffer and Pabo best you can… Look to Britu… I thought I would have more time…'

The king exhaled one last time and breathed no more.

Morgaine quietly sobbed, shoulders shaking.

Brigit let go his hand and placed it gently by his side. 'I had so much to tell him, but he is with her now,' she whispered. 'I sense they are together in paradise, surrounded by friends and angels.'

Merlinus reached for his wife's hand. 'Brigit sees the truth. There was never a braver or better king – to his last breath concerned only for his subjects, a paragon for others to follow.'

No one spoke, only the rhythmic splash of oars and the creak of the boat's timbers accompanied their private thoughts and prayers as they progressed across the Solway to Whithorn.

*

This journey did not have the same urgency as those they had undertaken in previous days, giving them time to reflect upon their grief, albeit salved by the beauty of Erechwyd which itself could not be dampened even by the squally showers that accompanied their travels. Both men spoke little, lost in their thoughts as they rode.

Agiluf mourned for his friend the king, taking little comfort from his assurance that he would return. The loss consumed him, and he could not even raise enthusiasm for his return to Armorica, though he knew he could not return to the ghosts and grief-soaked memories that awaited him in Elfed.

They followed the wooded valley past a long lake, then past the so-called temple of Myrddin, eventually arriving at the fork in the road he remembered so well.

'We walk from here. It's a miner's path that climbs past cascading waterfalls. Will you manage?'

'Yes, though I am frightened by what might be lurking up there in the clouds.'

'As was I when I came with Myrddin. It was a test of manhood I shall never forget.'

They walked through the fronds of bracken until they reached the stream.

'Do you think Arthwys will die?' asked Farddy.

'Though it grieves me to say it, yes. That wound would have killed most men within hours. Perhaps Morgaine and Merlinus will work some magic… There is always hope.'

'Then should we keep his sword in case he returns?'

'No. I dare not. There is more to this quest than we understand.' Agiluf paused. 'Do you believe in the one God?'

'Of course. I was taught to do so by Merlinus himself.'

'And what of the old gods, spirits and sorcerers?'

'Oh, I believe in those too, but the Lord God is supreme, watching over us and protecting us.'

'So, we pray to God but look over our shoulders, fearing the darkness because the old spirits are still potent?'

'Many believe they still influence our daily life. It seems imprudent to ignore that.'

'Myrddin believed in the old gods. He could summon the spirits and learn their secrets, but as is their way, there was a price to pay for that knowledge and assistance. There were always forfeits and obligations.' Agiluf paused again, watching his brother's reaction carefully. 'We are returning this sword out of one such obligation. Every warrior believes his sword is more than just metal, that the more lives it takes the more powerful it becomes, but Caledfwich was made by *the god of war*, Cocidius. Since ancient times, only the Bear of the tribes has been entitled to use it. It was hidden from the Romans, to protect it, its power lying dormant. The Druids always knew its hiding place, so when prophecy guided Myrddin that the time was right, he revealed the location to Arthwys and sent us on the quest to recover Caledfwich. But unknown to us, when brave Arthwys threw the sword into the tarn so that he might save my life on this mountain, it was received as an offering to the water goddess, Coventina. In that moment, she reclaimed the sword, only releasing it to Gwenhyfar so that she might give it to Arthwys to rid Britannia of the serpent from the east.'

'And you believe this?'

'What I believe does not matter. I do this for Arthwys, for he fears that Coventina might keep Gwenhyfar's soul hostage until this sword is returned.'

'Surely, that cannot be so. Pabo and I buried her with full Christian rites.'

'But she drowned mysteriously, Farddy. The goddess could have taken her, and we dare not risk otherwise.'

Farddy hesitated before answering, a tremble in his voice when he spoke. 'I loved Gwen with all my heart. The last few days have been... beyond bearable. What pain must she have been in to rather drown herself than return to us? Arthwys, famed King of the Britons, our mightiest warrior, was, nonetheless, a poor husband. He neglected his beautiful, courageous wife in preference for war. The trials Gwen suffered were undeserved by her.' He straightened his shoulders. 'We should do all that is necessary to ensure her onward journey to Heaven.'

Agiluf looked at his brother. Farddy was clearly overwrought, but then none could doubt he had tried the hardest of them all to protect and then rescue the queen. 'Farddy, Arthwys knew he had let both Gwen and Elfed down, but he was a man whose destiny was prescribed from birth. His whole life was a prophecy that tilted him toward war. It is difficult to spend days, months, years fighting battles, killing men, and still cherish a wife in the way she deserves. This is why so many warriors struggle to keep a home and family and why I have never married. But a king must have heirs, and he did love Gwen, though perhaps not in the way she would have hoped. There are many of us who truly believe the Britons would not have survived without Arthwys, and for that great achievement, he has had to make many sacrifices along the way, not least his own family. We must not hold that against him. I will return this sword because Arthwys has asked it of me. It matters not the reason, whether it is destiny, duty or because he believes it will ensure his queen's journey to Heaven. This is my service to him.'

Nothing further was said.

The large corrie soon opened before them. Low clouds swirled around the summit of Blencathra, cloaking it in mystery. As they walked toward the tarn, Farddy looked up the steep corrie slopes in awe. Agiluf felt excitement rise within him. This was where it had all begun. He sensed the import of completing the circle.

'See, up there? That is the dragon's back disappearing into the clouds, and over there is the gully and scree slope I slipped down. I might have died if not for Arthwys.'

Agiluf withdrew the sword from the blanket in which it had journeyed, careful to only touch the thick leather wrapped around the hilt. Then he walked to the steep bank below the dragon's back, stood on a boulder and cast Caledfwich out with all his might. The sword spun hilt over blade through the air and splashed through the still surface, ripples spreading out from where it entered the deep, dark pool.

'Is that it? The task is complete?' asked Farddy, his tone tinged with disappointment.

'What did you expect? The goddess to reach her hand out of the depths and catch it?'

They both laughed at the thought.

'Well, it would have terrified me, if she had, but I have to admit, I half-expected it.'

Agiluf gave his brother a playful shove. 'Come. Barinthus awaits us at Alauna. There are still more duties to complete, so let's make haste. A new start awaits us both in Armorica, if of course, we survive the voyage.'

Farddy looked ruefully into the tarn's depths. 'Do you think Caledfwich will ever be found again?'

'Other men will seek it, but none as great as King Arthwys. Few have been more deserving of a worthy gorchan, brother.'

'We shall compose it as we cross the sea.'

'Then only you will sing it.'

'Why so?'

'For I will be too busy retching over the side!'

They both laughed, and Agiluf put his arm around his brother to descend the steep path. Shafts of sunlight pushed through the cloud picking out different parts of Reged below.

'What is the name of your woman, brother?'

'She is called Diana.'

'And does she have sisters?'

Agiluf grinned. 'Yes, three. All spinsters who love poetry. I have told them all about you.'

'Will they like me?'

'*Like* you! You will be beating them off with a stick, brother – I can promise you that.'

'So, sing about the past but look to the future?'

'And we must never dwell upon either!'

Glossary of Fifth-century Terms, People and Place Names

I have used authentic place names and terms wherever possible. These are gleaned from an array of sources, in particular the annals, and monuments of the Romans and the Britons.

By the early fifth century, Rome had dominated much of western Europe for four hundred years. Latin became the language of the law, the military, religion and culture. Most ethnic languages endured, but the people who lived within or close by the Empire's frontiers came to adopt Latin terms, much like the English language now pervades modern global terms. The written word was mostly Latin, and later, ethnic writing was influenced by the phonetics of Latin speech. The poetry of the earliest bards was likely composed in either common Brittonic or archaic Welsh peppered with Latin. The 'Surrexit Memorandum' in the seventh-century Lichfield Gospels is the best example of this hybrid writing that developed over two centuries. Christianity, in particular, was taught in Latin. In this book, the elites and their militias would have messaged and written in Latin but likely conversed in Brittonic.

Seasons

ver	spring
aestas	summer
autumnus	autumn
hiems	winter

Calendar references

Ianuarius	January
Februarius	February
Martius	March
Aprilis	April
Maius	May
Iunius	June
Quintilis	July
Sextilis	August
September	September
October	October
November	November
December	December

Roman Provinces prior to AD 410

Maxima Caesariensis   The south and south east

Flavia Caesariensis   The East Midlands, East
                             Anglia and Norfolk

Britannia Prima   All territory west of a line
                             line from Chester to Dorset

Valentia   The territory between
                             Hadrian's Wall and the
                             Antonine Wall

Senior Roman military and civil appointments (in order of superiority)

patrician   highest class of noble
                             appointed by the Emperor

magister militum   master of soldiers, the most
                             senior general of a region, or
                             if empire-wide, 'magister
                             utriusque militum'

magister peditum   master of infantry

magister officiorum   head of the civil service

Count of the Saxon Shore   Comes litoris Saxonici,
                             general controlling south-east
                             Britannia and the coast of
                             northern Gaul.

Comes Britanniarum	Count of the Britons
Dux Britanniarum	Duke of Britain, general controlling northern Britannia
prefect	praefectus, high-ranking officer
decurion	Roman cavalry officer in command of a squadron (ala) consisting of three or more turmae
eques	knight, member of Roman equestrian order
optio	junior officer, similar to a lieutenant

Tribes and peoples

Alans	a tribe which allied with the Romans and were settled in central Gaul
Angles	one of the Germanic peoples who settled in Britain during the Roman period
Belgae	large Brittonic southern tribe
Bretons	Britons who emigrated to Armorica (Brittany)

Brigantes	large Brittonic northern tribe
Burgundians	Germanic tribe from the middle Rhine region
Carvetti	Brittonic tribe living in Cumbria, north-west Britannia
Cornovii	large Brittonic midland tribe
Cymry	a cultural grouping of Brittonic tribes some of whom, prior to AD 410 were Roman citizens, - a modern-day translation is 'the Welsh'.
Damnonii	Brittonic people who lived in the Kingdom of Strathclyde
Deisi	a tribe of people from ancient Ireland who settled in Wales
Dobunni	large south-west tribe based around Gloucester
Franks	Germanic tribe from the east bank of the lower Rhine
Frisians	coastal tribe from around the Rhine estuary

Gaels	group native to Ireland, who migrated to western Scotland and the Isle of Man
Gaini	Frank and Frisian tribes which occupied the east bank of the Trent
Goths	The collective name for Germanic people who originated from Poland and the western Steppes and migrated as different tribes to The Roman Empire
Gododdin	Brittonic-speaking people of north-eastern Britannia (now southern Scotland)
Huns	nomadic people who lived in Central Asia, and the Caucasus who grew by conquest to become as powerful as the Roman Empire
Jutes	Germanic people from Jutland who emigrated to Britannia
Novantae	tribe who lived in Galloway, south-west Scotland
Parisi	Brittonic tribe located in the east of Yorkshire

Picts	tribes who lived in Scotland north of the Forth–Clyde isthmus
Scotti	Irish raiders who colonised western Scotland
Suebi	Germanic people from the Elbe river region, now Germany and the Czech Republic
Syagrii	famous Roman family of which Aegidius is assumed a descendant
Vandals	Germanic people from southern Poland who swept across Europe and colonised North Africa
Visigoths	Germanic tribe first noted in the Balkans who eventually colonised southern Gaul

Other references

Agnes Dei	a liturgical chant 'Lamb of God'
Artio	Celtic bear goddess
atrium	a large open-aired reception space

bacaudae	groups of populist insurgents
barus	barons
basilica	a large building for civic use
Belatucadrus	Brittonic horned god of war
bucellari	barbarian escort troops
Caledfwich	famous sword known in legend as Excalibur
castrum	stone turret or watchtower
cena	dinner
Chi Rho	Ancient Christian symbol
cives	citizens
civitas	town
Cocidius	Brittonic god of war
Coeling	descendants of Coel Hen
Colonae	areas of settlement (Lincolnshire in the story)
corrie	circular hollow on a mountain
Coventina	Brittonic water goddess

culdeis	partners of God, Church-appointed representatives
Damnatio memoriae	Latin phrase meaning 'condemnation of memory', indicating that a person be excluded from official accounts, often applied to executed usurpers
draco	dragon
foederati	barbarian tribes bound to provide military assistance under treaty to Rome, also known as foedus
Gallic	the culture of Roman northern France
gladius	type of sword used by infantry
gorchan	a poetic elegy, commemorating fallen warriors
Janus	Roman god of transition and duality
kalends	first day of the month
labarum	a Christian banner and the imperial standard of Constantine the Great

Limes Germanicus	line of frontier fortifications stretching along the Rhine and the Danube dividing the Roman Empire and the Germanic tribes
Limes Saxonicus	Ambrosius' temporary frontier with the Saxons, being the lower half of Watling Street
lorica	a prayer for protection in Irish monastic tradition, associated with St Patrick
lusoria	Roman vessel used as a troop transporter
mansio	a large house used as a hotel or guest house
Pascha	the Christian festival of Easter
patria, the Patria	native country or homeland
peristylium	open inner courtyard surrounded by a row of columns
Praetorian Guard	the Emperor's guard
praetorium	headquarters of a Roman official

primogeniture	the right of succession of the firstborn child
publicanus	tax collector
Romanitas	Roman identity and culture
Saturnalia	an ancient Roman festival and holiday in honour of the god Saturn, held 17-23 December
seax	Saxon knife with a single cutting edge and a long, tapering point
siliquae	small, thin Roman silver coins produced in the fourth and early fifth century AD
solidi	pure gold coins issued in the late Roman Empire.
spatha	a straight, long sword used by cavalry
stola	a long, pleated, sleeveless robe, worn by Roman women
tanet	an area of land allocated for settlement
tarn	small lake or pool

the Bear	fictional name for the Carvetti and Brigantes' battle leader
the Purple	the epithet for the position of Roman Emperor
thegn	Anglo Saxon leader / landowner
tribune	an official leading a region
turma	a cavalry unit of usually thirty strong
Verbeia	a water goddess
vicus	village or part of a town
Wealas	Anglo-Saxon term for Britons, translates as foreigner or sometimes slave

Place names, Britannia

Afon Menai	Menai Straits
Alauna	Roman fort, just north of Maryport
Alt Clut	Brittonic fortress, capital of the kingdom of Strathclyde

Ambro Hill	hill in Leicestershire overlooking Breedon on the Hill
Angia	Jersey
Axholme	island to the west of the Trent
Badon	Bardon Hill, Leicestershire
Banna	Birdoswald Fort, Hadrian's Wall
Blencathra	mountain in the northern part of the Lake District
Breguoin	Breedon on the Hill in Leicestershire
Bremetennacum	Roman fort, Ribchester
Britannia	Roman Britain
Brovacum	Brougham Castle near Penrith
Bryneich	land between the Tyne and the Tweed mostly Northumbria
Caint	modern-day Kent
Caledonia	Scotland, north of the Forth
Calleva	Silchester

Cambodunum	Barwick in Elmet
Cambolann	a settlement by the Devil's Causeway north of Hadrian's Wall
Campocalia	earthworks near Thorner
Camulodunum	Colchester
Candida Casa	monastery at Whithorn
Cataractonium	Catterick
Causennis	Saltersford, Little Ponton
Celyddon	the northern part of the Great Forest near the river Don
Cheviot	a mountain between the rivers Tyne and the Tweed
Clausentum	Roman port, Bitterne, Southampton
Corieltauvorum	Leicester
Corinium	Cirencester
Crafen	Craven, a region of West Yorkshire
Corstopitum (Coria)	Corbridge

Crammel Linn	waterfall near Gilsland on the border of Cumbria and Northumberland
Crecganford	Present day Stamford Bridge
Criffel	prominent hill, Dumfries and Galloway
Danum	Doncaster
Derventio	a fort, Little Chester, Derby
Deva	Chester
Din Eidyn	Edinburgh
Din Guarie	Bamburgh fort, Northumberland
Dumnonia	Cornwall, Devon and part of Somerset
Dunnad	Scotti hillfort near Lochgilphead
Dunragit	fort of Reged, near Glenluce and Stranraer
Durnovaria	Dorchester
Durobrivae	Water Newton, Peterborough
Durovernum	Canterbury

Dyfed	county in south-western Wales
Eboracum	York
Edge, the	Wenlock Edge
Elfed	the kingdom of Elmet, now part of northern England
Episford	ferry on the river Trent also known in Welsh as Rither Gabail
Erechwyd	the region of the Lake District
Flavia	Roman province of central Britain sometimes called Flavia Caesariensis
Fortriu	Pictish kingdom
Gainnion	stronghold of the Gaini, Gainsborough
Gaulish Sea	the North Sea beyond the Wash
Glevum	Gloucester
Great Forest	the largest forest in Britannia, incorporating Charnwood, Sherwood, Elmet and Galtres,

	stretching from Leicester to beyond York
Guoloph	battle site, Nether Wallop, Hampshire
Gwynedd	region in the north-west of Wales
Heights, the	fictional Saxon reference to Bardon Hill and Breedon on the Hill
Hibernia	Ireland
Insula Manavia	Isle of Man, also known as Mannin
Isca Augusta	Caerleon, South Wales
Isca Dumnoniorum	Exeter
Isurium (Brigantum)	Aldborough, Boroughbridge, North Yorkshire
Itunocelum	Roman naval fort, Ravenglass, Cumbria
Lactodurum	Towcester
Lavatris	Bowes, County Durham
Letocetum	Wall, Lichfield
Lindinis	Ilchester, Somerset

Lindum	Lincoln
Linnuis	the kingdom of Lindsey, a large area of North Lincolnshire
Lisia, island of	Guernsey
Londinium	London
Luguvalium	Carlisle
Maglona	Old Carlisle, Wigton
Magna	Roman fort at Whin Sill on Hadrian's Wall
Mamucium	Manchester
Mediobogdum	Hardknott Roman Fort, Cumbria
Mona	Anglesey
Mons Badonicus	Bardon Hill, Leicestershire
Novomagus	Chichester
Orcades	the Orkney Islands
Pons Aelius	Newcastle upon Tyne
Ratae (Corieltauvorum)	Leicester

Reged	northern kingdom, covering north-west England and south-west Scotland
Rither Gabail	ferry on the river Trent, also known as Episford
Roman turf wall	the Antonine wall built between the Clyde and the Firth of Forth
Rutupiae	Richborough
Ryknild (Via)	northern part of the Roman road known as Icknield Street
Saxon Shore	military command of the Roman Empire consisting of a series of fortifications on both sides of the English Channel
Segontium	Caernarfon
Sorviodunum	Old Sarum, Salisbury
temple of Myrddin, the	Castlerigg stone circle, Keswick
Tigguo Cobauc	City of Caves, Nottingham
Traprain Law	Gododdin fortress, Lothian, Scotland

Tribruit	the shore of the Trent, near the junction with the Soar
Valentia	the fifth province of Britannia between Hadrian's Wall and the Antonine Wall
Vectis	Isle of Wight
Venonis	High Cross, Lutterworth
Venta Belgarum	Winchester
Venta Icenorum	Caistor St Edmund
Verbeia	Roman fort, Ilkley, West Yorkshire
Verulamium	St Albans
Villa Octavius	Harley, near Much Wenlock
Vinovia	Binchester, Bishop Auckland
Viroconium	Wroxeter
Wall, the	Hadrian's Wall, Northumberland
Whithorn	location of the monastery known as Candida Casa
Wippeds Fleot	Surfleet Seas End near the Wash

Wrikon, the	prominent hill near Wroxeter, known today as Wrekin Hill
Ypwines Fleot	Swinefleet near Goole on the Humber
Yr Wyddfa	Snowdon
Ystyuacheu	fortification at Stanage on the river Teme

Place names, Roman Empire

Aletum	St Malo, France
Ambianensium	Amiens, France
Antiochos, palace of	fifth-century palace in Constantinople
Aquitania	Roman province in south-west France
Aregenua	Vieux, Calvados, France
Armorica	Brittany, France
Arvernis	the Auvergne region around Clermont Ferrand, France
Aurelianum	Orléans, France
Autissiodorum	Auxerre, France

Avaricum	Bourges, France
Belgica Secunda	Roman province that combined Belgium and northern France
Bononia	Boulogne, France
Carthage	Roman city and port, now the capital of Tunisia
Chalons	the region between Reims and Troyes where Aetius fought Attila
Constantinople	Istanbul, Turkey
Dalmatia	historical region on the eastern shore of the Adriatic Sea in Croatia, sometimes known as Illyricum
Deols	ancient town in eastern central France
Gallaecia	northern Portugal
Gaul	France
Germania	Roman province bordering the Rhine and the Danube
Hispania	Roman name for the Iberian Peninsula

Illyricum	eastern shore of the Adriatic, Sometimes called Dalmatia
Juliomagus	Angers, western France
Lake Lemanus	Lake Geneva, Switzerland
Lutetia	Paris, France
Mare Nostrum	Mediterranean Sea
Noviodunum	Soissons, northern France
Pannonia	Roman province in the Balkans
Ravenna	fortified imperial palace, Emelia–Romagna province, Italy
Salona	ancient city and capital of the province of Dalmatia (Illyricum)
Tolosa	Toulouse, France
Trastevere	neighbourhood of Rome, Italy
Treverorum	Trier, Germany
Turonum	Tours, France
Via Egnatia	Roman road running across the Balkan peninsula, from

Dyrrachium to Constantinople

River names

Aire	tributary of the river Humber
Bassas	river Torne (or Thorne)
Dergeuntid	river Derwent near Derby, tributary to the Trent
Don	tributary of the river Trent
Eden	flows into the Solway Firth
Ellen	flows into the Solway Firth at Maryport
Esk	flows into the sea at Ravenglass
Garonne	flows through Toulouse to the Gironde estuary
Glen	flows into the river Welland
Humber	estuary, flows into the North Sea
Irthing	tributary of the river Eden
Loire	longest river in France, flows into the Atlantic Ocean at the Bay of Biscay

Skell	tributary of the river Don
Soar	tributary of the river Trent
Swale	tributary of the river Ouse
Teme	tributary of the river Severn
Trent	tributary of the river Humber
Welland	flows into The Wash

Central Characters

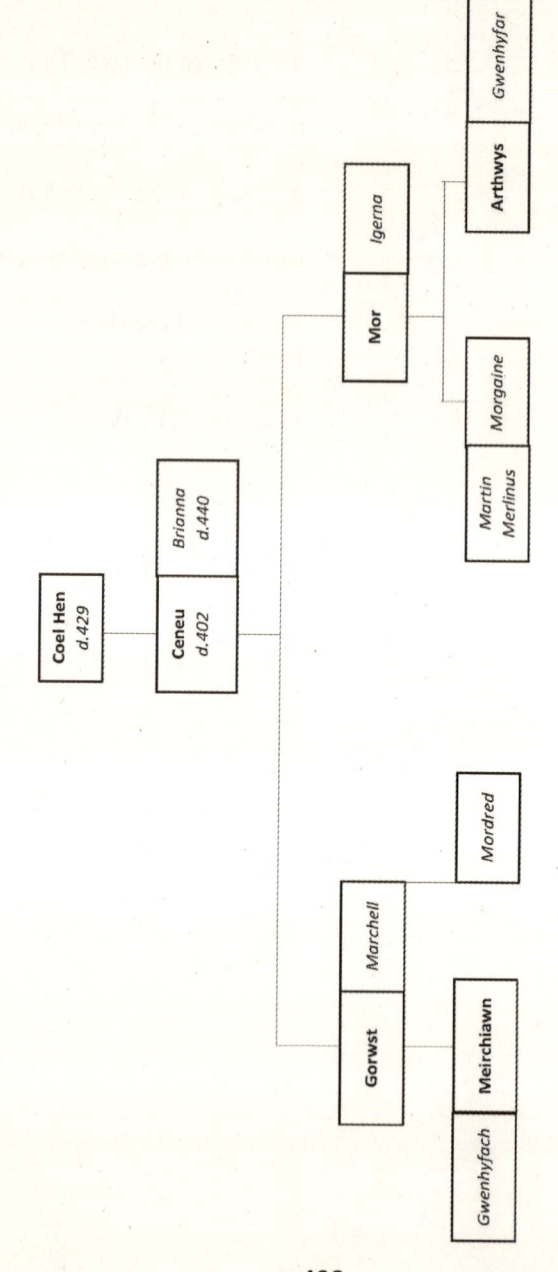

- **Coel Hen** d.429
  - **Ceneu** d.402 / *Brianna* d.440
    - **Mor** / *Igerna*
      - *Martin Merlinus*
      - *Morgaine*
      - **Arthwys** / *Gwenhyfar*
    - **Gorwst** / *Marchell*
      - *Mordred*
      - **Meirchiawn**
        - *Gwenhyfach*

Fictional additions to the 'Bonedd Gwŷr y Gogledd' (the Descent of the Men of the North) in italics

ROMAN BRITAIN'S ENEMIES AT THE CLOSE OF THE FOURTH CENTURY

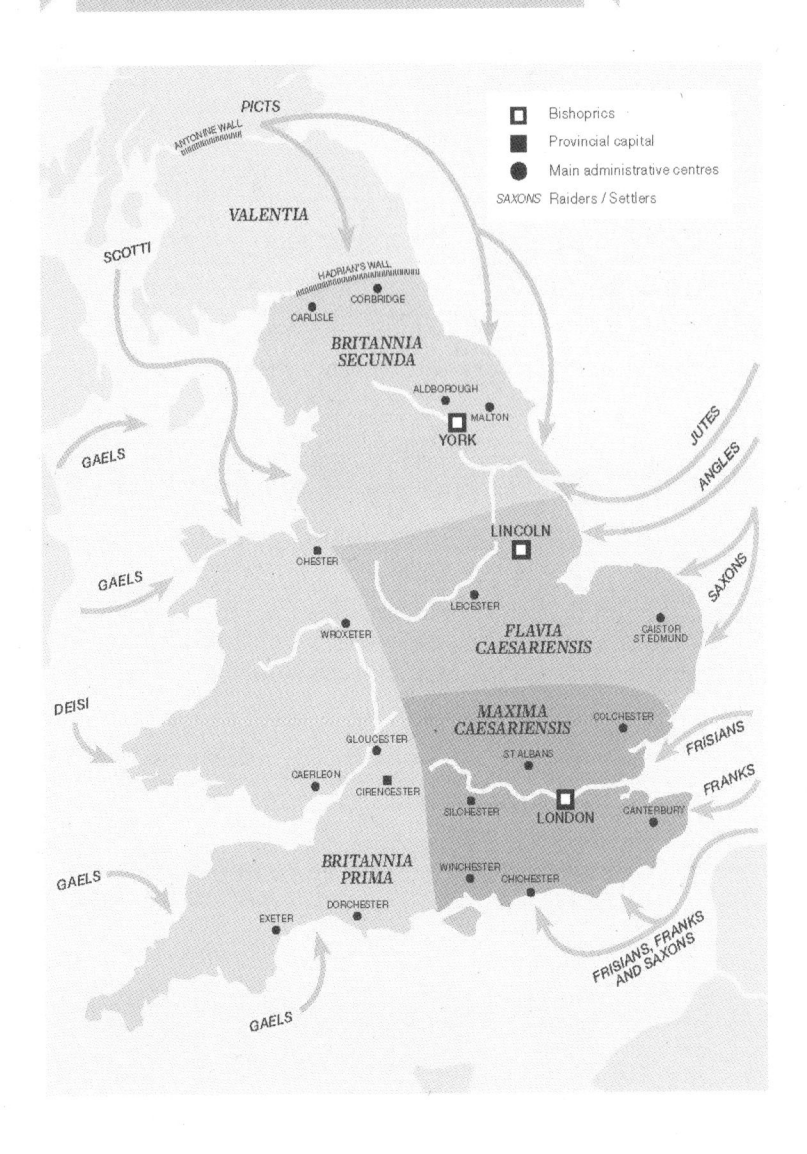

THE SAXON REBELLION AD 444 TO 456

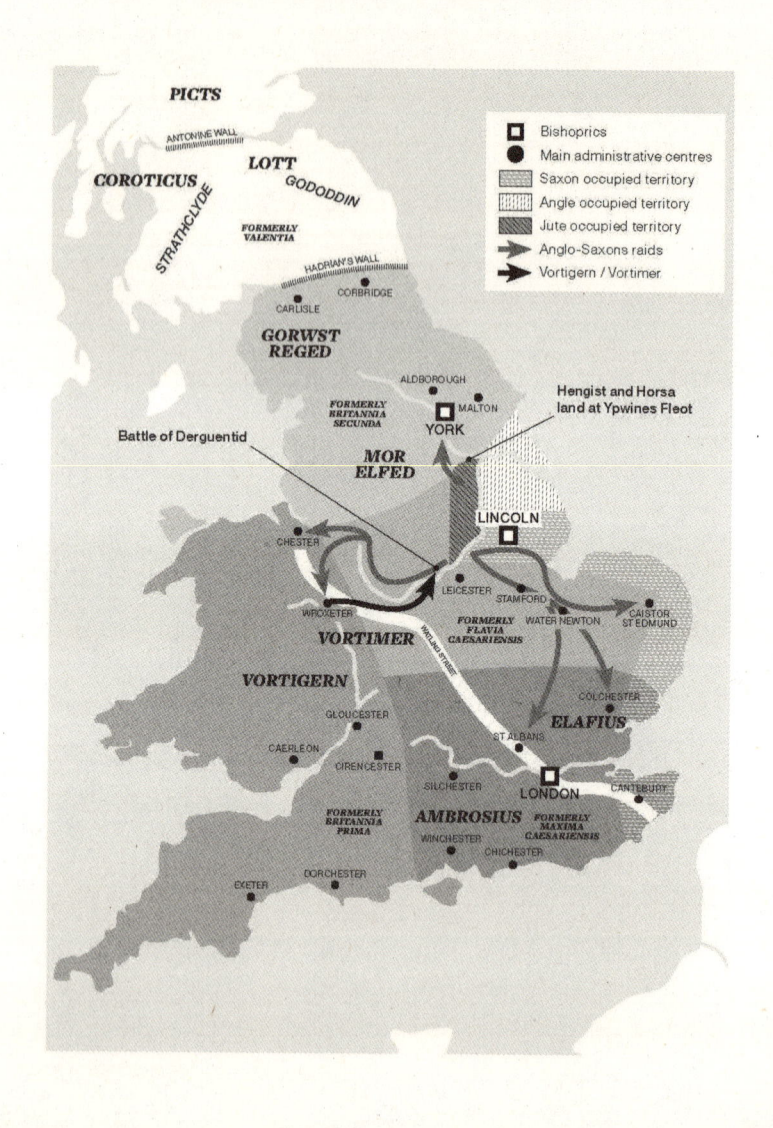

THE SAXON WAR
AD 460 TO 468

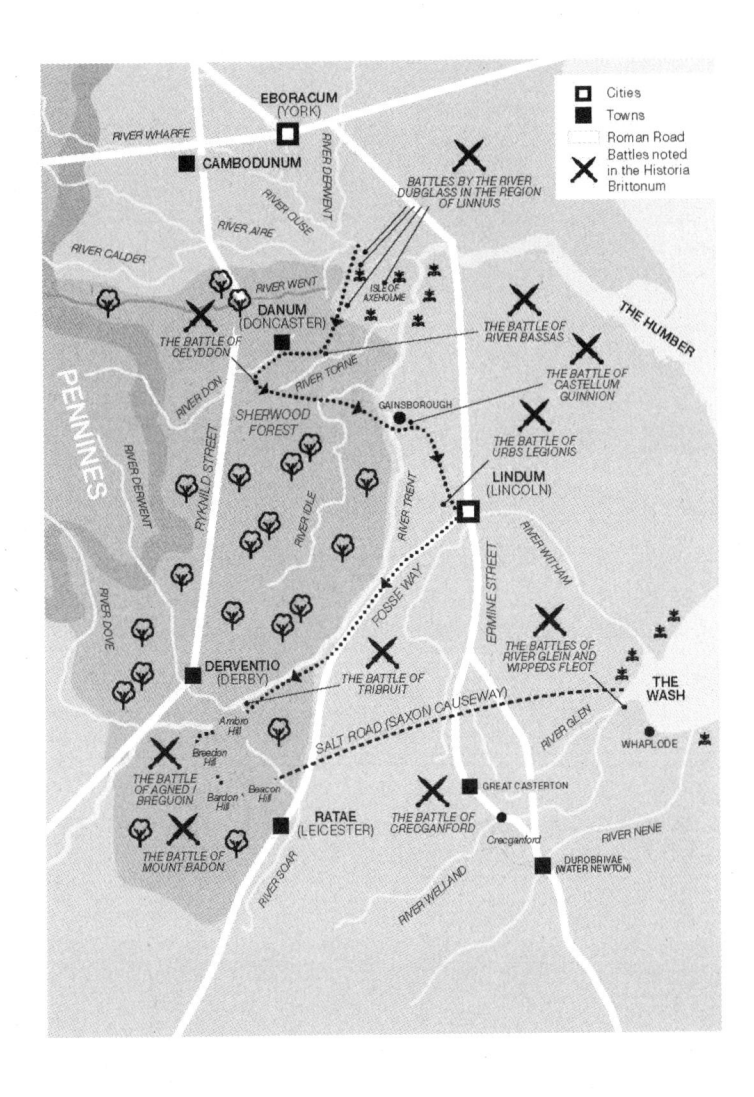

NORTHERN GAUL BY AD 470

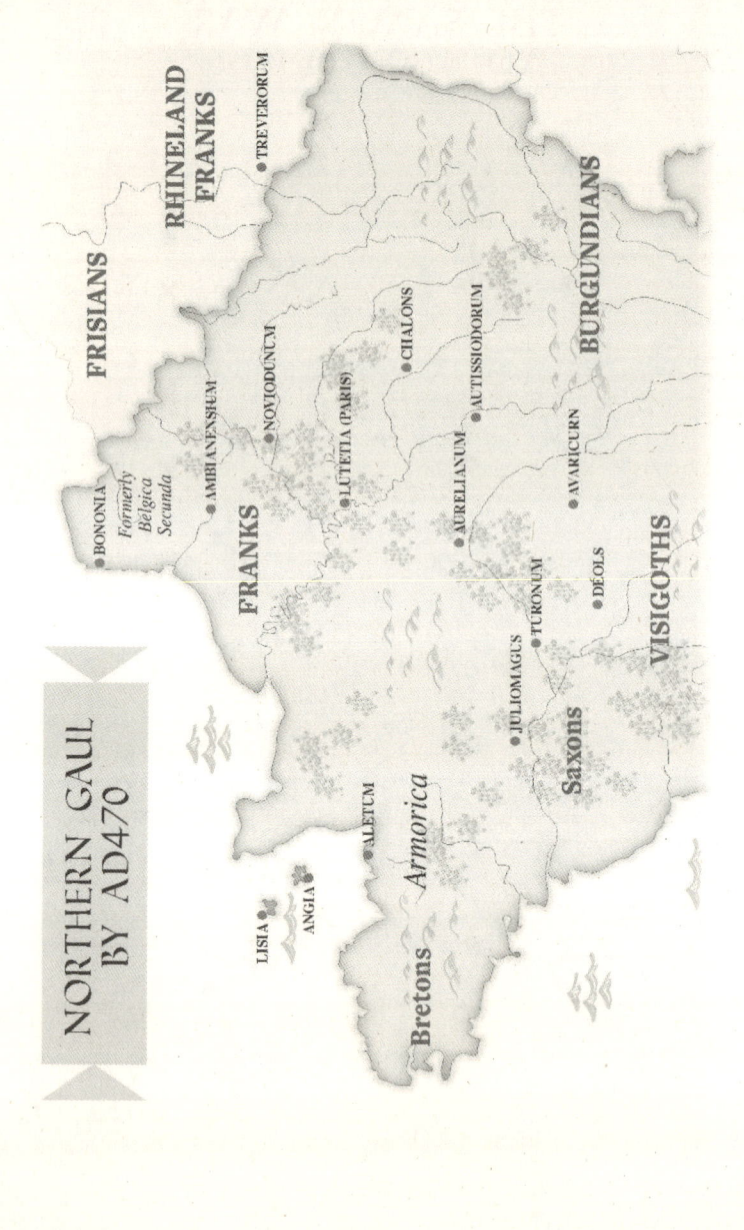

- BONONIA (Formerly Belgica Secunda)
- AMBIANENSIUM
- TREVERORUM
- NOVIODUNUM
- LUTETIA (PARIS)
- CHALONS
- AUTISSIODORUM
- AURELIANUM
- AVARICUM
- TURONUM
- DEOLS
- JULIOMAGUS
- ALETUM
- LISIA
- ANGIA

FRISIANS
RHINELAND FRANKS
FRANKS
BURGUNDIANS
VISIGOTHS
Saxons
Bretons
Armorica

The first title in this historical fiction series
The Genesis of Arthwys by Alistair Hall

The year is 412 AD. The Roman legions have all withdrawn from Britannia. The cives and tribes who remain no longer have the might of Rome at their backs or her foot on their throats. They must rally to fill the power vacuum and defend themselves against an array of seaborne enemies attracted by prosperous lands lightly defended. Meanwhile, the Picts of Caledonia seize their opportunity to invade and so begins sixty years of strife for the Britons. This is a story of those warlords that became kings and valiantly defended their religion and culture, ensuring their deeds passed down the ages into legend. The last Roman appointed Duke of Britain, Coel Hen, not only defended the North but also gave rise to a dynasty that would extend its grip on power, shaping kingdoms whilst facing the gathering tide of invasion from across the sea. *The Genesis of Arthwys* tells the story behind the rise of this illustrious northern dynasty. There is a prophecy that a serpent will come from the east, and the men of the North must be ready or risk losing all that they hold dear… only the Bear will defeat it.

Non-fiction history title by the author Alistair Hall   *Searching for Arthur .... Finding Arthwys*

In 383 the mighty Roman General Magnus Maximus set out from Britain to conquer the Western Roman Empire. Taking almost the entire British garrison with him, he defeated the Western Emperor Gratian near Paris and shortly thereafter was recognised as Augustus in the West. The audacious plans of Maximus included the re-organisation of troops for the defence of Britain and for the first time the chieftains of the Romanised Britons were given the responsibility to protect their regions from enemy raiders. This decision played an important role in the survival of Celtic Christianity and the successors of these chieftains were still fulfilling their duties as protectors a century later, one of whom became known in legend as King Arthur.

With a stunning new perspective, *Searching for Arthur ... Finding Arthwys* provides answers sufficient to not only justify the hero's historicity, but also to challenge the perceived chronology of the fifth century.